W9-CMB-712

WITHDRAWN
FROM THE BODMAN PUBLIC LIBRARY

PLAYING SAINT

Center Point
Large Print

**This Large Print Book carries the
Seal of Approval of N.A.V.H.**

PLAYING SAINT

Zachary Bartels

CENTER POINT LARGE PRINT
THORNDIKE, MAINE

RODMAN PUBLIC LIBRARY

This Center Point Large Print edition is published
in the year 2015 by arrangement with Thomas Nelson.

Copyright © 2015 by Zachary Bartels.

All rights reserved.

Scripture quotations are from the NEW AMERICAN
STANDARD BIBLE®, Copyright © 1960, 1962, 1963,
1968, 1971, 1972, 1973, 1975, 1977, 1995 by
The Lockman Foundation. Used by permission.

This novel is a work of fiction. Names, characters,
places, and incidents are either products of the
author's imagination or used fictitiously. All characters
are fictional, and any similarity to people
living or dead is purely coincidental.

The text of this Large Print edition is unabridged.
In other aspects, this book may vary
from the original edition.
Printed in the United States of America
on permanent paper.
Set in 16-point Times New Roman type.

ISBN: 978-1-62899-727-9

Library of Congress Cataloging-in-Publication Data

Bartels, Zachary.
  Playing saint / Zachary Bartels. — Center Point Large Print edition.
    pages cm
  ISBN 978-1-62899-727-9 (library binding : alk. paper)
  1. Large type books. I. Title.
  PS3602.A83855P58 2015
  813′.6—dc23
                                                    2015024344

RODMAN PUBLIC LIBRARY

To Judson Baptist Church,
for loving the gospel,
scandal and all.

38212006415472
Main Adult Large Print
Bartels, Z
Bartels, Zachary, author
Playing saint

PLAYING
SAINT

Prologue

Thirteen Years Ago

Danny sat quietly in the pew and waited for his exorcism.

It wasn't scheduled, but it would happen. He would make it happen. He'd been down this road countless times before—enough to know that all the elements of the equation were present here this morning. He would be *delivered,* at least that's what they would call it. He'd probably fall to the ground and writhe for a few seconds. He'd own the moment, milk it a little.

The prospect failed to thrill him. It had become banal, like waiting to be called in to the dentist's office, flipping through ancient, dog-eared magazines, or sitting at the DMV, fiddling with that little numbered tab of paper, willing your turn to come. And yet, a certain dampened twinge of excitement persisted. Not butterflies in the stomach. More like a tingle of expectation some-where deeper.

Which was fine. Stuffed full as it was with meat and grease, his stomach would not accommodate butterflies. Danny was a trim young man and usually ate little, but on these special Sunday mornings he always felt inexplicably compelled to stop at some rural greasy spoon and eat until he felt a bit queasy. It was like that old maxim about a pregnant woman eating for two. How many was Danny eating for now? He'd lost count.

And he had no choice but to continue feeding Them, to carry on with increasing momentum down this road, all the while pretending that he didn't know the truth: at the end of the day, he would be the main course.

One

Present Day

Detective Paul Ketcham did not need to flash his gold badge at the patrol officer covering the door —they knew each other on sight—but he did anyway. He liked the way it felt. He also enjoyed ducking under yellow crime-scene tape, but there was none here to duck.

"Let's get some tape up," he barked at the officer. "Press'll be here any minute. We don't need them contaminating the scene."

The house on Lane Avenue had lain vacant for nearly a year. Squatters found the body three hours earlier and, hoping to collect a reward, made the call to the Grand Rapids police. There was none to collect, so now they waited for the local news affiliates, thinking they might get some TV time in lieu of monetary remuneration.

Ketcham entered the spacious living room, noticing the hardwood floors and early twentieth-century leaded windows. It was clear that the house had once been beautiful, despite the years of neglect and the shirtless corpse lying in a pool of blood.

"Hey, Paul," called Corrinne Kirkpatrick, descending the curved staircase. "I've been here twenty minutes already. I can't remember the last time I beat you to a scene. Did you have to do your paper route?"

Like Ketcham, she was a senior detective with the Major Case Team. They weren't partners—there was no such official pairing in their unit—but they had been building a mutual respect and interdependence for the better part of a decade. Corrinne was the only person on the force who dared to call him Paul. To everyone else he was Detective Ketcham, save his superiors, who simply called him Ketcham.

In her midforties, she was almost ten years his senior, which somehow wound up as a source of ribbing in both directions. He also dished out frequent digs about her boyish haircut and severe pantsuits—both of which she took as compliments.

"This is already looking too familiar," he said, approaching the corpse.

The young man looked to be in his late teens,

his dark hair shoulder-length, his skin pallid, and his throat cut from ear to ear. On his forehead the number 666 had been applied in a dark red-brown. His chest bore a large five-pointed star in the same substance.

"Pretty uninventive," Corrinne observed with some disappointment. "I still give creativity points for painting on the guy with his own blood. But the star and the 666 are a little nineties, am I right? It's just like that corny movie; what was it called?"

"Hmm? I don't know. I don't watch movies." Ketcham ran a hand through his thick hair and squatted down for a better look. "It's definitely our guy, though. Same technique, same detail—looks like a pretty fine paintbrush. That didn't make the press, so we can rule out some copycat inspired by the headline."

"Nothing related to playing cards either. I guess they'll have to come up with a new name for the perp. The Blackjack Killer doesn't fit anymore."

"Yeah. Maybe the Pentagon Killer."

Corrinne shook her head. "A pentagon isn't a star. It's a five-sided shape, like the building in Washington, DC."

"Pentagram?"

"Yeah, maybe. Anyway, this changes the profile altogether. I don't think I'm jumping to conclusions when I see some definite religious overtones here. That's new."

"Hmm." Ketcham scribbled some notes in a pocket-sized spiral notebook. "And if we're not dealing with playing-card imagery, the whole thing about expecting four victims is out the window too."

"That was pretty thin anyway. I think Channel 8 came up with it. My real takeaway here is that our whole 'new gang' theory is probably off base. Gangs rarely employ Satanic rituals and symbolism, am I right?"

"I wouldn't think so." He rubbed his chin. "This whole thing is off. Two victims in two days. Ritualized killings. Looks like the work of a serial killer, but I'd expect another girl in that case."

"Why is that?" Corrinne folded her arms.

"Oh, save the feminism. We're talking about a murderer here. Guy's slicing people up; I doubt he cares whether his choice of victim is politically correct."

"And why exactly does the killer have to be a man?"

"If you're trying to advance the cause, I think you're doing it wrong." He turned his attention back to the body. "What have we got on the victim?"

She perused her own notepad. "His name is Benjamin Ludema. He was a senior at Central High. No arrest record. We're waiting to hear back from a school representative. I'd like to interview all of his teachers tomorrow morning."

"Yeah, that's good. Let me know if you need help."

"Now that you mention it, I was hoping you two might have some classes together. Are you friends with any upperclassmen?"

"Funny stuff." He pointed to the design on the boy's chest. "Did the lab ever confirm that the blood from yesterday's image was the victim's?"

"Type matched, but we're still waiting on DNA confirmation. I wouldn't stand on one leg until it comes in. I'll make sure they do the same tests on young Ben here, with a few unique samples."

"What's your guess at time of death?"

"Definitely within the last four hours. I'd be real surprised if it were any earlier."

"Sheesh. Killing for the devil on Sunday morning." Ketcham shook his head. "What's the world come to?"

"I know what you mean. In my day all the Satanic murders happened during the work-week. Between this and all the churches getting tagged, this town's really throwing in with Beelzebub."

He gave her a chuckle. "Those two vagrants out there waiting to give a statement?"

"No, they've been handled. Pretty much worth-less."

Ketcham was beginning to sweat. It was early October and still too warm for the lined trench coat he wore. "Techs should be here soon," he said, checking his watch. "You mind babysitting while I start the paperwork?"

"Of course the woman has to do the baby-sitting."

"You're a regular Gloria Steinem, you know that?"

Parker Saint had just seen a tear trickle down a cheek in the crowd, cutting slowly through a thick layer of foundation. This was important. A wet cheek was one of the last checkpoints on The List. He still carried an index card bearing The List in his jacket pocket, despite having long since committed it to memory. It was something of a good-luck charm.

For six years Parker had been preaching against an ultratight television schedule, and he prided himself on impeccable timing. A large digital clock, glowing red at the back of the auditorium, displayed the number of minutes remaining in the broadcast, and Parker knew where in The List he needed to be in relation to the number on the clock.

His sermons were twenty-eight minutes in length every week, not varying by thirty seconds. He always began with a joke, usually something a little on the folksy, heartwarming side. After that he would establish the vocabulary of the message: not theological jargon, but something catchy and appealing like "Unleashing Your Full Potential" or "Tapping into Your God-breathed Dreams."

Today it was "Moments of Majesty." Next, he would bring up some scriptural texts, weaving together several Moments of Majesty in the lives of biblical characters, all the while solidifying a principle around them.

When the clock read 0:14, he began identifying at least two practical action points. In his early years he had announced, "Now for the action points," but these days he brought them in more seamlessly. Finally, with six minutes left in the broadcast, the music would come in, all-but-inaudible at first, slowly swelling as Parker told a touching story—sometimes a personal experience, but more often something he'd read in a book or online.

This was the most delicate part of the process, and it made him grateful for the live audience before him. Parker would slowly turn up the emotional intensity until he saw a single tear on the face of a parishioner, then back off. In this case, the tear rolled down as he elaborated an account of an elderly married couple with dementia, living in a nursing home, reenacting their first date. It appeared just as the clock changed to 0:03. The credits would roll at 0:02.

Perfect.

The final checkpoint on The List was what he called "tying the bow," which meant summarizing twenty-eight minutes in a single statement. Parker was a master of tying the bow.

"My friends, God wants you to embrace your Moments of Majesty," he intoned, his words oozing with manufactured sincerity. "You may not recognize God's breath on your life today. The majesty of your destiny may be eluding your sight, but mark my words: your greatest Moments of Majesty are in front of you. Thank you for joining us today. And remember, God is awesome . . ."

"And so am I!" came the enthusiastic reply from the congregation, some 4500 voices strong. Parker beamed. The brilliant simplicity of his catchphrase never failed to delight him. He strode confidently from the stage, leaving the band to execute a bright praise song under the television credits.

Backstage he was met by his assistant, Paige, who gushed, "Seriously, Parker, that was one of your best messages yet!"

"You say that every week."

"It's true every week." She quickly took the wireless mic from him and smoothed his hair with several saliva-dampened fingers. "Houselights in less than a minute. You better go." She hugged him briefly. "Great job this morning. Seriously."

In the atrium after the service Parker stood behind a long table and greeted his admirers, as he always did. On either side of him volunteers sold DVDs of previous messages, but the real line was of people wanting to talk with Parker for just a moment. Many asked for an autograph on the morning's bulletin. With everything on large projection screens, there was really no need for bulletins except that Parker loved signing them. In a couple of months, though, he planned to phase them out altogether, as he would have something much more substantial to autograph.

"I can't wait for your book, Pastor Saint," a flustered, matronly woman said. "I'm planning to buy lots of copies and giving them away—give them away, I mean. For Christmas and such."

"I appreciate it. Thank you so much." He smiled, consciously flashing some tooth. He'd successfully quit smoking six months earlier at his mentor's insistence and was seeing improvement in the whiteness every day.

The line had begun to dwindle when Paige approached silently. "Parker, you've got an appointment in your office in five. The man from *Christianity in View*. He's in the greenroom now."

"I forgot about that. Thanks. Get me some water, would you, Paige? I'm parched." He lifted a hand to what remained of the line. "Sorry, folks, I've got to go! Remember, God is awesome and so are you!"

Brett LaForest was a short, balding man with a penchant for facts and no sense of humor.

"As I told your assistant on the phone, Reverend

Saint, *Christianity in View* is doing a cover story on fifteen up-and-coming figures in the church—authors, leaders, and preachers such as yourself who have a growing sphere of influence."

"I understand," Parker said, trying to sound both unsurprised and unimpressed with himself.

"Great. Let's start with the obvious then. You're thirty-seven years old, a third-generation preacher with a local congregation. A pretty common kind of pastor until a few years ago. Tell me how it is that you now find your audience on the verge of going national."

"Well, Brett, I'd like to think that's God's doing—that he's rewarding me for spreading the amazing news of his love. But I also know that God uses frail human beings like us to carry out his plans—and of course I can't answer your question without bringing up the name Joshua Holton. I'm sure you know what I mean."

"You're referring to your semiregular slot on Holton's program, *Live Your Dreams Now*. How did that come about?"

"Joshua Holton has been something of a mentor to me in recent years. We met at one of his conferences in Fort Worth, and he took an interest in me."

"I believe he's called you his 'great discovery.' What do you suppose he means by that?"

"I don't want to sound like I'm getting a big head over this, Brett, but I do believe God has brought Joshua and me together so that my message can reach his audience."

"But is your message any different from his?"

"I like to think it's nuanced a bit differently, yes. Of course Joshua Holton's been a great influence on me, and he and I have spent some significant time *visioning* together, so there will naturally be some overlap, but that's not a bad thing."

Brett flipped a page on the pad in front of him. "Most of our readers will be aware that Reverend Holton not only has a very highly rated television show, but his books, *Focus on Being You* and *(God Wants You to) Live Well Now*, have spent a combined forty-three weeks on the *New York Times* bestseller list."

It annoyed Parker that the reporter pronounced the parentheses in the book's title.

"And now your book is scheduled for release in the next season. Will you have an endorsement from Joshua Holton?"

Parker's eyes flashed slightly. "I'm not all that involved in the nuts and bolts of the publishing business, Brett, but trust me when I tell you this book will do its own publicity work when word starts to spread about all the changed lives and reborn destinies."

"Do you mind if we talk about your background a little?"

"Not at all."

"Your father and grandfather were both ministers

at Hope Presbyterian Church here in Grand Rapids."

"That's right."

"Were you on staff there as well?"

"Yes, for a while. I've joked that I had to leave Hope to keep it from becoming a dynasty. Dad was associate pastor with my grandfather for ten years. He took a few years away at another church, then came back and pastored for almost twenty years. During the last five I was on staff with Dad as an associate."

"While you completed your studies?"

"Correct."

"And then you started your own church, Abundance Now Ministries."

"That's not exactly accurate. My church grew out of Hope organically."

Brett looked at him blankly for a moment before saying, "I'm never sure what people mean when they say something happened 'organically.' "

"Well, my grandfather always had a radio ministry, even from his earliest days. In the eighties my father expanded that into a television ministry. It was called *Hope This Week*, and it started out as just his sermon from Sunday morning and a little closing thought.

"Near the end of his life, we began putting more and more emphasis on that aspect of the ministry. It actually caused a little bit of tension in the church. When Dad died it seemed natural for us to officially split the church proper from the television outreach. So Abundance Now sort of grew out of Hope Presbyterian."

"And you rebranded the television program as *Speak It into Reality*."

"*An Outreach of Abundance Now Ministries*."

"I'm sorry, what?"

"That's the full name of the show. *Speak It into Reality: An Outreach of Abundance Now Ministries, with Pastor Parker Saint*."

"That's a mouthful compared with *Hope This Week*."

"Sure."

"And you've gone in quite a different direction theologically."

"I don't know if I'd say 'quite different,' but yes, we have our own vision."

"How is the old church doing, by the way?"

Parker looked at his watch and everywhere but at the reporter seated across from him. "I'm sorry, is this interview about Hope Presbyterian or is it about me and my current ministry? Because I'd like to talk about some of the amazing things God is doing here and now."

Brett smiled politely. "Okay, let's talk about you. Your doctrine has come under fire by a number of conservative Christian leaders and self-described 'discernment ministries.' There are even a few blogs dedicated to 'exposing' your theology, or lack thereof. What is your reaction to that?"

"Well, Brett, I don't really sweat that. I preach what God wants me to preach. I'm sorry if some folks want to nitpick and divide, I really am. But I'm not going to worry about a few squeaky wheels when so many lives are being changed."

"So would you call your doctrine orthodox?"

"Yes. I certainly would."

"One Christian broadcaster recently called you a Modalist because of the way you spoke of the Trinity in your series on family dynamics."

He could see in the reporter's body language that he did not expect Parker to know what Modalism was. Parker was used to that. When they saw his television program and his style of preaching, the Brett LaForests of the world assumed that he was biblically and theologically illiterate—just some slick huckster and self-esteem expert who knew how to use quasi-religious language. Parker relished opportunities to prove them wrong.

"Again, I think that's just nitpicking and looking for a way to knock others down. Modalism teaches that God does not exist in three eternal persons. I've never taught that. All I did was use the Trinity as an illustration for how close Christians ought to be to one another. Jesus himself did the same thing in his high priestly prayer in John chapter 17."

If Brett was impressed, he hid it well. He skimmed through his notes and settled on, "You've also been accused of denying the historical and literal reality of hell, sin, and the resurrection."

Parker narrowed his eyes. "When have I done that?"

"Perhaps a better question would be: When have you affirmed those things in your preaching?"

"I preach about resurrection every week. Have you ever actually listened to any of my sermons?"

"I have indeed. While you do preach about the *concept* of resurrection in an individual's dreams or relationships, you almost never bring up the resurrection of Christ as a historical event. Not in the twenty sermons I watched on your website."

"You should read my book."

"I will, I'm sure. But can you just give me an answer now, for the article? Do you deny the resurrection?"

"You know what? I do deny it. Every time I walk past a hungry person and don't help them, I deny the resurrection. Every time I fail to see the divine in the other, I deny the resurrection."

"Mm hmm. And what about hell? Do you deny the existence of hell?"

"Look, you have to understand: I don't focus on that kind of stuff in my preaching. But I think we all deny those truths and we deny Jesus every time we fail to grasp our destiny." Parker hated evading questions with this kind of doublespeak, but Holton had convinced him that it was necessary in order to broaden his influence.

Brett scanned his notes, apparently on the verge of asking another question, then seemed to think better of it. He flipped closed his pad and held out his hand to Parker.

"Thank you so much for your time. I'm really glad I was able to get your perspective for this article. It's very helpful."

"The pleasure was all mine," Parker said. But he had a growing knot in the pit of his stomach, and it wasn't just the unease of a bad interview. The conversation about his ministry was just a reminder that tomorrow was fast approaching. And tomorrow, he'd have to fight to keep everything he'd built from crashing down.

Two

Three men in suits arrived at Brandon Crawford's door just after seven on Sunday night. They seemed to be standing in line youngest to oldest. On the left was a muscular kid in his twenties, his neck popping out of his shirt collar; next to him, a wiry man in his fifties with a neatly trimmed goatee and hair graying around the temples; and on the right, a rugged older man with a mop of white hair and unruly eyebrows that seemed to be reaching out in every direction.

The one in the middle spoke. "Is this the residence of Melanie Jane Candor?"

"It was."

"Yes, of course. Forgive me. I'm terribly sorry for your loss. I assume that you are Brandon Crawford, her boyfriend?"

"Fiancé," he corrected.

"Again, my apologies." The man's speech was soft and even. "We'd like to ask you a few questions if that's all right."

Brandon's face fell. "I've already talked to the police. For like six hours total. I've told them everything there is to tell. More than once."

The wiry man retrieved a badge from his inside coat pocket and held it toward Brandon.

"We're not with the police, son. This investigation has a much further-reaching scope than local law enforcement. My name is Frank Xavier. We would really appreciate just a few minutes with you."

Brandon opened the door. "Federal agents," he mumbled to himself. "For crying out loud."

He led them to a formal dining room, where a lone plate sat topped with most of a chicken potpie. "You can ask me questions while I eat," he said flatly, "or you can come back when it's not dinnertime."

"Not a problem at all," Xavier replied. "May we sit?"

"Go for it."

"I know you're tired of giving the same answers over and over, and I know you've been through

26

this before, but please, if you could . . . just start by telling us about Melanie."

Brandon thought for a moment. "Actually, no one's asked me to do that."

"*We're* asking you to do that."

He set his fork down and tipped his head back toward the ceiling. "She was amazing. She was everything I'm not: smart, capable, creative, talented, caring. She could listen to your problems, you know, and not say a word, just *listen.* And somehow everything felt better when you got done jawing at her. You weren't mad anymore or stressed out or . . ." He trailed off.

"She sounds incredible," the youngest agent said.

"She was. And for whatever reason, she loved *me.* I mean really, really loved me. I told her once that she deserved someone better, and she got so mad at me—for talking myself down like that. She gave me the silent treatment for three hours. That was the only time she was ever that mad at me. Can you believe that? For saying I didn't deserve her."

"How was Melanie's relationship with her parents?" asked Xavier.

"Good. Pretty good, anyway. They'd had some rocky times when she was in high school. She ran away for a few months one time, spent some time in a foster home. But lately it was good. If it weren't for me, it would have been better." He shoveled a bite of potpie into his mouth and kept talking. "They agreed with me that Mel deserved someone more at her level."

"How tense was the situation?"

"To be honest, they hated me. Her mom especially. But Mel took it all in stride. She told them she couldn't stay away from me because I was the inspiration for her art." He laughed a hollow laugh. "I doubt that. I can't even draw a stick figure."

"I understand she was studying art at university?"

"Yeah, illustration, at the Kensey School of Art and Design. This would have been her last semester. She could do amazing things with a pencil and a piece of paper. Look at this . . ." He disappeared for a moment into the adjoining kitchen and reappeared with a folio, from which he pulled a drawing of a woman half-submerged in a river, with the title *The Rise of Aquarius* in even block letters along the top.

"Impressive," the white-haired man said, his voice as crisp as his appearance was frowsy. "May I have a closer look?"

Brandon handed him the drawing, which he studied against the light for half a minute, making sounds of approval.

"Aquarius," he said, musing to himself. "The subject matter reminds me—we have some reason to believe that Melanie's murder and that of the boy who was found this morning may have been religiously motivated."

"You think the same person killed them both?"

"Similar markings were found on both victims," Xavier explained.

"Spades are religious now?"

"There may be more to it than that. Was Melanie a religious woman?"

"Not really. She was born a Catholic, I guess. Baptized as a baby, Catholic school as a kid, but she wasn't really into that. She wasn't a fanatic or anything." His voice cracked. "Love was her religion. She believed in kindness." He squeezed his eyes shut as hard as he could until the tears passed, unwilling to let them out.

"We're very sorry to be dredging all this up for you again, Brandon," said Xavier. "Just a couple more questions. Do you have any idea why Melanie might have been in the neighborhood where her body was found?"

"No. None. She was really careful about going out at night. She certainly didn't hang out in abandoned houses. Someone forced her to go in there. I know they did. Or they just dumped her body there when they were done with her. And if I ever find out who it was . . ." His face darkened. "Well, the way they killed Mel will seem like nothing compared to what I do to them. Love isn't *my* religion. Not anymore."

The three agents glanced at one another and stood in unison.

"Again, we are so sorry for your loss, Mr. Crawford," Xavier said, "and we thank you for your time. You've been very helpful. We'll show ourselves out. Try to enjoy your dinner."

The three men filed wordlessly out the door, down the steps, and into a late-model Cadillac sedan, the oldest man behind the wheel, the youngest riding shotgun, and Xavier in the backseat.

As the car pulled out of the driveway, the young man spoke up. "Stuff I need to get off my chest: first, I know you two are used to your good cop versus bad cop, diplomatic versus semiautomatic routine. You've been doing it forever. I get it. But remember who the Superior General tagged this time around." He shot a look at the old man behind the wheel, who just glared at the stretch of road ahead of him. "Also, let me go on record that I'm skeptical about the connections here. Tying the murders to the church burning and the vandalism seems like a stretch to begin with. But does anyone really think this has something to do with the Crown?"

The driver answered, his voice now thick with a Spanish accent. "Someone above us believes the two are linked or we wouldn't be here, Michael. Therefore, we approach this with an open mind."

"Yeah, I guess." The young man pulled off his

tie and clawed at the button on his collar. "Man, I hate these things." He tossed the tie on the dash and took a deep breath, rubbing his neck. "It's funny, I started wearing a clerical collar in seminary, what, seven years ago? All my friends from back home kept saying, 'Aren't they uncomfortable?' and 'It looks so tight!' but they'll wear these things to work every stinking day. It's a noose. How is this not a noose?" There was no response. "What are your thoughts, Father Ignatius?"

"I think you talk an awful lot," the older priest said.

"Just making up for letting Father Xavier do all the talking back there." He glanced back. "Let me add to the record that I don't like pretending I'm your intern or something. I've worked hard to earn this appointment, and now it's like I'm back in diapers."

Xavier answered from the backseat, his voice firm but gentle. "Father Michael, take some advice from a more experienced priest: you need to repent of your pride and think of the order, and the church, and the mission at hand. Being one of the Jesuits Militant means blending in with the expectations of others. Anything that would stand out, seem odd or memorable, we want to avoid."

They pulled to a stop at an intersection.

Michael sighed. "Father Ignatius, you do realize

that you can just roll on through yellow lights here in the States, right? That's allowed."

"As Father Xavier said, I am avoiding suspicion by obeying the laws of the land."

"No, stopping at a yellow *arouses* suspicion here. And your left blinker is on."

He turned it off.

Father Michael fought down a smile. "Look, I've been meaning to ask you something for a while now. When you were a young man, fighting the Moors in Spain, did you prefer the musket or the saber as your weapon of choice?"

Silence.

"Father Ignatius . . . ?"

"I get it. I'm old."

Michael slapped him on the knee. "Yes! You are. You're an antique. I, on the other hand, am young and fresh. But that's cool! We can complement each other." He gestured back and forth between them. "Old school; new school. Inquisition; intervention. Council of Trent; Vatican II. If you can set aside your grumpiness, I think we could have something snappy here. What do you say?"

The light changed and Ignatius slowly accelerated. "I say that I never question my orders from the Superior General. And he has decided that I answer to you for the duration of our time here."

"That's good to hear." Michael made eye

contact with Father Xavier in the rearview mirror. "You're awfully quiet back there."

"Leave me out of this."

"Fair enough. But really, you guys, let me just say that after all we've been through together, it's an honor to be telling you what to do. I mean that." He placed a hand firmly on Father Ignatius's shoulder. "And look, I'm sorry about all that Moors and muskets stuff. That was out of line."

"Yes, it was. It was disrespectful and unprofessional."

"I totally agree and I apologize. Just tell me one thing, though: did you wear a cape back then? Because I think capes are awesome."

Sunday afternoon, in theory, began Parker's day off. He liked the thought of unwinding after all the stress of the previous week, which had slowly built up to the climax of the morning's broadcast. But it was just a theory and it rarely happened. Someday he would have a large enough staff to deal with every little detail, he often told himself. For now, he'd have to settle for a little time off here and there.

The Reverend T. Charles Watkins, however, always took Fridays off. He worked like a dog Saturday through Thursday, but Friday was sacrosanct. How he could rest and unwind that close to Sunday morning was a mystery to Parker, but that was one of the things he loved about Charles. Charles could let go of it all.

"Pastor Saint! How are you doing today?" Tasha, the young receptionist at Holy Ghost Tabernacle, smiled up at him.

"Charlie's got you working on Sunday afternoon now?" He shook his head slowly. "That's reprehensible. I'll talk to him for you."

"Don't mess this up for me," she warned. "He's letting me skip out tomorrow and Tuesday to visit my sister."

Parker laughed. "I won't say a word. Is the Right Reverend in by chance?"

"Nothing's by chance, but yes, Pastor Watkins is in his office. I'll tell him you'd like to see him." She held a brief exchange through her headset. "He'll be out in just a second," she chirped. "How's the church coming along? I heard you were up near five thousand last week."

"We're getting there. I keep telling Charlie he should come out on a Sunday and show them how real preaching is done."

"I'm afraid I have a standing engagement on Sunday mornings, Parker." Charles stood in the doorway to his expansive office and beckoned his friend. "But I have a few minutes for you now. Come on in. And Tasha, are you done filing those quarterly reports?"

"Almost done, Pastor."

"I see. And I see you filing your nails in the reflection on the window."

Her smile disappeared. "I was just, um, taking my break from before, because—"

"It's okay. Just try to have it done before the evening service, okay?"

Charles closed the door and motioned for Parker to have a seat on a black leather couch, while he took a chair on the far side of a stylish coffee table.

"I hope this is just a social call, Parker." He smiled broadly, causing his brown skin to crinkle a bit around his eyes. He could have been fifty or seventy. Parker guessed closer to the latter.

"Yes, partially. I also brought this." He slid an envelope across to his friend.

"That's not necessary. I've told you."

"This should cover their share of the utilities for a few more months and the use of whatever rooms they're occupying."

"Parker, we're happy to have them here. And I'm happy to do you the favor. What has become of the body of Christ if one church can't open her doors to another when they lose their building?" He chuckled. "Even if they are Presbyterians."

"I know, it's just—"

"Young man, do you remember when Holy Ghost Tabernacle had that fire? It was probably twenty years ago. We'd been meeting in a leaky little building on Division that used to be a barbershop."

"I remember. I was a teenager. It was just before my grandfather died. You lost everything."

"Not everything, Parker. The church was untouched. We just lost a building. But my point is that your father reached out to me and offered to let us meet at Hope Presbyterian while we found a new facility. Four other churches made the same offer. We wound up in with some Baptists a block away."

"And that was nice of my father, but this situation may be more permanent, Charlie. Hope Presbyterian is dying. It's slowly shrinking toward nothing."

"You aren't to blame for that, Parker."

"I know. It's not guilt. It's compassion. I care about these people. Did you know I met with a banker when they lost the building, to see if I could get a loan and pay off their mortgage?"

"No, but that doesn't surprise me."

"Well, after my book comes out, I may be able to do just that—get the building back for them. In the meantime, if you won't take the money today, I'll just mail the church a cashier's check."

Charlie handed the envelope back to Parker. "Give it to Tasha. At least she can give you a tax receipt, and you can write it off."

"Thanks, Charlie."

"It's no problem. But next time I see you, it had better be for some real fellowship."

"You got it."

"Good. You may be getting big, but you're never too big-time for old Charlie."

• • •

Dinner was in the oven, some smooth jazz on the stereo, and Isabella Escalanté looked more put together than she had in weeks. She glanced at her watch. It was 8:43 p.m. Leon had promised he'd be there by a quarter to nine, but there was still construction on I-96, so she had her doubts.

She hadn't seen her boyfriend in nearly a month. Leon's decision to tackle eighteen credit hours this semester was already taking its toll. Rather than commute every day, he'd gotten an apartment in Ann Arbor, near campus. They'd been talking every night on the phone, telling each other it would be worthwhile when he got his degree almost a year early, but that did nothing to ease her pain now.

She turned up the stereo. Jazz was best appreciated at low levels, but the woman in the apartment downstairs was half deaf, and her television continually blared judge shows. Always judge shows, as if she had access to some all-judge-shows satellite channel. At first this had annoyed Isabella to no end, but considering the paper-thin walls, she had come to appreciate the "cover" it provided and the accompanying sense of privacy for the other three units in the building.

The intercom buzzed, and she ran to the bathroom door to give herself one last check. She was more than satisfied with what she saw. Another buzz. She laughed. Leon had somehow lost the third key she'd given him, and still it came off as a lovable quirk.

"Come on up, baby," she said into the intercom and buzzed him in. She opened the door just a crack and then assumed the pose she'd practiced in the mirror that morning—head tilted and knees together like a magazine cover girl. She wished the only door to her apartment didn't enter into the kitchen—she was certain she could look more glamorous in the living room—but she'd make the best of it. Besides, the curried chicken smelled perfect, Ramsey Lewis was coming from the speakers, and she could barely even hear the two former best friends suing and countersuing each other over a car they'd bought together.

She heard footsteps coming up.

And then a man she'd never seen before walked into her apartment. He was the opposite of Leon in almost every way. Slim, white, ugly, dressed all in black with long, dark hair falling in his eyes. His standing there in her kitchen was so unexpected and bizarre that it took a moment for the panic to set in.

"Who are you?" was all she could get out.

"Hello to you too, Bella." He spoke softly, a strange combination of comforting and cruel.

"I don't know you."

"But I know you. I've been getting to know you for a while now."

He took a step toward her. Her heart was

thudding so hard she could feel it in the tips of her toes.

He sniffed the air. "Is that some kind of pork dish I smell?"

"Chicken," she whispered. She was thinking of her cell phone, plugged into the charger next to her bed. The man took another step toward her.

Isabella ran to her right and pivoted, turning toward the door. She'd been a basketball player in high school and could move when she needed to. But not in heels.

The man caught her easily and shoved her back into the kitchen. "I just got here," he said with a malicious grin. "Where are your manners?"

"My—my boyfriend will be here any minute." Her voice sounded foreign to her. "I think I hear him now. Leon!" she shouted. The word melted into the music behind her and the empty hallway below.

She tried to think clearly, to channel her fear into anger. "He's huge. He can bench-press four hundred pounds. And he's got a temper. If he finds some goblin-lookin' white boy in here bothering me, I don't know what he'll do."

"That's an interesting prospect. What *would* he do?" The man reached into his black trench coat and pulled out a shiny black knife with a diamond-shaped blade.

"He carries a gun," she sobbed. "My boyfriend does. I'm not kidding."

"I know he does. Leon Price, third-year senior at the University of Michigan, studying criminal justice. Smart kid, thinks he's already a cop and carries a Glock 17 in his waistband, right about here." He pointed to his side.

"How do you know that?"

The man slammed the door shut and threw the dead bolt. His face darkened and his body tensed. "We know that because we've done our homework. We're very precise about what we do. We need you to know that. The papers will call this random, but we've planned every last detail. You were dead when you woke up this morning, Bella."

Isabella threw the sugar bowl in his face and lunged for the knife block on the counter, coming away with a long, serrated steak knife. "Stay away from me."

The man smiled. "This is priceless." Isabella's hands were shaking. "Well, don't just stand there. Use it," he urged, striding toward her. She held the knife up with both hands and closed her eyes tight, crying. A moment later she felt her arm twist roughly behind her back. The knife fell to the floor, and she went sailing into two chairs.

The intercom buzzed.

"Leon!" she shouted, reaching out and barely making contact with the button. The intruder slammed her back to the floor. "Leon!"

The man pointed the knife at her and covered

her mouth. "Will young Leon be joining us this evening? This just keeps getting more interesting."

It buzzed again. Then Leon's voice: "Bella, are you there? I lost my key, baby. Buzz me in."

"You're in trouble now," she said. "You should just leave. Go down the back stairs. I promise you, he'll kill you if he finds you in here."

There was a loud thud from below. They both paused and listened to the stifled sound of footsteps coming up the stairs, then a pounding on the door. "Isabella? Are you in there? Is everything all right?"

She tried to shout his name, but the man had his hand on her throat. All she could hear was the TV downstairs. Those stupid judge shows.

And then nothing.

Three

Evert Carlson could never just meet with someone—he always had to "break bread" with them. Evert preferred Chinese restaurants, so there was usually no bread per se, but "breaking egg rolls" just didn't have the same ring to it.

Parker had agreed to meet him for an early lunch Monday at the Ming Tree, a small family-owned restaurant in downtown Grand Rapids. Evert was in his late seventies, retired for almost fifteen years, but unlike most of his contemporaries, he hadn't downgraded to sweatpants and T-shirts. His suit was the same charcoal gray as Parker's, only thirty years older.

The waitress had just brought the bill and the fortune cookies on a little plastic tray, which Evert snatched up with surprising speed for a man of his age.

"My invitation, my treat."

Parker knew from experience not to argue. "Thanks, Dr. Carlson."

"Call me Ev, boy. You're making me feel older than I am." He handed Parker a cookie. "Here. Tell me your fortune."

Parker popped open the little plastic pouch and cracked the stale cookie in two. "It says, 'One who is true is worth three who are wise.' I don't know what that even means."

Evert frowned. "That's not a fortune. That's a nonsensical proverb. You should ask for another one."

"No, that's okay."

"No, really. You should." His voice was rising, drawing some looks from adjacent diners. "It's called a fortune cookie, which clearly implies that it contains an actual fortune," he fumed. "Have you heard of the Michigan Implied Warranty? If you sell me something, it has to do what the name implies. That's the law."

"Calm down, Ev. Look, we can interpret it as a

fortune. It's telling me that I should stay true. Good things will happen if I stay true. That's a fortune."

"Well, are you?"

"Here we go." Parker sat back in the booth.

"You brought it up. Are you staying true to who you are?"

"Yes, I believe I am."

"You know who stayed true to his last breath? Your grandfather."

"How did I know you were going to bring him up?"

"He was my mentor during my darkest days, son. And he was my pastor and my best friend, apart from my wife. What do you think Pastor Brian, Sr. would think of the way you've gone?"

Parker sighed. "I know you don't like big churches, Dr. Carlson. And I know you've got some beef with the charismatic camp, but—"

"You know better than that," Evert scolded. "You know the friends I've had over the years and the partnerships in ministry. I believe that our Pentecostal brothers and sisters bring something to the table that no other tradition can. And I've got no problem with megachurches either, if they grow because they've focused on proclaiming the gospel—not on scratching people's itching ears."

"And that's what you think I'm doing."

"I don't know for sure. All I know is that you graduated seminary with a fire lit under you like

I've never seen. And then that fire was doused with record speed."

"My father died, Dr. Carlson. Someone had to take over his ministry, or everything we'd been building for twenty years would have been down the drain."

"You may have taken over his ministry empire, but what about the church he pastored? The church that your grandfather pastored for thirty years, the church he brought back from the brink of apostasy and built up into a strong outpost of the kingdom of God? That church is in danger of closing its doors forever, Parker. Aren't you worried about all of *his* work having been for naught?"

"I'm not going to answer to my father or my grandfather, Evert. Or to you. Ultimately, I'm only going to answer to my heavenly father."

"Seems to me you mostly answer to that Joshua Holton fellow."

"You don't need to tell me again how you feel about Joshua Holton."

"The things that man offers his followers are the same things the devil has been offering since the beginning: wealth, satisfaction, all your dreams coming true right now at your very whim!"

Parker forced a laugh. "You're telling me that Joshua Holton is in league with the Prince of Darkness? You've obviously never met him."

"Met him? Son, I wrote my dissertation on the devil."

"I meant Joshua Holton."

"Hmm. Maybe not, but I've met his type a thousand times. Satan masquerades as an angel of light. That's basic theology. You know why it was a serpent in the garden of Eden? Not because serpents are gross or slimy—they're not!—it's because they're beautiful. They move seductively. The devil doesn't look like Anton LaVey or—what's his name?—Marilyn Manson. The devil looks a lot more like Joshua Holton: slick hair, nice suit, gleaming white smile."

"You're wearing a suit too, sir."

"You know what I'm trying to say. I don't doubt your motives in getting wrapped up with him, Parker. But I worry where it will go. You remind me of the apostle Peter in the Gospels. You want to serve God, but you're impetuous. You want to do it your way—a way that looks a lot like the world's idea of success."

"I don't think God dislikes success. Neither does Josh Holton. And he preaches from the same Bible you do."

"Even the devil quoted Scripture to Jesus in the wilderness, and twisted it into something that appeals to the flesh."

Parker smirked. "I just don't see the devil waiting around every corner, especially not in a fellow pastor's ministry."

"As I said, you remind me of Saint Peter. It was Peter who wrote that the devil 'prowls around like a roaring lion, seeking someone to devour.' And yet, Peter wasn't ready for the devil when he came as a serpent. You have to be ready for both."

"I should get going, Doc."

Evert put his hand on Parker's. "The church needs you. I want you to think about taking this star power of yours and using it for good. Your grandfather's pulpit—your father's pulpit—is vacant. You could build that church back up."

"Why don't you take the job? You're passionate enough about it."

Evert gazed out the window. "My last cardiologist appointment was not encouraging. I don't have much time left, Parker. I'm a pilgrim nearing the City."

Parker's annoyance with the old man sank away in a moment. "Dr. Carlson, I don't know what to say."

"You don't have to say anything, son. I know my only hope in life and death. I'm more worried about you. You're on the top of the world right now—from the world's own point of view. It's when you hit bottom that you'll understand what Jesus meant about being poor in spirit."

Parker looked at the time on his phone. "I have another appointment I have to get to, sir. Thanks for lunch. Let's get together again soon."

"God willing." He gave Parker's hand one more squeeze and then began the project of getting up from the booth.

"Aren't you going to look at your fortune, sir?"

Evert shook his head. "Never do. I already know my fortune."

Parker left the restaurant and headed up Division at a brisk pace. As he waited for the signal to change at the intersection, he took in the quintessential Grand Rapids corner: three out of four buildings were churches. One bore a large For Sale sign. He felt a twinge of guilt.

What a strange situation. His home church had lost its building, while dozens of church buildings sat on the market to be grabbed up and either bulldozed or converted into office space. But Joshua Holton had hammered this point home over and again: if you're going to grow, you need something bigger, something that looks less churchy. Holton had snatched up the bankrupt Fort Worth Civic Center, which he filled to capacity each week. Parker had started smaller, purchasing a shopping center.

The signal changed. Parker picked up the pace. He couldn't be late for court.

Downtown Grand Rapids was inordinately clean and bright. Every third street corner showed visitors their location on a map, a large dotted circle bragging that one was almost always less than a five-minute walk from any other point downtown. Today this worked in Parker's favor.

He sprinted up to the Kent County Courthouse, huffing and panting, with three minutes to spare.

If things went well, this would be his last trip here, which suited him just fine. Overestimating his own renown, he donned a pair of dark glasses and made his way through the security screening at the entrance.

Mark Walsh, Parker's lawyer, was waiting impatiently on the other side, tapping his briefcase against his leg. "Parker, baby. Let's *go!* If we're late, bad things happen. Follow me." They power walked twenty yards down a side hall.

"Sorry. I was having lunch."

"Right. How could you possibly have foreseen that need? Catches me by surprise every day."

"Do you bill extra for sarcasm?"

Mark came to an abrupt stop in front of a closed door—one of thirty just like it—causing Parker to bounce off of him. The lawyer looked at his watch. "We're okay. But before we go in, let me warn you. This is not exactly what we were hoping for."

"What do you mean?"

"It's going to be more complicated than we thought. But it's not anything I could have predicted."

"You said one more meeting and we were home free."

"Last-minute change. It couldn't have been predicted."

"So you keep saying. Just tell me there's no chance I'm going to jail."

"You know I can't tell you that. Come on, we'll be late." He opened the door.

The room was smaller than Parker expected, and lit with the kind of fluorescent lighting that made him think of incarceration.

Three people were already seated at a conference table, papers spread out before them. Parker immediately noticed that the combed-over little weasel from the prosecutor's office—the one Parker had been dealing with since this thing began—was not there. Instead, Ashley Englesma, the Kent County prosecutor, sat at the head of the table. Next to her was Brynn Carter, the woman who had caused all this. And next to her a man he'd never seen before.

The prosecutor pointed to the clock. "You're late, Walsh."

"Not by my watch."

She rolled her eyes. "Please, have a seat. You too, Mr. Saint, wherever you like." Parker's knees wobbled as he lowered himself into the faux leather chair.

She looked him in the eyes intensely. "Mr. Saint, you do realize that this is not an arraignment or any type of official legal hearing. You're not being formally charged with anything today. There's no judge and no jury. Do you understand?"

"So help me God," he quipped.

She gave him a dead stare for a moment and then shook her head slightly. "I'd like to start by reviewing the facts. Mr. Saint has been accused of threatening and physically assaulting one Brynn Carter, an employee of SkyTown Airlines, on the eighteenth of August this year." She pulled a typed statement from a manila folder. "She has indicated that Mr. Saint, quote, 'Shouted at me in a threatening manner.' When told that his ticket to DFW was nonrefundable, he asked, 'Don't you know who I am? I don't deserve this . . .'"

"My client knows what Ms. Carter has accused him of. Can we just skip ahead?"

"No, I'd like to sum up where your client's case stands, if you don't mind."

"With all due respect, Ms. Englesma, my understanding was that this would be an informal meeting to tie up some loose ends."

"Whoever gave you that idea?"

"You did. I was under the impression from our previous conversation that this was just a formality, and we could lay this matter to rest today."

"So you thought this would be an informal formality?"

"Well, when you put it like that, it sounds . . ."

"May I continue, Mr. Walsh?"

"Why not?"

She found her place in the document. "According to Ms. Carter, Mr. Saint then 'shoved the contents of the counter in my direction, causing a plastic literature rack and a bottle of hand sanitizer to fly toward me and make physical contact with me.' He then told her, quote, 'You'll regret this. I promise.' "

Parker scoffed. "Miss Englesma, I've already told your assistant, this is not how it happened. Was I rude? Yes. Was I condescending? Maybe. Did I 'assault her verbally'? I don't know."

"Parker, shut up," his lawyer murmured.

"I did push her hand away when she stuck it in my face, but I didn't throw anything at her, I didn't push anything at her, and this whole thing is just plain stupid. And worst of all, she knows it."

Brynn didn't look up from the table.

"That was quite a closing statement," Ms. Englesma said. "But as I told you, you're not on trial today. I'm just reviewing the details—for my own benefit as much as anything else. Now, I understand that Ms. Carter would no longer like to pursue a criminal case against Mr. Saint. I also understand that, via their private legal counsels, Mr. Saint and Ms. Carter have come to a tentative financial settlement in a pending civil suit stemming from the same altercation."

She looked from Parker to Brynn. "First of all, let me say that I'm impressed with how quickly you've worked all this out. Just record time. Unfortunately for you, Mr. Saint, any civil action against you is unrelated to these criminal charges."

"But you said yourself, she wants to drop the charges," he protested, his stomach in free fall. "They can't go forward now, can they, Mark?"

"It's highly unusual, but yes, they can continue to pursue the case if they want. Seems like a bit of a suicide mission."

The prosecutor leaned her elbows on the table. "We *could* subpoena Ms. Carter and let her decide whether or not to contradict her earlier written and videotaped statements. But we don't want to do that."

"Of course not," Mark said. "Now we're coming to the pitch."

Ms. Englesma turned to Brynn and said firmly, "I'd like you to go and wait in the room directly across the hall. I'll follow up with you shortly." Brynn gathered her belongings and left without a word.

When she was gone, Mark placed his palms flat against the table. "Okay, Englesma. What do you want from my client?"

She gestured to the man next to her. "This is Detective Paul Ketcham of the Grand Rapids Police Department's Major Crimes Team."

Parker exploded. "Knocking over some brochures is a major crime?"

"No. But interrupting me gets a little closer."

"Sorry."

"Detective, it's all yours."

Ketcham opened an accordion file folder and retrieved a small stack of papers. "You've probably heard by now that another two victims of the so-called Blackjack Killer were found this morning. That makes number three and number four. And according to the newspapers, three makes a spree."

"You've got our attention," the lawyer said.

"Based on the two most recent victims, it's now clear that the perpetrator of these crimes is motivated by some sort of religious ideology. I would like Reverend Saint to work with me and my team in analyzing these crimes and working toward the apprehension of a suspect."

"Are you talking about a plea deal?" asked Parker.

Ms. Englesma answered, "No, it's not a plea. We've postponed your arraignment three months. Cooperate with Detective Ketcham and his team in the meantime—offer your assistance in his investigation to the best of your ability—and the charges will simply be dropped by the prosecutor's office. You won't need a plea deal, and you won't have a criminal record."

"I'd like to discuss this with my client, please," Mark said.

"Of course," she replied. "Detective Ketcham and I will be outside."

When they'd left, Mark threw up his hands.

"What choice do you have, Parker? I'd grab this in a heartbeat."

"I'm still trying to figure out what is going on here. If the so-called victim wants to drop the charges, why would they burn taxpayer money prosecuting me?"

Mark considered this for a moment. "I think two things are going on. First of all, they know you're a prominent minister in town. They know you can't afford to be accused of assaulting a woman. Whether you're convicted or not is almost irrelevant. You know that, right?"

Parker nodded.

"Secondly, both the prosecutor and the detective out there have a vested interest in catching this killer quickly and getting a conviction. It'll be a feather in both their caps. I guess they see your predicament as an opportunity to get an expert at their beck and call."

"*Expert?* I'm not an expert on killers. Where did they get that?"

"Maybe they just want to be seen consulting with high-profile clergy—Grand Rapids politics. I don't know. But the deal she offered was that you help 'to the best of your ability,' not that you prove to be useful. If we can get that in writing, you've got nothing to lose."

"There's no other option?"

"Hey, I'll be honest. I only stand to gain if we go to trial. I can bill you for another pile of hours, and

I know I'd win the case. Heck, *she* knows I'd win the case. And I don't think she's bluffing. That's why I advise you to just play along."

Parker thought about the beating he'd taken from the *Christianity in View* reporter. He knew that if news of this mess were to hit the papers, the next ten interviews he did would be about his supposedly assaulting a woman for doing her job. Forget a book tour; he'd need a damage-control tour. Everything he'd been working toward was hanging in the balance.

"Okay. Tell her I'll do it."

Parker phoned Paige while he waited at the corner of Lyon and Ottawa for the detective to pull his car around.

"How did the meeting with Mr. Walsh go?" she asked, her voice hopeful.

"Not great, but it could have been worse."

"What does that mean?"

"For starters, it means that you need to cancel the three appointments I have this afternoon and hold off scheduling anything else for the time being unless you coordinate it directly with me."

"You're not going to jail, are you?"

"No. But for a while we're going to have to work my ministry schedule around some volunteer police work I'm doing."

"Volunteer poli—*huh?*"

"It's a plea deal from the DA. Or it's like a plea deal. If I do this, the charges go away."

Paige stifled a laugh. "No offense, but how in the world are you qualified for any type of police work?"

"You've heard of the Blackjack Killer?"

"Don't tell me . . ."

"They need some help analyzing 'religious motives' in the crimes."

"Parker, this is incredible for us."

"Come again?"

"If they catch this murderer while you're working the case—I can't believe I just said that—if you're helping with the investigation and they catch him, can you imagine what it will do for book sales? Seriously. I'm going to call Charter House and tell them we may be doing some rewrites to capitalize on this. We're looking at *Good Morning America* if this works out. Barry is going to be ecstatic."

"Let's not get ahead of ourselves. I have to go. The detective's here."

Parker surveyed the 1986 Bonneville as he climbed into the passenger seat. The back was full of large, square plastic containers, and the floor in front was littered with empty paper coffee cups, rattling all around Parker's shoes.

"Budget cuts, right?"

The detective shot him a sharp sidelong glance. "This is my personal car. It's also my office and my friend. Show some respect, Reverend Saint."

"You can call me Parker."

"Okay, Parker. You can call me Detective Ketcham. And since you bring it up, the reason I drive this classic example of Detroit design and reliability is because I like things that are genuine." He still hadn't left the curb in front of the courthouse. "I don't like new cars, which are basically plastic bubbles. I like cars that have straight edges and are more than fifty percent metal. My car is genuine. And I'm going to be genuine with you right from the get-go. Securing your services was my idea, and I'm hoping you're the genuine article as well."

"I'll do my best."

He grunted. "I hope you have a strong stomach."

"Why?"

"We're headed to the crime scene." Ketcham shifted into drive and merged into traffic. "You don't mind if I smoke," he said, drawing a cigar from a plastic tube and striking a match.

"Well, actually, I'd—"

"I wasn't asking."

After half a minute of awkward silence, Parker pointed to the containers in back. "What's in there? Some kind of high-tech, crime analysis equipment?"

"It's files."

"Oh. That's a lot of files."

"I know. I don't like computers. I don't like

scans and I don't like e-mails. I like paper. It's genuine."

Parker had no response but wanted to avoid more silence. "So, did you get into police work because of your name?"

"Excuse me?"

"Like, there are bad guys out there and I need to Ketcham."

"Huh. I've never noticed that before. Did you get into preaching because of your name?"

Parker, who had been born Brian Parker III, had no desire to discuss names any further.

"Do you think we're going to solve the crime today?" The moment the question left Parker's mouth, he realized how ridiculous it sounded.

"No, I don't think we will. Detection is more art than science and it takes time. Forget your stupid procedural police shows where they find a flake of the guy's skin and a supercomputer tells them the perp's ID ten minutes later. We'll be talking to a lot of people in the days to come. I need you to be listening, noticing anything that might relate to your area of expertise. I know you're used to blabbing. Can you listen?"

"Yes, I'm trained to be a very good listener."

"Good. And to answer your question, yes, I will solve this case. I've done it before; that's why it was assigned to me. I'm the one who identified James Patrick Cramer."

"Who's that?"

"He killed four prostitutes a few years ago."

"I remember that. He wound up killing himself, didn't he?"

"Oh, stop it. You're breaking my heart."

"Paul's here," Corrinne announced. "Oh, and he brought a friend! Awww . . ."

Ketcham tried not to smile. "Parker, this lovely brute is Detective Corrinne Kirkpatrick—"

"Hey!"

"—and the guy staring at the dead girl is Detective Troy Ellis. Try to bear with him. He was born without sense."

"You're hilarious, you know that?" Troy was in his early fifties and had the build of a high school athlete who had replaced exercise with beer the moment he turned twenty-one. He was several inches taller than any living person in the room, although the dead man in the doorway came close.

Parker had been asked to step over the body to enter the apartment. Instead, he'd pressed his back to the doorframe and shuffled past the dead man, his eyes trained on the far wall, much to the delight of the detectives. He was now wishing he could do it over and step confidently over the corpse without flinching, so that he could interpret the step over the body as a metaphorical step into a whole new world of excitement and intrigue.

But he couldn't.

"I think you both know what Parker is doing

here." Ketcham inspected the soggy, chewed end of his cigar. "He's a minister. He's been to minister school. What do you call that, Parker?"

"Seminary."

"Right. He's here to unravel some of this devil-worshiping stuff that's been carved into our victims. Troy, this is your crime scene, I suppose. What have you got?"

Parker held up a hand. He wanted to keep the focus off the carnage for a moment longer if he could. "I'm sorry," he said. "I'm new to all this, so I'm just trying to understand how things work. Is a different one of you investigating each separate incident?"

"Technically we've got three crime scenes, so they've been assigned to three of us," Troy explained. "But Ketch here solved the big hooker case, so we're following his lead."

"He's kind of coordinating things then," Parker said.

"That's right." Troy nodded. "If I were Corrinne, I'd make some wise-guy comment about him, but I actually think Detective Ketcham is a brilliant investigator."

"He has to be nice to him," Corrinne chimed in. "Paul's his nephew."

"No, he's not," Troy said. "Anyway, what I've got is this: two young kids with bright futures who should not be lying here at room temperature. Probably the work of one man: a complete sicko who gets off on Satanism. First victim is a twenty-three-year-old female, Isabella Escalanté. Height: five foot seven. Weight: 121 pounds. Race: half black, half Mexican."

"Is that the politically correct way to put it?" Corrinne asked.

"I dunno. How would you say it?"

"I guess, half black, half Mexican."

Troy pointed at Isabella with his clipboard. "Just like the last two vics, cause of death was loss of blood due to a knife wound to the throat. I'm sure Dr. Potter will confirm that. As with the other one, no sign of sexual assault."

"What did she do?" Parker asked. "For a living."

Troy frowned. "She was a nurse's aide. By all accounts, she loved what she did and her patients loved her."

"Let's move on to the artwork," Ketcham said.

"The upside-down cross isn't much more creative than yesterday's," Corrinne said with a touch of disappointment. "But what's this word: *nex?*"

"No idea. Preacher?"

"Um, how's it spelled?" Parker asked.

Ketcham palmed the back of Parker's head and directed it toward Isabella's body. "Remember what I said about listening? Well, looking is just as important with this job. What do you see?"

An inverted cross had been painted in blood on her sternum, partially obstructed by her low-cut blouse. On her forehead, the letters *N E X* had been painted in all caps with the same careful strokes. Parker tried with all his resolve not to look at her throat, cut deeply from one side to the other, dried blood clinging to the skin.

He felt the Chinese food coming back up his throat. He slapped a hand over his mouth and ran into the cramped bathroom, slamming the door behind him to block out the sound of the three detectives guffawing in the kitchen.

Do not throw up, he commanded himself. *Get ahold of yourself!* He swallowed hard, forcing his lunch back into place. He was about to face the jeers of his three new colleagues when an idea struck him. He pulled his phone from his pocket and opened an Internet search.

Nex? He had no idea what *nex* was. Seminary had covered the biblical languages, Hebrew and Greek, comprehensively. And, unlike most of his colleagues, Parker had kept up on them. But he was almost certain that *nex* was neither language.

He typed the word into the search bar on his phone. The first two pages of results were for telecom companies and gadget websites. He started over and typed "nex translation." The third hit was a Latin to English dictionary. He opened the web page. It was blank save for the words, "Nex: death" and "Back to index."

Parker smacked his lips and frowned. Despite having kept his lunch down, his mouth still tasted like vomit. Setting the phone on the sink, he fished around in his back pocket for a foil pack of prescription nicotine gum. He popped a piece from a little plastic bubble and wrapped it in a stick of tooth-whitening spearmint gum. Joshua Holton had taught him that trick. Quit smoking and kick-start your winning smile all at once. He felt a little rush from the nicotine as he sank his teeth into it.

"You okay in there?" Ketcham called from the other side of the door.

Parker pocketed his phone and emerged from the bathroom.

The detectives were gathered around the dead man in the doorway while Troy read from his clipboard. "Leon Price, student at U of M. Twenty-year-old black male, about six four and 235 pounds. He'd been dating the other victim for nearly three years."

Ketcham relit his cigar. "Looks like the boyfriend broke the door down, had a gun in his hand, and still couldn't save the day. What happened?"

"Knife to the throat again," Corrinne observed.

"It's different though," Troy said. "He died from a single stab wound to the jugular. When the knife was pulled out, it opened the vein about an inch, and he bled to death very quickly."

Ketcham furrowed his brow. "How do you know that?"

"I sent some pictures to Dr. Potter with my phone," Troy confessed. "Said the killer was either real lucky or insanely skilled to put the knife dead center in the jugular with a single stroke and enough force to puncture it."

"And all while his victim is holding a gun," Corrinne added. "Anything else?"

"Yeah. Dr. Potter thought N-E-X might be some kind of numbering system, like the equivalent of 666 or something."

The detectives all looked to Parker. He could sense this was a test. If he couldn't deliver in this moment, Ketcham might second-guess the decision to bring him in. Isn't that what he wanted? Then he thought of the string of recent clergy scandals. He thought of Brynn Carter's voice cracking while she did interviews on cable news programs, political cartoons of him in the local paper.

. "I think the doctor has seen too many movies," Parker said, chewing his gum rhythmically, suddenly calm and in control. "It's Latin. It means death."

Ketcham chuckled. "He killed her and then he wrote *death* on her? That's kind of redundant."

"Not just death, but carnage. Destruction. Genocide." Parker was making things up now. "This might be a warning that there is much more to come."

There was a moment of silence, then Ketcham

clapped once. "I told you this was our guy, didn't I? I was about to give up on you, Parker."

Parker forced a smile. "We wouldn't want that, Paul."

The smile disappeared from Corrinne's face. "Don't call him Paul."

Thirteen Years Ago

Danny tuned out the announcements and invocation and passed the time leafing through a special edition King James New Testament. It was in every sense a prop, and as such, he had learned how to attract attention to it in just the right way —to showcase the words *12-Step Edition* on the cover without being too obvious about it. He'd found the gem in a secondhand bookstore six months earlier and knew right away that it would help The Project. An unspoken battle with drugs and drink worked wonders at building credibility and filling in the grim backstory.

A rotund man with a pink face invited the congregation to stand and sing a chorus from a yellowed, comb-bound booklet in the pew rack. Danny stood with the rest, thoroughly despising the saloonish bounce of the untuned upright piano, but moving his mouth with the words all the same. There was no need to draw attention to himself just yet. He was still invisible and that was good.

Churches were funny that way. A pretty, young lady in a sundress or a middle-aged couple with two children would attract an ad hoc welcoming committee within moments of entering the building. But a dumpy guy in his early twenties with unkempt hair, thick circles beneath his eyes, and worn, ill-fitting, thrift-store clothes would only be noticed by a very particular type of person. And yet, this type could be found in most every church, and these were the people with whom Danny needed to make his initial contact. Spotting them and, in turn, being spotted was not an exact science, but it was one that he had been developing for nearly two years.

The first time had just sort of happened. It was early spring his sophomore year at Wayne State, and Danny hadn't slept for three nights. The nightmares had been getting worse back then, and he had found that chemically keeping himself awake was the best defense. One Sunday morning at about six thirty—his classwork complete and his few friends unconscious in their bunks—Danny had gone for a drive. He cracked the windows, cranked the music, and followed a state highway north. Before he knew it, he was out of Detroit and up into what Michiganders call The Thumb, flanked by fields of corn and soybeans.

A little before nine his fuel gauge told him it was time to refill, and his better judgment added that it was time to head back. He began looking for a gas station. Two popped up in the course of ten miles, but the first was closed on Sundays and the other didn't open until noon. Another three little towns came and went without any hint of where their residents procured fuel. The car began to intermittently shake and chug, the final warning that the bottom of the tank was near.

Danny remembered having seen a pay phone outside a convenience store a few towns back. He could possibly make it. Then again, what if there was a gas station just over this hill? It would be stupid to turn around and miss it. He cursed his luck and his life and decided to push ahead until the old car stalled out, which happened just as he crested the hill.

And he was sure that no one had ever been as glad as he was in that moment to see Don's Beer Bait and Gas shining like a jewel in the valley, a red neon Open sign glaring in the window. The car coasted easily down to the entrance where Danny guided it into the parking lot and up to a pump. Obeying at least a dozen hand-lettered signs distributed around the grounds demanding that he Pay First, Danny headed into the charmless little store.

"Fifteen dollars on pump one," he told the clerk, presumably Don, who held out his hand dispassionately without so much as glancing up from a two-page glossy spread full of guns.

Danny put his hand into his back pocket in

search of his wallet. Nothing. The other pants pockets were empty too, as were his coat pockets. With a burst of clarity, he remembered tucking the tattered brown billfold into the front pocket of his backpack the night before. It was in his dorm room.

"Oh no. This isn't happening." He surveyed Don's—or whoever's—face for any trace of compassion but came up empty. "Um, I can't believe this, but I left my wallet back in my room. In Detroit."

"You don't say."

"I know how it sounds, but I'm completely empty out there at the pump. I'm sure the thing won't even start. I'll mail you the money. Plus interest."

"No credit. No checks. No loans. This is a gas station and a bait shop, not a charity."

"I'm not asking for charity. I could leave you my watch for collateral. It's not much, but—"

"Save it. You want charity, the Jesus freaks across the street are about to start their meeting any time now. I'm sure someone over there will give you a handout."

The Prince of Peace Gospel Church was a two-minute walk from Don's no-longer-jewel-like establishment. Danny had entered five minutes into the service, slipping into a seat near the back.

He'd never been a churchgoer. A religious friend in high school had goaded him endlessly, but Danny had never seen the point.

The service was more or less what he expected: uninspired music and an unremarkable pep talk about living a "victorious life." He endured it without participating, waiting for it to be over so he could undertake the uncomfortable chore of asking for money. Before the minister gave the benediction, he invited anyone who "had a need" to come to the front for prayer, counsel, and support from the church leaders. This seemed the best chance Danny would get. As the congregation filed down the center aisle, he made his way up the side.

Judging by the brightening of the pastor's face, Danny guessed it was rare for someone to take him up on the offer of a postservice meeting. He gave Danny's hand two vigorous pumps while bellowing, "Jim! Eddie! Need you up here!" to a pair of men busily herding women and children out the back.

They in turn tapped a few others, and before he knew it, Danny was surrounded by a group of seven concerned church members.

"You need prayer. I can see it in your eyes," said a white-haired woman. There was a general murmur of agreement that persisted until the pastor held up a hand for silence.

Eddie, an enormous man in a worn button-up shirt, gripped Danny's arm a little too hard and looked him in the eyes. "Tell me, son, are you having a problem with drugs?"

"Yes," he answered, although he wasn't sure why. Danny hated anything stronger than caffeine and B12, but it was clearly the answer they wanted. Noticing the exchange of concerned glances, he added, "But I'm six weeks sober last Thursday."

Their smiles returned. The pastor patted Eddie on the back as if he deserved the credit for this development.

"I'm not feeling too good, though. I haven't slept in days." He was surprised how the truth felt no different from the absurdity of his lie, even to him. "I've run out of money, and I'm afraid I'll fall back in with the old crowd."

"Can we pray for you?" the pastor asked.

"Yes, I'd really appreciate that," Danny lied.

In unison, seven hands pressed into him, spread out all over his head, shoulders, and back. He took the hint from their firm downward pressure and fell to his knees.

The pastor's voice dropped to a raspy half-whisper. "Lord, we pray for this young man, that you bind the spirits of addiction that are terrorizing him. Give him the strength to push forward. Give him sleep. Give him rest in you. And Lord, if there are any demons oppressing him, we break their hold over him in the name of *Jesus!*" He punctuated the last word with a squeeze to the back of Danny's neck, pinching a bundle of nerves.

Danny flinched and sucked in a breath. The group collectively gasped, and for a moment, all seven hands were lifted from his body. When they returned, they were placed gingerly, with an added sense of reverence.

Emboldened by this little victory, the pastor's voice doubled in volume and intensity. "Father, we pray that all evil spirits leave this man for good, never to return!"

Playing to his audience, Danny let out a little yelp, followed by a shudder. There were a variety of *amens* from the huddle around him and then the prayer was over.

When he opened his eyes, he was met with a wall of awe. They all gaped at him like he'd just broken a home run record or dragged a child from a burning building. Then the awe matured into the pride of builders surveying their work. He was their project and they were all pleased with the outcome.

Two hundred and thirty-seven dollars was quickly amassed. It was all they had on them and they insisted he take it. They would be thinking of him, they vowed, remembering him at their weekly prayer meetings. Everything would be better from here on out.

Only it wasn't. For a few days, the dread he'd been carrying around seemed to lighten. The nightmares even went away for a couple of nights. But when they came back, they were all the more terrifying.

The next Sunday morning he found himself strangely drawn to a little Pentecostal church in Lapeer, where he began to hone his performance as the man who needed prayer and deliverance. Within three months he felt like he could write a book on the subject. Refusing to take money was his first breakthrough. He slowly learned that peppering his speech with Latin phrases, a low growling laugh interspersed with weeping, and a pretended sense of confusion helped as well—as long as he didn't overdo it. Less was more, he learned. And, of course, the churches had to be far enough apart from one another to avoid any kind of overlap.

For the better part of a year Danny did not understand his compulsion to return to these little churches, seeking out an informal ritual from ordinary folks who had never taken part in it before—a ritual he himself did not believe in.

Then came the quiet voices. And the unmistakable presence, like the nightmares spreading into his waking hours. At first he thought of it as a battle—him against Them, as if he was dealing Them a blow on Sunday mornings. Eventually, though, he realized that They actually *wanted* him to go to the churches. They wanted him to be *delivered* each week. They had been the ones compelling him all along, coaching him as he worked on his craft.

They had also compelled him to kill two people. The most recent was just last night. Danny shifted in the pew a little impatiently, bending the *12-Step Edition New Testament* nearly in half one way and then the other. The song leader gave the universal sign for *you may be seated* and whispered, "Thank you, Jesus."

A blond woman in her fifties took to the pulpit and asked the group, "Before the pastoral prayer this morning, do we have any special prayer requests?"

Danny raised his hand as timidly as he could.

Four

"Good work today, Parker."

Ketcham's car rattled away from the crime scene. "And listen, don't be embarrassed about losing your lunch. It took all of us a little while to harden our nerves and stomachs."

"I didn't throw up," Parker insisted.

"Sure. You'll feel better after you get home and get some more food in you. I've got a pass for most of the parking ramps downtown, so I can take you right to your car if you like. Where'd you park?"

"I actually walked to the courthouse. I can walk home from there."

"Nonsense. Where do you live?"

Parker gave him the address.

"So what's in the cards for the preacher tonight? Is dinner waiting on the table?"

"No, I'm not married," Parker answered.

Ketcham nodded approvingly. "Me neither. Never have been." He pulled a pack of cigarettes from his inside pocket and held it out to Parker. "Smoke?"

"No thanks. In fact, I just quit, so the less smoke I smell, the better for me."

"I see." Ketcham lit a cigarette and inhaled deeply. "I'm afraid it's a matter of principle with me. I smoke when I can, and the only place you *can* smoke anymore is locked in your own vehicle with the windows sealed tight. Can't even smoke at a bar. Stupid nanny state."

"It does seem a little extreme, I guess." Parker loved the smoking ban. Smoking in restaurants had been his downfall the first three times he tried to quit. Now it was illegal.

"And yet anyone can carry a gun," Ketcham said. "Unless you're a felon. Did you know that, Parker?"

"I'm sorry?"

"In the state of Michigan, they have to issue you a concealed pistol license if you've never been convicted of a felony. I guess they figure if you haven't held up a liquor store, you deserve a chance."

"I didn't know that."

"*You* should probably get one, though." He pulled on to the Ford Freeway and poured on the gas.

"A gun?"

"And a permit to carry."

"You don't think the killer will come after me, do you?"

Ketcham laughed. "No I don't. It's just that you're a pretty high-profile guy and you only seem to be getting famouser. Ashley Englesma told me you have a big book coming out soon."

"March is what they tell me."

"Well, you never know when some nut will read your book and start stalking you."

Parker was strangely flattered at the thought but said, "Sounds unlikely."

Ketcham shrugged. "My motto is Always Be Prepared for the Unexpected. That's why I carry two sets of handcuffs."

"I'm not really the gun type."

Ketcham lit a fresh cigarette off the butt of his first. Parker couldn't believe how fast he'd smoked through it.

"It's not about being a 'gun person.' It's like . . . my sergeant at the academy taught me—and I teach my rookies—that 80 percent of the population are sheep. They just move in herds. They've got two modes: graze and stampede."

"Do sheep stampede?"

"Of course they do. Anyway, the sheep have no

interest in trouble. If they see it, they'll go the other way. They only want to go to work, go home, eat dinner, have a drink, go to bed. Another 10 percent of the population are wolves. They prey on the sheep, take advantage of the fact that they want to avoid trouble at all costs. Most wolves won't carve a Latin word into your forehead, but they'll take advantage of anyone if they can get away with it."

"What's the last 10 percent?"

"Sheepdogs. People like me. We protect the sheep from the wolves. That's our calling. And we need every advantage we get. That's why we carry guns."

"I'm glad you do. I sleep better at night."

"My point is that you don't have to be a cop or a soldier or a fireman to be a sheepdog. There are people everywhere who have an innate desire to protect others. I get that vibe from you. I don't know. Maybe I'm misreading you."

Parker thought for a moment. "I'd say I'm neither a sheep nor a sheepdog. I'm a shepherd. That's what *pastor* means. And I don't need a gun for that."

"Like 'the Lord is my shepherd, I shall not want'?"

"Exactly. The Scriptures tell us that Jesus is the Good Shepherd and we pastors are his under-shepherds. Shepherds don't generally carry artillery."

"What about 'Thy rod and thy staff, they comfort me'? A rod can come in handy for a shepherd when wolves come around."

"Nice try. But the rod and staff in that passage are figurative."

"That's convenient."

"They are. The Hebrew is *shebet*, and it's almost always figurative. The pillar or rod of God symbolizes his authority, his reign."

"My Beretta symbolizes my authority too, I suppose."

Parker chuckled. "Good enough. Take a right here. I'm off Cambridge." They rode in silence for a few blocks. "You know the Bible a little bit," Parker observed.

"Yeah, a bit. I don't know the Hebrew word for *rod*. Then again, you may have just made that up for all I know."

"Do you attend church?"

"I used to go every Sunday. Haven't in quite a while. I've caught your program a couple times though."

"I'd think that in your line of work, a church base would be crucial. I can't imagine looking at all that blood and guts every day. The hopelessness. Seeing the handiwork of all those evil people. Studying it, even."

Ketcham took a long drag on his cigarette. "It's that kind of junk that keeps me from going to church. I don't think I could sit in a pew and worship a God that would allow those two kids to be sliced and diced to death before they've even started their lives."

"How do you deal with it then?"

"What do you expect me to say? I go for long jogs? Lift weights? Meditate? Drink? The truth is, I don't do any of that stuff. I deal with the grit and the garbage by . . ." He grappled for the right word.

"That's my house."

"Wow. Nice place, Preacher." He guided the car up the driveway and put it in park. "Do you know where the police station is down-town?"

"Yes."

"Good. I want you there tomorrow morning at oh-eight-hundred. Not a moment later."

Parker pulled out his phone and brought up the calendar. "Okay, I'll be there. If it's not too much trouble, maybe we could schedule the other times you'll need me, too, so I can work my program prep around that."

"I don't think you understand, Parker. You're with me every day for the foreseeable future. Take your little phone and block off at least a week. Maybe two."

"Detective Ketcham, I can't just throw something together for Sunday morning. What I do requires hours of preparation."

Ketcham shrugged. "Can't you play a rerun?"

"It's not a sitcom. People come to our church to worship and be spiritually fed."

"Get a guest speaker then. I'd do it for you, but I'm not the guy who chucked a stapler at a stewardess."

"That's not what—"

"8:00 a.m. See you then."

"Yes, sir."

Paige Carmichael was one of the smartest, most capable women Parker had ever met. A Vassar grad, she had worked for a television producer in New York for two years before moving back to Grand Rapids. Her skills were a perfect match for her job with Parker's ministry. This was all a happy accident though, as Parker had largely hired her for the image of success she projected. She was a pretty, nubile little thing with short red hair and piercing blue eyes. She was exactly Parker's type, and their chemistry and rapport were thick from day one. A romantic relationship had seemed on the verge of developing when Joshua Holton warned Parker to cut it off at the pass.

"Paige is a great assistant, Parker, but she looks like a stripper. She's got trailer-park lips. When choosing a wife, you have to think about your image," he'd said in that easy Texas drawl of his. "Not that there's anything unbiblical about factoring in the length of a woman's legs, the width of her hips, and the size of her bust when choosing a life mate. The Bible's full of that sort of thing. Just look at the Song of Song."

Song of Songs, Parker had wanted to correct, but he'd grown used to biting his tongue. He'd also grown accustomed to fighting down the urge to strangle the Southern preacher when he went off on these sexist tangents. For all the opportunities and advancement Parker got from his association with Holton, his tongue was taking quite a chewing.

Parker found Paige working furiously in her office at Abundance Now Ministries, her fingers flying over the keys of her laptop. She was unaware of his presence until he flopped down in a leather chair next to the desk.

"Are you looking for the one-armed man?" she joked.

"I'm not a fugitive, Paige. I'm practically an honorary cop after today."

"It went well?"

"You sound surprised."

"I didn't realize you knew a lot about occult symbolism," she said, gesturing toward a copy of the day's *Grand Rapids Press*.

"I don't know anything." It felt good to admit it to someone. "I had a great seminary education. They covered systematic theology, preaching, Greek, and Hebrew, but they sort of glossed over church history, at least from before the Reformation. A little light on world religions too."

"That stuff seems kind of important."

"It's not that they skipped it entirely. I had a few credits here and there, but how much do I remember fifteen years later? Not a ton."

"But you do more research than anyone I know."

"Paige, you've heard me preach. The last thing my fans want to hear about is demons and candles and black masses."

"Do you need me to buy you one of those *For Dummies* books?"

"Not necessary. But I would like you to track someone down for me. Do you know where my class notes are?"

"Yeah, they're in the file room."

"Find a class I took in Bible college. Undergrad. It was about occult topics or cults or something. They covered Satanism and witchcraft and that sort of thing. The prof was this oddball. Dr. Grant, I think. Make me copies of any notes and see if you can track down the professor's contact information."

"I'll get right on it. Would you like me to make an appointment for you? You have openings tomorrow and Wednesday."

Parker sighed. "Paige, I have to go in to the police station tomorrow morning at eight. And every morning after that for at least a week."

She closed her laptop and squinted at him, trying to read if he was joking. "No you don't."

"I'm afraid so. It's that or a very public trial

dragging on, smearing my good name, tanking my book sales."

"But what about Sunday morning? When will you find time to prepare?"

"Honestly, I could probably throw something together if I had to—wing it a little. But let's see if Tony Rex can take over the show this Sunday."

"I'll see if he can preach the service," she gently corrected.

"Right. And clear my schedule for the rest of this week."

Paige nodded and scrunched up her nose. "I hope you catch the bad guy fast. Every week you're off the air hurts our momentum."

"By the time the book comes out, this will be ancient history."

Parker had just arrived home and dropped his keys in the dish on the mantel when the doorbell rang. He looked through the peephole to find three men in clerical collars standing shoulder to shoulder on his porch.

Could this day get any weirder? He opened the door.

Father Xavier spoke. "We're looking for the Reverend Saint."

"That's me."

"Splendid." The priest smiled and bowed slightly at the neck. "How are you this evening?"

"I'm well, Father. How are you?"

"We are blessed by God the Father and our Lord Jesus Christ. We realize this may be inconvenient, but could we possibly have just a few minutes of your time?"

"How could I tell three priests no?" he laughed. "Come on in, gentlemen."

At his invitation, they sat down on a designer sectional in the living room.

"So, what can I do for you?" Parker asked wearily. "I'm sorry to be so abrupt, but I've had a very long, very strange day, and tomorrow's not looking much better."

"We understand," Xavier said, "although I'm not sure where I should begin. Perhaps it would help if you could tell me what you know about the Jesuits?"

Parker thought. "The Society of Jesus? I know a little bit. It's a Catholic order started by Loyola, right? Francis Loyola."

"Ignatius de Loyola," Father Ignatius corrected.

"Yes that's right. Ignatius de Loyola. Part of the Counter-Reformation, I believe."

All three men stiffened.

"We call it the Catholic Reformation," Father Michael said.

"Oh. Sorry. I know a couple of Jesuit guys through the Christian TV station in town. I love what they do for the poor and downtrodden. They're always working to change the system for the better. Great guys."

Ignatius scoffed. "You are speaking of the so-called 'option for the poor.' Secular liberal causes, political action. These things are innovations, leading the order astray."

"Um . . . sorry?"

"Father Ignatius misspoke," Michael said. "He meant to say . . . nothing. He meant to say nothing. The fact is that we're members of the Jesuits Militant, a very different branch of the order than your friends. A much less public branch, with a different goal and different methods. But we aren't here to discuss religio-political issues in modern Catholicism, are we, Father Ignatius? We're here because of the destruction of churches in Grand Rapids."

"You're talking about Valley Christian."

"Yes, Valley Christian was burned to the ground—intentionally, we believe. But I'm also talking about the fire at St. Casimir's and a wave of vandalism and property damage at St. Mark's Episcopal, Fountain Street Church, Immanuel Lutheran, and a handful of others."

"What about it?"

"We are investigating these events on behalf of the Holy See."

Parker smiled. "The Vatican? Sure. And what would the Vatican care about teenagers spray-painting Protestant churches in the American Midwest? It seems like they would have bigger fish to fry."

"St. Casimir's is one of ours," Ignatius said.

Xavier quickly added, "And, of course, we don't want to see any church building defaced. We're rather more ecumenical these days. Isn't that right, Father Ignatius?"

Ignatius grunted.

"The paper said St. Casimir's fire was caused by a wiring problem," Parker said. "That happens all the time with churches. A friend and I were just talking today about how he lost his first church in an accidental fire."

"Even granting that possibility," Xavier said, "you cannot deny the sharp uptick in occult-related crime in this city." He reached into his messenger bag and pulled out several photographs, paper-clipped together. "Esoteric symbols spray-painted on church buildings, mysterious fires, and now, murders with Satanic overtones. These things are harder to explain away when you take them as a group." He handed the photos to Parker. They were pictures of graffiti on the outer walls of various church buildings.

"I don't understand what any of this has to do with me," Parker said. Fatigue was pressing in on him, and he wanted nothing more than to order in some Lebanese food and go to sleep.

"Because you're on the inside of the police investigation into these crimes," Father Michael said.

Parker stood. "I'm not sure how you know

that, but I think it's time for you to leave."

Michael pulled a portable video player from Xavier's bag and set it down on an end table.

"We'll be on our way in a moment." Michael beckoned Parker to sit next to him. "First, I want to show you something." He pushed Play, and a familiar image of Brynn Carter appeared on the small LCD screen.

"He was out of control," Brynn was saying. "He slapped my hand and then he just . . . *shoved* everything that was on the counter right into me." She began to cry.

"Where did you get this?" Parker demanded. "You shouldn't have this." He was not generally given to fits of rage like the one being described on the video, but he felt one boiling under the surface now.

"Let's say the Freedom of Information Act," Michael answered. "No one cares about this little clip right now. No one knows about your little outburst. What if this clip were on the Internet though? Or mailed to the local paper?"

"Am I really being blackmailed by three *priests?* Because I'm pretty sure that's illegal."

Michael feigned offense. "I'm not blackmailing you. We're just watching a video together like a couple of buddies and having a conversation. And in that conversation, I'm telling you this: all we're asking for is a little inside information that might help us protect the churches of this city.

That seems like something you'd want to do."

"I should call the police. In fact, I'm going to be at the police station first thing tomorrow morning. I think I'll tell Detective Ketcham about this."

Ignatius frowned. "I suppose you could do that. You could have us arrested. Upon further investigation though, the police would find us to be genuine ordained priests, citizens of Vatican City, and official envoys of a sovereign state. With diplomatic immunity, naturally."

Michael nodded. "It's a good deal if you can get it. Kind of like being the grandson of the old guy your dorm's named after at boarding school."

Parker's head was spinning. "What are you telling me?"

Ignatius's accent surfaced for a moment. "We're telling you that we could burn down your Washington Monument, and the very worst they could do to us would be send us home."

"Well, I don't think you could burn down the Washington Monument," Michael said, "since it's made of, ya know, *stone*. But that is the general idea."

Parker laughed, overselling it. "Vatican envoys with diplomatic immunity? This is like if a guy brags he knows karate, then he doesn't. Right? If you guys were really secret Vatican assassins, why would you tell me?"

"We aren't assassins, Parker." Michael shook his head slowly. "We never said that. And we're telling you who we are because you're not going to utter a word of this to anyone. Because you're scared to death of that video entering the public consciousness." He removed the disc from the video player and held it out in front of him. "The good news is that *this* is the original. They're still using DVDs down there. Can you believe it? And this one disappeared mysteriously from the archives today. We'd like you to have it in exchange for your help in this matter. You could do whatever you want with it. Burn it, shred it, blend it."

"I don't suppose you men have any sort of ID on you."

"You can probably imagine why we're not issued laminated badges. But here's my card." Michael pulled a bone-white calling card from a silver case and extended it to Parker between two thick fingers. On the front it read *Fr. Michael Faber* in a sans serif font. Below the name was a graphic—the letters *IHS* interposed on a cross. The reverse side bore two phone numbers: one international and one domestic with a 410 area code.

Parker's eyebrows went up. "This is your identification? Color me unconvinced."

Father Ignatius stood and reached into his jacket. "Perhaps this will help," he said and pulled out a nickel-plated semiautomatic pistol with the same crest engraved on the custom pearl grips.

"Whoa!" Parker was up and halfway to the door before he knew it. Michael caught his arm.

"Ignatius, what are you doing?" he shouted at the older priest. "I'm sorry, Parker. He's not always this psycho."

"What is the problem?" Ignatius asked incredulously. "The Superior General gave me this gun to commemorate thirty years of service to the order. I thought it might convince our friend."

"He's convinced. Just put it away already."

Parker studied the card. "So you basically want me to call you and give you updates on the investigation."

"No need," Xavier said. "Feel free to call us if you need anything, but we'll be contacting you soon with some specific questions."

"I don't usually give out my number," Parker said.

"No need," Ignatius echoed, heading for the door. "We have it."

Five

Parker felt a little silly to be standing in his closet, trying to decide what to wear to police headquarters. He wished he'd paid closer attention to Troy's and Ketcham's clothes the day before. As it was, he had it narrowed down to three suits, but they all seemed a bit much.

His phone vibrated on the nightstand.

"This is Parker."

"Good morning, Officer."

"Paige, I was just thinking about you. I wish you were here to dress me this morning."

"Umm . . ."

"Yeah, that came out wrong. What I mean is I can't decide what to wear for my first full day on the job with the detectives."

"You realize how that comes across, don't you?"

He chuckled. "I suppose it's a little juvenile. I just don't want this to be any more uncomfortable than it has to be."

"Well, I can't help you with that, but I have come through on another front. I found the number for Dr. Geoffrey Graham."

"Who?"

"The professor you wanted me to track down. The class was called Contemporary Occultism. You must not have been as excited about it as you remember; you took all of three pages of notes for the whole semester."

"I hadn't found my focus yet during my undergrad years."

"That's normal, I guess. There was a phone number on the syllabus, so I tried giving it a call. It's current."

"Does he remember me?"

"No idea. I got his voice mail, saying he's on a

mission trip until Wednesday. I left your number and asked him to call you."

"Rats. I was hoping he might give me some pointers on dealing with all of this."

"You'll do fine. Just turn up the charm."

"You like the charm, eh?"

She giggled. "It's all right in small doses."

"How's Sunday's show shaping up?"

"The service is coming together well. Tony Rex is lined up to preach. He offered to do next week too, if need be."

"Try and string him along on that until we're absolutely sure we need him."

"Already on it."

"You're a doll. I have to go. Don't want to be late on my first day."

Parker swallowed hard as he approached One Monroe Center, the recently revamped headquarters of the Grand Rapids Police Department. He loved the modern feel and open floor layout of the atrium—not at all what he expected, having watched dozens of eighties crime movies full of grim, ill-lit rooms and packed with jaded cops and dirty bureaucrats.

A pretty, young uniformed officer greeted him from behind a circular information kiosk as soon as he walked in.

"Good morning," she said pleasantly.

He wasn't quite sure how to begin.

"Hi there. I'm, um, here to see Detective Ketcham. My name is—"

"Pastor Parker!" She smiled brightly.

"Yes, that's right. Have we met?"

Her eyes dropped to the sign-in sheet on her desk. "I've, uh, gone to your church for five years."

"Oh! Yes. I didn't recognize you in your uniform."

Suddenly cold and businesslike, she reached under the counter and handed him a small manila envelope with his name on it. "The detective unit is on the second floor. There's an ID card in here. It will give you access to the second floor only and only between the hours of seven and five."

He hovered by the desk, wanting to smooth over his gaffe. "I guess I'm going to be here quite a bit for a while. I'm helping the homicide detectives with the serial killer case."

"That's great," she said curtly. Then, looking past him, "May I help you?"

Not a great start to my first day, he thought.

He entered a glass elevator with a GRPD logo emblazoned on it and pushed the button for the second floor. Nothing happened. He fished the ID card from the envelope. It bore his name, an ID number, and the words "Consultant— MCT." In the upper corner was a publicity shot from his ministry's website, which looked more than a little odd on a government ID. He swiped the card through a reader strip and pushed the second-floor button again. He was moving up.

When he got off the elevator, everyone seemed to know who he was and where he needed to be. He guessed that at least fifty people were working on the floor, and all greeted him with a smile, a nod, and directions to Detective Ketcham's desk.

When he found it, a hand-scrawled note instructed him to report to Room 8B, where he found Ketcham and Troy Ellis gazing at a map full of dots and overlapping circles, spread out over a conference table. The room's walls were covered with crime scene photos, more maps, and other documents—each of three walls dedicated to one of the three incidents. But the first thing Parker noticed was that neither man was wearing cuff links. How Parker wished he had just one button-down shirt that did not require cuff links.

"He's on time!" Troy announced.

"Good morning," Parker said, his eyes drifting from photo to map to photo.

"Get a cup of coffee if you like," Ketcham said. "It's behind you on your right."

"No thanks."

Ketcham furrowed his brow. "Don't tell me you drink tea."

"No, I love coffee, it's just . . . it stains your teeth."

"And your teeth are your livelihood, right?"

"I don't know. What's all this?" He gestured around him.

"We call this the Command Center. It's our temporary workstation for the Blackjack Killings. We've got this setup so we can focus entirely on getting this nutcase off the streets and behind bars. Feel free to look around."

"Are you sure the same person killed all four victims?"

"No, we're not sure, but that's our working assumption."

"Assumption?" Parker mumbled to himself, surveying a large flowchart of Melanie Candor's friends, family, and acquaintances.

"I'm sorry, what was that?" Ketcham asked.

"Nothing. Talking to myself."

"Look, Parker, I know you've got years of experience solving crimes, but let me explain something to you. Grand Rapids usually has about a dozen murders per year. Of those, a good number are open-and-shut domestic disputes gone bad. A few are random, mostly gang-related, and more or less unsolvable. Until last week, none of them were Satan-inspired voodoo killings. Now we've got four victims in three days with devil-doodles all over them. If we keep piling up bodies at that rate, we're pretty quick going to run out of manpower. We're treating these murders as a single investigation out of necessity."

"I understand," Parker said.

"And you tell any of that to the press, I'll see you in jail. In fact, anything you might learn in the course of working as my consultant is to be kept in absolute confidence. You understand?"

"Yes, sir."

Troy snickered. "I'm gonna tell Corrinne you said 'manpower.' She'll let you have it."

"Oh, shut up, Troy."

A uniformed officer knocked on the open door and poked his head in.

"Detective Ketcham? Jason Dykstra. You wanted to see me?"

Ketcham folded the map in half, concealing its contents. "Yes, Jason, have a seat. You too, Parker." He turned his attention to Troy. "Detective Ellis, can you do me a favor and try and locate Isabella Escalanté's next-door neighbor. She has to be somewhere."

"Not a problem, Ketch."

"And maybe you could get me an actual time when Ben Ludema's mother will be home. I need to follow up on this scant statement from Sunday"—he tapped a sheet of paper—"but I can't pin her down. Her kid dies, there's a lot of planning and running around to do, I get that, but I want to sit down with her personally. Today." He turned to Parker and clarified, "Ludema was the kid we found in the red-tagged house yesterday morning."

Troy nodded. "I'll send a cruiser to wait at her place and see if I can track down a cell phone number."

"Thanks, Troy. You're the walrus."

Troy grabbed his coat and clicked the door shut on his way out.

Ketcham's attention returned to the man across from him. "Officer Dykstra, I'd like to introduce Parker Saint. He's working as a special consultant during this investigation."

"Hello," Parker said feebly.

"You're the TV preacher I heard about?" The young cop squelched a laugh.

Ketcham ignored the comment. "Jason, I understand that you were the responding officer to two complaints recently—one Sunday and one yesterday—in which you discovered victims related to this investigation."

"Yes, that is correct."

"Why?"

"I'm sorry, sir?"

"Why you? Two times in a row—that's just weird."

"I—I don't know. I guess he likes the South Service Area."

"You think he lives nearby?"

"It's possible. How should I know?"

"Watch your tone, Officer."

"I'm sorry, sir."

"Jason, I called you up here because, although we spoke briefly at both crime scenes, I need more information from you. I want to encourage you to take some time to think about the two scenes together as a unit. Think about common elements to the calls, what you found when you responded, and how you found it. Look for patterns."

Jason chewed his lip for a moment. "I can't think of any, sir."

"You don't have to put it all together this second. Just roll it around in your head a little. Sleep on it. Then I want you to write up a report for me on any common threads you discover, no matter how insignificant they might seem. I'd like it tomorrow morning if possible, but no later than Thursday."

"Will do, sir."

"Thank you. Please shut the door behind you."

When he had left, Ketcham motioned at the door with his head. "What'd you think of that man?"

"Seems nice enough, I guess."

"Yes, he does. But think about this: there are 225 patrol officers in our department. Seventy of them are in the South Service Area. What are the odds that the same officer would respond to two random killings by the same perp during two different shifts?"

"Math was never my thing, but I'd guess the odds are pretty slim."

"Yeah. Slim."

Troy and Corrinne returned a little after one o'clock. Ketcham ordered in pizza—a working lunch for the four of them, barricaded in the

Command Center. Parker listened as Corrinne recounted her interviews with Ben Ludema's teachers and two school administrators. For his part, Troy had been successful in locating Isabella's neighbor and in setting an appointment for Ketcham to meet with Ben's mother at three. The detective deemed his colleagues' morning exploits a success. Only then did he allow the pizza boxes and two-liters to be opened.

While they ate, Troy asked Parker, "What do you think of the place so far?"

"It's not quite what I expected," he admitted. "I thought you guys would be going over the crime scenes inch by inch, looking for drops of saliva and that sort of thing."

Troy nodded. "You're thinking of crime scene technicians, not detectives. They showed up after you left yesterday. Our job is to talk to people and sort through all their BS."

Ketcham choked on some soda. "Did you just say BS? Wow, we bring in a TV preacher and this guy's language suddenly goes PG."

Troy plopped two more slices on his grease-stained paper plate. "Don't listen to them, Parker. I'm as pure as the wind-driven snow."

Ketcham dumped his plate and paper cup, wiped his hands, and announced, "All right, geniuses, let's hear some mind-blowing insights."

Before he had time to think it through, Parker raised his hand.

"The pastor's having a vision. Let's hear it."

He cleared his throat. "Last night, I was at home thinking about all of this. And it occurred to me that there's been quite a bit of church vandalism lately. And some of the graffiti has been along the same lines as our murders." He took the pictures Father Michael had given him from his back pocket and laid them side by side on the table. "Seems like maybe too much of a coincidence."

Ketcham perused the pictures. "Where did you get these?"

"Um, a colleague in ministry gave them to me. I think they came from the newspaper's website."

Corrinne was around the table in a moment, inspecting the pictures as well. "You might have something here, Preacher," she said.

Parker smiled proudly. "Yeah, it sort of seemed like the killer's MO."

"MO?" Corrinne asked amusedly.

"You know. *Modus operandi.*"

"I know what it means."

Ketcham shook his head. "First BS and now MO? Somebody shoot me."

"Sorry, I was trying to use the . . . lingo." Parker tried to recover his momentum. "Anyway, in addition to the graffiti, there have also been two church fires lately."

"Both of those were electrical problems," Troy said.

"Maybe, maybe not."

Ketcham was engrossed in the pictures. "You're way ahead for your first day in the inner sanctum, Parker. Don't push your luck. The fires were accidental." He quickly gathered the photos into a stack and set them aside. "Let's keep this in mind going forward. I'll dig up statements and incident reports on each of these.

"But for now, I want to move on to what I've learned about Mr. Leon Price." He walked over to a wall where two photos of Leon were pinned up side by side, one smiling, holding a drink, and full of life; the other, very dead.

"I think we can all agree that, even with the bloody symbols and the Latin word, the strangest part of the scene yesterday was this guy lying there dead, holding a gun. I couldn't make sense of it myself.

"I mean, think about it: our subject is either in the process of killing, or has already killed, Isabella Escalanté, and in barges this set of six-pack abs with legs—former star running back and salutatorian for Grand Rapids Central—gun in hand, and he winds up killed with the same knife that killed his girlfriend."

"Medical examiner confirmed it was the same knife?" Troy asked.

"Yep. Killer wiped the blade on the tablecloth before he left, and the victims' blood was intermingled. But the real question on my mind was: who's fast enough to kill a guy with that kind of reflexes and that much strength without his so much as squeezing off a round?" He let the question hang in the air for a minute. "Are you ready for this? The knife was thrown."

Troy and Corrinne both groaned their skepticism.

"Forensics is certain about this. It happened," Ketcham insisted. "The knife used was something like this one." He pulled a five-inch-long knife from a cardboard box on the table. It was shiny and black with four holes down the handle. "Doesn't look like anything special, but it's perfectly balanced for throwing."

Corrinne was smirking. "Let me get this straight, Paul. Our killer threw a knife across the room, directly into this man's jugular? So we're looking for some sort of ninja, then? Why don't we put out an APB on anyone in black pajamas in the greater Grand Rapids area?"

"It's not that uncommon a skill. Sure, your average schlump can't just chuck a throwing knife with no practice and expect to hit a target, but with a little work it's not unheard of. A specialized skill, sure, but not as rare as you might think." He paced off seven feet. "This is how far away forensics is guessing our subject was when he made the throw. We stand farther away playing darts at the bar. Trust me, there are plenty of people out there who could hit a small target at this distance."

Troy nodded. "Yeah, my roommate at the academy had a wooden target up in our room and five or six knives, a lot like that one. He'd come back to the room after an exam or a bad date and throw those things for an hour at a stretch. He hit the bull's-eye four out of five times—and from farther away than your seven feet. It was really annoying. *Thud! Thud! Thud!* I wanted to cut his throa . . ."

"Lovely," Corrinne said. "So the point is that knives are easy to throw."

"Not at all," Ketcham said. "It takes dexterity and practice." He held the knife out to Parker by the blade. "Give it a shot, Preacher," he said. "Try and stick it in the bulletin board."

Parker wound up and sent the knife spinning in the direction of the wall. It went high, and the handle collided with a wall clock, cracking the glass.

"See?" Ketcham said. "It's hard to master, but for certain people it makes sense to put in the time. Just think about it: someone with a handful of these knives and the ability to throw them accurately can kill from a distance without alerting everyone in the vicinity with the sound of a gunshot. And knives never run out of bullets, don't leave casings behind, and can be reused indefinitely. I'll have to double-check, but I'm pretty sure Special Forces learn knife-throwing as part of their training."

"So our guy could be ex-military," Troy offered.

"Maybe. Or he could be your old roommate from the academy. Or he could just be some guy who bought a set of knives and a DVD on the Internet and taught himself in his basement." He studied the photo of Leon's dead body for a moment. "Still, this looks pretty professional. It wouldn't hurt to keep an eye out for military backgrounds. Whatever the case, the second the door swung open, that knife went into Leon's throat and that's all she wrote."

Ketcham put the knife back in the box and replaced the lid. "Let's move on to the artwork. Parker, this is your area. You already came through yesterday. Let's see if you can wow us all again."

Parker's hands started to sweat.

Ketcham pointed to a series of close-ups of the victims. "The common element at all three scenes is that our subject has painted detailed images onto his victims with their own blood. You don't see that every day. Seems to be a fairly skilled artist too. The subject matter on victims two, three, and four is pretty vanilla, pop-culture, devil-worship stuff, but what do we make of the first one?" He dropped a color photo of Melanie Candor's lifeless body on the table in front of Parker.

"The first victim was decorated with two images," he continued, "which appear to be a spade and a snake, the spade being more prominent. As you know, this led the press to dub our subject 'The Blackjack Killer.' And you could almost feel their collective disappointment when the second victim didn't sport a heart, diamond, or club.

"Before victim two was dropped on us, we exhausted several gang-crime databases for any connection with a spade or a spade-snake combination and came up empty. So, Parker, we're all ears. What are we looking at?"

Parker leapt up from the table. "I'm getting a call," he announced, pulling his phone from his pocket. He pushed it to his ear. "Hello?" After a beat, he covered the mic and said, "Detective Ketcham, can I leave you hanging for just two minutes? This is a very important matter with one of my parishioners."

Ketcham gave him a dubious look.

Parker whispered loudly, "He has *can*-cer."

The detective waved him away. Parker left Room 8B and moved off a ways from the door. He tried to look as if he were on the phone, while also bringing up an Internet search screen. It was a failed project. He noticed the sign for the men's room and relocated to a private stall.

Parker typed the search terms "Satanism spade symbol" and hit Enter. The whole first page of results was filled with multiple instances of the same article, entitled "Calling a Spade a Spade:

Satanism, Catholicism, and the Jesuit Oath." No help.

He restarted the search, this time entering the terms "religious symbols spade." The first three matches contained information about Saint Maurus, the patron saint of charcoal burners and coppersmiths. He quickly skimmed one of the articles. It was not much help either. He hit the Back button and checked the next result, a website about tombstones and religious symbolism. The entry simply read, "Pall, pick, spade: Symbols of mortality." Parker noticed the time and headed back to the Command Center.

As soon as he entered the room, Ketcham held out his hand. "Give me your phone. I don't want us to be interrupted again." Parker obeyed. Ketcham fumbled with it, pushing on all sides. "How do you turn this thing off?"

Troy snickered. "Technology hates you."

"The feeling's mutual," Ketcham said. He finally gave up and slipped the device into his pocket. "Okay, Parker. What do you know about spades?"

"For starters, spades are used on tombstones as symbols of mortality."

Ketcham sighed. "Again with that? This seems like déjà vu. Apparently, our subject likes killing people and then labeling them dead in creative ways. This is not very helpful, Parker. What else you got?"

"In Christian iconography, spades are a symbol of Saint Maurus."

The three detectives stared blankly at him.

"Who's Saint Maurus?" Corrinne asked.

"He's, uh, the patron saint of charcoal burners and coppersmiths."

Corrinne nodded. "That makes perfect sense. There was a charcoal grill in Melanie Candor's backyard."

Troy tapped the table excitedly. "And I think she had some pennies in her pocket. The killer probably flew into a copper-and-charcoal-fueled rage. We've seen a lot of those lately."

"Almost a cliché at this point," Corrinne agreed.

Parker's phone began to buzz in Ketcham's pocket. He flinched, unused to the sensation, yanked it free, and thrust it at Parker.

"Here. Answer the stupid thing. Just be ready to leave in ten minutes. You and I are interviewing Ludema's mother at three."

Parker checked the display. The number had a 410 area code, like the one on Father Michael's card. He left the conference room and found a quiet corner near an emergency exit.

"Parker Saint."

"This is Father Michael. Can you talk now?"

"Not really."

"You sound upset. Is everything all right?"

"Why couldn't you have called when I needed a lifeline five minutes ago?"

"Huh?"

"Just hurry up and tell me what you know about Saint Maurus."

"Saint Maurus . . . Let me think. Traditionally, he's the first oblate."

"What's an oblate?"

"Never mind. Let me ask Father Xavier; he knows his saints a lot better than me." There was a rustle and some muffled talking before Michael came back on the line. "Father Xavier says Maurus is the patron saint of charcoal burners and coppersmiths."

"That's very helpful, thank you. But I can't talk right now."

"When should I call you back? I've got some questions for you."

"Don't bother. I'll call you tonight."

Six

Meredith Ludema lived in a low-end apartment complex that billed itself as a "townhouse community" on account of the vertical orientation of the units. Her front room was packed with outdoor Christmas decorations, empty pizza boxes, and other miscellany.

Despite the chill in the October air, only a ripped-and-mended screen door stood between the men and Mrs. Ludema, whom they could barely make out through the obstacle course.

"Come in," she called, her voice hoarse and emotionless.

The men entered the apartment and stepped carefully around a large, plastic Santa, wrapped in a clear garbage bag, standing sentry.

"Ms. Ludema?" Ketcham called.

"Miss." Her dull brown hair was pulled back into a tight ponytail, stretching her skin but not quite erasing her crow's-feet. A cereal bowl filled with cigarette butts sat on the ratty couch cushion next to her, while she worked on adding another.

"I'm Detective Ketcham. This is Mr. Saint. We're here to talk with you a little more about your son. May we sit down?"

"That's fine." She was looking in their direction but focusing on nothing.

The men squeezed into the only other available piece of furniture—a small love seat—uncomfortably close to each other.

"First off, how are you doing, Miss Ludema?" Ketcham asked, his voice thick with concern.

"How do you think?"

"I imagine you're feeling pretty overwhelmed. Not to mention angry, brokenhearted, guilty—"

"I don't feel guilty," she snapped. "I didn't kill him."

"Of course not. But guilt is a normal emotional response for a mother. Guilt for being angry, guilt for feeling guilty. Guilt for not feeling guilty.

If you need someone to talk to, the department can provide you with that."

"I don't need to talk to anyone. Youse guys are the ones who said you need to talk, so let's talk."

"Okay, Miss Ludema." Ketcham opened his notebook. "You mentioned to my colleague on Sunday that your son was having trouble with a group of boys at school. I'd like to hear more about that."

She shook her whole body *no*. "The trouble didn't come from anyone at school. It was all that Damien man. He tells them what to do and they do it. They all do it. He's got spells and curses and he controls their actions. Teenage boys aren't the smartest tools in the shed, ya know."

"Who's Damien?"

"The leader of the group. He's a grown man. What's he doing hangin' out with a bunch of kids? Having them over in his house. That's not right. I called you people two weeks ago, but you did jack."

"You called us about this Damien?"

"Yeah, and what did you people do? Nothin'."

"Do you know Damien's last name?"

"Nope. I've got his address, though. I followed Benny one night." She pulled a vinyl billfold from her purse and riffled through a pile of paper scraps. "Here it is." She read out an address on Garfield.

Parker nudged the detective. "That's two blocks from where we found the body."

"Of course," she said. "They're all around there."

Ketcham slid to the front of his seat, pen poised. "Can you describe this Damien to us?"

"Guy's a freak. In his thirties, maybe. He has those big earrings that stretch out your ears and you can see right through them. Weird tattoos too and long black hair. He's always surrounded by a bunch of kids who look just like him. He's a nightmare."

"When you say kids, you mean—"

"Some high school age, most a little older, I guess. A bunch of them live there with him. Place is one nonstop party."

"Did Ben spend time there as well?"

"He used to. I told him about three weeks ago that he wasn't allowed to see Damien no more. He wasn't to go to his house or hang out with that crowd. He was eighteen, but like I told him, as long as he lived in my house, it was my rules, ya know? He needs to do well in school so he can get a good . . ." Her voice trailed off.

"How did Ben receive that prohibition?"

"How what?" she asked.

"Was he angry when you forbade him from visiting Damien?"

"Not really. It felt like he was waiting for an excuse to break it off. You have to understand, my son was just looking for a place to fit in. He wasn't really like them."

"Was there any one incident that led you to put your foot down?"

"A few things. I found him with weed a couple times. He admitted Damien gave it to him. I'm not real strict about that stuff, but that's not all they were doing down there. Damien is into hard drugs. And he worships the devil. I heard Ben and his friends talking about it one day. I don't go to church or nothin' and I had Benny out of wedlock, but I'm a Christian woman. I didn't want Benny getting into any of that."

"And what occasioned your call to the police?"

"Damien called here and threatened me and my son."

"When was this?"

"A couple weeks ago. I know it was him. He said Ben still owed him something. I told him where he could go. I said I wasn't afraid of him. And he told me he put a curse on us and he wouldn't lift it until Ben was back where he belonged. I thought he was just trying to scare me. How could I know what would happen?" She sobbed lightly.

"You can't blame yourself, Miss Ludema," Parker said. "Besides, Ben wasn't killed by a curse. He was killed by a knife."

She began to cry harder. Ketcham shot him a look that said both *Nice job* and *Shut up*.

Meredith tried to say something else, but her words were unintelligible through her tears. Ketcham pulled a handkerchief from his pocket and handed it to her, patting her hand.

Parker shifted uncomfortably. He hated dealing with tears. His father would have known exactly what to say in this situation. He'd have prayed with the woman, quoted Scripture to her, given her some peace. Parker, on the other hand, just sat there, frozen, watching her cry. He could deal with the cameras and the masses, but one-on-one he felt useless.

She regained her composure with a few deep breaths. "I'm afraid he's going to curse me now," she said. "I got Jesus in me, ya know, but what if Damien puts a curse on me? I'm afraid for myself. That's not right."

Ketcham gave Parker another look. This one said *Say something, you idiot.*

"I know you're afraid, Miss Ludema," he said, his voice shifting into preacher mode. "But let me set your mind at ease. I'm an ordained minister, and I can tell you that you have nothing to worry about. If you've put your faith in Jesus, no curse and no spell can get a hold on you."

She wiped her eyes. "Really?"

"That's what we believe, isn't it? That Jesus broke the curse when he died on the cross. He did that for you, Miss Ludema."

She tried to smile. "You can call me Meredith."

"Okay, Meredith. And you can call me Parker."

"Parker?" Her eyes snapped to his face. "You're the guy on TV. You're on right after Joshua Holton."

"Why, yes. That's me."

"I never miss your show. I DVR it every week. Just watched you this morning."

"Aw, that's great, Meredith. I hope it was a great comfort to you."

"It wasn't," she said flatly, the emotionless wall returning.

"Oh." He fumbled for words. "I'm, uh, sorry that—"

"You were talking about big success moments in people's lives. Like if I had enough faith, I could live my dreams right now. How does that comfort me when I just lost my son?"

"I . . . don't know."

"I really needed something from you this morning, Parker. Something from God to give me hope for me and for Benny. You let me down." She sniffed. "I want you guys to leave."

"Yes, ma'am," Ketcham said, rising and pulling Parker firmly from the love seat by his arm. "I'm going to leave my card here. If you think of anything else, please don't hesitate to call. And again, I'm very sorry for your loss."

They walked back to the Bonneville and drove two blocks to a convenience store parking lot.

Ketcham killed the engine and turned to look Parker in the eye.

"Hear me good, Parker. You can't take any of that junk personally. Do you understand?"

Parker was in a daze. "She's right, though. I dropped the ball."

"No you didn't. This is normal in my line of work. Every cop has had a victim lash out at him at some point or another. They need someone to blame, and we're sitting right there. There's no way your TV program could have said exactly what that lady needed to hear today. And even if it had, what about all the other people watching? They can't all hear exactly what they need from you all the time." He put a hand on Parker's shoulder. "To do this kind of work, you have to wall yourself off. You listen, you understand, but you don't absorb. Got it?"

"All right." Parker nodded.

"Good. Pardon my reach." Ketcham opened the glove box, retrieved a large, blocky cell phone, and dialed a number.

"Troy. Ketcham here. Just got done at the mother's house. We've got a lead. She gave us a partial name and an address. I need you to cross-reference these for me." He gave him Meredith Ludema's phone number and the address on Garfield. "She said the guy's name is Damien something. Get me a full name and bio if you can.

"Apparently she filed a complaint about two weeks ago when the guy called her at home, threatened her and the kid. If you can pull that file too, I'd appreciate it." He listened for a moment. "No, get what you can in the next twenty minutes, and meet me at that address in thirty. I want to bring him in for questioning today if we can. I'll track down Corrinne too. We might need some muscle." He chuckled. "Okay, see you in half an hour."

Damien Bane's large, two-and-a-half-story house was eighty years old and showing manifold signs of aging. The blue paint was peeling, the shingles molting, and the yard ungroomed, but it maintained a certain undeniable charm. Six rusty cars were parked in a line on the gravel drive, and a uniformed police officer was quickly surveying them, peering into the side window of each, his hand resting on his gun.

Parker had been instructed to wait in the car, which was precisely what he had hoped to do. As he watched the three detectives mount the steps to the long, wooden porch, he marveled at their courage. They were actually *hoping* this was a murderer's house. Unbelievable.

He had a great view from the passenger seat of Ketcham's car, parked on the street. A tall, beefy young man answered the door. He had stringy red hair and was dressed in black from head to toe. A brief conversation followed, after which he disappeared, replaced a moment later by a thin man in his thirties with long black hair and a neatly trimmed goatee. His body language revealed nothing as he spoke to each of the detectives in turn, at one point peering out from between them to see the uniformed cop waiting on the street.

Parker couldn't hear what they were saying, but the man seemed unflapped by their sudden arrival, as if the police came for him every afternoon. He disappeared from view again for half a minute and then came out onto the porch in black boots and a long black trench coat. Troy led him down to the black-and-white—which was really blue and red, but Ketcham had called it a black-and-white—and escorted him into the backseat, hands uncuffed.

"That was easy," Ketcham said to Parker, sliding back in behind the wheel. He withdrew a cigar from a plastic tube and ignited it. He was flushed and seemed a bit flustered.

"This is always a little tricky," he explained. "We don't have grounds to arrest him just yet, but we can be a lot more effective questioning him downtown rather than on his turf." He took a few puffs, calming down a bit. "Convincing a suspect to come with you is an art. I was sure this guy would give us grief, but he agreed to come right away, which is not necessarily a good thing. He maintains more power. It'll be hard to put the pressure on him now." His brow furrowed thoughtfully. "You know what? Hang on."

He exited the car and jogged a few paces up to the police cruiser, just pulling away from the curb. It came to a stop. Ketcham and the officer spoke through the window for a short time. Then the officer got out of the cruiser, and Ketcham got in.

The uniformed cop trudged back toward Parker, keys in hand. His voice betrayed his annoyance as he said, "I guess we're playing musical cars. The detective wants to transport the suspect himself. He would like you to ride with Ellis and Kirkpatrick."

Troy's backseat only had lap belts—no shoulder harnesses. Maybe that's why Parker felt more like a little kid than a criminal as the two detectives escorted him back to police headquarters. They took a circuitous route and seemed to violate every statute and traffic law along the way.

Corrinne flipped open the visor mirror and reapplied her dark red lipstick. She puckered and smacked at herself several times before noticing Parker watching from behind.

"So, Preacher," she asked, "how do you like working with Paul?"

"It's fine. A bit of a change from my normal schedule."

"I've never been able to figure out what

preachers do all week. You talk for half an hour on Sunday. Is the rest just praying and eating bonbons?"

"Do you really want to know?"

"Not really." She flipped the visor closed. "Paul seems to like you, am I right? That's lucky for you. When somebody rubs him the wrong way, look out."

"Have you seen his cell phone?" Parker asked.

Troy laughed. "I think it's the prototype. The first phone that didn't need a suitcase with it. Of course, Ketch sees no reason to upgrade. All he does with it is make calls anyway."

"Rarely even does that," Corrinne said.

"I wish he checked his e-mail rarely. It's more like never."

"I don't think he knows how." She cranked her neck back toward Parker. "Here's what you need to know about Paul: he's a fedora short of a cartoon."

"What does that mean?"

"Let's just say I knew him before he made detective. He was the most serious cop I ever met. His shoes were always polished so you could see your face in them. He had more gadgets on his belt than Batman. He never called in sick or came in late, nothing like that. Then, the day he made detective, he became this hard-boiled investigator. He must have gone to a secondhand store and bought a trench coat that looked like it had seen some mileage, started smoking those cheap cigars."

"Those cigars," Troy laughed. "They must be a nickel apiece. He buys them by the gross."

"Oh, they're terrible," Corrinne agreed, "but it's the image he wants to project. I think he wishes he had an alimony-hungry ex-wife and a teenage daughter he never sees, just to make him all the more grizzled. Of course, he'd barely be old enough to have a teenager."

"Does he keep a bottle of Scotch and some tumblers in his desk drawer?" Parker asked.

"Nope," Troy answered. "He doesn't drink." He and Corrinne both pointed at their heads and in unison recited, "Got to keep it swept clean."

The two detectives laughed.

Corrinne led Parker down a hall and up to a door marked Interview D.

"Stay," she ordered. "I'll tell Paul you're here. And remember—you repeat anything we said in the car, and I'll have you picking up trash on the freeway in an orange jumpsuit, *capisce*?"

"Mum's the word."

She winked at him and disappeared behind an unmarked door. Almost immediately, Ketcham emerged.

"Parker, you're coming into interrogation with me," he said. "Are you okay with that?"

"I suppose."

"And just so we don't have a replay of this afternoon, let me lay down some ground rules. You do not speak unless I give you the signal, understood?"

"What's the signal?"

"I'll look at you. And I won't be talking. And it will be obvious that I want you to talk. That's the signal. Otherwise, you do not interrupt. You don't try to steer the conversation. You don't speak unless you get the signal.

"Or, if the suspect should start to make a connection with you, which is really unlikely in this case, I'll just find an excuse to leave the room. If that happens, don't worry. I'll be right on the other side of the glass, listening and watching. In that case, just keep him talking. Any hint of a threat, and we'll be at your side in a heartbeat."

Parker swallowed hard. He felt some dread building in his gut. "Is he in there already?"

"Yeah, we like to let people cook by themselves for a little while before we start any questioning. Something I've learned: people have a habit of knocking down their own defenses if you leave them alone with their thoughts long enough. They stare into that mirror and start to second-guess the stories they've concocted. Hopefully that's what he's doing."

"Do you really think he could be the killer?"

"Never ask that, Parker," Ketcham chided. "What's the matter with you?"

• • •

Damien was tipping back casually in the institutional gray chair, a smile tugging at the corners of his mouth.

"Detective, I'm glad to see you again," he said with mock excitement. "I was getting bored. And who have we here?"

"Don't worry about my associate, Mr. Bane. We're not here to talk about him. We're here to talk about you and Ben Ludema." He sat across from Damien and motioned for Parker to take the seat next to him, their backs to the one-way glass.

Damien's smile vanished. "I already told you. I barely even knew the kid."

"But you did know him."

"Yes. Barely."

"You already said *barely*."

"Because I barely knew him." He pointed at Parker. "Seriously, what's he doing here? You think I don't know who that is?"

"He's just sitting in on our conversation if that's okay with you. If not, I can ask him to leave."

"What about separation of church and state? Are we dropping all pretense now? The police department is now an unapologetic member of the Christian Imperialist Elite?"

"Parker is not on the police payroll. He's here as a consultant because of his area of expertise. If you'd rather he step out, that's no problem."

"Nah, let him stay." He flashed a dark smile at Parker.

"Fine," Ketcham said. "Now, what were you telling me about Ben Ludema?"

"That I barely knew him."

"But you know that he died."

"It was on the news."

Ketcham tilted his head. "How did he die again?"

"I believe his throat was cut."

"And the killer painted some pictures on the boy with his own blood. Don't forget that. Some Satanic stuff—your kind of stuff, I understand."

"You people are so small-minded. I don't even believe in God, but you think I worship the devil? A literal devil?" He gave a derisive laugh.

"So you're not a Satanist?"

"Not the way you mean it. I'm not into mainstream religions of any kind, much less pentagrams and six-six-sixes."

Ketcham perked up. "Who said anything about pentagrams? That wasn't on the news."

"You told me. In the car on the way here. There was a pentagram on the dead girl."

"No I didn't. How did you know about the pentagram?"

Damien smoldered. "*You* told me."

"Mr. Bane, we did not have a conversation on the way here. The cruiser's recorder will bear me out. On the drive over, I asked you several questions, which you did not answer. You just sat in the back and pouted. No one mentioned the pentagram."

Damien glared. "You're ridiculous."

"Tell me about your phone call to Ludema's mother."

"I never called her. She called me. She told me to back off, that Ben was finished with all of us 'freaks' and that we'd never see him again. I said fine, but he owed me money."

"And then you threatened them both."

"I don't do threats and I don't do violence. I do occasionally employ curses and spells."

"Spells? By the look of you, I'd be surprised if you *could* spell."

"I'm a college graduate, Detective. I'm a scholar."

"Of course you are. Did you put a curse on Ben Ludema, then?"

"Is that illegal?"

"Not in itself. At least, I don't think so. But have you heard of motive? Intent? If you put some kind of a curse on the victim two weeks before he was killed, that would show both. And we've got a statement from the victim's mother indicating that you did. All we need now is opportunity and this case is looking good for us."

Damien was drumming his fingers quicker and quicker against the table. "Can I smoke in here?"

"*I* can't even smoke in here. Not anymore."

Ketcham tipped a file folder in his direction and perused the information Troy had gathered. "You've got a couple aliases, it seems. What's your real name?"

"Knowing a man's name gives you power over him."

"I've got power over you either way, and I can find out. Let's save some time here so you can go home."

"My name is Legion!" He slammed his palm against the table, causing Parker to jump six inches out of his seat.

Ketcham chuckled. "Legion? You're going with that? That's the tiredest answer in the book. Everyone says 'Legion' when they're going for the scary vibe or an insanity plea. I honestly expected better from you."

Damien bared his teeth. "You don't know what you're dealing with."

The detective sighed. "Okay, Legion—do you mind if I call you Lee for short? Let's get to the point. Where were you Sunday morning between the hours of two and five-thirty, Lee?"

"I was home. I have witnesses. Lots of them."

"I'm sure you do."

"I'd like to call my lawyer."

"Do you really have a lawyer?"

He hesitated. "Not yet."

"Are you nervous about something, Lee?"

Damien shrugged. "I don't trust you and I don't

like being here. That may be what your amazing skills of detection are picking up."

Ketcham reached into his worn sport coat and pulled out an antique, metal cigarette case. "I tell you what," he said. "You can't smoke, but I find it helps me think if I chew on one of these." He flipped it open to reveal about fifty wooden toothpicks inside.

"I think I'll pass," Damien said.

"Suit yourself." Ketcham set the case on the table, open. "How about if I just ask you a couple more questions, then we call it a day?"

"I don't think so, Detective. I'm growing tired of you. But maybe you'd let me talk to Parker here for a while."

Ketcham rolled the request around in his head for a moment. Under the table, Parker grabbed the detective's sleeve and held firm.

"That's fine by me, Mr. Bane. Parker, I'll be right outside if you need me." He scooped up the file folder and freed his sleeve with a hard yank.

In a few seconds, the two men were alone.

Damien studied the minister. "I scare you, don't I, Parker?"

Parker set his jaw. "Of course you don't scare me."

"We watch your show sometimes at the house. *Speak It into Reality.*" He snickered. "Your little sermons are a drinking game. Did you know you're a drinking game? The boys do a shot every time you say *destiny*."

"That's not as funny as you think."

"Who said it was funny? You don't make me laugh; you make me sick. The other preachers on TV—the homophobes and the anti-evolutionists and the hellfire-and-brimstone types—at least they believe in what they're selling. At least they have some conviction. You're just selling it for profit. You epitomize the hypocritical elite."

Parker could feel his face reddening. He cleared his throat. "I don't have to sit here and listen to you drag my good name through the mud," he said defiantly. "If you'll excuse me, I have to check on something with Detective Ketcham." He got up from the chair and walked purposefully to the door. It was locked. He stood there awkwardly for a moment before returning to his seat.

Damien didn't laugh. "He told me about the pentagram in the car, you know. He really did." He picked a toothpick out of the case and began chewing on it.

"No offense, but I'll believe a highly decorated police detective before I believe the likes of you."

"Why? Because I have long hair and tattoos? Because I don't fit in to your little picture of what society should look like? Your society demands a scapegoat when something like this happens. I'm an easy scapegoat, aren't I?"

"Mm hmm. Some kind of vast conspiracy. What did you call it, the Christian Imperialist Elite? Somehow I doubt that."

"Do you know where the word *scapegoat* comes from?" It was a test and Parker knew it.

"It's from Leviticus chapter 16. The high priest would confess the sins of the people over a goat and then send it out into the desert."

Damien nodded slowly. "How enlightened is that? How very sophisticated. You can't really believe in that nonsense. A goat?"

"I do believe it."

"Do you believe in hell, Parker?"

"That depends on what you mean. I believe that people tend to make their own hell."

"You don't believe in eternal conscious torment though, do you? I didn't think you would. Why do you bother to preach from that stupid book of fairy tales when you don't even believe what it says?"

"I do believe it," Parker repeated. "My father taught from that Book and so did my grandfather, and I won't be second-guessed by a grown man in makeup."

"You know what my father taught me? He taught me how to dodge an ax handle in the hands of an angry drunk."

The edge left Parker's voice. "I'm sorry to hear that, Damien." He was expecting a wave of compassion to flood over him, but it didn't. So he tried to force it. "Our earthly fathers can let us down, but the good news is you do have a heavenly father."

"My father broke two of my ribs when I was nine. He hit my mother so hard that she permanently lost the vision in her right eye. Do you really think I'm longing for another one of those? One who beats me over the head with commandments and guilt and shame instead of a stick? You think I've got some God-shaped hole in my heart? I don't."

Parker was at a loss. "I'll pray for you," he said feebly.

"You know what you can do with your prayers?" Damien's answer was specific, if not inventive.

"There's no need for that kind of talk."

Damien leaned across the table, filling Parker's field of vision. "Oh, I'm sorry, did you think this was the conversion scene? Is that how your mind works? You thought I'd find my scapegoat, cut my hair, put on a suit, and start living for *Jay*-zus? Let me tell you something, Saint: once you accept there's nothing but dirt and decay on the other side, it's all uphill from there."

The door opened and Ketcham reentered, skimming a sheet of information.

"Forget Lee," he said. "I think I'll call you Daniel. Or how about Danny?"

Damien clenched his fists. "Don't you dare."

Ketcham resumed his seat. "But that was your

name, wasn't it? Daniel Banner? Until you legally changed it four years ago." He locked eyes with Parker. "Seems everyone's changing their name these days."

"Daniel is a Judeo-Christian label," Damien ground out through clenched teeth. "It describes a slave to the Christian imperialists. You know what it means?"

"It's Hebrew," Parker answered. "It means 'God is my judge.' "

"God will have to wait in line," Damien said.

Parker's phone began to vibrate loudly. Ketcham kicked him in the shin. The caller ID showed a 410 number. Father Michael again. He pressed Ignore.

Damien stood suddenly and asked, "Am I under arrest, Detective Ketcham?"

"No, you're not."

"Then I'm going home now. I'll have a friend pick me up."

"That's fine." Ketcham said, standing as well. "I can take that for you." He held out his hand and gestured to the toothpick.

Damien deposited his saliva-laden toothpick into Ketcham's hand, and the detective unlocked the heavy door to let him out. When Damien had gone, he returned to the table, took the seat across from Parker, and pulled a small plastic ziplock bag from his coat pocket, carefully depositing the toothpick.

"And now we've got something to match DNA against," he said with a smile.

"Brilliant."

"You did a good job with him, Parker. You had him off-balance. Stupid nanny state did us in. If that guy had an ashtray and a full pack in front of him, he'd still be sitting here talking to us, and we could have been a little more discreet about the saliva sample. But nice work on your part."

"Thanks."

"Troy's been in the observation bay watching this Bane guy's video channel on the Internet. It's called *The Devil's Humanist.* The guy claims to be indwelled by a 'spirit guide,' goes off on long, paranoid rants with no point, makes veiled threats against city employees, loves spells and curses and such. This is exactly the kind of stuff we brought you in for, Parker. I'd like you to watch some of those videos tonight and bring us a report tomorrow."

"Yes, sir. I'd be—" His phone rang. The 410 area code again.

Seven

Paige found herself a bit conflicted about her employer's extended absence. While certainly less than ideal, it did have its upside—namely that Parker's office was at least two and a half times

130

larger than her own and was feng shuied to perfection with top-of-the-line office furniture and an air purifier that added a subtle hint of vanilla to its output. Whenever Parker left for a day or more, which was rare indeed, Paige relocated. She scrunched and stretched her toes in her nylons and smiled at the sight of her feet up on the mahogany desk. Parker wouldn't mind—far from it—but it was still fun in a semirebellious way.

She could just barely make out the deep red nail polish through her dark stockings. She'd removed and reapplied the polish again last night, though she was unsure why. No one but she had seen her bare feet in months. Despite being a short drive from the picturesque shores of Lake Michigan, yet another summer had come and gone without a single trip to the beach. She told herself it was because redheads don't tan well, but she knew it was really because her entire life was wrapped up in this place. This job. This man.

It would be worth it, though. She could feel the stars beginning to align. The increasing visibility. The syndication deal on the horizon. The book. Parker had the vision for it all, but they both knew it was Paige who made things happen. At least twice a week he posed the question, "What would I do without my Paige?"—aloud, to no one in particular—but Paige wondered it silently far more often than that. When their time came, she knew he would reward her loyalty. For now, though . . .

The phone rang.

"Parker Saint's office," she said. Even with her feet propped on the enormous desk, the headset Paige wore made her feel like an overqualified receptionist.

"This is Mason Fitch calling on behalf of Pastor Joshua Holton."

"Hi, Mason," Paige chirped. It was her own private game to see how cheerful and personable she could be with Holton's robotic assistant. "How are things down there in Texas? Still hot, right? We're just starting to—"

"I'm calling to let you know that Parker missed his weekly call this morning." Mason left a window of silence, as if he were letting the news of a train wreck or air raid sink in.

"Okay . . . ?"

"Yes. And I don't think I need to tell you that Mr. Holton takes his time very seriously."

"Does he really?" She dropped the cheer and matched her colleague's annoyance. "Parker's dealing with some personal stuff up here at the moment. I'm sure he'll make up the call when—"

"We're all dealing with personal stuff all the time, Paige. And there are no makeups." His tone reminded Paige of schoolchildren claiming no tag-backs. "Tell Parker we expect to hear from him next week at the usual time."

Paige opened her mouth to respond, but the call

had ended. For the tenth time today, she thought of the e-mail she'd been saving in her in-box—the one from the firm in Indianapolis. It came three weeks ago and she had yet to respond, so the position had likely been filled, but she held on to the possibility like a security blanket. It was twice the money in a bigger market with a team of three working under her. But your Parker Saints didn't come along every day. She thought about the way he commanded the crowd, how they hung on his every word, how he looked behind this very desk as he painstakingly crafted each line of each sermon. She knew there were many reasons she was staying close to Parker. Some professional, some not so much.

Perhaps she'd better call him. Just to let him know that Mason was on the warpath, which meant that Holton was at the very least perturbed. Her computer told her it was nearly five. Maybe she'd wait another half an hour, just to make sure he was finished at the police station. She had no plans tonight, as Tuesday and Wednesday evenings were generally working dinners for the two of them. Planning and brainstorming—big-picture stuff. Maybe they could still get that in tonight. She missed the synergy.

For the moment, though, she had work to get done. Just as soon as she reread the message from the firm in Indianapolis.

● ● ●

It had been years since Parker's first—and last—visit to a bar. He'd been to many restaurants and grilles with a bar in the back, but he hated the idea of patronizing an honest-to-goodness tavern. Perhaps it was beneath him. Perhaps it was his introverted nature—something that no one expected of a man in his position. Whatever the case, he hadn't dared refuse Corrinne.

"It's a rite of passage," she'd told him flatly. "We have a round and we shoot the breeze. If you want any chance of fitting in around here, you can't say no." Troy and Ketcham had exchanged a look but made no attempt to contradict her, so Parker had agreed to meet them.

The entryway to Marc's Watering Hole was so thick with smoke that Parker's eyes began to water. Once within the smoke-free building, though, he recovered quickly. As his vision returned, he skipped his eyes down the bar and then to each table in the place, hoping to spot his new friends quickly. Nothing was less desirable to Parker than waiting in an uncomfortable place with people he didn't know. He came up empty and was considering whether to just pull the plug when a woman rose up in her bar stool and waved him over.

She wore a knee-length skirt and a spaghetti-strap top and could almost have passed for Corrinne, if not for the eye makeup and intentionally disheveled hair. And the skirt. Parker made his way over and awkwardly mounted the stool next to her.

"You look . . . different tonight," he said, chiding himself as he spoke. He thought of those romantic movies he'd been forced to endure with his high school girlfriend, in which the ugly duckling friend takes off her glasses and lets down her hair to reveal that a beautiful, graceful young woman has been hiding under the nerd, jock, or grease-monkey persona all along. He hated those movies.

She smirked. "Just because you never shift out of R-E-V, don't assume we're all wound up that tight." She drained her drink and caught the bartender's eye. "I got him," she said, tipping her head toward Parker.

He kept his eyes on Corrinne for just a moment too long and said, "I'll have a Sprite."

Corrinne reeled and laughed, slapping the bar so hard it shook. *I'll have a Sprite!"* she howled, and laughed some more. When she'd recovered, she leaned onto the bar and clapped her hand over his. "You're the real deal then, huh?"

"I don't know about that," he answered, accepting his drink from the bartender and trying to ignore the colorful paper umbrella.

"He's just having fun," Corrinne said, removing the cocktail favor and tossing it down the bar. She smiled at him, wheels obviously turning in her mind.

Parker smiled back. He loved her slight crow's-feet and the way her hair fell over one eye. She hadn't changed at all, he realized. He just hadn't taken any notice of her beyond her role in this particular hoop through which he must jump. He sipped his drink and wondered just how often this happened without his ever recognizing it. He was aware, in ever-increasing waves, of his growing self-centeredness and was continually putting off the chore of addressing it.

A group of men in work clothes entered the room and swarmed the bar, taking every remaining seat.

"Guess we'll have to get a table," he said.

"Why?"

"For Troy and Detective Ketcham."

Corrinne smiled and looked down. "They're not coming, Parker. Come on now."

He squinted at her.

"Would you be more comfortable at a table?" she asked, scooping up her drink. "Pick one."

Parker surveyed their options and came to a realization. He was on a date. With Corrinne. This was happening.

"But be honest," Corrinne said, gripping Parker's arm and shaking it a bit too harshly. "You wouldn't want to be rescued by a woman. That's all I'm saying."

"I guess that might hurt my ego a little bit," he admitted.

They were in an ill-lit corner booth—sitting on the same side of the table, which hadn't been Parker's call but suited him just fine. He was on his third Sprite and Corrinne on her third whatever-it-was, and they'd been talking for almost an hour. She'd told him all about growing up in a house full of brothers, how she'd dropped out of cosmetology school to get her bachelor's in criminal justice, how she'd been valedictorian of the same graduating class as her captain and been passed over for detective twice while less-distinguished men rose in the ranks. Her ire increased as she related all this, but she kept patting Parker's knee, as if to assure him that she didn't blame him for the transgressions of his fellow males.

All at once she switched topics. "So, Paul says you changed your name."

He felt blood pooling in his cheeks. "Um, yeah. About four years ago."

"Why?" She leaned back in the seat and looked at him expectantly. No one had ever asked him this question, but he'd long ago prepared the perfect answer—one that didn't sound superficial or showy. One that would not come to mind right now.

"It was just . . ." He grappled. "This guy who mentors me told me that the name Brian lacks gravitas. It doesn't sound prophetic. It sounds like a guy in a cubicle or something."

"A mentor?" She put her hand to her mouth, mortified, and glanced at his soft drink before asking, "Are you an alcoholic?"

"No. His name is Joshua Holton. He's a pastor like me. You've probably seen him on TV."

"I don't own a TV," she said, her easy confidence returning. "So, what, this guy tells you to change your name, and you just do it? That's some kind of power he's got over you."

"I didn't *have* to do it," he answered, more defensive than he intended. "I trust him, that's all."

"I couldn't deal with that. I can't stand people who think they know what's best for me. That's why I don't date cops."

Parker was surprised at the little jolt of elation this news brought him. "So, you and Ketcham aren't . . ."

"Don't finish that sentence," she said, "or you're going to find out where I keep my gun when I'm out about town."

They enjoyed a comfortable silence until it was no longer comfortable. Corrinne drew in a breath and shook her head. "Changing your name is kind of like changing who you are, though, am I right?"

Parker said nothing. He'd asked himself this question a thousand times. A cloud of self-doubt he'd been successfully ducking for months was re-forming over him. Joshua Holton was undoubtedly trying to turn Parker into another version of himself. This he knew, but he told himself that he was still in control. He could chew the meat and spit the fat, so to speak. But was that true? Was he losing himself to gain the world?

"I said, your phone's ringing," Corrinne said, putting her elbow in his ribs.

"Oh. Sorry." He retrieved it and checked the display. Paige. A sudden wave of shame gripped him. Why did he feel like he was somehow cheating on her? They were friends and colleagues, he and Paige, nothing more. Not officially, anyway. Still, he couldn't bring himself to answer it.

"I have to go," he announced, and placed the phone back in his pocket.

"Me too," Corrinne said, pulling herself from the booth and hefting her ample purse onto her shoulder. "Walk a lady to her car?"

They exited the bar together, through the cloud of smoke outside and down to the street.

"Is that yours?" she asked, pointing at Parker's BMW.

"Yeah, that's me."

She strode up to it and peered in through the tinted windows. "Not bad," she said.

"Where are you parked?"

"Oh, I'll have a friend pick me up. Got places to go."

"I get it. You're my armed escort. You just didn't want to say it."

She shrugged. "Like I said, nobody wants to be rescued by a woman." She took a step toward him, penetrating his personal space by an inch or so.

"Doesn't sound so bad."

They stood for a moment, neither sure what to say.

Corrinne broke the silence. "My pastor's name is Brian," she said. "Seems fine to me."

"You go to church?"

"I'm glad that shocks you," she laughed.

"No, I didn't mean—"

"It's okay. I don't go as much as I should. A few times a year: Christmas, Easter, um . . ." She laughed. "Just Christmas and Easter, I guess. I'm just saying, you seem like a good man, Parker. Whoever this mentor guy is, don't let him change you, okay?" She pushed two fingers against her lips and then toward his, pulling up at the last second to press them against his nose. "See ya tomorrow, Preacher."

She stepped quickly back into the bar in her brown skirt and Birkenstocks. Parker watched her disappear and then plopped down behind the wheel and smiled despite himself. He could still smell the generic perfume she'd been wearing, and while he was fairly sure he had lipstick on his nose, he didn't check.

Twelve Years Ago

Danny had notebooks full of research. After the first few exorcisms he'd made a trip to the university library, expecting to find only a handful of books on demonology and the like. But there were dozens—two full shelves. The more he studied, the more he found that the nightmares no longer bothered him. He still had them; he just didn't mind.

He'd stay up late while his roommates slept, trolling the Internet for videos of exorcisms, which he would watch over and over. He learned how to act, how to move—what people expected of a demoniac and what would get a rise out of them.

Before long he was an authority on the subject, although he told no one. He knew how to respond to holy water or a crucifix in a charismatic Catholic Church, and which Scriptures should make him squirm in a Baptist congregation. He began attending Pentecostal deliverance services in the city, hanging back, watching the crowd react to the demons supposedly coming out of their friends and co-workers.

An unintended side effect of all this study was Danny's growing ability to differentiate the fakes from the real thing. And with it, his certain knowledge that he himself was no longer faking it. He was, without a doubt, the genuine article.

Within six months, The Project had taken over Danny's life. He grew his hair out longer and dyed it dark for the benefit of his audience. He kept two wardrobes—one for church and one for everything else. When he entered a church, the people there did not see a calculating individual who had been planning his attendance for more than a month, a college graduate with a firm control over the direction of his life. They saw what he wanted them to see.

Danny found that he had to travel farther and farther in order to avoid short-circuiting his progress. Now living alone, he kept large charts and maps in his bedroom, plotting where he'd been and where he planned to go. Some weeks he would do advanced scouting. He could pick just the right church based solely on the construction of the building and the slogan on the movable-type sign. Soon he'd exhausted the rural churches in a forty-mile radius of his apartment as well as the inner-city black churches. That's when he started in on the suburbs.

The suburbs breathed new life into The Project. Soon Danny stopped looking for churches with a developed theology of "spiritual warfare," realizing that people who had never dealt with the demonic often received him most enthusiastically.

He would occasionally attend a church for two or three weeks before manipulating a prayer of deliverance from the leadership, then come back for another two or three afterward, slowly reforming his appearance each time, just to study the way the event had changed the church's culture. But it was not long before he needed each Sunday to count. He was beginning to realize that the real change taking place was inside of him.

He could no longer live a bifurcated life. He could no longer appease Them by giving Them attention one day a week. They were rushing back in quicker and stronger each time, demanding more. And he was happy to give it.

Eight

Parker's neighborhood had been gentrified long before *gentrify* was a household term. He was comfortable in his home and rarely went out at night. Having no outward vices to speak of, he stayed inside and unwound in two ways: his treadmill and long, in-depth Internet searches. He kept a list throughout the day of items that interested him, things he wanted to know more about. Then, before bed each night, he would look them all up on knowledgeshare-beta.org, an open-source online encyclopedia full of cross-referenced hyperlinks.

These wanderings down the side streets off the information superhighway gave birth to many a sermon illustration for Parker. He would sometimes become so entangled in the Web that he'd forget what he had looked up in the first place and wind up reading about the most obscure people or events, barely able to keep his eyes open. He loved the idea of drifting off to sleep having just fed his brain a heavy meal of new knowledge to digest.

The night before, he'd been so exhausted he had foregone the ritual, so there were several items on his list tonight. Damien Bane, of course, was one of them. But before he even punctured the seal on that one, he typed "Jesuits Militant" into a search box. He scanned the first few pages of hits. Plenty of historical information about the founder of the Jesuits, St. Ignatius de Loyola, who had been a military man in his first career. Interspersed among those were several fundamentalist sites with a decidedly anti-Catholic bent, attempting to expose the ignoble intent of the "ecumenical movement."

Parker suddenly remembered his first search in the bathroom stall that afternoon. What was the wording? He tried typing in "spade symbol Satanism." Jackpot! Fifteen occurrences of an article entitled "Calling a Spade a Spade: Satanism, Catholicism, and the Jesuit Oath" by one Reverend David Black. Parker began skimming the article. Halfway through, the grammatical and spelling errors were more than he could take. Still, there was something about the subject that wouldn't let him go—something providential about his stumbling into this space where the two worlds had intersected.

He opened a new search window and looked up "Jesuit Oath." This yielded 36,000 matches, most containing the phrase "Jesuit Extreme Oath of Induction" in their titles. The first page of results seemed evenly divided between those attempting to debunk the Oath's authenticity and those appealing to it as a means of debunking the Jesuits themselves.

But what was the Oath? Parker had never heard of it. He began clicking and reading. Apparently, the Jesuit Oath had entered the public consciousness in 1843 in a book called *Subterranean Rome* (although Parker could not find a scanned copy online anywhere, or even a rare hard copy for sale). It was immediately clear why emotions ran so high around the words, which almost seemed like a series of intentionally incriminating and incendiary statements strung together with little to connect them.

Parker copied and pasted a few choice passages into a text document to further digest later. The Oath of induction apparently began with the priest initiate naked on his knees with a dagger to his heart, while a superior said these words:

My son, heretofore you have been taught to act the dissembler: among Roman Catholics to be a Roman Catholic, and to be a spy even among your own brethren; to believe no man, to trust no man. Among the Reformers, to be a Reformer; among the Huguenots, to be a Huguenot; among the Calvinists, to be a Calvinist; among other Protestants, generally to be a Protestant, and obtaining their confidence, to seek even to preach from their pulpits, and to denounce with all the vehemence in your nature our Holy Religion and the Pope; and even to descend so low as to become a Jew among Jews, that you might be enabled to gather together all information for the benefit of your Order as a faithful soldier of the Pope.

Parker thought of Father Michael's incriminating DVD and Father Ignatius's comment about burning down the Washington Monument. These Jesuits certainly did not seem to be sneakily obtaining anyone's confidence.

As the Oath continued, the initiate repeated a series of promises:

I do further declare that I will help, assist, and advise all or any of his Holiness's agents in any place wherever I shall be, in Switzerland, Germany, Holland, Denmark, Sweden, Norway, England, Ireland, or America, or in any other Kingdom or territory I shall come to, and do my uttermost to extirpate the heretical Protestants' or Liberals' doctrines and to destroy all their pretended powers, regal or otherwise.

I do further promise and declare that I will have no opinion or will of my own, or any mental reservation whatever, even as a corpse or cadaver, but will unhesitatingly obey each and every command that I may receive from my superiors in the Militia of the Pope and of Jesus Christ.

It was the final vow that filled Parker with an almost insurmountable skepticism as to its authenticity.

I furthermore promise and declare that I will, when opportunity presents, make and wage relentless war, secretly or openly, against all heretics, Protestants and Liberals, as I am directed to do, to extirpate and exterminate them from the face of the whole earth; and that I will spare neither age, sex, or condition; and that I will hang, waste, boil, flay, strangle, and bury alive these infamous heretics, rip up the stomachs and wombs of their women and crush their infants' heads against the walls, in order to annihilate forever their execrable race. That when the same cannot be done openly, I will secretly use the poisoned cup, the strangulating cord, the steel of the poniard or the leaden bullet, regardless of the honor, rank, dignity, or authority of the person or persons, whatever may be their condition in life, either public or private, as I at any time may be directed so to do by any agent of the Pope or Superior of the Brotherhood of the Holy Faith, of the Society of Jesus.

After speaking these words, the young man would supposedly receive the Sacrament before being given the charge,

Go ye, then, into all the world and take possession of all lands in the name of the Pope. He who will not accept him as the Vicar of Jesus and his Vice-regent on earth, let him be accursed and exterminated.

Parker thought about the three men sitting in his living room the night before, trying to imagine them reciting these terrible vows. He needed to know where he stood on this. He prepared some green tea and began reading articles from both the pro and con camps. Those who maintained the Oath's veracity inevitably appealed to its presence in the United States congressional record a hundred years ago and in the Library of Congress. But a little more digging on Parker's part revealed that one could submit any document to the Library of Congress by simply filling out a form and paying a small fee, and that the congressional record in question was simply a transcript of an unsuccessful candidate making a protracted charge of divided loyalties against his Roman Catholic opponent. The whole thing seemed like a house of cards to Parker.

Then he thought about Father Ignatius's gun with the Jesuit crest on the handle, and he was inclined to believe every word of the Oath. His stomach tightened at the memory. He tried to calm himself with some centering breathing. A man in his position had to avoid internalizing sources of stress, he reminded himself. After all, Father Michael hadn't called back since Damien's interrogation. Parker checked his watch. Maybe he'd be lucky and never hear from them again.

Seeing that it was nearly eleven, he decided to start on his homework for Detective Ketcham. He began with a search on Damien Bane, which led him to Damien's video channel, *The Devil's Humanist*. The picture at the top had been taken in an alley, converted to black-and-white, and inflicted with no fewer than fifteen filters and effects, by Parker's estimation. The focal point was meant to be Damien's eyes, dark and mysterious, semiconcealed behind his long black bangs.

Parker brought up the feed and hit Play on the most recent video, which had been posted the afternoon before. The clip showed Damien sitting cross-legged on the floor, a short table covered in strange symbols before him and a banner bearing the words *Satan, Self,* and *Will* behind him.

"Greetings, freethinkers, nontheists, polytheists, spiritualists, and revolutionaries," he said with such a rote cadence that Parker assumed this to be some kind of recurring catchphrase. "Today I want to continue my sixteen-part series on the many tentacles of the Christian Imperialist Elite. I begin with an observation: as I speak, there are activists out there—commendable activists—trying to push for the inclusion of America's reprehensible colonialism in our children's history textbooks. And while I do respect these activists, they're dead wrong when they try to relegate colonialism to the past tense. It's a very present reality. Today, I offer proof." Parker noticed the thirty-eight-minute length of the video and switched to a clip from a week earlier.

"Greetings, freethinkers, nontheists, poly-theists . . ."

Parker scoffed at the words "Number of views: 146" beneath the video. He couldn't help but think of the last time he'd appeared on Joshua Holton's show. Seven *million* had watched him at home. Holton had warned Parker never to appear on small-time news programs or other broadcasts that might dilute his brand. "Let someone else spoon out the soup or emcee the coat drive," Holton had advised. "It's good work, but it's not for us."

Parker was about to shut the computer down when he noticed a new video at the top of the list, activated just two minutes earlier. He opened it.

"Greetings, freethinkers, nontheists, polytheists, spiritualists, and revolutionaries," Damien recited, his voice quivering. "I'm a little shaken today, as you can see." He held a hand up next to his face to prove it. "I've been accosted and accused by the Christian Imperialist Elite. I actually spent the whole day at the police station being lied to, yelled at, and interrogated. I was denied access to my attorney. I was treated as less than a human being.

"This does not surprise me. Apparently I've been asking the wrong questions for too long, and now it's catching up with me. I knew this was coming. The majority religious system cannot tolerate dissent." He paused to take a drink from a bottle of spring water.

"How do I know the hypocritical Elite was behind it, you ask? Because they sent their captain: this man." Parker's publicity headshot momentarily replaced Damien on the screen.

"His name is Parker Saint. You might know him as the syrupy, insufferable Christ-monger often seen licking the boots of Hypocrite General Joshua Holton. Perhaps you've played the destiny drinking game while watching his sermons. I know it's a favorite at my house. But this man is now working with the police. If this surprises you, then you haven't been listening to me for the past two years."

The blood was pounding in Parker's temples. He'd been the subject of many a critical Internet video in recent years, but this one raised the wrong kind of questions. His mind was already in overdrive, trying to spin the facts before they hit the public. Should he be proactive and issue a press release about his volunteering to aid the police? Maybe he could cut the head off this problem before it grew legs. Then he remembered Damien's week-old video with fewer than two hundred views, and the panic subsided.

His phone buzzed against the surface of the desk. The display read "Private Number." Father Michael again, he assumed. Time to put an end to this.

"This is Parker Saint."

"Are you enjoying the show?"

Parker's stomach dropped two stories at the sound of Damien's voice.

"How did you get this number?"

"Everything can be bought. You of all people should know that." There was an unnerving growl present beneath Damien's voice. Parker wondered if it was some sort of modulator or voice synthesizer. He hoped that was it.

"What can I do for you, Damien?" He tried to sound cool and collected.

"You can't do a thing for me. And you can't

do anything *to* me, either. But I've already done something to you, Saint."

"What have you done?"

"Do you believe in curses, Parker?"

"I'm hanging up now."

"Sleep tight, Parker." The line went dead, and at the same moment an orange glow backlit his curtains at the rear of the house. He scrambled to the window, peering around the drapes into the backyard.

Parker gave an involuntary yelp. In the hub of his Japanese Zen garden stood two figures, all in black. He recognized the redhead from Damien's house. The other was shorter and thicker around the neck. Between them they'd driven a dowel, a little taller than a man, into the ground. At the top was a dead animal—a raccoon, Parker thought—burning with a bright, tall flame. The young men spotted Parker at the window and smiled wickedly in his direction for a few seconds, planted there on either side of the burning creature. One of them held up his middle finger. Then they scrambled over his back fence and disappeared.

For half a minute Parker searched frantically for his phone before realizing that he still had it locked in his hand. He wanted to call Detective Ketcham but did not have his home phone number. Should he call 911? What could he say without opening up the whole affair? How could he explain the squad cars to his neighbors? How could he keep this from snowballing into a Brynn Carter exclusive interview on the nightly news?

The smell of burning hair wafted into the house, but one thing he knew for sure: he wasn't going to put out that fire. He could just imagine dark figures hidden in every shadow, baiting him out into his own backyard, fire extinguisher in hand. He'd stay inside and let it burn itself out.

The phone vibrated, causing Parker to startle, and the 410 number appeared on the display.

He answered it. "Father Michael, it's not a good time."

"Never seems to be with you."

"I'm sorry, but something really serious just happened. I'm thinking of calling the police."

"What's going on?"

"I just got a visit from some devil worshipers. They set a dead animal on fire in my backyard."

"Yeah, that happens sometimes."

"This isn't funny to me, Michael. I think I'm going to hang up and call the police now."

"Are they still there?"

"No, I haven't called them yet."

"I mean the devil worshipers."

"Oh. No, I think they're gone. I saw two of them jump the fence."

"Stay inside and keep the doors locked," Michael instructed. "We can be there in a couple minutes. We're just a few blocks away."

Of course you are, Parker thought.

● ● ●

Parker could not retrace exactly how he'd wound up in the backseat of a luxury rental car next to Father Ignatius. He was not sure if it had been his idea or the priests', and he was not sure where they were going. He was, however, sure of several things. He was sure the car wasn't inexpensive. He was sure they were headed west on Michigan Avenue, toward downtown. And he was absolutely sure that Father Ignatius wore too much after-shave.

"I completely understand your not wanting to stay there," Xavier said from the passenger seat. "When our sanctuaries are violated, it's a horrible feeling."

"Sure is," said Parker.

"Lucky for you, we were on our way back from St. Nicholas Orthodox Church on the east side," Michael explained, weaving through traffic like a New York cabbie. "We're sort of on patrol this evening."

"Patrol for what?"

Xavier handed Parker a photocopied map. "I've analyzed the locations of the nine churches that were vandalized, including the two that caught fire. Then I cross-referenced the results with the remaining churches in the city. That gave me a list of the five most likely to be targeted next."

As he studied the map, Parker felt Ignatius's eyes boring into him. A glance to his right confirmed that the old priest was glaring at him. Just glaring. It was then that Parker noticed the older man's tabbed collar. The other two priests were dressed in casual clothes and jackets, while Ignatius wore full clericals.

"We've already been to three of the churches this evening," Michael said. "All locked up tight, not a soul around. The other two are downtown."

"What are you going to do if you find the vandals?"

Michael ignored the question. "I just had a great idea," he announced. "Both church fires were downtown, right? I'm thinking that makes these last two the most likely targets on our list. Why don't we give them each a more in-depth look? I can drop my two colleagues off at St. John's. And Parker, you and I can have a look at St. Andrew's. That will give us a chance to talk, and you can tell me why devil worshipers would want to have a barbecue on your lawn."

Nine

Sneaking around a 150-year-old church in the dark was not exactly how Parker wanted to spend the balance of his night, especially given the evening's earlier events. But the thought of returning to his empty house, going up the poorly-lit stairway to his bedroom, was even less attractive. At least this way he wasn't alone. And as far as bodyguards go, one could do a lot worse than the muscle-bound, presumably gun-toting Father Michael Faber—even if he had black-mailed Parker the night before.

They dropped Xavier and Ignatius at St. John's Anglican Church and agreed to meet there at the corner exactly one hour later. If either party ran into anything suspicious, they would call the other for backup. Parker, who rarely stayed up past eleven thirty, felt like curling up on the heated backseat and going to sleep. The purring of the engine and slow passing of streetlights weren't helping either.

"We'll park here and leg it," Michael said, putting the car at a meter half a block from the church.

The chilly night air immediately revived Parker, as did the chill he felt at the thought of skulking around the nineteenth-century cathedral towering before them.

"There's no alarm here," Michael assured him, as he produced a small, zippered lock-pick kit and went to work at a side door. "Did you know this is the mother church for the diocese?"

"You don't say."

Michael stowed his tools in his leather jacket and motioned for Parker to enter.

"Are we looking for something in particular?" Parker asked.

"I'm gonna say no."

Parker could see the headlines now. Brynn Carter was small potatoes compared to breaking and entering at a church. And the mother church of the diocese, at that. He followed Michael down a short hall by the light of emergency exit lamps.

They turned a corner. Parker flinched.

"What is it?" Father Michael suddenly held a black handgun in his sizeable mitt. He scanned their dim surroundings, alert to any possible threat.

"I'm sorry," Parker whispered. "It was actually that." He pointed to a large, realistically painted crucifix in a niche on the wall. "Those have always given me the willies."

The priest shook his head and holstered his gun. "An icon of our Lord Jesus on the cross gives you 'the willies'?" He pushed ahead, resuming his slow, systematic circuit of the church.

"You have to admit, it's a little grim. A little macabre."

"No, I don't," the priest answered.

"Well, to me, the cross is a symbol of victory and life. Why put a dead man on it?"

"The cross is a symbol of life for sinners by the death of Jesus—God in the flesh. Why *wouldn't* you portray the Christ on the cross? That's the most important part."

Parker shrugged. "I don't know. I've just never really liked those things."

"I think that's a pretty common reaction.

Protestants are trained to be offended by certain aspects of the Catholic faith. Careful on the stairs."

"No, that's not it. I cooperate with Catholics all the time. And I sit on a national, interfaith dialogue board. I don't have a problem with your faith."

"Then why aren't you a priest? It's not like you're married."

"I wasn't raised Catholic."

"Neither was Father Xavier. He converted. Something's got you going a different direction."

"Okay, I guess I do have a few objections."

"Hit me."

"Well, we studied the Reformation pretty hard in seminary, and I always have a hard time getting past indulgences—John Tetzel, going from peasant village to peasant village, selling pieces of paper to pay for all those beautiful Vatican buildings. You know, 'When the coin in the coffer clings, the soul from purgatory springs.' That seems wrong."

Michael came to a stop and locked eyes with Parker. "I admit that wasn't the Church at her best. But can I speak plainly with you?"

"I think it's a little late for that question after last night."

"Fair enough. But tell me this: How are you any different from Tetzel? I checked out your website a couple nights ago, and it was pretty much the same thing. Tetzel was selling release from purgatory after this life; you're selling people their dreams come true, wealth, and success right now in this life. You say Tetzel's product was a mirage, that it had nothing to do with the gospel. Maybe it didn't. But a lot of people would say the same thing about yours."

"I don't think that's a fair comparison."

"Neither do I. At least Tetzel was trying to build up the Church that he believed in—something greater than himself. He wanted to bring glory to the Body of Christ on earth, even if his methods were misguided. You just want to build your own name and influence. Maybe that's why you don't like crucifixes. They remind you that Jesus called us to die to ourselves and our little empires."

"You're speaking plainly, all right."

"Saves time, you should try it. For example, why couldn't you just tell me you're not Catholic because you believe in salvation by grace alone through faith alone? You're not Catholic because we differ in how we describe and divide the process of salvation and what it means. It's not always better to gloss over differences. We can identify them and then move from there. But that's just my perspective."

"You've got it all figured out, huh?"

Michael's eyes calmed a little. "I'm sorry if I'm being too direct." He began walking again. "I get passionate easily. You've already noticed that, I'm sure. But it comes from a good place. I try to live my life by the Jesuit motto, *Ad Majorem Dei Gloriam*: 'everything for the greater glory of God.' They really pounded that into us at Stonyhurst. It's a Jesuit-run school." He turned on a small flashlight and led the way into a boiler room.

Parker was trying to keep his mind off the creepiness of their surroundings and the inky blackness ahead. "Is that how you got into this line of work?" he asked. "Some kind of ROTC for Jesuit-prep-school kids?"

"That's not as far off as you might think. My parents died when I was twelve. They left money and instructions in their will that I was to attend Stonyhurst in Lancashire. That's England. My family has connections to the school going way back. I excelled there academically and athletically. I also fit a certain 'psychological and spiritual profile,' and so the Jesuits Militant recruited me on my sixteenth birthday."

They came back out of the boiler room and made their way to a flight of stairs. Parker was thankful for the streetlights streaming weakly in through the windows.

"Father Michael, can I ask you a question along the lines of 'speaking plainly'?" ·

"I guess that's fair."

"When you were sixteen and they recruited you, did you strip naked, put a dagger to your chest, and take an oath that you would burn, flay, strangle, and bury people alive?"

Michael spun and faced him, his face emotionless. "What did you ask me?"

"It was something I read on—nothing, never mind."

The priest's face hardened. "I'm afraid I have to kill you now, Parker."

"You have to—what? Why?" He wanted to run, but his feet felt glued to the stairs.

Michael burst out laughing. "I'm just messing with you. You're talking about the Extreme Oath of Induction. It's a fake. Basically every nasty anti-Catholic rumor ever spread, all rolled into one. The idea of an oath might have come from some kernel of truth—the early Jesuits were pretty active in fighting Protestantism. But then again, John Calvin was active in fighting the Catholic Church too. I like to think, five hundred years later, we might be able to let some of those old grudges go."

"What does Father Ignatius think about that?"

"Well, he's five hundred years old, so he gets a pass," Michael joked, flashing a goofy grin. "But really, if you knew his background, you'd understand."

Parker thought of Ignatius glaring at him in the backseat. "Try me."

"You know those families where every generation has a fireman or a soldier or a cop? It's passed down father to son to grandson to great-grandson—a straight line down the family tree?"

"Firsthand."

"Well, in Father Ignatius's case, it's like a slalom run down the family tree. Every generation for at least twenty has had one Jesuit Militant. His uncle was one, and his great-uncle. And his great-uncle's uncle. He's had some of the old ideas kind of bred into him."

"So what's his position on us Protestants, really?"

"Let's just say I wouldn't leave you alone with him."

"I can't tell if you're kidding, Michael."

"I am. I think. But he really is old-school. I mean, it never crossed my mind to drop him off here. This church is a ministry of the Paulist Fathers, who are most well-known for their work toward Christian unity. Incredible priests—it just wouldn't sit well with him."

"But he hasn't flayed, strangled, or buried Protestants alive. Has he?"

Michael laughed. "Of course not. Father Ignatius likes to talk like it's the Middle Ages, but even then, we've honestly never been above the law. We're subject to the Scriptures and the rule of the Church. Like any Christian, we can only take a life in a just war or to protect ourselves or someone weaker than ourselves."

"For the record, I'm a lot weaker than you."

They had come full circle to the narthex of the church. Michael opened one of the large oak doors and signaled for Parker to stay behind him as they entered the nave. Passing a small font, the priest dipped two fingers and crossed himself. He dipped them again and splashed a few drops of water onto Parker's face.

"Let this water call to mind your baptism into Christ," he said with a solemnity Parker could not have imagined a moment before. "Christ who has redeemed us by his death and resurrection. Amen."

"Amen. Thank you, Father Michael."

"You're welcome."

"Can I ask you one more thing? You know, speaking plainly."

"Sure, Parker."

"Would you really have sent that video to the newspaper? You seem like such a nice guy."

Michael grinned sheepishly. "Of course not. I've actually been meaning to give this to you." He brought the DVD out of his pocket and handed it over.

"This is really the only one?"

"It's the original anyway. I shouldn't have taken it, and I really shouldn't have used it like that. I'm sorry." He sat down on a back pew and motioned for Parker to join him. "They're not allowed to contradict me directly, but both of my colleagues thought my approach last night was way over-the-top. And they were right. Like I said, I get too passionate too easily. And I suppose I'm a bit overeager to prove myself. It's my first time in charge."

"I don't get that. How can you be in charge of those men? What are you, twenty-five?"

"Twenty-four, actually. We have a pretty unusual hierarchy in the Jesuits Militant. We're divided in teams of three, each team member complementing the skills and abilities of the others. When we're sent on assignment, the Superior General tags one of us as leader for the duration, based on our gifts."

"So next time, Father Ignatius might be in charge?"

"He almost certainly will be."

"And yet you keep poking the bear, so to speak?"

"He's a teddy bear."

"And Father Xavier?"

"I'd be answering to him if we were here investigating a weeping statue or an alleged miracle. That's his area of expertise."

"And what is yours?"

"I'm good at inspiring people to tell the truth."

"Are you talking about interrogation?"

"Not exactly."

"Torture?"

Michael bobbed his head from side to side, as if to evade the question. "Father Ignatius says torture is 'a crude and imprecise word.' I kind of agree. I almost never need to touch someone to make them tell me the truth. I can read them and get inside their defenses. It's a gift."

"And what gifts does Ignatius have?"

"He's just good to have around. Trust me. The guy's fought in wars, taught literature at university, speaks twelve languages fluently. He's even a certified exorcist."

Parker suddenly thought of Damien, his eyes dark and cruel, shouting *I am Legion*. "But you're not?" he asked. "You can't cast out demons?"

Michael shook his head. "No, I haven't been qualified for that particular ministry."

"Father Ignatius hasn't given you any pointers?"

"Not really. You have to remember: in the Holy Catholic Church exorcism is a formal rite, and only those who are authorized can carry it out. And even then, only with ecclesial permission."

"What if there's an emergency and there's no time to get permission?"

"I know of one method. But it's undesirable. And messy."

This whole situation seemed undesirable and messy to Parker. "How does something like this end for you?" he asked. "You can't make an arrest on American soil, can you?"

Michael shrugged. "Honestly, this kind of thing usually goes unsolved. My guess is, it will just stop happening and people will eventually forget.

We don't get many *wins* in this game. That's just the nature of the beast. Literally."

Michael's phone buzzed in his coat pocket. He read a short text message and jumped to his feet. "Xavier says they may have something. Let's go."

The four men met up in the narthex of St. John's Anglican Church.

"That light in the sacristy came on less than ten minutes ago," Xavier whispered.

"Could be someone defiling the Sacrament."

"Or poisoning it."

Father Ignatius drew his gun and clicked off the safety. "That can't happen," he gritted. "Protestant, you stay to the epistle side of the church, up against the wall."

"Which side is that?" Parker asked. The older priest expelled an annoyed sigh and pointed to the right.

They entered silently, walking quickly through the nave: Michael in the left aisle, Xavier in the middle, and Ignatius on the right, Parker sticking close. Converging behind the altar, they could hear someone moving around in the sacristy . . . heavy breathing, some sort of chanting.

Michael was gazing into the edge of his flashlight's beam—dilating his pupils, he would later explain. He signaled that he and Xavier would breach the small room while Ignatius hung back.

Parker's heart thudded in his chest, stealing his breath. He thought about his warm bed. His nightly routine. Even the burning carcass in his backyard seemed warm and inviting now.

Xavier yanked open the door and Michael disappeared into the sacristy, Xavier behind him. Parker heard shouting and crashing. Father Ignatius launched himself toward the door, and without thinking, Parker followed him into the small room. A squat, sweaty man with thick, round glasses was holding a pump-action shotgun in Xavier's face. Three feet away, Michael had his weapon trained on the man's head. All were yelling some variation of "Put it down!"

At the sight of Ignatius's clerical collar, the man went silent. He pulled the earbuds from his ears but kept the gun up.

"I think he's the janitor, guys," Parker said, pointing at the large, plastic trash can on wheels and the dozen bottles of cleaning solution.

The man swung the thick gun in Parker's direction. "I'm the custodian, not the janitor. Night watchman too. What are you doing in my church?"

Ignatius quickly stepped between Parker and the shotgun. "Please calm down. I'm with the diocese," he soothed, his voice reflecting a perfect Midwestern accent. "These men work for a private security firm—part of our effort to step up safety and security in our local parishes. Weren't you told about this?"

The custodian slowly lowered the shotgun. "No, nobody told me."

"Are these your normal hours?" Michael asked.

"So happens they are. I come in three times a week. This ain't my real job. I clean the church when I get done at UPS."

"You always carry a gun while you work?"

"You bet your life," he said, patting it lovingly. "No one's going to lay a finger on my church. I've been going here for forty-five years." He pushed his glasses back up his broad nose. "You think I don't see what's going on out there? Father, you've got the right idea, bringing in some muscle. And I'm glad to see you're packin' too."

"Just don't get caught with that thing," Michael advised.

The custodian safetied the gun and slid it between the cart and the trash can. "I won't be caught without it, kid."

"We apologize for the scare," Father Xavier said. "Carry on."

The four of them filed wordlessly out the front of the church, everyone a bit embarrassed.

On the sidewalk outside Xavier finally broke the silence. "He was a bit of a loon, no?"

"He seemed an exceptional servant of the Church to me," Ignatius said.

Michael rolled his eyes. "Of course you liked him. He's the American You."

They were all silent for a beat.

"That could have gone smoother," Michael admitted. "Sorry, guys."

Ignatius squeezed his shoulder briefly.

"This might not be the time," Parker said, "but can I ask a question? What's the PX thing on the altar in there? I've always wondered about that."

Ignatius's face soured. "A PX is a candy store, Protestant. The symbol on the altar was a Chi-Rho, the monogram of Christ."

"I know. Just trying to lighten the mood."

"No more for me, please," Parker told the waitress, laying his hand over his cup. "I've got an early appointment tomorrow morning."

"It's decaf, sir," she said.

"It still has trace amounts of caffeine, which can affect sleep patterns. I'm not supposed to drink coffee anyway. It stains your teeth."

The waitress snuffed and made her exit.

The priests had convinced Parker not to go directly home to bed, keyed up as he was. Best to wind down a little after having a shotgun poked in your face, to talk things out, they had explained. It made sense to Parker.

They had found Café 37, a twenty-four-hour diner off the highway, where a table in a dark corner provided plenty of privacy for Parker to recount Damien Bane's alleged connection to the murders, his response to Parker at the interrogation, his videos on the Internet, and the visit to Parker's home that evening.

The smell of grease and meat had revitalized Parker's appetite with a vengeance. He set aside his usual culinary snobbery and ordered a plate of something called volcano fries. The three priests all had questions for Parker, but he was unable to answer most of them. He did give them Damien's address and a few other tidbits. All in all, the priests seemed pleased.

"We have a suite at the Grand Plaza," Xavier said as they paid the bill. "If you're worried about sleeping at home tonight, we could have them bring up a rollaway."

"No thanks. They were just trying to scare me. You can take me home."

"Actually, we've got one more place to go," Michael said.

"But it's 1:35 in the morning."

"It'll be quick, Parker. I promise."

Father Xavier pulled the Cadillac up to the curb.

"What are we doing here?" Parker demanded, panic edging his voice.

"You recognize this place?" Michael asked.

"Of course. That's Damien's house up ahead. I don't want to be here. Will you please take me home?"

"You don't have to leave the car," Michael assured him. "You'll be safe here with Father X.

I promise. We'll be back in a few." He and Ignatius stepped out of the car and approached the house on foot.

"What are they going to do? Are they going in there?"

"No," Xavier said. "And don't worry; the windows are tinted. They can't see us."

Parker watched the two priests walk past the house and disappear into an alley.

"Now, I want you to look carefully," Xavier said, "and tell me if you recognize anyone."

"You mean, do I see the guys from my back-yard?"

"Or Damien himself. That would be even better."

The house was alive with young people—coming and going, drinking on the porch, milling on the lawn. Occasionally a group would emerge from the backyard, laughing and weaving. Parker let his eyes drift across the scene from face to face.

"No. I've never seen any of these people."

"We'll just wait a little while."

"Sir, I'm really tired. I'm afraid I'm going to fall asleep right here."

"Please just give us five minutes, then we'll take you home."

Parker leaned his head against the soft leather headrest and let his eyes half close. His stomach full to bursting with junk food and his mind running on fumes, he began to drift.

"That Michael's a good kid," Xavier said, a transparent attempt to keep Parker from dozing off.

"Yeah, he's a nice guy. I like him."

"I think it's a mark of incredible piety that you can say that and mean it, considering your first impression."

"He explained himself. There's no harm. I can't imagine the pressure for someone that young in his position."

"He's a bit of a loose cannon now, but by the time he's my age, he'll be one of the best."

"As long as he and Father Ignatius don't kill each other out there."

Xavier chuckled. "Unlikely. Don't buy into their bickering. The reason they get on each other's nerves is because they're so much alike. And they're closer than you would ever guess. Michael lost his parents at a young age, and Ignatius has been like a second father to him."

"How long have you three been a team?"

"Father Ignatius and I have been working together for twenty-two years. Michael joined us fresh out of seminary, a little more than five years ago."

"He must have been some kind of prodig— Wait." Parker leaned forward in the seat, squinting toward the house. "That's them."

"The three coming down the steps?"

"Two of them, anyway. I didn't see the guy with

the black hair. He might have been there, I just didn't see him."

"That's not Damien?"

"No. Damien's older."

The three young men cut across the grass and headed down the street, away from the car.

Xavier pushed a button on his phone. "Parker's houseguests are headed your way now."

"No Damien?" Michael asked.

"Negative. They'll reach your position in approximately forty seconds."

"Copy," came the reply.

"Will they hurt them?" Parker asked, slightly concerned. "They really didn't do much of anything. Just a prank, if you think about it."

"Don't worry. They'll just—what's the American phrase?—put the fear of God into them."

There were train tracks a block from Damien's house, and the neighborhood had once been on the right side of them. The tracks hadn't moved, but in the past few years a distinct shift had occurred. Damien's presence had everything to do with it.

Three stoned hooligans whooping their way down the street, discarding bottles in the gutter, was no longer an unusual sight. A seventy-four-year-old priest walking alone at two a.m., his coat wrapped tightly around his frame, was.

"Guys! What am I seeing? Am I seeing this?" one of the punks called out, pointing toward the sidewalk with one hand and holding up his sagging pants with the other. "What is this?"

"That's a member of the Christian Imperialist Elite."

They closed in on him like a pack of hyenas, their eyes red and their breath foul. The malice in the group was almost tangible.

"I heard that if you hit these guys, they can't hit you back."

"No, that's Amish, man."

"Priests too."

"Let's find out," the tall, ruddy one said, taking a last drag on his cigarette and flicking it into the darkness of the railroad crossing. "How about it, Grandpa? Can you take a hit?"

He wound up and slapped the priest's face, sending him staggering back two steps. This brought a chorus of laughter from the trio.

"You gonna turn the other cheek, Padre?" He slowly pushed his dull red locks from in front of his bloodshot eyes, then backhanded the older man with a sudden jerk of his arm.

"Lemme try, man." The fat one in the hoodie jostled past his friends and gave the priest an experimental shove.

"Hit him, Jared," the others urged.

Jared shoved the priest again, harder. "Where's all that wrath of God I keep hearing about?" He balled a fist and swung it at the priest's jaw.

The punch never connected.

Jared noticed the dull, bitter taste of the black-top before the sharp pain in his shoulder, where the ball and socket were making the best of a long-distance relationship.

Father Ignatius poked his pistol against the fat man's temple. "Thou shalt not put the Lord your God to the test."

The ringleader reached frantically into his faded army jacket, his hand groping. He didn't see Father Michael moving silently up the train tracks behind him.

Michael gripped the punk hard around the throat and held his own handgun up at eye level.

The third punk looked from one priest to the other and put his hands in the air, sending his pants down around his ankles. He reached for them.

"Leave your dignity on the ground," Ignatius commanded.

"Please," Jared pleaded, "don't go all Crusades on me."

"Crusades? My order had no part in the Crusades," the old priest answered evenly. "The Inquisition, however—that was ours."

Michael yanked the redhead's coat down past his shoulders, pinning his arms, and snatched the revolver from his inside pocket. He shoved him toward his exposed friend.

"Makes you feel tough, preying on the weak,"

Michael said, a gun in each hand. "I bet you just love violating the sanctity of a man's home, too. Giving him a good scare." He stuffed the battered revolver into his coat pocket. "Parker doesn't know we're talking to you like this. Suffice it to say, he wouldn't approve."

Ignatius took two steps back from the young man heaped at his feet. "You will not bother Mr. Saint again. If you do, there will be consequences. This goes for your friend Damien as well. You may know where Parker lives, but we know where you live."

Ten

"Time to get up." Father Michael was standing next to Parker's bed, shaking him roughly.

"My head hurts. Give me five more minutes."

"No, you don't even have time to shower. It's 7:35. Do you want to be late?"

Parker was too miserable to notice the oddity of the situation—a priest he'd met two nights earlier waking him for work. They had brought Parker home at nearly two thirty in the morning and given the house a thorough sweep, just to be sure. Michael had offered to keep watch on the first floor during the night. Parker's objections had been feeble and quickly melted away. He had fallen into a fitful sleep at about four.

"Ugh. My stomach feels like a clenched fist."

"I told you not to get those tornado fries," Michael said.

"Volcano."

"Whatever. Here, I made some coffee. The grounds were stale, but the caffeine's still good."

"I'm not supposed to have coffee."

"I'll leave it on the nightstand in case you decide you want it," he said. "And I mean it—get up," he added over his shoulder as he left the room.

Parker slowly sat upright on the edge of the bed. He stared at the coffee mug, steaming and inviting. He decided it was worth compromising his principles to take the edge off his headache. He took a long gulp, immediately regretting it as his stomach began to bubble and percolate. He fell back on the bed and lay for another two minutes.

Michael banged on the door. "Are you up? It's almost twenty till."

Parker hurriedly dressed and dashed out the door. By five minutes to eight he was parking his car in a municipal lot near the police station. He entered the elevator with two minutes to spare.

"I know about your little rendezvous last night," Ketcham said, his face as stern as his tone.

Parker's stomach tightened all the more. His mind groped for a way to spin the events in the church, the guns, and whatever had happened in the distance beyond Damien's house.

"I was . . . I mean, I can explain."

The detective laughed. "No need. And don't bother resisting. What that one wants, she gets. Believe me."

"Oh, you mean Corrinne."

"Yeah. She's a predator, that one. Watch yourself."

Parker felt a sudden urge to defend his new friend, but fought it back down. "We just had some drinks and talked for a while. That's all."

"Mm hmm. Well, you look like garbage, Parker. I didn't think preachers were supposed to party."

"I wouldn't say I *partied*."

"I really don't care, just as long as you don't let it affect your work with us. There's way too much of that in law enforcement. It's unprofessional to come in functioning at 35 percent because you spent the night chugging liquid depressants. That's why I don't drink." He pointed to his head with two fingers. "Got to keep it swept clean."

"I'm fine. Really."

"Good. I need you to keep it together this morning. We're going to an autopsy at ten."

"Whose autopsy?"

"Melanie Candor, the first victim. We're sparse on anything useful with this girl. Hopefully Dr. Potter can give us something new to go on."

"But why do I have to go?"

"What are you, ten years old? You're going.

You're going because you chucked a fax machine at an airline stewardess."

"But isn't an autopsy for when you don't know how someone died? Melanie Candor's throat was cut. We already know that. Can't we just skip it?"

"Actually, that's not up to us. The county medical examiner determines when an autopsy is necessary. In this case, he believes it is. We're attending in order to preserve and protect evidence of the crime and to learn everything we can about this killer and how he operates."

"Fine," Parker pouted.

"By the way, did you do your homework?" The detective raised an eyebrow like a stern schoolmaster.

Parker had been debating whether to tell him about Damien's phone call and the midnight visit. He'd decided to keep the details sparse, in order to avoid opening a door to the events at St. John's. Worlds, as they say, were in danger of colliding.

"I was working on it last night when he called me."

"Who?"

"Damien. He said he was putting a curse on me."

"He called you at home?" Ketcham's voice raised a touch.

"On my cell."

"And you didn't think to call and tell me?"

"I didn't have your number. Besides, what could you do? He blocked the caller ID. It's my word against his."

"Did he identify himself?"

Parker thought. "Not in so many words."

"But he was trying to intimidate you."

The image of a burning animal on a pike flashed into Parker's mind. "I would say so."

Ketcham seethed. "I'm going to nail this little mutant to the wall."

Troy and Corrinne breezed into the conference room, all smiles.

"We've got something for you, Detective Ketcham," she said, beaming. "Last night—"

Ketcham cupped his hands over his ears. "I don't want to know about last night!"

Corrinne's lips twisted into a little smile, and her eyes met Parker's for a moment.

Troy chuckled. "This is work, Ketch. There was a community memorial service for Ben Ludema at Central High School last night." He set up his laptop on the conference table. "We got video of the crowd. Wait till you see this."

He loaded a clip and hit Play. The lighting was low and so was the video quality—probably a cell phone, Parker thought. The video had been slowed down and was continually looping a pan down the second to last row of seats.

"They're all Goth," Ketcham observed.

"I don't think 'Goth' is a thing anymore, is

it," Troy said, more a statement than a question.

"You know what I mean. Emo. Whatever."

"Yeah, that doesn't mean what you think," Corrinne said.

"They're all dressed like it's Halloween," Ketcham said emphatically.

"They're definitely together," Troy agreed. "Watch how they act."

"There's Danny Boy." Ketcham pushed a finger onto the screen. "And this guy answered the door yesterday." Parker's pulse quickened at the sight of the red-haired man, whom he'd last seen walking down the street, away from Damien's house, at two in the morning. For a moment he wondered if he was looking at the image of a dead man.

Corrinne paused the video on a frame where all eight faces were visible.

"We ran this by a school administrator at Central," she said, "and she was able to identify everyone pictured here with Damien as either a current student or a dropout or graduate from the last five years. I've got names, Paul."

"Names are good," he allowed. "But Damien already admitted to knowing Ludema. He'll say he was just paying his last respects."

"There's more," Troy said, suspending his large frame over the computer and pecking at the keys. "They had a candlelight vigil for Melanie Candor at Kensey Sunday night."

"No one waits for funerals anymore," Ketcham said.

Troy pulled up another video file. "We got the security footage."

"That was my idea," Corrinne said. "And we barely got it too. They would have overwritten the tapes today."

"I don't know that it was all *your* idea," Troy mumbled. "Okay, check this out."

The footage was black-and-white and the angle was bad, but Corrinne zoomed in with the mouse until the screen was filled with just three people.

"This is Damien." She pointed with her pen. "There's no doubt of that."

Ketcham grinned. "We've got a dumb one, folks!"

"Yeah, going to the memorials is stupid. Or else maybe he *wants* to get caught. Remember, he talked about a lawyer yesterday, but didn't demand one."

"Good point."

"He doesn't want to get caught," Parker said with authority.

Ketcham threw his hand up. "There you have it. From a trained criminal profiler."

"You don't need to be a psychologist for this. It's simple. On his website Damien claims to be a secularist, a humanist, and a Satanist. Satanism is—practically speaking—just a celebration of self-indulgence and pride. For Damien to get caught and incarcerated is detrimental to both. Can you imagine how a guy like that would be treated in prison? No, he's shoving what he's done in your faces because he doesn't think you can pin it on him. He's convinced he's the smartest man in any room and everyone else is just *sheeple*. If you think about it, that's your edge."

There was a pause while the three detectives took this in.

Ketcham whacked Parker between the shoulder blades. "We're keeping this guy."

Corrinne directed their attention back to the screen. "There's one more thing on the tape. We've got a mystery man here. I'm pretty sure this big guy next to Damien is the ginger we met at the door. His name is Dylan Eiler, by the way—juvie record as long as Parker's mailing list. But who is this kid?" She tapped the image of a sullen teenager with a collection of lip rings and a crusty blond spike.

"We checked with three schools," Troy said. "Nobody can identify him."

"And he wasn't at the service for Ludema yesterday." Ketcham furrowed his brow in thought. "There may be more than one defector in the group."

"That would possibly put this kid in some danger," Troy said.

Parker half-raised his hand. "Don't you have

facial recognition software or something?" He felt silly the moment the words left his mouth.

Ketcham scoffed. "You watch too much TV, Parker."

"I don't, actually. I never watch TV."

Troy closed the laptop. "Let's just keep an eye out for him. He might have been sick yesterday. Or maybe it was his turn to stay home and stir the cauldron. Who knows?"

"Either way," Ketcham said, sitting back in his chair, "we've got a real suspect now. He's in the crosshairs for the time being. I want to match any partial prints from the crime scene. I want DNA. And maybe you two could head back over to the Monster Mash house later today and get some statements from any 'witnesses' who want to cover for Damien during the Ludema murder. If there's anyone credible there, I need to know."

"Where are you going?" Corrinne asked.

"Autopsy."

The first thing that hit Parker was the smell—like a high-end butcher shop in which every surface had been scrubbed down with ammonia. It got exponentially stronger as Ketcham led him into a windowless room, somehow nondescript and macabre at the same time. The fluorescent lights were thrumming loudly, bathing the place in a sickly greenish glow.

Parker put his hand over his nose and mouth.

"Here," Ketcham offered, holding out a baby-food jar full of brown mush.

"What is this?"

"Coffee grounds. Put some in your nostrils. If you think it smells bad now, just wait."

Parker tried not to look at the counter against the wall, filled with a collection of electric saws and cutting implements, but he couldn't help it. His stomach began to accordion again.

He redirected his eyes to the steel table—the most prominent feature in the room—and tried not to think about what would soon be happening there, just several feet from where he stood. The table was built at a slight angle, Parker observed, thinking that it would make more sense if it were constructed level. Then he noticed a series of built-in drains and realized why. The room was a little cooler than was comfortable, but Parker was starting to sweat.

An obese man in a lab coat came bustling into the room, his eyes glued to a clipboard. He looked up, startled to see the two men.

"Oh, great. The fuzz is here," he deadpanned.

"Choke on it, Uncle Fester," Ketcham said.

They glared at each other for a moment, then broke out in smiles and shook hands heartily.

"Dr. Potter, this is Parker Saint. He's a TV preacher and, for the moment, special consultant to the Grand Rapids Police Department."

The doctor gave a slight bow. "Reverend," he

said, "good to have you here. I'm agnostic, but I have enormous respect for your kind."

"My kind appreciates that."

"Terri's getting the subject now," the doctor said, looking at his watch. "She should have been here already." He opened the door and poked his head into the hall. "Terri!" he bellowed.

"Quiet as a morgue has lost its meaning," Parker mumbled.

"Here she comes." The doctor smiled like a proud father presenting a gift to a child.

A young woman wheeled a bagged body into the room on a gurney. Dr. Potter helped guide it up next to the table and then began to unzip.

It suddenly occurred to Parker that this young woman would be naked; he'd seen enough police procedurals to know that. His discomfort level increased threefold. He was thinking less about himself—although he did have a policy of avoiding female nudity—and more about the girl in the bag who had already died a desperate, undignified death.

As a pastor, Parker had been around dead bodies many times before, having done his share of funerals—particularly early on in his ministry, while an associate at Hope Presbyterian. But those encounters had done nothing to prepare him for this. If anything, they'd done the opposite. A pastor's involvement with the dead takes place after all the grisly preparations, when the deceased has been drained, treated, embalmed, and is wearing a nice suit or a dress and pearls. His or her dignity is protected in those situations with mafioso vigilance. And Parker was used to being part of the dignity protection racket.

Terri peeled the bag away from the feet first and then the head, as if removing the plastic wrap from a Twinkie, Parker thought.

Melanie Candor was not naked; only her shoes had been removed. Parker breathed a sigh of relief, though he knew this only postponed the inevitable. Dr. Potter and Terri carefully moved her body to the table on a three-count with speed and gentleness, like two paramedics afraid of further hurting an injured patient.

Parker grimaced. "So, 'toe tag' isn't just an expression."

"No, Parson. That's how we keep track of them. Can you think of a better place to put it?"

"Not really."

Terri read the name and serial number from the tag, while Dr. Potter confirmed it on the clipboard.

"That's our girl," he said. "Look at that birth date. So young. What a sad thing." His face fell momentarily before regaining its shine. "Ah, we're getting tattoos on the bottoms of our feet now," he observed.

Parker noticed a small, star-shaped design next to where the toe tag rested. He realized anew that this body on the metal table had been a vital, living woman just a few days earlier—with a beating heart, a sense of humor, and a favorite restaurant. He couldn't help but think that the little star looked like an asterisk, referring the doctor to some fine print.

"At least it's easy to hide down there," the doctor continued. "My daughter Anne got a sea turtle tattooed on her neck, can you believe that? I said, what about job interviews? She tells me she can cover it up with a turtleneck, which I guess is ironic or something." He looked at Parker expectantly. "You know, because she already has a *turtle neck*."

"Why are there plastic bags on her hands?" Parker asked.

Ketcham cleared his throat. "This might go faster if Dr. Potter doesn't have to explain every step of the process."

"No, that's fine. I appreciate the interest. Most people don't want to know. The bags are put there by crime scene technicians. It allows us to get samples from the palms, fingertips, under the fingernails. In this case, it's also holding in some blood from the defensive wounds to her hands, but there's not really a way around that."

Potter walked over to the long table full of saws and snips. Parker's vision dimmed around the edges until the doctor settled on a small ruler.

"We can often find very important evidence

under the fingernails in homicide cases," he continued. "Even if an attacker is wearing gloves, it's almost impossible to cover up all of your skin, and some of it can end up under the victim's nails. It's a great source of DNA if you have a suspect to check against, which I understand we do in this case."

Dr. Potter measured two tears in the blouse and a long black scuff on the skirt, dictating the information to Terri, who recorded it on the clipboard and took digital photos. He then tipped the body onto its side and examined the back of the clothing, making several more observations.

"I'm going to take the bags off now," he told Parker. "You'll see how carefully we analyze the hands and how many samples we can get from such a small space."

Parker was becoming a little more comfortable with the idea of an autopsy, to the point of being rather fascinated as he watched the hand examination stretch on for nearly twenty minutes. He mentally added "autopsy" to his list of search terms for the evening.

His comfort evaporated when Dr. Potter began unbuttoning the blouse. Parker averted his eyes slightly at the sight of a white lace brassiere.

"What's that tray for?" he asked, knowing he was stalling, trying to temporarily derail the progress.

Ketcham answered, "The rib cage will be placed

there during the internal examination. That will give Dr. Potter easy access to her organs."

Parker's stomach began quivering and complaining. What was left of the volcano fries was in danger of erupting.

"And that bucket closer to you is called the brain bucket," he continued. "I'll give you two guesses what that's for."

Dr. Potter snatched a pair of small wire cutters from the table. "You find a girl yet, Ketcham?"

"That's a negative, Doc. No time. But speaking of, how's Katie?"

Potter paused before snipping the underwire. "How do you know my wife?"

"I bumped into you two at that new restaurant on Market a few weeks back, remember?"

"Oh, yeah—Tangy Bones. Amazing ribs, that place. Terri, come here and help me lift up her hips." He returned the wire cutters to the exact spot where he'd gotten them. "All-you-can-eat ribs will be my death. I must have gone through about fifty of those wet naps that night. Those ribs are good but they sure are messy."

Parker felt the contents of his stomach backing up into his throat. He wanted to turn and run out the door, up the hall to the restroom they'd passed, but he knew the very act of turning would just increase the projectile nature of what was about to happen. So, instead, he lurched forward two steps and emptied his guts into the brain bucket.

"You're not the first one to do that. Don't worry," Ketcham assured him a few minutes later, out in the hall. A smile was tugging at the corner of the detective's mouth. "At least the brain wasn't already in there. That would have caused some problems."

Parker had apologized profusely and repeatedly, but Ketcham was clearly more amused than annoyed. Parker hadn't stuck around long enough to learn how Dr. Potter would react.

"Go home and get some rest," Ketcham said. "I've got some solo work to do this afternoon anyway. I'm going to compare statements and do a little digging into Damien's background. I'll get you copies of anything that might be up your alley."

"Thank you, Detective Ketcham."

"No problem. Gargle some mouthwash and get some sleep. I've got to get back to the autopsy."

Parker loved the idea. He wanted nothing more than to shut his curtains and curl up in his bed. But when he pulled up to his house, the Jesuits' Cadillac was in the driveway.

Ten Years Ago

Danny sat in his car, parked under a bridge. He locked the doors, pulled his keys out of the ignition, and tossed them under the seat. It was better if they weren't easily accessible.

He could sense that They would be back any minute now. It was a familiar but still disconcerting feeling. His mind was spinning, refusing to land on any one thought. This in-between time was complicated for Danny. He felt emptied, in both a good and a bad way. There was a certain freedom to be enjoyed during these brief windows, but an intense longing as well. He knew Their return would be painful yet ultimately satisfying.

There would be more of Them this time. A lot more. That's what he really cared about. More in number and more in power.

This unexpected side effect of repeated expulsion had prompted the change in Danny's motivation. He was no longer driven by the attention or the sense of awe focused on him by a group of perfect strangers. Nor was it the perks that came with it, numerous as they might be.

As he'd moved into the affluent suburbs of Grosse Pointe and Farmington Hills, the treatment from churches had gone deluxe. The bigger ones had green rooms, where they would bring Danny after the service. They'd give him a six-dollar bottle of sparkling water and treat him like a king. Danny had eaten this up at first, but now it just got in the way. It wasn't about attention anymore. It was about the power that increased each time They came back.

The temperature in the car began to drop quickly. Or at least it seemed to. Danny sucked in a deep breath and held it. With a jerk, he arched in his seat and ground his teeth. Dread always came first, but then a kind of contentment took its place. The whole process was getting quicker each time. Within three minutes he was calmly pulling his keys from under the car seat and turning on the ignition.

Perhaps the reason it had taken him so long to realize he was no longer pretending was that Danny remained fully aware of what was going on. He didn't black out or lose time. He was fully conscious and usually in complete control of himself.

Danny was still Danny. But he was more.

Eleven

"Home for lunch already?" Michael asked, peering over Parker's backyard gate.

"No, I'm done for the day."

"We came back to dispose of the burnt cat," Michael explained. "You heard me, the sickos burned a *cat*. Can you believe it? Probably had a name. We didn't want you to have to deal with it."

"I would have had to. How could I explain that to anyone else? Thanks."

Michael opened the gate and emerged from the

back, pulling off a pair of long rubber gloves. Ignatius came up behind him, holding a shovel, followed by Xavier.

"This works out well," Xavier said. "We were going to ask you to accompany us to the Church of the Transfiguration later this evening, but now would be better. Are you free?"

"How do you break into churches during the day?"

The priest laughed. "We're not breaking in. We have an appointment with the parish priest."

"I'll pass on this one. I need to get some sleep."

"I wouldn't do that," Xavier warned. "You'll confuse your internal clock. You wouldn't want to wake up at 3:00 a.m., wide-awake. Better to power through and sleep well tonight."

"You may have a point."

Michael flashed a smile. "It won't take long. We'll buy you lunch. What do you say?"

Parker's stomach had calmed down after he vomited, but the thought of putting something else in it caused it to rebel again.

"The last thing I want is to eat right now," he said.

"Good. Because we just had omelets. Big ones. You can ride shotgun."

"This church wasn't on your list last night, was it, Father Xavier?" Parker asked.

"No, that list analyzed vandalism. I don't expect we'll hear about much of that here. My experience tells me that people in this sort of neighborhood respect the Church. In fact, I would pity the young delinquent caught by the locals while defacing this building."

There were a dozen cars in the lot of the old brick edifice. Michael put the car in park and looked earnestly over at Parker.

"Now, there *are* going to be crucifixes in here. You gonna be okay?"

"Very funny."

"Just warning you."

Father Ignatius scowled. "What is this talk?"

"Inside joke." Michael twisted in his seat to address his fellow Jesuits. "When we get in there, forget the charade. I'm taking the lead this time."

Father Xavier looked dubious. "If you think they'll buy it."

"There's nothing to buy. I'm leading this investigation."

"We have no objection," Xavier said.

Ignatius nodded.

They entered through a 1940s addition to the church. Parker surveyed the foyer.

"These old buildings must be a bear to heat and maintain."

Ignatius snorted. "Did you say *old?*"

Michael leaned in to Parker. "Father Ignatius

was baptized and confirmed in a fourteenth-century Spanish monastery, so . . ."

"Well, it's old to me. Our facility was built in 1981."

There was an explosion of clerical garb as Michael and Xavier collided with a speed-walking priest rounding the corner. The large beads of his rosary clacked, and his salt-and-pepper beard reverberated with the impact.

"Excuse me, friends," he said with a voice much smaller than his frame would have suggested.

"It was my fault," Father Michael said, holding out his hand. "You must be the Reverend Monsignor John Naughton."

"I am indeed." The priest gave Michael's hand a single weak shake.

"I'm Father Michael Faber. Do you have a few minutes to speak with us?"

The monsignor's face brightened. "You must be the men from the Vatican." He looked to Xavier expectantly.

"Indeed we are," the priest replied with a slight French accent Parker had not yet heard. "I'm Father Xavier and this is Father Ignatius. And this is Parker."

"Father Xavier, Father Ignatius, Father Parker," he said, shaking each man's hand.

"Mr. Parker," Ignatius corrected.

"Reverend Parker. Reverend Saint, actually," Parker said.

The bearded man drew up his brow, impressed. "Parker Saint? Do we have a local celebrity in our midst?"

"Well, I don't know about *that*."

"How on earth did you get mixed up with the Vatican's men?"

"It's a long story."

Ignatius shook his head. "A short story. We commandeered him."

The monsignor laughed. "And you've got a young protégé as well. Sounds like a good arrangement."

"He's still in training," Ignatius said, mussing Michael's hair. "You're doing *very well,* my son."

"We were hoping to speak with you for a few minutes this afternoon," Xavier explained. "We apologize for the short notice, but it concerns some rather pressing church business that cannot wait."

"The bishop told me to expect you at six o'clock this evening," Naughton said with a pained expression. "I'm afraid I'm supposed to be hearing confessions for the next two hours. I have people waiting."

"Not a problem. Father Ignatius can hear the confessions while we talk."

Michael held up a finger. "Are you sure that's—"

"It will be fine, Father Michael. Don't you think?"

Ignatius waited, his eyes on the young priest. "Yeah, I guess it will be fine."

Ignatius bowed slightly and followed the monsignor's simple directions to the confessional. Michael's eyes followed after him, full of concern.

"He doesn't like hearing confession?" Naughton asked.

Xavier waved a hand. "It's not that. Father Ignatius has been serving the Church in a very different capacity for many years. But hearing confession is like riding a bike, as they say. Besides, we hear each other's confessions regularly, and I can attest that Father Ignatius is more than capable."

"Yeah, no one's getting away with anything today," Michael mused. "May we follow you to your office now, Monsignor?"

"Of course."

They passed under an archway and down a few stairs to a door adorned with a nameplate and a large framed placard bearing the words War Is Not the Answer. The parish priest unlocked the door and invited them to sit in two high-backed leather armchairs facing his desk. Father Michael grabbed a stackable metal chair from the corner and sat between them.

The Reverend Monsignor Naughton slipped in behind his desk and silently studied his guests. "I have to admit I've been relentlessly curious all day, wondering what the Holy See could possibly want with our church."

Xavier spoke, friendly but efficient. "We'd like to discuss three items with you today. The first, and most mundane, is the question of whether your church—particularly the building—has been the victim of any occult-related crimes. Any sort of defacing or desecration?"

Naughton pursed his lips in thought. "None that I can think of, no. I'd be very surprised by any defacing or malicious property damage here. We've done quite a good deal of mercy ministry in this neighborhood. We help ex-cons transition back into society, support addicts trying to kick their habits, and we feed a hundred and fifty people three times a week. Our church building is safe here because we are well thought of in the community."

"That's what I was telling Pastor Parker. There's more respect for the Church in the inner city than most other places."

"We prefer to call this a 'transitioning neighborhood,' but yes, I agree. Does that cover item number one?"

"It does."

A young man, sloppily dressed, shifted uncomfortably in the confessional.

"I'm not sure about all this. A little archaic, isn't it?"

Father Ignatius never got sidetracked during confession. "Yes, the Rite of Reconciliation is an ancient sacrament of the Church. Now, please begin."

"It's just, I'm not really used to—"

"I realize that I'm not your parish priest, but be assured that I have taken my vows and have been a priest for almost fifty years. I am more than qualified to hear your confession."

"I'm not used to being in here is all," the young man said. "Anyway, this week has been a little better than last."

Ignatius sighed. "You're getting ahead of yourself. How long since your last confession?"

"A week. I come every Thursday and meet with Father John."

"And yet, the confessional seems foreign to you. Why do you suppose this is?"

"Because we don't use it. We meet in Father Greg's old office. There's couches."

"You do confession face-to-face?"

"Well, yeah. It's sure not like this." He poked at the screen. "It's more like a counseling session."

"A counseling session," Ignatius repeated, horrified.

"Yeah, we talk about my spiritual life. My struggles, my successes. That's how a lot of churches are doing it these days. Like a counseling session."

"Does Father Naughton assign penance?"

"Well, yeah, but it's mostly exercises to help me with my struggles, so I can grow spiritually."

"Like what, for example?"

"Last week, he had me write down one thing I did each day that made God smile. I have it with me if you want to hear—"

"No! I've heard enough. Your confession has been vulgar and blasphemous. Your penance is sixty Our Fathers, one hundred Acts of Contrition, and forty Hail Marys."

"But I haven't even gotten to my sins yet," the young man objected.

"If they're worse than what you just told me, I don't think I could bear hearing them."

"Item number two," Michael said, "is the girl who was murdered Sunday night."

"Isabella." Sadness stole over the monsignor's face.

"She was a member of your church?" Xavier asked.

"Technically, yes. She was baptized here, catechized here, and made her First Communion. But we haven't seen her lately. She kind of . . ." He grappled for the right word.

"Lapsed?" Parker offered.

"I suppose, but that word describes a whole generation. These young adults raised in the church are functionally no different from their peers. They want to be moral and they believe that

God looks out for them, but they see no need for devotion or piety, much less attendance at a local church."

"So she never came to Mass," Michael said.

"Once in a while. She usually came on Mother's Day as a gift to Rosa—that's her mother, of course. I'm afraid that Isabella viewed the sacrament as something of an occasional magic pill that got her off the hook with her Creator. Much like what the Protestants accuse us of teaching." He gestured to Parker. "No offense."

"None taken."

"And yet, I wonder how many of her generation take time to fathom the mystery of the Eucharist, the power of what Christ accomplished for us and its potential to change this world."

"Will you be saying her funeral Mass?" Xavier asked.

"Of course. We're waiting for the police to return her mortal remains to the family."

Parker thought of Melanie Candor on that metal table, the rib tray, and the brain bucket. He felt sick once again.

Rick made his confession every year on his birthday. Apart from that, he never entered a church.

"My friends call me Rick the Closer," he often told clients, "because I close deals like nobody's business." But he had few friends, and none had ever called him that. He was splayed in the confessional, stroking his neatly trimmed chin beard and hitting the highlights of another debauched trip around the sun.

" . . . then, six months ago, I brought Candy up to the lake house for the weekend. She was all worried that my wife would be there, and I'm like, 'Babe, my wife's swimmin' with the dolphins in Florida right now.' Well, I was wrong. So Candy and my old lady get in this knock-down, drag-out, all-on fight, and I'm like, 'Whoa, I know this is all wrong, but this is totally turning me on.' So, then—"

"I'm going to stop you a moment and give you some penance. Just to clear the slate."

"I've never heard of that."

"All the same, get on your knees and give me fifty Hail Marys."

"Not really, though," Rick chortled.

"I'll wait."

Rick the Closer glanced from side to side, as if to be sure no one was perched in the corner of the booth watching him, then shrugged and plopped to his knees.

"Hail Mary, full of grace. Blessed are—"

"In Latin, please."

"I don't know Latin."

"Not even the Hail Mary?"

" 'Fraid not."

"Get out," Ignatius growled.

Rick curled his lips into a slick smile. "Look, baby, you have to listen to me. It's your job to absolve the Closer."

"I will drag you to the street by your throat and give you Last Rites."

Rick the Closer scrambled out of the confessional.

"The third matter is rather sensitive," Xavier told the monsignor. "By bringing it up, I am betting the integrity of our assignment here on your reputation for absolute discretion."

"You can trust me to keep whatever we discuss in the strictest confidence," Naughton assured him. "But are you sure you want to discuss confidential Church matters in front of—" He tipped his head toward Parker.

"Don't worry about him," Michael said. "He's cool."

"As long as he's *cool*," said Naughton.

Father Michael leaned forward dramatically. "What do you know about the Crown of Marbella?"

"Absolutely nothing," Naughton answered. "What is it?"

"It's a relic. Or it was. We're not sure which."

"I've never heard of it. A relic of which saint?"

"Not a saint," Xavier answered, excitement infusing his voice. "It is said to be the true crown of thorns worn by our Savior."

Parker stifled a laugh.

"Something funny, Parker?" Michael asked.

"I'm sorry. It's just—I think of Martin Luther's line about how there were once so many 'pieces of the true cross' that Jesus must have been crucified on an entire forest."

Xavier nodded. "Since Father Ignatius is not in the room, I can admit that Luther had a point. But the Crown of Marbella is different. It can be traced with absolute continuity back to a time before the age of multiplying relics and pilgrimage for profit. There is even a strong tradition tying it to the Sudarium of Oviedo."

"I don't know what that is either," Parker admitted.

"It's a cloth," Naughton said, "from the sixth century or earlier. Supposedly the facecloth of Jesus at his burial."

"There is a leaner manuscript trail for the Crown," Xavier said, "but it can be traced back in a way similar to the Sudarium. It was widely accepted as a true relic from early on because of a miracle attributed to it. You see, the Crown was in the hands of private individuals—noble families—for hundreds of years. Then some time in the early ninth century, it was becoming so very brittle that, even without being handled, it began to crumble—sitting as it was on a golden plate.

"And so to keep it from turning to dust, an artisan was hired, a glassblower, to craft a glass globe, a permanent protective vessel. The Crown was placed inside with the utmost care. Then the glass ball was fire-closed, sealing the relic inside."

"What was the miracle?" Parker asked, mentally adding "Crown of Marbella" to his search terms list.

"Within a day, vitality returned to the relic. It was no longer crumbling and dry. Within two days, it began to bud. And within a week, it began to bloom—flowers that remained until the relic was lost."

"Lost how?"

"It's a bit ironic, really. Because of political turmoil—and possibly for some financial remuneration—the Pasquale family donated the Crown to the Iglesia de la Encarnación in Marbella, Spain, sometime in the early 1570s."

Michael interrupted excitedly. "Have you been there?" The other three men shook their heads. "It's about a fifteen-minute drive from where Father Ignatius grew up. He took me once. It's incredible, the majesty of the place."

Xavier resumed his history lesson. "Well, it may be beautiful, but the Crown would only remain there for about seventy years. In hindsight, it was precisely the wrong time and place to bring such an artifact into the public consciousness. Local rumors—or perhaps *legends* is a better word— began to grow and circulate."

"What kind of rumors?" Naughton asked.

"That the Crown possessed the power to forgive sins—all sins, even those of the impenitent and the heathen. The bishop decided to jettison the Crown before it became bogged down in superstition.

"To that end, in 1641 it was brought by Hernando Escriva to the Jesuit College at Saint Omer, which was for the moment under Spanish control. After the Crown was nearly destroyed on several occasions by fire and the constant threat of Protestant persecution, it was decided to move the relic once again.

"The Crown survived the voyage to Baltimore, Maryland, in 1761, transported by a company of Jesuits. The idea was twofold: to escape the religious powder keg of the Franco-Spanish border and to breathe a renewed sense of religious zeal into a New World colony that was becoming less Catholic every day. The plan obviously failed in regard to the latter goal, but the Crown remained safe, housed in St. Luke's Church, where it stayed for 135 years, through three new buildings, protected and cared for by the clergy there."

"But here's where the intrigue comes in," Father Michael said, rationing his eye contact between Parker and the monsignor. "In 1893—"

"1891," Xavier corrected.

"In 1891, Jonathan Wescott, the bishop of Northampton in England, was getting into all sorts of trouble for his radical views on a whole slew of topics—ecclesiastical, political, and beyond. He was shipped over to America and busted down to parish priest."

"Can they do that?" Parker asked.

"They did it. The idea was that Wescott would be out of sight, out of the loop, living out the rest of his days in obscurity in a place where radical views were the norm. As a friendly gesture to honor his former rank, they gave him St. Luke's, a prominent Baltimore church. Good place to be semiretired. Problem is he started gaining a following in Baltimore. Before long it was clear that he was more of a problem as a priest in America than he had been as a bishop in Britain."

Michael paused to take a breath, and Xavier took the opportunity to jump back in. "The archbishop of Baltimore wanted him defrocked. But Wescott still had a lot of friends in prominent positions. So they transferred him again, this time to the newly formed diocese of Grand Rapids, Michigan.

"In an infantile act of revenge, he hid the Crown in with his baggage and spirited it up here with him. Within a short time he had made connections with a group of Protestant clergy in the area. One day he brought them all together, showed them the Crown, and told them about some plans the bishop had to build a chapel, where the Crown would be an object of worship."

"It was a lie," Michael said with a sneer.

"Of course it was a lie. There were no such plans. For 135 years it was rarely even displayed; the Crown was kept in a reliquary in the sacristy at St. Luke's. But the Protestant clergy were quick to believe it. Swearing secrecy, resisting the pope's 'evil plans'—these were the types of romantic adventures they had fantasized about as seminarians. They told Wescott that they understood why he had to take it, why such an important object could be neither worshiped nor destroyed. And so he charged them with keeping the Crown of Marbella safe, hidden, and away from the hands of Rome."

"How do you know all this?" Parker asked.

"The Jesuits have come into possession of the diaries of two of those ministers. Both documents agree on the general arc of events, although one claims that twelve churches were represented in the group, while the other remembers only seven. Unfortunately, neither lists the congregations involved."

"In 1891? There can't be that many to choose from."

"It was 1893 by the time he arrived in Grand Rapids. And I think you'd be surprised at the list. The church where you cut your teeth is one, in fact. It had a different name back then, but there is still continuity—the same church charter, an unbroken succession of elders and clergy."

"Do you have the Crown at home, Parker?" Michael joked. "Just tell us."

"Hope Presbyterian was not that kind of place," Parker said. "The only ancient treasures you'd find there would have been flannelgraph boards and filmstrip projectors. Trust me."

"Worth a shot." Michael shrugged. "What about you, Monsignor? And let me remind you that if you know where it is, you are required by the very authority of the Holy Father to tell us."

"Why on earth would I know that?"

"My research tells me you've built more interchurch relationships than any other priest in the area," Xavier said. "You might be able to give us some direction."

Parker interjected, "Can I ask why you're even bringing this up after 125 years? This seems really random."

The monsignor stroked his beard slowly. "That's a misnomer, Pastor Saint. There is no such thing as 'kind of random' or 'really random.' Something is either random or it is not. And our friends here don't think that any of these events are random. Am I right, Fathers?"

"You are correct," Xavier affirmed. "We are inclined to believe—or at least to explore the possibility—that all of the events we've been investigating are connected at one point, and that point is the Crown of Marbella."

"How?" Parker asked, gesturing widely.

"It's a bit of a web. There's no one telltale connection to point to, but the reason we're even here in this city is this: every church that's been vandalized or experienced a fire in the past three months, save one, was founded before 1893."

"Older churches are in rougher neighborhoods," Parker said. "And they have older wiring."

"No, four of them have fled outward as their neighborhoods changed."

"But what would someone have to gain by spray-painting churches that may or may not have been part of a secret cabal more than a century ago?"

"We suspect that someone, or a group of people, is searching for the Crown, covering their tracks as they go, perhaps disguising it as a string of vandalism. There have been different levels of destruction at these churches, from merely cosmetic damage to break-ins to what we believe is arson, but each has been written off as the work of teenagers with too much time on their hands, and therefore not given an in-depth investigation. We believe the graffiti, the fires—even the murders—may be part of a campaign to find the Crown. Part distraction, part treasure hunt. The subtle occult element in the graffiti implies that their motivation in finding the Crown is not monetary gain. They're marking these houses of worship as they go—some of them more thoroughly than others."

"But the one church that burned down has got to be the one founded after 1893," Parker said. "I can't believe Valley Christian is that old."

"Believe it or not, Valley Christian—or at least the original congregational church—is one of only two churches that we know for certain was part of the group. Their original pastor wrote one of the diaries I told you about. They 'relaunched,' as their website calls it, in 1992, but that just entailed an unofficial name change and public relations campaign. It's still the same church."

Naughton sighed loudly. "I'm afraid I won't be of any help to you gentlemen. I had hoped your visit would be about the work of the Church, feeding the hungry, proclaiming the release of captives, and the forgiveness of sins. Instead, I think you're letting your minds do what the human brain does best: find patterns where none exist."

"Forgive me, Father, for I have sinned," Andrea said in little more than a whisper. "It has been two weeks since my last confession. I accuse myself of these sins: I have failed to love and honor my husband, Jeff, as my spiritual head."

"Go on," Ignatius said, relieved to finally have an informed penitent in the booth.

"Father Naughton?"

"Why does that matter?"

"I guess it doesn't." She sucked in a long breath. "I am filled with bitterness toward Jeff. He won't work. He's not injured, but he gets disability. All he does is sleep and watch TV, and I get so frustrated. I know it's wrong, Father. And I know that he only gives me what I deserve, but when he hurts me . . . sometimes I hate him."

Father Ignatius snapped to attention. "Hurts you?"

Twelve

"But assuming you're right," Parker continued, "and not just inventing patterns like our friend here said, why would anyone go to such great lengths to try and find this thing now? I mean, killing people, burning down churches—it just doesn't make sense."

"We're not entirely sure," Xavier said. "It may have to do with the legend that the Crown had the power to atone for sin. Whoever is looking for this relic might have any number of motives. It could be that someone is looking to make up for a lifetime of evil in one fell swoop."

"Or it could be," Michael said, "that someone wants to desecrate one of the holiest relics of the Christian church, but one that remains, conveniently, in obscurity."

Xavier stood. "At any rate, I believe we are in danger of overstaying our welcome with the Reverend Monsignor. Naughton. I thank you for your time and your hospitality, sir, and I will commend you and your work to my immediate superior." He threw Michael a sidelong glance that said *Consider him commended.*

"Thank you," said Naughton, rising from his desk to shake each of their hands again. "I'll walk you back to your colleague. I can finish hearing the confessions myself."

They retraced their steps under the arch and down the hall.

"Do your parishioners partake of the sacrament of Reconciliation often?" Xavier asked.

"Not most of them," Naughton answered. "I have six or seven who come quite regularly. In a given week I'd say I usually have about ten, which isn't bad these days."

They entered the sanctuary and approached the confessional. A note taped to the door read Back in 30 minutes.

"What a boob," Michael said under his breath.

"Why's that?" Xavier asked.

"Back in thirty minutes? When did he write it? Two minutes ago? Twenty-nine minutes ago?"

Father Xavier shrugged slightly. "I don't know, but I can't believe he heard all those confessions in that short amount of time. That's what I call a priest."

Jeff and Andrea's house was a silent victim of neglect. The large porch leaned to the right,

215

making the front doorway a slightly different shape from the front door. Andrea tried to lead Father Ignatius as quickly as possible down the narrow aisle between cubes of beer cans and garbage bags full of empties.

"I really think this is a bad idea, Father. Jeff has a temper."

"I only want to talk with the lad," Ignatius said. "I'll be gentle."

She took a deep breath and slid the key into the lock. Jeff sat slumped on the couch, his back to the door, eyes glued to an old television set where a handful of cars continually circled a track. His beer belly betrayed his present sloth, but large, tattoo-filled arms suggested a past full of military service and automotive work.

"Didja get my cigarettes?" he slurred.

"No, honey. I was at church."

He pulled himself to his feet. "Are you kidding me? You forgot my—" He locked eyes with Ignatius, and his next words became "Forgive me, Father, I didn't know you were there." He sobered instantly, quickly covering the space of the living room and giving Ignatius's hand a firm, friendly pump.

"I'm Jeff. Nice to meet you, Father—?"

"Ignatius. I am glad to make your acquaintance as well. Thank you for welcoming me into your home."

The priest did not wait for an invitation but

sank into a battered recliner, picked up the remote control, and clicked off the television. Jeff returned to the couch, trying and failing to mask his annoy-ance.

"I'm going to get right to the point," Ignatius said. "Jeff, I'm here to talk with you about some spiritual matters. Specifically, those related to your marriage and the way you treat your wife."

Jeff's posture changed. "Did she tell you to come here?"

"No, your wife did her best to dissuade me from coming and to defend you as a decent man and a good husband. Unfortunately for you, I remain far from convinced."

"Yeah, well, sorry Father, but you'll have to come back another time. I'm a little busy right now." He reached for the remote, but Ignatius snatched it up first.

"If it were my life and my marriage, I would make time for this."

"Look, no disrespect, Father, but my marriage is none of your business. And if I want to see a priest, I'll go to confession with Andie."

Father Ignatius tugged at his clerical collar, his temper rising.

"Sometimes, my son," he said, a hint of his Spanish accent showing through, "confession comes to you."

"Well, not today. Now get lost."

Ignatius stood and walked wordlessly toward

the door. He paused before a small metal desk stacked high with bills, papers, and magazines.

"I am doing my best not to blame you for being a disrespectful whelp. You've clearly had no formal religious instruction," the priest said.

Jeff rounded the couch, abandoning the act. "What did you just call me?"

"I'm here to help, Jeffrey. I'm going to teach you to respect a man of the cloth." He opened the desk drawer and roughly riffled through its contents.

"Get out of my stuff, old man!"

Ignatius found a foot-long wooden ruler.

"Ah. This will do." With unexpected speed, he scooped up Jeff's right hand and brought the ruler down on his knuckles with a *crack*. Jeff yelped and shoved his injured hand down between his knees, ejecting a string of curses.

He lunged for the priest.

"Disrespect and profanity too." Ignatius side-stepped the clumsy man and whacked the ruler on his temple. It broke in half with a shower of splinters.

"You're dead." Jeff grabbed an old rotary phone off the desk and swung it at Ignatius, who leaned back coolly, avoiding the blow by an inch.

Jeff's inertia sent him sprawling past the priest, who tightly wrapped the phone cord twice around the stocky man's neck and, with two fists full of cord, slammed Jeff into the wall.

Ignatius pinned him there with one hand, while the other retrieved the large nickel-plated handgun from the small of his back.

Jeff began to whimper at the sight of the barrel, now inches from his face.

"Let me save us both some time here," Ignatius said, his voice gravelly and controlled. "How long since your last confession?"

"Two weeks."

Ignatius twisted the phone cord, tightening the loop.

"I dunno," he croaked. "Fifteen years maybe."

"That explains much. But let us just start with two weeks."

"I been drunk."

"Let's narrow it down some more. What have you done to your wife?"

"I've yelled at her."

"And . . . ?"

"I roughed her up a little."

"Why did you do this?"

"Because she's always nagging me and waking me up at like seven in the morning and telling me I need to get off the disability and find a j—"

"Wrong. The reason you hurt your wife is because you're a pathetic little excuse for a man. Say it."

"Go to—"

The priest cocked the gun.

"Okay," Jeff shouted, "it's because I'm a pathetic excuse for a man!"

"That's right." Father Ignatius chewed his lip in thought. "This is a tough one, Jeff. It may be beyond my abilities. Perhaps I should send you up the chain to St. Peter and let him decide your penance."

Andrea, standing frozen behind the couch, let out a squeak of protest.

"Please don't," Jeff said weakly.

"What about you, Andrea dear? Do you think there's a good man in there somewhere?"

"Yes! Please don't hurt him."

"Jeffrey, your penance is as follows: You will go to early Mass every morning. You will do this indefinitely. You will go to confession every week. You will find a support group for little men with big tempers and attend it faithfully. You will love your wife as Christ loves his bride the holy Church and gave himself for her. You will not shout at her. You will not beat her. Do you hear me?"

"Yuh-yes. Whatever happened—"

"I'm not finished, Jeff. Listen carefully. If you lay a finger on her again, I'll take your eyes. Do you believe me?"

"I believe you!" he croaked.

"Good. And remember this: You live directly between two churches. Those two churches are *my* eyes. And if my eyes tell me that you're not following through on your penance, I will come back here and put a period at the end of this sentence."

"Yes, Father."

"Good. Now, you had a question for me?"

"It was just . . . I was going to ask whatever happened to saying a few Hail Marys?"

Ignatius shrugged. "We do things differently these days. It's more like a counseling session."

He released his grip on Jeff, who slid to the floor, grappling at the phone cord around his neck. The priest made his way to the foyer, opened the front door, and looked back at the married couple, very involved in the project of untangling Jeff.

He made the sign of the cross. *"Deinde, ego te absolvo a peccatis tuis."*

They gave him back a blank stare.

Ignatius sighed disgustedly. "Through the ministry of the Church, may God give you pardon and peace, and I absolve you from your sins in the name of the Father, and of the Son, and of the Holy Spirit."

"I'll be the first to admit I'm no expert on church history, but it seems like I should have heard of this Crown." Parker was in the backseat of the Cadillac as they headed toward downtown. "Why isn't it famous like the Holy Grail?"

"The Holy Grail is 99 percent myth, Protestant," Ignatius said, craning his head back from the driver's seat. Parker thought the old priest seemed a little more laid-back than usual. "Those stories grew up at just the right time to become syndicated in poems and adventure tales. The Crown of Marbella is the very opposite. Even before it was lost, it was lost to the world, lost in a cloud of false relics and fantastical claims. There were dozens of 'true crowns of Christ' in the sixteenth century, but none of them stood out."

"Do you think there's a chance it's authentic?"

"Authentic or not, it is the rightful property of the Holy See, and we will recover it if we can. And if someone is burning churches and killing innocents in pursuit of the Crown, we will stop them with all the fire of our faith."

"I'm famished," Michael proclaimed from next to Parker. "Who wants lunch? Too late for lunch, I guess. How about an early dinner? Parker, where's a good place to eat around here?"

"I don't really know this side of town," Parker answered, realizing that he, too, was intensely hungry. He hadn't eaten since two this morning, and whatever had been left of that was expelled at the autopsy.

"Try the NavStar, Father Ignatius," Michael said.

"What is that?"

"It's a service that comes with the car. It connects you to someone who can get you tables at restaurants and that kind of thing. Just push the button." A buzz followed. "No, that's the window. That's the power lock. Up on top there. No, that's the moonroof. Nope. Nope."

"This is Nathan with NavStar. How may I help you?"

Ignatius veered from his lane in surprise.

"We're from out of town and looking for a good place to have dinner." Xavier spoke upward, toward the mic.

Ignatius checked the cross street. "We are currently on Division Ave, headed—"

"I know where you are, sir."

"How do you know that?"

"Global positioning transmitter in your car. What's your price range?"

"Midpriced," Xavier answered.

"I'm cross-referencing positive reviews and your location," Nathan said. After a brief pause, "Top three choices are Paddy's Irish Pub, Flinger's, and Tangy Bones—a new location on Market Avenue."

"That's a rib joint," Michael said. "It's supposed to be really good. What do you think, Parker?"

Parker's stomach twisted. "Can't we just go back to your suite at the Plaza?"

Xavier nodded. "That's a very good idea. We can get room service and have a working dinner with some discretion. Thank you, Nathan. That will be all."

"My pleasure. Have a wonderful night, and thank you for using NavStar."

"Let's hit the convenience store on the way up," Michael said. "It's not too far out of the way."

Ignatius looked back with concern. "How do we know that he's not listening?" He pointed upward.

"He's always listening. You're a priest. I'm surprised you didn't know that."

"I mean this Nathan person."

"I think we're safe. Anyway, why would he care that we're stopping at a convenience store?" Michael held his hands up and wiggled his fingers spookily. "The intrigue never ceases."

"All the same, perhaps we should speak in the ecclesial tongue."

"Do you mean Latin?" Michael asked. "Because no one speaks conversational Latin. That's why they call it a dead language."

"I speak Latin."

"Well, I don't. So take your pick: I can speak English, French, or Italian. My Greek is passable."

"I taught you Deutsch."

"What? When did you teach me Dutch?"

"*Deutsch*. German. How is your German, Father Michael?"

"*Mas o menos*."

"That's Spanish."

"No, no. My Spanish is *muy poco*."

"Then how do you read the writings of St. Ignatius de Loyola?"

"English translations?"

"I cannot believe I have to report to you."

"Argh! This insolent boy speaks no Latin," Michael mimicked, poorly.

"You need to work on your accents as well. What was that supposed to be?"

"Give me a break. I'm Canadian. We're historically unable to shake our accent."

Ignatius pinched his lips together, holding his ire until it passed. "My son, I still have hope for you. St. Ignatius de Loyola was thirty-five before he learned Latin."

"Parker, you go in first," Michael said. "Pretend to be a customer. Scratch that; actually *be* a customer." He handed Parker a five-dollar bill. "I want a Slim Jim and a Watt energy drink."

They were parked at the Quality Dairy Mart on Franklin.

"Yeah, okay, but you haven't told me why we're here."

"That's because we're not sure if Nathan is still listening," he quipped.

Xavier tried to cover his laughter with a cough. "Melanie Candor worked here," he explained. "We have a few questions to ask her former co-workers. Do me a favor and walk around the back of the store so you can enter from the west."

Parker felt a prickle of excitement at being included in the Jesuits' covert operations.

"Got it," he said. "So what's the angle here?"

Xavier shook his head slightly. "The angle?"

"Yeah, what's my role?"

"It's essential," Michael said. "You're the guy who buys the Slim Jim. Just keep your ears open."

A cold blast of wind as he rounded the building gave Parker a rush of clarity. Fatigue had been overtaking him in successively stronger waves. He entered the store to find an endcap full of various jerkys staring him in the face—no fewer than twenty varieties. He studied his options. *Is Michael more a Blazing Hot kind of guy or a Smoky Original?* he wondered.

"Hello, my name is Xavier. This is Ignatius and Faber. We'd like a word with the manager on duty."

Parker saw Xavier quickly flash a silver badge at the slack-jawed kid behind the counter. All three men were now wearing white button-ups and polyester neckties under their black sport jackets. Parker wondered how they could possibly have changed that quickly.

"Hold on," the kid said. He picked up a phone and punched a few buttons. "Greg, there's cops or something here."

Greg emerged from the back room, wiping his hands vigorously on his pants.

"I'm the shift manager, Greg Barnes," he said. "What can I do for you gentlemen?"

Xavier flashed the badge again. "We have a few questions about one of your former employees, one Melanie Jane Candor."

"One of your colleagues was already here two days ago. We couldn't tell him much."

"That would have been a detective with the police," Michael said. "We're with an agency that has a bit broader scope."

"Wow," Greg said, impressed. "I'll do my best. Shoot."

"How would you describe the late Miss Candor in one word?" asked Xavier.

The clerk snickered, and Greg shot him a sharp glance.

"Pleasant," Greg said. "Very pleasant. She was working her way through art school with this job, and she put in a ton of hours each week. But I never knew her to have a negative attitude like some people." He paused and locked eyes with the young clerk. "And she never called in sick. A model employee, I'd say."

"Did she ever speak of having a religious affiliation or a commitment to a particular faith?"

"Not really. Not that I remember."

"So you didn't know that she was Catholic," Michael said.

"Nope. I didn't know that."

"Because she wasn't," Ignatius mumbled.

"She never spoke of a former time in her life when she may have been more involved in matters of faith?" Xavier asked.

"You know, we didn't really have a lot of deep discussions, Melanie and I. A lot of my job is done in my office. Scheduling and such, handling the business end of things."

"What about you, young man?" Ignatius asked the young slacker behind the counter. "Did Melanie ever speak to you about her religious beliefs?"

"No."

"All right. Thank you for your time."

As they turned to leave, Parker grabbed Michael's beefy arm. "Excuse me, you men look like you know your snack meats. Do you think I'd like a blazing hot or a smoky original Slim Jim?"

"They're both good," Michael answered, "but the important thing is pairing it with the right energy drink. I'd make sure you got a can of Watt. The low-carb kind. It's really easy to forget the energy drink."

Thirteen

The Grand Plaza was a five-star, turn-of-the-century hotel in the English style, with some significant updates, namely a huge, reflective glass tower that had been appended to the original structure in the early eighties. Peaking at an angle like an enormous chisel, the building had once defined the Grand Rapids skyline, but a recent upwelling of new skyscrapers had left it some-what obscured.

They left the car with the valet and entered through the swanky lobby.

"Wait here a minute," Michael commanded. "I'm going to see if we've got any messages from the Big Man." He headed to the desk.

Parker felt another wave of exhaustion coming over him. The room was very warm, and the plush surroundings weren't helping; everything looked soft and comfortable. He toyed with the idea of calling a cab and heading home but abandoned it when he looked at his cell phone for the first time all day and found it dead. He kicked himself for not plugging it in before crawling into bed that morning.

A sudden jolt of adrenaline tore up Parker's spine and awakened him with a start. Standing at the check-in desk next to Father Michael—a Texas Rangers ball cap pulled low over his eyes and a single rolling suitcase at his feet—was Joshua Holton. Parker squinted and shook his head violently. When he opened his eyes, Holton was still there, receiving a key and directions to his room.

A sense of panic closed in on him. What could Holton be doing there? If he was visiting town, why wouldn't he have told Parker in advance? What was with the stupid disguise, and where was his staff? It made no sense. Joshua Holton never came to the Midwest unless he had sold out an arena. For some reason, Parker was sure that this could not be a positive development. Then again, for all he knew, perhaps Holton frequently slipped out on his own, hiding his famous mug and toothy grin beneath a ball cap.

"Okay, let's head up," Michael said, walking past and wrenching Parker from his stupor.

The Jesuits Militant had hired a suite on the twenty-third floor of the tower—the kind of lavish accommodations that Parker was just getting used to as his star was rising. He was tired, confused, and parched. He took a short bottle of water from the minifridge and cracked it open.

"You owe the holy Church four dollars," Ignatius told him.

They ordered room service at Michael's insistence. Parker chose salmon on a bed of greens, as it was the only entrée on the menu that he was sure wouldn't remind him of the medical examiner's office and the autopsy that he hadn't actually witnessed, but felt like he had.

While they waited for the food to arrive, Xavier and Ignatius unlocked a large garment bag and unloaded eight wide, foam poster boards full of photos, notes, diagrams, and the like, setting them up around the room with quiet efficiency. Before long, the suite looked an awful lot like the Blackjack Killer Command Center at police headquarters—except that each board also included possible connections between the events and individuals involved and the Crown of Marbella.

Parker slumped on the settee while the priests arranged their visual aids, adding with Sharpies what little new information they'd acquired during the day. The next thing he knew, Ignatius was shaking him awake and thrusting a plate of perfectly cooked salmon at him.

Michael made the sign of the cross and recited, "Bless us, O Lord, and these thy gifts, which we are about to receive from thy bounty, through Christ, Our Lord. Amen."

They wordlessly wolfed down their dinners, all of them ravenous, but none more than Parker. He finished his food before the others and went looking for a vending machine, which he didn't find. The Holiday Inns and Howard Johnsons where his family used to stay on road trips always had vending machines. A candy bar always tasted better in a hotel room, while enjoying cable television, another rare treat.

When he returned to the room, the empty dishes were stacked on a cart in the hall. Michael let Parker in and invited him to have a seat. The furniture had been rearranged into an arc, completing the circle begun by the photos and charts.

"We were just discussing you, Parker," Xavier said. "We were wondering if you could fill in some missing information about Hope Presbyterian. Of all the congregations I researched for this investigation, that church was one of the most elusive."

"What do you want to know?"

"First and foremost, did your father or your grandfather ever tell you anything about the history of the church, its origins in the late nineteenth century or anything about interchurch relationships with other congregations?"

Parker suddenly came to an overdue conclusion. "That's why you dragged me into this whole thing! You thought that maybe my grandfather told me something about the Crown of Marbella." He laughed, astonished.

"That's one reason, yes." Xavier nodded. "But we knew that was unlikely. There was also your connection to the police investigation. We always like to know what *they* know and where they're focusing their efforts. But more than any of that, we brought you in because the Crown's whereabouts is a local Protestant matter. And we are neither local nor Protestant. You, however, seem to know everyone. Or at least they know you. You're our ambassador. You get our foot in the door, if you will."

"He will," Ignatius said.

"I still can't get my head around this." Parker stood and looked at the largest bulletin board, full of pushpins, photos, and notations. "You really think all this has to do with a glass ball with an ancient artifact inside?"

"There are only fifty-seven Jesuits Militant in the world, Parker," Michael said. "We wouldn't have been sent here for some random string of church vandalism, or even for occult-related murders. The truth is, they sent us because this town is red-flagged to begin with. If the Crown still exists, it's here somewhere. We're going to get to the bottom of it, and we'd like your help."

Parker had another mini-epiphany. "And that's why we were creeping around those churches last night, isn't it? You were looking for the Crown. That's what your list was about."

"Again, that's partially true," Xavier said. "We were also hoping to bump into the culprits, as we said, although that, too, was a long shot. We've been through fourteen church buildings in the last three nights, looking for any sign of the relic or any sign of trouble."

"To be realistic, though, the Crown was probably tossed out by an overzealous custodian years ago," Ignatius said with a scowl.

"But what about the league of pastors sworn to protect it?"

Michael flopped down in an armchair. "There's no league of clergymen, Parker. Not anymore. You don't have to study this stuff long to realize that these secret fellowships rarely outlive the first generation. Add to that how frequently Protestant clergy move around, and there's virtually no chance of succession for a group like that. It's not like in the movies where thirty generations later, they're all still organized, wearing matching outfits, eager to give their lives for the cause. There is no cause, because there is no threat. The group just fell apart. I'd bet my beads."

Xavier nodded. "But that's not to say its memory doesn't live on in some sense, through individuals and individual churches. Father Michael is right about these secret groups. And our job here is harder for it, but not impossible." He gestured to a picture of Melanie Candor. "Her uncle was on the ministry staff at the First Methodist Church. He set up a mission in the 1970s, a major player in the ecumenical scene." He gestured to a diagram of churches and ministries, full of crisscrossed, interconnected lines.

"Isabella Escalanté." He moved to the next collection of photos. "Her paternal grandfather was the pastor of a Lutheran church in town. For nearly fifteen years."

"This is all pretty underwhelming," Parker said. "Uncles? Grandfathers? What about her fourth cousin, twice removed?"

Xavier didn't laugh. "How about this, then, Parker?" He pointed to a branch of names and photos. Their point of origin was an intentionally mysterious, black-and-white photo labeled *Damien Bane (Birth Name: Daniel Banner).*

Beneath it was a school yearbook picture in which Damien looked the part of a classic high school misfit: close-cropped hair, acne, and an ugly sweater.

Parker was impressed. "You got all that on Damien already? You were busy this morning."

"This man's life is an open book; it didn't take much. Damien's mother gave up her parental rights when he was nine. He bounced around to different foster parents for most of his teen years. When he was sixteen, he spent six months living with the Reverend Clinton Raybrook, a fourth-generation Baptist minister in East Grand Rapids."

Parker considered this. "So you think he might have heard—or overheard—about the Crown through his foster parents, then done some research on the matter and found the legends behind it. Then—what?—got into Satanism and decided he had to have the thing at any cost for some dark, ignoble purpose?"

"I'm open to that possibility," Xavier answered. "Are you?"

"I guess. He talked about curses and spells. If he knew about the Crown, I can't imagine he wouldn't want to get his hands on it. And maybe it gave him an excuse to kill a few people in the meantime," he said, gesturing at the victims' photos, "however tenuous their connection."

Michael clarified, "*If* he's even responsible for

the murders, which I'm nowhere near ready to concede. What can't be denied, though, is that the Protestant churches involved in the recent rash of occult-inspired vandalism are all first-round draft picks for those seven—or twelve—slots in the Secret Protectorate of the Crown. Or whatever you want to call it."

"That has a nice ring to it," Parker said.

"Thanks. I thought so."

"But they're all mainline churches as well," Xavier said. "It could just be a big coincidence."

"Not even a *big* coincidence," Parker agreed. "Almost anyone with roots here is going to have some ancestral connection to one of those congregations. Everybody's got a minister in the family. This city churns them out. The Baptists have a seminary here. So do the Christian Reformed. The Puritans even have one on Leonard Street. Who knew there were still *Puritans?*"

"That's why we've got to stay focused on the center of all this," Xavier said, "which I believe may be the Crown of Marbella. Something you may not have known, Parker: the second pastor of Hope Presbyterian Church was a close personal friend of Anthony VanderLaan, the author of one of the diaries confirming all this. I would bet my reputation that your grandfather's church, your father's church—your old church—was part of this conspiracy in 1893.

"We haven't checked the church out yet,

because frankly I can't figure out if it still exists. The phone number is disconnected, and the web page has been utterly neglected for quite some time. More than a year ago they seem to have folded or split or relocated. Which is it?"

Parker felt the familiar stab of guilt. "They lost the building," he said plainly. "And they're currently without a pastor. I got them some space in a friend's church. Holy Ghost Tabernacle. There aren't many people left at Hope, but they still come together faithfully each week."

"What is the building like? The new building?" Ignatius asked.

"It's state of the art. Holy Ghost just built a new auditorium, and Charlie offered to let them use their old sanctuary for free."

"So this is shared space?" Michael asked.

Parker nodded.

Ignatius was fixing a drink. "This is a 'church' like the one on your television program—lights and screens and smoke machines?"

"More or less."

Michael frowned. "Even if someone had the Crown in their possession a generation ago, they wouldn't have moved it there. I need you to think, Parker. Did your father or your grandfather ever say anything about a church secret of some kind? Could have been an object that he was entrusted to protect, a sacred duty, even something vague?"

Parker closed his eyes. "I don't think so." He was having trouble concentrating with his current sleep deficit. "Wait." A memory was emerging from the jumbled archives of his childhood, something he hadn't thought about in twenty years. "Wait a minute, maybe . . .

"When I was a little boy, back when my grandfather was still preaching and my father was the associate pastor, there was a break-in at a nearby church. The Foursquare Gospel Church, I think. It really shook up my mother. I remember before that we used to keep the doors unlocked almost all the time so people could come in and pray. But my father insisted that we start locking up. They argued about it for hours—pretty heated stuff.

"I remember asking my grandpa if the communion ware was made of gold. He laughed and said it was worth less than his watch, but that someone might *think* it was valuable. He told me there were people who didn't know Jesus and didn't know any better who might try to steal from the church.

"I asked if the church had *anything* valuable and he told me, 'There is one thing, but no thief could carry it away, and no thief would even know it was a treasure to begin with.' "

Michael was on his feet. "I swear, Parker, if you're messing with me . . ."

"I'm not. I haven't thought of that in forever, but it's as clear as anything to me now. I'm sure that's what he said, almost word-for-word."

"A thief could not take it away, nor could he identify it as a treasure," Ignatius repeated. "If he *was* referring to the Crown, it sounds to me like the relic may have been built into the structure of the church building itself. How else would it be both hard to detect and immovable?"

"Worth a look," Michael said, then asked Parker, "Is there another congregation in the old building?"

"As far as I know, it's still vacant. And you won't even need to break in—I still have a key."

Fourteen

The nightclub was called Church, and it was located in the old Hope Presbyterian building. A long lipstick-red banner announced the grand opening, but it was battered and shredded by the wind, suggesting that the place had been around for a while. If Parker had thought he was sick at the prospect of the brain bucket, it was nothing compared to this. Rather than emptying his stomach, he felt like someone had emptied his soul.

He considered a hundred what-ifs at once. What if he had never left the parish? What if he'd found a way to take out a line of credit and rescue the building? What if he'd used his television time to do a sort of save-the-local-church-a-thon before it was too late? What if he'd gone against his father fifteen years ago and voted to register the building as a Michigan historical landmark? He was pretty sure if they'd done that, he might still be looking at an empty building, but he doubted he'd be looking at a nightclub called Historic Church.

In the back of his mind Parker knew he'd still been planning to make this right—to ride in some day, buy the building for a song and some back taxes, and deed it back over to the congregation. And he'd been afraid this would happen. That's why he never drove by, never checked up on the place. He thought he could keep it exactly as it had been in his mind until he came to the rescue in real life.

"Church: A Nightclub," Ignatius read. "Inventive."

Michael extended a small monocular with a flick of his wrist and peered through it. "They're open," he said. "Until midnight on weeknights. What time is it?"

"It's ten after ten," Xavier said.

"It *is?*" Parker wished he were in bed, asleep. What on earth was he doing sneaking around another old church with these men?

"I've got ten-fifteen," Michael said. "It took forty-five minutes going back to your house to find the stupid key. I could have had that lock open in forty-five seconds."

"Well, it's not locked now," Xavier observed. "What's to stop us having a look?"

Michael's laugh echoed up the alley. "*Us?* No. Parker and I will go in. No offense, Father X, but you and Eisenhower here would probably stick out just a bit. Lose the tie, Parker," he said. He pulled off his own.

Predicting metal detectors, Michael left his hardware with Ignatius and led Parker across the street to the entrance.

"Do you think we'll get in?" Parker asked.

"Get in? This isn't Manhattan. I'm sure everybody gets in."

At the door he passed a twenty to the lethargic bouncer, more than enough for the cover charge for both men. As they entered, Parker barely recognized the foyer, now covered in stylized fluorescent graffiti, bathed in black light. He tried not to imagine it as it used to be. They ascended some stairs and entered a large, open space where about forty twentysomethings were flopping back and forth to the repetitive squeal-thump of the techno music.

"This sucks," Michael declared, surveying the scene, "even for a Wednesday." A small huddle of young men, spray tanned and mostly unbuttoned, snickered at the priest and the preacher.

"I think we still might be overdressed," Parker shouted at Michael's ear.

Two young women approached them, stuffed

into minidresses and spackled with makeup.

"There you are," one of them said, her breath reeking of alcohol. "We've been looking all over."

"I don't think we know you, sweetheart," Michael said.

"Yeah, we know you. You're the guys who want to buy us a drink." She giggled, then flashed a practiced smile.

"I'm afraid I've taken a vow of celibacy. And my friend here is old enough to be your father. Or maybe your uncle. He's really got an uncle vibe, doesn't he?"

"I'm a square," Parker confirmed.

"I can make you break that vow," she said, swaying near, her perfume wafting in.

"You're better than this," Michael answered without condescension. "Trust me; I have a gift for reading people. You don't have to act this way." She stared at him for a long time, then spun on her heels and walked away, tugging her friend along behind her.

"I don't belong here," Parker said.

"No. No, you don't. Be thankful for that." Michael quickly analyzed what he could see of the interior and formed a plan. "Let's pretend we're looking for someone and make our way around the outside of the room. We're looking for any kind of artistic glasswork, hidden cabinet, or some other architectural anomaly."

"This whole place is an anomaly."

"That's why you're here, Parker. Try and picture it as it was."

"Minus all the metal, fog, and strobe lights."

"Exactly."

They moved slowly, and it took twenty-five minutes to make the circuit back to the door. A dozen young toughs arrived halfway through their survey, rowdy and roving, and Parker got the distinct feeling that he would have been beaten for sport had he not been accompanied by Father Michael.

"This place just isn't happening," the priest said. "I wonder how much of the building is accessible. Where was the pastor's study?"

"This way." Parker led him out the back of the large room and down a hall, the walls covered in chain-link fencing and illuminated by hundreds of red Christmas lights.

Halfway down the corridor a large, bald black man sat on a stool in front of a velvet rope, blocking access to the hall. He was reading a thick book by the light of a little LED flashlight and didn't notice Parker and Michael until they were on top of him. He quickly shined the light in their direction and hopped off the stool.

"I'm sorry. This is the VIP area. VIPs only," he said, not quite sounding like he believed his own words.

"It's cool," Michael reassured him. "We're VIPs."

"I know VIPs. And you're not. You want to

head back that way." He shined the light back the way they'd come.

Michael produced a small roll of bills and peeled off a few. "Do we look like VIPs now?" he asked, extending the money.

"Almost," the bouncer said, pushing the bills away. "Unfortunately, the VIP area is spoken for until closing tonight. But you can be VIPs tomorrow."

"Thanks anyway."

"No problem." He hopped back up on his stool and turned his attention back to his book.

The men retraced their steps, descended the stairs out of the building, and strode back across the street, the cold air a welcome, invigorating change from the steam bath of breath and sweat inside the club.

"Anything?" Xavier asked.

"It's too dark," Michael answered. "And too many people. Could be in there, though. The place has been given a face-lift, but it's all cosmetic. They didn't knock down any walls or even plaster over the mosaic of the crucifixion behind the DJ stand. I want a better look at that place."

"It's a little more than an hour before they close," Xavier said. "Shall we make the rounds and come back?"

Parker's collar was damp and cold from the steady cascade of drool he'd deposited while he slept. He had tried to bow out of further nighttime adventures, but the priests had convinced him that without him as a guide, another trip into the club would be pointless.

The last thing Parker wanted was to go back in there, to see even more clearly what they'd done to the church where he'd grown up.

"I know it makes you sick," Michael said, "but think about this. You might rediscover the most precious lost treasure of the Christian church."

Lacking the energy for a debate, Parker had caved—under the condition that he be allowed to nap while they drove all over town, swinging by each of the churches on Xavier's list yet again. He had only been out for twenty minutes when the car came to a stop, jarring him from his shallow doze. The drool welcomed him back to the land of the living, as did a persistent crick in his neck. These little pockets of sleep weren't helping.

"What time is it?" he asked.

"Twelve thirty," Michael answered. "We don't know how long it takes them to clean up and close down, so Father Xavier has gone to have a look."

The two-way on Michael's phone chirped annoyingly. "Parker's key doesn't work," came Xavier's voice. "But I had a look inside. No sign of anyone."

"The cameras I saw?"

"Took care of them. What do you think?"

"White smoke, new pope," Michael answered. "Let's go."

The three of them moved through the shadows up to the front door, which Xavier opened from the inside, permitting quick access. Three heavy, D-cell flashlights came to life, their beams moving in a coordinated way as they passed through the entryway.

Walking into what had been the nave, Ignatius stopped.

"This is sacrilege," he said, sweeping his flashlight to and fro. The floor was covered in glitter. Several cages, each large enough to accommodate a dancing human, were suspended from the ceiling. The priest looked from one wall to the next, disoriented by the bar and the DJ's booth. "Protestant, tell me how this space used to look. Where was the chancel?"

"The what?"

"The raised platform with the rail."

"Oh, the stage."

Ignatius opened his mouth, but said nothing.

"You want to burn me at the stake right now, don't you, Father Ignatius?"

"No comment."

"The *chancel* was up here," Parker said, making his way to the far wall. Not holding a flashlight, he was walking by faith into the moving arc of light.

Ignatius zeroed in on two bolt-holes in the floor.

"Is this where your father stood to preach?" he asked.

"No, but my grandfather did. When the television ministry took off, Dad replaced the two podiums with a Plexiglas stand in the middle. Right about here." He pointed, and Michael's flashlight beam illuminated a lacy undergarment, abandoned on the floor. "Maybe it wasn't there," he said, his voice quavering. "Sorry, I haven't been here in years."

They spent half an hour studying the walls and columns, finding nothing. Michael then led the group down the hall to the VIP area, where they found the door bolted.

"We should hurry," Xavier said. "Clearly, they farm out janitorial services. Who knows when the cleaning crew arrives."

"Agreed. I just want to check one more thing. This was the pastor's study," Michael explained, while he quickly had his way with the lock. The door swung open to reveal a velvet love seat, plush purple carpet, and a spent condom on the ground. Parker, nauseated and light-headed, leaned against the wall.

"Let's go," Michael said after a moment. "There's nothing left here."

"You got that right," said Parker.

"Your grandfather was probably speaking metaphorically," Xavier said. They were parked in

Parker's driveway, the engine idling smoothly. "He might have meant that the Church itself or the sacraments or the gospel of Jesus Christ were a treasure that a thief would not recognize and could not take."

"Hadn't thought of that," Michael admitted. "Are you sure you don't want to stay at the Plaza, Parker? I know you must be on edge after last night."

"No, I'd like to sleep in my own bed," Parker answered. He glanced at his watch. It was 1:40 a.m. The thought of sleeping in his own bed was the only thing that could have motivated him out of the plush seats of the car.

Ignatius met him halfway up the drive, having made a circuit around the house. "No signs of forced entry, Protestant. And no charred animals. I hope you sleep well."

"Believe me, I will."

Parker slogged his way up the steps and wrestled with the dead bolt. He was three steps inside the house when he sensed that something was wrong. He heard a door clicking shut. *The bathroom? That or the spare bedroom,* he thought. A sense of panic overwhelmed him, demanding that he retreat out the front door, but stealing his ability to do so.

Footsteps were coming his way, quick and relentless. It took what seemed like thirty seconds to unfix his feet from the hardwood floor and reverse the direction of his body. He lunged toward the doorknob, hand reaching, but collided with a pedestal, knocking it over and sending a hundred jagged pieces of broken vase sliding along the ground in every direction. He landed hard in their midst.

The footsteps were just a few feet away. His eyes searched around frantically, not really wanting to see what or who was out there in the darkness, just beyond his field of vision.

The overhead light came on with a click, and Parker shielded his eyes.

"Seriously, Parker," Paige said, "you're a real girl sometimes."

He rolled up off his back and let his eyes adjust to the light before fixing her with a firm, disappointed look. His heart was still pounding and he was embarrassed, and both of those things could be channeled into blame.

"How did you get in here, Paige?"

"You gave me your spare key last year after you locked yourself out," she reminded him. Paige lived just a short walk from Parker's house. "Since you're not answering your phone today, I figured waiting for you here was the only way to catch you. And I was about to give up on that."

His anger quickly subsiding, Parker apologized. "Sorry. My phone died today. I've been so busy I forgot to plug it in last night."

"Well, I tried to call you seven times and left you seven voice mails."

"The battery's still dead. Why don't you just give me my messages now? The short version." He led her into the living room, and they both sat.

"Fine." She seemed to be working hard to maintain an edge to her tone, while not crossing the line into insubordination. Pulling a leather-bound planner from her purse, she flipped to a page of notes and settled back in the armchair. "A woman named Corrinne called for you at the church at about two. She said she wanted to tell you a funny story about Paul, whoever that is."

Parker smiled despite himself, but the smile quickly faded at the obvious jealousy in Paige's eyes.

"Paul's a detective," he explained. "And so is she. I'll hear the story tomorrow."

"Can I say something, Parker?"

"I've always encouraged you to be candid with me."

She took a deep breath. "I feel like you're enjoying this too much. Like you're not trying to jump through this hoop and put it behind you. It's like"—she frowned—"like you're happy to be away."

"Not in the least," he said with all the conviction he could muster. "I'm just making the best of the situation. It would be pretty hypocritical if I did anything but, wouldn't it?"

"You haven't checked in with me once in two days. Your mail is piling up. I have no idea what to tell people about rescheduling your appointments and appearances."

"I'm leaving all that in your capable hands, Paige. You said you got Tony Rex to do the show, and I know you can handle everything else."

"The service is covered, but that's not all we've got going on, is it? Do you remember that you have a book coming out?"

"Yes, I remember that I have a book coming out," he droned, annoyed at her condescension.

"Well, you may not. Some guy from Charter House called today, and they're not happy. He said they've held up the book as long as they can, waiting for Holton's blessing and his blurb. He used the word 'self-absorbed' like four times."

"The book is coming out," he assured her. "I've got a contract."

"Your contract says they'll publish the book, but we both know they won't put any effort or expense into promoting it if you keep this up."

"I'm sure Josh is just running behind."

"Holton is never running behind. If his staff hasn't sent up an endorsement, there's a reason."

Parker felt a stab in his guts as the truth of Paige's words sank in, followed quickly by the image of Holton at the desk of the Grand Plaza Hotel, that stupid cap pulled down over his eyes. In the fog of fatigue and power naps, he was only about half sure that he'd really seen him, but it scared him nonetheless.

In many ways, Joshua Holton was the key to his future. Parker's first book, *God Is Awesome (And So Are You)* had been contracted by Holton's own publisher, at Holton's insistence. Parker had gotten a hefty advance and turned in the manuscript, and the planned release was perfectly timed with a syndication deal due to take effect in March. The idea was that his book could ride the wave of a hugely expanded, national TV platform, giving Parker a share in ten times as many markets as he now enjoyed. But without Holton pushing the book . . .

"Do you even realize that you missed his call yesterday morning?" Paige demanded.

The knife in his guts was twisting. How could he forget his weekly call with Joshua Holton? He hadn't missed even one in the last two years. It was during these calls that Parker got direction and mentoring and reported back how things were going. He wanted to punch himself in the jaw.

"I don't know how I forgot," he said weakly.

"You would have just needed to duck out for fifteen minutes."

"Believe me, I know," Parker spat. "Josh can never spare more than fifteen minutes for someone like me."

She slapped the planner down on the coffee

table and threw her hands in the air. "What's going on here, Parker?"

"Nothing's going on. I'm just tired of how one-sided this whole thing is. I've flown down there, what, fourteen times? Why doesn't he ever come up here?" Once again the image of Holton at the hotel desk flashed through his mind.

"He's busy."

"He's using me, Paige."

She scowled, an expression that Parker usually found unbelievably cute. "Maybe he is, but if we're going to use him back, you need to smooth this out and get that book endorsement."

"I'll try to find some time tomorrow."

"You'll try to find—? I'm going to ask this one more time: what's going on with you?"

"I don't know what you mean!"

"I tried to reach you at the police station this afternoon, and someone told me you had left before lunch. I think it was that Corrinne woman, and she asked me why I needed you, and she called me 'hon.'

"If you weren't with them, where have you been all night? Where were you last night? It may be none of my business, but I need to know what you're into if it's going to affect our work."

Parker weighed the prospect of telling her about the Jesuits Militant. On one hand, he was afraid he would be unable to explain his getting dragged into their investigation. Still, he was longing to share the whole affair with *someone,* and Paige was the best sounding board he knew.

He decided just to push through and give her the long version. He prefaced it with, "I know this is going to sound crazy, but—" and then walked her through every event of the past three days, leaving nothing out—nothing but his date with Corrinne. Paige's expression went from disbelieving to incredulous and back again as she listened.

When he had brought the narrative full circle to his breaking the vase, he flopped back on the sofa and waited for her reaction.

"You're not serious."

He nodded.

"Secret agent priests." She shook her head. "Tell me you checked up on them."

"With who? I don't have any contacts at the Vatican. Besides, between the detectives and running around with these guys, I haven't had a spare moment to even think about it."

Paige stood stiffly and gestured with short cutting motions. "Has it occurred to you that they may not be priests at all? Have you thought about that?"

"They're priests," he said. He understood her concern and knew all too well how farfetched it all sounded, but the idea—that Father Michael especially was not who he claimed to be—seemed somehow ludicrous.

"How do you know that? They could be with one of those breakaway-fundamentalist, splinter groups I've read about—some weird sect with stockpiles of weapons. These do not sound like people you want in your life, Parker."

"Well . . ."

"And even if this Crown thing is real, how do you know they aren't the ones burning down churches looking for it? Have you ever actually heard of Catholic priests carrying guns? Baptist pastors, maybe . . . but priests? I went to Catholic school for six years and, trust me, priests aren't like that. They're all about love and peace and feeding the poor, not breaking into churches and packing iron."

"There are only fifty-seven of them in the world. They're a secret order." He knew it sounded stupid as the words came out of his mouth.

"Seriously, Parker. Secret priests from the Vatican, diplomatic immunity, guns, hidden treasures . . . and it never occurred to you to check their credentials?"

"One of them gave me his card," Parker offered lamely, producing the calling card.

Paige snatched it and flipped it over twice. "Oh, well, why didn't you say so? No way they could fake this. I doubt that kind of technology even exists!"

Parker knew that when Paige got sarcastic she was feeling protective, so he endured it without complaint. He suddenly realized that as they'd been talking he'd been sliding down the sofa, so that he was now about two-thirds lying down.

"I really have to sleep," he said. "Any other pressing matters?"

"Yeah, Bishop Jackson called to confirm that you would be at his revival tomorrow night. I told him I'd have to double-check with you."

"Why didn't you cancel that for me?"

"Because I didn't know about it, Parker. When you make plans for yourself and you don't tell me, I can't be responsible for them."

"Call him back tomorrow. Tell him I'll be there. I'm taking a break from all this craziness tomorrow night. I promise. I'll call Joshua and patch things up. And I'll plug the book at the revival."

"Okay," she said, resuming her seat and picking up the planner. "Just two more things."

Parker stood abruptly, suddenly very irritated. Why couldn't they all leave him alone for even a few hours so he could sleep? Why did everyone want to cash in on him? It wasn't just Holton using him. It was everyone.

"I'm going to bed, Paige. You can either come up with me or go on home."

She stared at him for a few seconds, her reaction unreadable.

"Why would you say that to me?" she asked, her voice quivering with anger. "Why would you say that?"

She clomped to the door and let herself out without so much as a good night, giving the door a healthy bang behind her. Parker wanted to indulge in some self-loathing, but he was far too tired. Besides, he knew there would be plenty of time for hating himself tomorrow.

He went up to his room, plugged his phone in, and dumped it on the nightstand. When he had returned from brushing his teeth, the display alerted him to eleven messages waiting. Knowing he couldn't sleep until he'd heard them all, he punched the button for voice mail.

The first two were from Paige. He knew what they would say but listened to them both in their entirety anyway. He loved her voice. His regret was mounting, and he wanted to call her right this minute, apologize for being a jerk, for taking all this stress out on her. But he knew her well enough to let her calm down before he made that move.

"Hey Preacher, it's me." Corrinne's voice, lower, laid-back, and a little scratchy, was almost the opposite of Paige's, yet just as inviting. "I hacked in to Paul's computer to get your cell number," she said. "And by 'hacked in,' I mean I looked at it when he went to the bathroom. And by 'computer,' I mean this really gross, grease-stained spiral notebook he keeps in his jacket pocket." She laughed—far too briefly for Parker, to whom the sound was like a drug.

"Anyway," she said, stretching the word out in a playful singsong, "I have to tell you something hilarious that happened after you left today. So call me back. It's three thirty. Oh, and I don't think the secretary at your church likes me. What's her deal?" She laughed again, and Parker caught his reflection in the mirror, grinning like an idiot. "Really, though," she said, "call me if you get a chance. Bye."

Parker kicked himself for not charging his phone. He was sure it looked like he was intentionally dodging Corrinne, just as surely as it had seemed to Paige.

He saved the message and quickly listened to and deleted the next six, five of which were from Paige and the other from Bishop Wayne Jackson, trying to make sure that Parker would be making an appearance at his church the following night and asking if he would please return the call because everyone would love to see him. Parker pressed Delete.

The next message was in an unfamiliar voice. "Brian Parker, this is Dr. Geoff Graham. I'm just getting back into town, and I have a message from your secretary. She said you wanted to meet with me. I'm pretty open tomorrow, just unpacking and such. Why don't you give me a call back? If this is about a grade I gave you twenty years ago, please know that I can be bought. I love Chunky Monkey ice cream." He laughed at his own joke.

Parker jotted down Dr. Graham's cell number and stuck the note in his money clip on the nightstand.

The next message began, "This is Joshua Holton." The voice sent the little hairs on Parker's neck at attention. "You missed our call yesterday, and now you're not answering your cell phone. I just wanted you to know that I'm in Colorado right now, and I passed up an appearance on a national television show this morning so that I could have my weekly update time with you. I'm feeling unappreciated and a little angry. I just needed you to know that." *Click.*

He's in Colorado? Was his clone in Grand Rapids? Or was he lying? Despite Parker's promise to Paige, he decided right then not to return Holton's call until this whole thing had blown over. He'd successfully kept the entire Brynn Carter affair below Holton's radar, certain that he would not be okay with this sort of accusation, litigation, or the complication of police involvement. Better to call him after the fact, hopefully having helped to catch a serial killer—good news for the book—apologize profusely, and get things back on track.

Parker inserted himself between the sheets and found his mind instantly alert. He spent nearly an hour tossing and turning, trying not to think about Damien and the bodies, the Jesuits and the Crown, Paige and Joshua Holton.

At three fifteen he hit the treadmill, running three miles. Then a shower. He finally drifted off a little after four.

Six Years Ago

The woman sinking into the swamp was number sixteen.

The first three had been spread over a decade. The rest had happened in half that time. He was beginning to discern a rhythm involving the exorcisms, the returns, and his compulsion to kill.

It was as if each time They returned, They tightened a spring inside Danny. When it was as tight as it could get, he needed release. Twelve women and four men had died to provide it. Each time, They made sure to tell Danny exactly how, who, and when to achieve it.

But each time They returned, They wound the spring a little tighter than they had the time before, and the increasing frequency of the killings was a cause for some concern. Danny was already being proactive, though, implementing a system for managing the situation. He had kept his head through all of this, if not his soul.

He watched the body disappear from view. His black trench coat flapped in the wind. He was dressed specifically for the occasion, every element designed to shock and terrify. When he'd begun The Project (back when it *was* a project, before it had become his life), dressing all in black—with black eyeliner; long, greasy hair; and mismatched, color contact lenses—was a pretty common cultural phenomenon, showing up on horror movie posters and heavy-metal album art. It had come and gone from pop culture, but Danny still found it effective in eliciting the desired response from his victims.

The woman now slowly making her way to the bottom of the swamp, three cinder blocks chained to her waist, was a member of a church Danny had visited two years earlier. She'd given him a look full of judgment when he settled into his pew, then flip-flopped with the rest of the sheep when he had responded favorably to their offers of prayer. She was all smiles after that and made a show of hugging him several times, although he could tell by the way she tensed up that she hated every moment of it, suffering through it for show.

Danny hadn't thought of the woman in months when They brought her to his mind one Tuesday afternoon. They wanted her, and Danny was more than happy to deliver. He had enjoyed the shock of recognition on her face. He had savored her tears, which welled up when he recounted her hypocrisy and how he'd noticed her playing to the crowd, even as he had played the same crowd.

Tomorrow Danny would go in to work, and no

one would suspect that he had killed a woman less than ten hours before. No one would look at him with a newfound sense of awe or fear or disgust. But he hadn't done it for his colleagues and co-workers. He hadn't even done it for himself.

As with everything in his life, he did it to please Them.

Fifteen

"He's not here," said a wormy, little man of indeterminate rank and function, hunched over his desk filling out a stack of forms, "but he wants you to wait for him in the conference room." He looked up at Parker with undisguised glee. "He was *not* happy."

"Wonderful."

Parker had awakened with a start at 8:05, his head buried in the folds of a comforter under piles of pillows, oblivious to the racket blasting from his alarm clock. As he entered the Command Center, he felt decidedly like a kid doomed to wait outside the principal's office for a tongue lashing. The effect was enhanced by a sneering Officer Jason Dykstra tipping back in a chair at the head of the table.

"Billy Sunday," he said.

"Officer Dykstra," Parker said with a nod. "How are you this morning?"

"I'm doing just fine. Getting paid to sit and wait for Detective Ketcham because he insists that I put this right into his fingers." The cop held up a piece of ruled notebook paper, upon which he had scrawled a list of superficial similarities between the two crime scenes.

"I'm sure you'll get an A," Parker said, taking a seat at the far end of the table.

Dykstra waited for him to settle, then held a Styrofoam cup up to his lips. "Do me a favor, Parker. Say *destiny.*"

"Destiny? Why?"

The cop threw his head back and drained what remained of his coffee. He laughed derisively. "You didn't know? You're a drinking game. I found it on the Internet."

"You've been reading about me." Parker felt his pride rising up in self-defense. "Funny, I haven't thought about you once since we met."

The officer sneered and flung his empty cup at the trash can. It went wide.

"Is today the day you're gonna crack the case, Preacher?" He laughed again, the way a school-yard bully laughs at a mark.

"I think we're making some progress. I'm probably not supposed to share any information with you, though. Need-to-know basis—you understand." Parker prayed he'd never be pulled over by Officer Dykstra. A ticket would be the least of his worries.

Dykstra fiddled with the retention snap on his holster. "You know you don't belong here, right? You went to college and learned about—what?—fairy tales. Now you think you're a detective? Ketcham doesn't need you. You're just a gimmick."

Parker knew Joshua Holton would object to diluting his brand on an audience of one, but he couldn't resist. "It's funny," he said, "I've heard people refer to the Bible as a book of fairy tales before. But it makes no sense. Fairy tales take place in unspecified magical kingdoms, long ago and far away. They aren't stories about historical people in real places at specific times, like we find in the Bible."

Dykstra folded his arms across his chest. "I don't think Jesus is historical. Most people don't anymore. He's as make-believe as they come."

Parker chuckled. "You might as well say that Alexander the Great never lived. We have infinitely more evidence from the life of Jesus."

"Maybe Alexander didn't. You don't know. You've never seen him and neither have I. Can't go dig up his grave, can we?"

"What about George Washington?" Parker asked. "I've stood at his tomb on Mount Vernon, but I've never looked inside. Have you?"

"No, but that's different."

"How?"

"Because we live in America. Because there *is* an America. We aren't bowing to the queen and speaking English and all that stuff. That's because of George Washington."

"We don't speak English?"

"You know what I mean."

"Sure. You mean that everywhere we look, we see firsthand the effects of his life."

"Right."

"I rest my case." Parker's phone rang and he ducked out.

"Parker Saint."

"Hello, Brian. Or Parker—sorry. This is Geoff Graham."

Parker suddenly remembered his old professor with absolute clarity—his ticks, his quirks, his sense of humor. He could see his baby face, his Hawaiian shirts, and his bony hands full of ink from permanent markers, which he used instead of chalk, taping newsprint up all over the room.

"Dr. Graham, it's great to hear from you. Thanks for returning my call." Parker held the phone close and spoke quietly.

"My pleasure. As I said on the message I left, I got a call from your secretary. I'll admit, I'm curious. What can I do for you?"

"I'd like to get together and discuss some things. Soon, if you're available. Kind of a long story, best done in person. It's right up your alley: devil worship, spirit guides, church burnings, even murder. I'm afraid I'm in a little over my head here."

"Were you thinking today?"

"Today would be good, but I'm tied up for the time being."

"Are you at your church?"

"No, I'm actually going to be downtown for meetings all day."

"I'll tell you what—I have to run some errands and have lunch with a friend. What say I meet you at Rosa Parks Circle? About two forty-five?"

"That should work."

"Parker, put that phone down!" Ketcham's voice filled the detective's unit.

"I've got to go, Dr. Graham." He ended the call and stuffed the phone into his pocket, instinctively backing into the Command Center to avoid a public dressing down. Ketcham followed him in and slammed the door behind them.

He was flushed with anger. "When I give you the afternoon off, that's a gift. It doesn't mean you can start showing up late, chatting on your phone, wasting my time!"

"I know. I'm sorry, sir." Parker felt at least three flecks of the detective's spit resting on his face, and it took every bit of willpower not to wipe them away.

"Do you think it makes sense for me to sit here waiting for you to roll in when we're overdue for another dead body?" He poked a finger at Parker's chest.

"No, sir. It won't happen again. I promise."

"What are you smiling about?" Ketcham demanded of Officer Dykstra, who had been thoroughly enjoying the show.

"Just in a good mood is all. Here's the report you wanted." He handed the wrinkled page to Ketcham.

"*This* is your report?" Ketcham scanned the handwritten list with a mixture of anger, disgust, and pity.

"That's it."

"Fine, you've delivered it. Now get back out there. You're not paid to sit in here with that stupid grin on your face."

The patrol officer left slowly, eyeing Ketcham with concern.

When they were alone, the detective crumpled the paper and tossed it into the trash, then rested his chin in his hand and studied Parker silently.

"Are you waiting for me to say something?" Parker finally asked, unable to take the awkward silence.

"No, I'm deciding if I've yelled enough."

"You have. Again, I'm very sorry. I hope you can forgive me."

"Why do you have to put it like that? Geez, Parker—you're a preacher; I *have* to forgive you. Come on, let's go."

Lecture over, Ketcham beckoned him to follow.

"I spoke with Ben Ludema's mother again this morning," Ketcham said as they zipped down US 131, southbound.

"What did she have to say?"

"Nothing useful. But she was a lot more forthcoming this time."

"I would imagine. That woman really did not like the sight of me."

"It wasn't you. In fact, she made me promise I'd pass along an apology on her behalf. It's like I told you, Parker. You can't take any of this stuff personally."

"Right." Parker was generally the poster child for not taking things personally. But he'd been avoiding any thought of Meredith Ludema and her rebuke, and had no desire to discuss her now. "You haven't told me where we're going."

"To interview the last person who saw Melanie Candor alive. Apart from the guy who killed her."

"I thought that was her boss at the convenience store."

"So did we, until yesterday afternoon. Come to find out, not only was she beautiful, smart, talented, et cetera, but the late Miss Candor volunteered twice a week, reading to kids at a community center on Division. Half an hour here, forty-five minutes there. She stopped by Saturday night. I want to know if she mentioned anything about where she was going or her plans for the night."

Ketcham reached into his backseat, selecting one large file case from his not insubstantial collection. He hefted it onto Parker's lap. "And as penance for being late," he continued, "you're going to spend the afternoon going through all these crime scene photos and incident reports from the church vandalism cases. Let's see if you can turn your hunch into something a little more concrete."

"You sound skeptical," Parker observed. "Don't you think it sounds like something Damien would do, to have his minions spray-paint church buildings, stick it to the 'Christian Imperialist Elite'?"

"Sure, sure. But when you charge someone with four ritualized murders, you don't usually bother to add five counts of vandalism. When we were running around blind through needle-in-a-haystack country, I thought the church connection might help us find our suspect. But now we've got a suspect."

"So my penance is pointless busywork."

"Maybe not." Ketcham framed his words carefully. "Just between you, me, and the stack of dead bodies at the morgue, we don't have quite as much as you might think on Danny Boy. Sure, he knew one of the victims, went to a couple of their memorials. But it's all circumstantial. It's the very definition of circumstantial. We'll have preliminary DNA results tomorrow. If Damien's a match, we're on track. If not, what do we have? A trollish little guy we don't like because he looks weird and talks about magic spells? The prosecutor's office won't touch it."

The detective picked up and shook three empty plastic tubes from the floorboards, where they'd been rolling around his feet, before finding one that contained a cigar. He lit the stogie and gave a few thoughtful puffs. "It really feels like there's something else holding it all together," he said. "Something else or *someone* else—in addition to Damien—that can tie a bow on this whole thing."

"And you think the answer might be in these crime scene photos."

"Not really. It's a Hail Mary, but you're not on the payroll anyway, so what do we have to lose? I skimmed through the reports myself last night— reminded me why we chalked it all up to gang activity."

"Why?"

"Granted, I'm not an ordained minister or anything, but I saw very little along the lines of devil worship or occult crime—some possible religious overtones, but mostly overlap with common gang symbols: five-pointed stars, pitchforks, crowns, that sort of thing."

"Crowns?" Parker's pulse doubled.

"Right, the People Nation uses a five-pointed

crown as an identifier. There's a lot of photos in there. I hope you have a long attention span."

"The longest." Parker was looking forward to a research project, having missed his extensive web searches for the past two nights.

"Good, because it'll probably take all afternoon. The real glorious side of police work."

Parker suddenly remembered his appointment with Dr. Graham. "This may be the worst possible timing, but about this afternoon—"

Ketcham flicked a sharp sidelong glance at him. "You've *just* reentered my good graces. Step carefully."

"No, you'll like this. I got a call back from a friend of mine this morning, a college professor. His name's Geoff Graham, and he teaches classes about cults and that sort of thing. He just got back into town, and I set up a tentative appointment with him for two forty-five." He tapped the file case in his lap. "I can show him these photos and bounce some of these symbols off of him." He sensed that Ketcham wasn't biting. "He's really an expert. He would see a lot more than I would, looking through something like this."

The detective exhaled loudly. "Don't mention names, and make sure he knows this is all confidential."

"Of course."

"And this doesn't get you off the hook. I still want you to go through every photo in that box yourself, and I want you to check up on Damien's Internet videos. Troy said there were a couple new ones. Were you planning on coming back to the office after your meeting?"

"I . . . I guess I could. It's just, I have this revival thing tonight—I forgot to tell my assistant about it—and they usually want me to—"

"Fine. Take the afternoon, but I want reports on this meeting and on those photos—written and verbal reports—on my desk tomorrow morning at eight o'clock. And by eight o'clock, I mean eight sharp. You got all that?"

"How can I put a verbal report on your desk?"

"Shut up, Parker."

H.I.S. Youth Center, near the corner of Franklin and Division, was an old converted movie theater, still sporting the long row of cinematic lights—most bulbs missing or broken—and a marquee, which now read "Loving Children—Changing Lives."

Ketcham rang a buzzer at the door. The words "How may I help you?" or something close blared from a distorted, old speaker.

"I'm with the Grand Rapids Police Department. I called earlier."

"Come on in." The door clicked and buzzed.

The foyer was polished and restored, compared to the façade. A large mural full of rainbows and smiles covered the near wall, and the smell of buttered popcorn filled the space. A college kid with an intentional gait approached them. "We didn't call the police today," he said. "Everything's okay."

"I'm a detective with the Major Case Team," Ketcham said, flashing his gold badge, "and I'd like to speak with the person who supervises the volunteers."

"That's Sara. Hang on." He freed a walkie-talkie from his belt and said, "Sara, this is Ryan. Are you available right now?"

"I'm about to start a tour for a donor," came the reply.

Ryan lowered the radio. "Can you gentlemen wait for a while, or would you like to come back later?"

"Tell her we'll join the tour," Ketcham said.

Within thirty seconds of receiving the message, Sara whooshed into the foyer, followed by an elderly man in a powder blue suit.

"I'm Sara Morse," she said, matching the firmness of Ketcham's handshake and then some. "I understand you'd like to see the facility."

"You understand correctly. I'm Detective Ketcham, GRPD, and this is Mr. Parker Saint; he's helping us out with an investigation."

"May I ask what investigation?"

"The Blackjack Killer."

She momentarily deflated. "Oh. You're here because of Melanie."

"Yes. But we really would like the tour. I haven't been here since I was a patrol officer."

She forced a smile. "Gladly. I never get tired of showing off our facility. And we do value our relationship with the police department. By the way, this is Dr. James Creswell. He's with a mission organization looking for a worthy cause, so I'd appreciate a lot of *oohs* and *ahhs* to help win him over."

"Pleased to meet you," Dr. Creswell said, shaking hands with Ketcham. His Minnesota Nice accent complemented his easy manner. He turned his attention to Parker. "And you too, young man," he said, locking eyes. "A pleasure."

Parker squelched a gasp. Dr. James Creswell was not a philanthropist from the North Star State. Under a generous helping of pomade, Father Ignatius was now shaking hands with Parker.

"The pleasure's mine, Dr. Creswell. I've been on a few mission boards myself. Which agency did you say you were with?"

"I'm here on behalf of Midwest Ecumenical Baptist Outreach." The words of the Jesuit Oath, *a Protestant among Protestants,* echoed in Parker's head.

They began the tour, but Parker's mind was preoccupied with what on earth Father Ignatius might be doing there. The detective's mind was clearly wrapped up in Melanie Candor and the details of her last night alive—as evidenced by his many questions. Only Dr. James Creswell seemed to enjoy the tour for its own sake, posing questions and voicing approval at all the right moments.

H.I.S. Youth Center did incredible work as far as Parker could tell. Born and raised in Grand Rapids, he had spent literally no time in this part of town. While he was aware of child hunger, the lure of gangs, and the dangers of the streets as abstract concepts or statistics, it was comforting to simultaneously encounter the reality of the stories Sara shared and this place that addressed those problems. He decided that, whatever Dr. Creswell's fictitious organization determined about sponsoring the youth center, he would be sending a fat check.

As they neared the end of the tour, Sara brought them all to a set of double doors under twin glowing exit signs.

"This is a new part of the tour," she said, her voice growing somber. "This is where I point to the bloodstains on the carpet. These emergency exits are locked from the outside, but anyone can open them from within. Fire code and all that. There used to be an alarm when these doors were opened, but it hasn't worked in more than a year. And the lock sticks.

"Two weeks ago some local teenagers came in here and attacked one of our fifth graders. They said he had squealed. I don't know the whole backstory, but I know that what we do here is needed more than ever in order to give these kids a positive alternative. And yet we still haven't fixed the door lock or the alarm because we can't afford it."

"Have you had a locksmith out?" Parker asked.

"No. We're operating in the red right now. To be quite frank, we might lose the building in another two months if we don't get some sizeable gifts. There are a lot of little projects like this one that simply can't be addressed right now."

Parker felt a pang of guilt as he considered his own real estate situation. He owned the former shopping center that housed Abundance Now Ministries free and clear. The building itself had been donated—under the condition that it be used as a church or charity—and Parker had been able to pay off the surrounding land inside a year, careful to keep his name, not the church's, on the deed. He rented the space to the church for a dollar a year.

Joshua Holton had insisted on this arrangement, warning him not to trust boards of elders and trustees. Nearly a million dollars in renovation had been required to transform the defunct shopping center into a state-of-the-art church and soundstage, but those funds had been borrowed by the congregation and were all but repaid.

How many months could the youth center subsist off of a single week's giving at Abundance

Now, Parker wondered. He wished he could partner with them, organize trips to come and fix the doors, read to children, give them hope—but with his burgeoning national reach, and with Holton's strict regulations about diluting one's brand, that was not possible.

And Parker knew it.

The three detectives and their clergy consultant sat around the conference table in the Command Center, sharing information and strategizing. Parker had grabbed the seat next to Corrinne and tried to reestablish their chemistry, but was unsuccessful. When he apologized for not returning her call, she waved it away, and when he asked about the hilarious event he'd missed, she decided it hadn't really been all that funny unless you were there.

As the other detectives settled in, they matched their colleagues' malaise. There was a general sense of disappointment in the air, and basic agreement that the investigation was in something of a rut.

"I need to hear what you two came up with on Damien's background. Wow me."

Corrinne held up a file folder. "The guy's childhood was a nightmare," she said. "Father abused him, then killed himself. Mother renounced all parental rights when he was nine years old. He bounced around from foster home to foster home.

Booted from one for starting fires and fights, pulled from another because the foster parents sexually abused him. The *foster parents.* That's some bad luck, am I right?"

Everyone nodded, but Parker sensed a collective hesitancy to start down the road of sympathizing with the suspect.

"Have a look at these," she added. "Definitely possible seeds of violence later in life." She handed a file folder to Parker. He got the impression it was supposed to make the rounds, and wondered if it would be bad etiquette not to have a look inside. Maybe just a glimpse to appear engaged.

Parker cracked the folder and let out a little girlish gasp. The photograph on top was labeled *Daniel Banner, Age 6.* The boy in the picture was unmistakably Damien, his little face a mixture of sadness and anger. Both of his eyes were black, and his arm hung in a sling.

"He had a broken collarbone in that one," she explained.

"That's horrible," Parker said quietly, handing the folder to Ketcham.

"We're dealing with a troubled man," the detective said, nodding. "That angle will be attractive to his attorney."

"But he beat the odds and went to college," Troy said. "Got a bachelor's degree in philosophy. What kind of job can you get with that?"

"Not much," Corrinne answered. "Might push me into devil worship too."

Ketcham stood. "Okay, let's pause here a minute. I want your gut feelings. You too, Parker—are we convinced that Damien Bane is involved in these murders?"

Corrinne nodded emphatically. "Involved? Yes."

"I agree," Troy said. "But there's something missing. I don't know what, but I think we should consider the possibility that a number of people are involved. Maybe Damien has a partner—someone smoother, a little more connected, a little more 'on the grid.' "

Ketcham grunted his agreement. "I was saying the same to Parker this morning. It's almost like Damien's too obvious a suspect. I've been in this line of work long enough to get nervous when something's too obvious. Although I'm sure the preacher here disagrees, don't you, Parker? A guy looks like the devil himself, of course he's doing the devil's work, capable of all manner of evil. End of story, right?"

"Not at all," Parker answered. "In fact, the Scriptures tell us that Satan masquerades as an angel of light and his servants as servants of light. Anyone could be doing the 'devil's work.' " He thought of Evert Carlson's distinction between the lion and the serpent. "In fact, he specializes in *not obvious*."

"So you're saying that, according to the

Bible, everyone's a suspect?" Ketcham asked.

"I don't know if I'd put it like that, but sure."

"I like that. You could be the killer, Parker. You're a messenger of light, aren't you?"

"Parker's not our killer," Corrinne assured, her pep coming back. "If he was, there'd be little piles of puke at every crime scene."

Troy bellowed a laugh, uncomfortably loud in the small room. "And we'd find him passed out next to the body!" The laughter rose a notch.

"Oh, look at the time," Parker said, tapping his watch. "I've got some police work to do. You kids have fun."

"Eight sharp, Parker!" Ketcham called out after him.

Sixteen

The air was brisk as Parker made his way up Monroe Center, past vendors, boutiques, and a herd of large people on rented Segways. It was just a few blocks from police headquarters to Rosa Parks Circle, a small amphitheater situated between the art museum and the Grand Plaza, surrounded by fountains, trees, and several alleged pieces of public art.

Parker spotted Geoff Graham sitting on a bench a ways off. He wore a bulky jacket—the kind one might buy for a trip to Alaska, with a ring of faux fur around the hood—unzipped, revealing a bright red Hawaiian shirt. He spotted Parker a moment later, broke into a grin, and stood to envelop him in a bear hug.

"Good to see you, Parker," he said warmly. He smelled mildly of mothballs and Altoids, a smell that propelled Parker back to his under-graduate years—memories of sitting through early morning classes like Logic and the Philosophy of Religion. And not just sitting through them, but loving them.

He looked almost exactly as Parker remembered him, except a little swollen around the middle and under the eyes. They sat on the bench and looked out at the city, beautifully fringed with orange, red, and yellow foliage.

"I'd like to catch up on the past fifteen or twenty years, Parker, but I already know what you've been up to, and I'm more than intrigued by all your talk of murder and demon possession. So let's skip the formalities and get to the meat."

Parker tried to channel Ketcham's authoritative tone, saying, "You have to understand that what we discuss today is completely confidential."

Dr. Graham smiled—the beginning of a laugh—but then backed off at Parker's grim expression. "Okay," he said. "Confidential."

"I've been working with the police department as a consultant for the Blackjack Killer investigation."

"The what now?"

"The serial killer. He's murdered four people in the past week."

"I've been in Chile for ten days. I'm afraid I'm a bit out of the loop."

"I can fill you in on the details, but here's the short version: four people killed by having their throats cut and Satanic symbols and that sort of thing all over the crime scenes. And our prime suspect claims to be indwelled by 'spirit guides,' which sounds like demon possession by any other name. I called you because I'm in over my head. I remembered that you taught the class on cults, and I thought you could give me some pointers."

"Well, that wouldn't be much help, would it?"

"Come again?"

"A class on cults would be irrelevant to your investigation. Luckily, the class you're thinking of was Contemporary Occultism. That's a whole different field of study."

"You see? I'm learning already."

"Why don't we start with what you think is going on here, Parker? You were always one of my sharper students. What's your take?"

"My take is a very fluid concept right now. I'm trying to nail it down. But, of course, it's hard to nail down something fluid. I was hoping you could rehash the highlights of your teaching on the subject. You know, the twenty-minute version of a semester-long class."

Dr. Graham puffed his cheeks and exhaled. "Where to start . . ."

"How about demon possession?" Parker could not shake the memory of that low growl under Damien's voice on the telephone. "I remember you joked that your kids called you the Christian Reformed Exorcist; how does that work?"

"My kids called me that to get under my skin. I'm not an exorcist, I'm a missiologist. I used to run a ministry that specialized in setting people free from spiritual bondage. That's a far cry from being an exorcist by trade."

"But you had stories about possessed people."

"I've always tried to avoid that term, actually, but yes, I have certainly seen enough during the course of my career to know that there are spiritual powers out there, and that they are working counter to the gospel. Haven't you?"

Parker waffled. "I do believe people can become trapped by their own demons."

"Their own demons? You don't believe in real demonic beings—personal, spiritual beings—like Scripture teaches?"

"I sure don't believe in the horror-movie version. The little girl whose head spins around while she spews pea soup all over the place and can throw grown men across the room. That's just embarrassing."

Dr. Graham's face darkened. "That's your inexperience talking, Parker. I've seen demonized people do incredible things when cornered or challenged. No spinning heads, but certainly showing strength they did not have in the flesh."

Parker leaned in, intrigued. "Go on."

"I'm not going to indulge you with ghost and goblin stories, Parker. If you really want to discover the truth about these things, open your Bible. The Gospel of Mark, chapter five. Jesus and his disciples are in the middle of a missionary speaking-slash-healing-slash-deliverance tour, crisscrossing the Sea of Galilee in a fishing boat." He pulled a worn, thinline Bible from the inside pocket of his enormous coat and quickly flipped to the right page.

"Then they arrived at the region of the Gadarenes, and the evangelist tells us that a man with an evil spirit lived there among the tombs. This guy was a local legend. People had tried to chain him up, shackle his hands and feet, and yet he always tore the chains apart and broke the leg irons to pieces."

"I'm familiar with the story," Parker said.

"It wasn't weight lifting that made him strong enough to break chains. It was the unclean spirits. But look what Jesus did." Dr. Graham began to read aloud.

"Seeing Jesus from a distance, he ran up and bowed down before Him; and shouting with a loud voice, he said, 'What business do we have with each other, Jesus, Son of the Most High God? I implore You by God, do not torment me!' For He had been saying to him, 'Come out of the man, you unclean spirit!' And He was asking him, 'What is your name?' And he said to Him, 'My name is Legion; for we are many.'"

"Damien said that to me," Parker interrupted. "He said his name was Legion."

"Who's Damien?"

"Our suspect." *Don't use names,* Ketcham had ordered.

Dr. Graham frowned. "Take it from someone who's been around the block a few times: that's a red flag."

"Red flag for what?"

"A poseur. And not even a very slick one. That's not the real thing."

"What does the real thing look like?"

"There are more than forty indicators by my count, but most of them can be faked by someone looking for attention—things like blasphemous tirades, self-mutilation, and the like. The unmistakable signs are harder to counterfeit—the kind of superhuman strength Jesus encountered in the Gadarenes, for one. Speaking in a language he or she couldn't possibly know, or having knowledge of future events."

Parker squelched a laugh. "You're serious?"

The old professor flipped some more pages. "Let's look to God's Word again and see what it has to say. In Acts 16 Luke, writing about his missionary journeys with Saint Paul, says,

"It happened that as we were going to the place of prayer, a slave-girl having a spirit of divination met us, who was bringing her masters much profit by fortune-telling. Following after Paul and us, she kept crying out, saying, 'These men are bond-servants of the Most High God, who are proclaiming to you the way of salvation.' She continued doing this for many days. But Paul was greatly annoyed, and turned and said to the spirit, 'I command you in the name of Jesus Christ to come out of her!' And it came out at that very moment."

"Our suspect is oh-for-three so far."

"What makes you think he's demonized to begin with?"

"He told us as much when we brought him in for questioning."

"Another red flag. Anything else?"

"Well, if he's the one who killed those four people, there's that. And the bodies were covered with symbols, like pentagrams and inverted crosses. Those are occultic, right?"

"That's not a word, but . . . yes."

"And there's the way he dresses and all his piercings and such. I mean, I try not to judge people, but look at this man." He pulled out a photo, printed from Damien's website, and handed it to the professor.

Dr. Graham's face drained of color. His mouth fell open. "I think I've dealt with this man," he said quietly.

"Are you sure?"

"No, I'm not sure. But the hair, the dark eyes, the black clothes. He looks an awful lot like a man who walked into Broken Bondage Ministries shortly after we founded it. He told us he'd been on drugs and that he heard voices. He manifested a number of very unusual signs of demonization —the sort of things that don't even occur to the fakers. My partner and I tried to hold him down while we prayed for the demons to leave him, which they eventually did. Then we counseled him for a time, walked him through the gospel, gave him our contact information, and asked him to keep in touch."

"Let me guess; you never saw him again?"

"No, that's the strange thing. He never called us, but I did see him again, maybe three years later. I was visiting my brother in Lowell, and we attended his little storefront church. And this same man was there visiting, looking exactly the same. He stuck around after the service and asked Jerry and the elders to pray over him. Of course, considering my work, Jerry invited me to join them, and we cast the demons out again. It was like déjà vu. He fell to the ground, and the spirits came out, and he responded with the same sense of gratitude and peace, even the same words he'd said to me years earlier—almost verbatim."

"So he was a poseur."

"No. He was the real deal."

"I don't get it."

Dr. Graham was flipping again. "You remember Luke 11. When Jesus's enemies publicly accused him of serving Satan, he asked them, 'If I drive out demons by Beelzebub, by whom do your followers drive them out?' Then Jesus gives what I believe is a description of what happens when the Pharisees—or anyone—drive out demons without the demonized person putting faith in the Savior. Listen:

> "When the unclean spirit goes out of a man, it passes through waterless places seeking rest, and not finding any, it says, 'I will return to my house from which I came.' And when it comes, it finds it swept and put in order. Then it goes and takes along seven other spirits more evil than itself, and they go in and live there; and the last state of that man becomes worse than the first."

He closed his Bible. "I think that young man was going back for seconds, in a sense. Or, more likely, he was way beyond seconds, like he was seeking out more unclean spirits."

"Is that uncommon for victims of demon possession?"

"That's the point, Parker. He wasn't a victim—at least he didn't see himself that way. When Jesus cast the legion of demons out of the Gadarenes demoniac, the man's immediate response was to worship Jesus. He wanted nothing more than to follow him—literally. He became an evangelist, proclaiming the freedom from bondage that can be found in Christ. The same thing happened with Mary Magdalene. Jesus drove seven evil spirits out of her, and she was his servant to the very end, even to the grave and beyond. In fact, she preached the first ever Easter sermon: *I have seen the Lord!* That's almost always what happens in Scripture when someone is delivered from this sort of oppression. But not with this man."

"Do you have any idea why not?"

"I'm going to go out on a limb here, Parker, and buck the party line a little bit. A lot of people in my circles want to allegorize Jesus's teaching about the demon who returns with seven more and finds the place swept clean—to make it into a parable, a simple spiritual truth. But I think that misses the bigger point. Whatever spiritual truth we can glean from this, it's clear that Jesus actually meant what he said here."

"But most theologians don't take it literally?"

"I don't think it's a question of literal versus spiritual. This text, rightly understood, teaches that outward reform and religious rituals are no permanent remedy for the soul because the problem lies in the heart and will. Jesus is using this one example—exorcism—to teach that truth." He hesitated a moment, then asked, "Do you want my theory?"

"Of course."

"I'm only telling you this because you already said our conversation is confidential. My thought is this: what if a person could somehow leverage this phenomenon? What if they experienced this increasing of their capacity for evil, increasing power—and started wanting more and more? A wicked man could seek out exorcism from different channels, different traditions, even different religions for that matter, sweeping the place clean, adding square footage, installing more bunks and bathrooms, to press the analogy. He would make himself more and more inhabitable, more hospitable. If I had to guess, I'd say that's what he was doing."

"But if that's possible, why wouldn't more people do it? Or maybe they do, right? Maybe every pro athlete is really packed full of evil spirits . . ."

Dr. Graham shook his head violently. "No, no, no. Being demonized is not like taking steroids or getting superpowers. It's a horrible thing.

Terrifying. That's one reason why everyone delivered from demons in the New Testament is endlessly thankful. Evil spirits tend to torment people, throw them into fires, cause them to cut themselves. If I'm right about this, there must be something different about this particular man. Or maybe he has a high tolerance for torment. Maybe he even likes it."

"Do you happen to remember this man's name?"

"It wasn't Damien. Well, it might have been, but he didn't call himself that." He pursed his lips in thought. "Both times I saw him, he called himself Danny."

It was Parker's turn to lose all color. He realized he was squeezing his hair at the roots, and returned his hands to his lap.

"His given name is Daniel Banner," he said, gesturing at the photo. After a short silence he added, "I'll admit, Dr. Graham, I'm scared. I was hoping you'd tell me something that would make all the angst and fear melt away. No such luck, huh?"

"If you're afraid this man is going to kill you, I don't have a remedy for that."

"That's not it. If he wanted to kill me, I think he would have done it already. What I'm afraid of is some kind of spiritual confrontation—me versus the powers of darkness. I'm afraid I'd choke."

"*You* versus the powers of hell? Yes, you'd be hamburger, and so would I. Remember the Epistle of St. Jude—'But Michael the archangel, when he disputed with the devil and argued about the body of Moses, did not dare pronounce against him a railing judgment, but said, "The Lord rebuke you!"' If you make it your personal battle, you'll fall. Do you remember the seven sons of Sceva, the high priest?"

"Sure. That's in the Book of Acts. They were casting out demons in Jesus' name, but they were using it as a magic charm or something."

"Exactly. And the demonized man turned on them and beat the tar out of these seven strapping, young men."

"I understand," Parker said.

"Do you?" The professor zipped up his coat and looked off in the distance. "You want a strategy for spiritual warfare? Is that what you're looking for?"

"I'm not sure. I guess so."

"Well, listen carefully, because this is complicated: 'submit to God, resist the devil, and he will flee from you.' "

"It's that simple?"

"It's simple, but it isn't easy. There are a whole lot of people running around out there wanting to defeat the powers of darkness, thinking they can resist the devil and send him running, without first submitting themselves to God. If you skip step one, it doesn't work."

"What does that look like? Skipping step one?"

"Like the seven sons of the high priest, like Peter swinging his sword in the garden. And it looks a little like you, Parker. It looks like your positive pep talks on TV, your appearances at all the big events, but without calling anyone to true repentance and the forgiveness of sins.

"You know what you need? You need a scandal; that's what your ministry has been missing."

Parker's scalp prickled, and his mind was again filled with the image of Brynn Carter and her ever-evolving version of events. He locked eyes with Dr. Graham. How did all these people already know?

The old professor balked briefly at the intensity in Parker's eyes. "I'm being clever, of course," he said, his tone smoothing over. "Our word *scandal* comes from the Greek *scandalon*. It means a stumbling block, something you trip over. The Scriptures call the cross a *scandalon*. People trip over it and fall away if they haven't been born again. Remove the scandal and you can grow a big audience, but what's the point?"

Dr. Graham tilted his head and tucked his chin, as if finally making a frontal assault on an enemy. "I've been following your meteoric rise, Parker. You need to learn the lesson that Satan learned the hard way: a meteoric rise, without submitting to God's will, is the setup for a meteoric fall. Jesus said he saw Satan fall like lightning. I don't want to see that happen to you."

"Well, don't sugarcoat it." Parker was tired of hearing different versions of the same speech.

"I'm just trying to help you. Speaking the truth in love, as the Word says. And if I had to guess, I'd say you're nowhere near ready to resist the devil. I think your fears are well-founded."

"So, what then? If it comes down to it, the devil will just claim my soul?" Parker asked, his tone sharpening.

"I hope your soul is already claimed. And that's your edge. That's where you turn. When you confront evil, whether it's a trial in your life, a temptation, or a full-on frontal attack, just look to the cross. Look to the man bleeding and dying there for your salvation. If you've given yourself to him, you can't be overtaken by the evil one.

"Right after Jesus described the temporary nature of heathen exorcism, he told a quick little parable." Dr. Graham flipped back to the Gospel of Luke. " 'When a strong man, fully armed, guards his own house, his possessions are safe. But when someone stronger attacks and over-powers him, he takes away the armor in which the man trusted and divides up the spoils.' When you've got the Holy Spirit, no one can bind *that* strong man. No one can come in and claim your soul, Parker. Take comfort in that."

Parker believed Dr. Graham with every ounce of his being, and he knew it should comfort him. But for some reason, it had the opposite effect.

His phone buzzed, and Parker grabbed the distraction.

"Parker Saint."

"It's me," Father Michael said on the other end. "We want to drop off a package for you to look at, but Xavier is paranoid about leaving it at the police station. You think they'd open your mail?"

"I'm not there anyway. I'm meeting a friend at Rosa Parks Circle."

"Any chance we could meet up when you're done? This would be better discussed in person."

Parker glanced at his former professor, who was staring straight up into the sky. He could sense the older man waiting for an opening to restart the lecture. "We're actually just finishing up, Michael. Where do you want to meet?"

The Basilica of St. Adalbert was a hundred-year-old Romanesque church, her three jaded copper domes jutting up alongside an elevated freeway downtown, amidst office buildings and high-rises. Parker met the Jesuits at the rear of the nave. He hadn't known what a nave was, much to Father Ignatius's horror, causing Parker to bump "church architecture" to the top of his list of Internet search terms.

"Do you see this, Protestant?" Ignatius asked, gesturing all around them. "The columns, the sculptures, the baldachin suspended over the marble altar, the purposeful combination of

Roman, Byzantine, and Gothic influence, the sheer majesty. *This* is a church!"

"Yeah, it's nice, I guess," Parker said, goading the priest just a little.

Michael cut the exchange short by thrusting a manila envelope toward Parker. It was labeled *Reverend Parker Saint* in Sharpie. Parker carefully bent back the metal clips and tried in vain to fold up the flap, which was securely glued down.

"Let me save us all some time," Ignatius said, snatching the envelope and producing a shiny black knife from his belt somewhere beneath his jacket. Parker felt a spike of adrenaline at the sight of it—an almost exact duplicate of the throwing knife Ketcham had shown the detectives back in the Command Center. He took an involuntary step back. *I will hang, waste, boil, flay, strangle, and bury alive these infamous heretics.*

"Don't worry, Protestant. The Inquisition is on hiatus," Ignatius said wryly.

In the envelope were three forensic photos of the back of a woman's neck, a gloved hand holding her long black hair off to the side.

"Who am I looking at?" Parker asked.

"Isabella Escalanté," Michael answered. "I was able to gain access to the GRPD's crime scene photographs this morning."

"You hacked into their computers?" Parker was doubting anew his alliance with these men.

"Of course not. I slim-jimmed the detective's car while you and Father Ignatius were keeping him occupied at the youth center. But look here." He pointed to a small black symbol on her light brown skin. It was an intersecting of four wedge-shaped lines. "Do you recognize this character?"

"No, I've never seen it."

Xavier said, "It's a Sumerian cuneiform character called a dingir. It denotes deity."

"That's odd."

"The evidence technicians cataloged it as a tattoo," Michael said, "but it doesn't look like one to any of us. Looks like marker. We followed up with Isabella's mother, and she knew nothing of any tattoo. Apparently Isabella had always been very much against them—thought they were 'trashy.' "

"Which means," said Xavier, "that either she had a sudden change of heart, which is certainly plausible, or this is not a tattoo."

Parker held the photo up near his nose and tried to focus. "But why would this symbol be so different? The others were in plain view and done with such demented creativity, painted with her blood. Why would the killer also draw this little thing in marker where no one would likely find it? And the Samaritan letter for 'deity'? That's just strange."

"Sumerian," Ignatius corrected, "as in, the cradle of civilization."

"Right, sorry."

Xavier withdrew a few more photos from a folio and handed them to Parker. They showed Melanie Candor, dead, an image of a spade beginning at her throat and filling her sternum. Beneath it was a smaller image of a snake.

"I would suggest that the stars, the 666, and the lightning bolt were for the police, the press, and the public, while the dingir was for the benefit of Merodach."

"I don't believe I've met Merodach," Parker said.

"Perhaps you know him by another name: Marduk, a Babylonian sun god who essentially swallowed up many of the other heathen deities in the ancient Near East—Baal, Shemesh, and others. We read about him in the book of Jeremiah. He's largely forgotten today, but clearly someone still remembers him."

"Why do you say that?"

"In Babylon, the two main symbols used for Merodach were the spade and the serpent or dragon."

Parker weighed this new information. "No offense, Fathers, but this could mean anything. Sometimes a spade is just a spade. It's not always an obscure Babylonian reference."

Xavier shook his head. "The combination of these symbols and the unmistakable image of the dingir is just too much to be a coincidence."

"What about Ben Ludema? Did he have any Babylonian imagery on him?"

"Don't know," Michael answered. "There were files from at least ten different cases in that guy's backseat. By the time I found the right one and started scanning, Father Ignatius gave me the signal that you and the good detective were on your way back out."

Xavier fixed Parker with a solemn look. "We'd like you to try and gain access to the rest of these crime scene photos. I suspect there may be more of these subtler touches, perhaps overlooked by the police."

"I can probably do that. Ketcham seems to be running out of uses for me. He's just giving me busywork now. Working through photographs keeps me occupied and out of his way."

"Great," Michael said. "And keep in mind—it might be anywhere on their bodies. Doesn't have to be the neck."

"Wait!" Parker shouted, pointing at the photo of the dingir. "That symbol was on the bottom of Melanie Candor's foot."

"Are you sure?"

"Yes. The coroner thought it was a tattoo, made some smart-aleck remark about it. I'd bet anything it was this exact symbol. And, really, who gets a tattoo on the bottom of her foot?" He furrowed his brow. "But I don't get it. Ketcham has been through all those photos, and he went over every inch of the crime scene. Why wouldn't he so much as mention that symbol to Troy and Corrinne?"

Michael shrugged. "These days it seems like everyone in their twenties has a foreign letter tattooed somewhere on their body. It wouldn't seem important if you didn't know what you were looking for."

"Agreed," Xavier said. "What I find strange is the lack of continuity. The dingir and the emblems of Merodach hearken back to some of the most ancient heathen worship on record. Then, the killer's subject matter suddenly jumps forward thousands of years to the current pop-culture caricature of Satanism, the kind of thing popular in recent decades in the West—both amongst self-styled devil worshipers and in the reactionary American church. Instead of the religious culture of the Uruk period, we've got goat heads, pentagrams, and inverted crosses."

"Exactly," Father Michael agreed. "It's the difference between a wannabe occultist and someone who is deeply into the world of the demonic."

"What do you mean 'wannabes'?" Parker asked.

"Most of what we call Satanism can't be traced back much further than the early twentieth century, when it was cooked up by Aleister Crowley. It got a face-lift in the fifties and sixties by Anton LaVey and a few others, but its rituals, symbols, and catchphrases have absolutely nothing to do with ancient occultism."

"Are you sure about that? My old neighbor claimed to be a Wiccan. She had this bumper sticker with a big pentagram on it, and it said 'The Religion Older than Christianity.' "

Father Michael laughed derisively. "Wicca's even newer. Everything about it—the symbols, the *Book of Shadows*—it's all made up in the last 125 years. Even the five-pointed star and inverted cross were actually Christian symbols centuries before anyone associated them with the occult." He scoffed. "Older than Christianity—that's a laugh."

Father Ignatius said, "And yet, this murderer seems to have a foot in both worlds."

"So what does this tell us about our perp?" asked Parker.

An awkward silence followed.

Father Michael tilted his head inquisitively. "Did you just say *perp?*"

"I guess I, uh—"

"It tells us that our *perp* has great knowledge of ancient spiritualism and the occult, but wants to appear to be in the same category as some metal-head kid who watches one too many eighties slasher flicks, puts on a hockey mask, and chops up his whole family."

"Any theories as to why?"

"We think that the press was too dull to catch

on to the Babylonian occult connection, as were the police—"

"And their clergy consultant," Ignatius interjected.

"—and so the killer kind of dumbed himself down on purpose, as if to announce, 'I really am a devil worshiper and these killings really are occult related!' Why would he want to do that? Search me."

"Or it could be more complex," Xavier said. "There could be two different agendas at play simultaneously—one public, one private. Where the two intersect is the disturbing part. I see in our killer a man who would desperately want the Crown of Marbella for obvious reasons, and would do anything to get his hands on it."

"But could that be Damien?" It didn't quite add up for Parker.

"That's what we're going to find out," Father Michael said.

Seventeen

Parker ate dinner at the Clear Water Grille, one of his favorite restaurants. He ordered cedar-plank salmon and a peasant salad, hoping to distract himself from the increasing backlog of questions swirling in his mind. As the hostess walked him past the bar, he overheard the word *destiny* from a herd of college boys, who laughed and went bottoms-up to Parker's health.

The food was exquisite, but it did nothing to distract him from thoughts of cuneiform writing, stolen church artifacts, and Damien Bane seeking out the rite of exorcism again and again in order to increase his demonic prowess.

He pulled up a Bible program on his smartphone and reread Luke's account of the Gadarenes demoniac over some herbal tea. It made him shudder. Damien was a rather slight man, physically speaking, but Parker found himself wondering if he could break chains and snap leg irons. Then he felt silly for wondering.

When he'd finished his dinner, Parker made the short drive to the Rivers of Life Worship Center, a megachurch on the north side of town. As he neared the church, his anxiety over seeing Paige again so dwarfed his other concerns that he was almost thankful for it. Paige could hold a grudge with a single-minded commitment that few possessed. But Parker had taken her for granted and said just the wrong thing before and had always been able to recover using a combination of charm and contrition.

The building reminded Parker of a giant cinnamon roll, every entrance designed to keep the crowds moving, funneling worshipers clockwise into the enormous auditorium. He entered a hall behind the stage door and found

Bishop Jackson sitting in front of a sprawling mirror while a scowling middle-aged woman teased and sprayed his thinning hair.

"I'm sorry, I must have the wrong room," Parker said. "I thought this was a church office, not a beauty parlor." He did not like Wayne and found that he could best disguise his genuine distaste in the form of lighthearted jabs.

"Parker," the man called, standing abruptly, "I'm so glad you could make it."

"I said I'd be here."

"That book done yet?"

"Yeah, it's in galleys. Should hit the shelves in early spring."

"Get a blurb from Joshua Holton?"

"Of course," Parker said, not sure if he was lying or not. He was well aware that Bishop Jackson was using—or attempting to use—him as a means of getting in with Joshua Holton and his scads of viewers. Parker resented that, but it also gave him a bit of a rush to be in such demand.

"Well, you can build anticipation tonight," he said, handing Parker a printed schedule. "We'll have you up at the beginning of Act Two. We'll pick a few people from the audience for you to pray with. Feel free to use the opportunity to plug the book. We're on Tri-State Christian Network tonight. It's no Joshua Holton program, but we're looking at a potential viewing audience of two hundred thousand."

"Sounds good, Wayne. I'll go for ten minutes. That sound about right?"

"I have you scheduled for eight, but we might end up ahead of schedule. Any extra time is yours. We'll give you the standard thirty-second warning, naturally. By the way, your girl's already in your dressing room, 116."

"My girl?"

"Yeah, the redhead. I told her she looked nice. You know what she said to me?"

"Drop dead?"

"More or less."

"That's because you're a slimeball, Wayne. I'll see you onstage." Parker walked slowly down the hall, collecting his wits and pre-chewing his pride so it would go down easy. Pausing outside room 116, he thought about how most pastors would probably pray before walking into such a touchy situation.

He found Paige curled up on a large plush chair, engrossed in her cell phone. She glanced up at Parker for a fraction of a second before returning her attention to the device in her hands.

"Hello, Paige."

"Hello," she said, her voice covered in frost. She continued clacking at the tiny buttons of her phone.

"Can I talk to you a minute?"

"That depends. Have you learned now how to talk to a woman?"

"I'm sorry. Can I lead off with that? I'm incredibly sorry."

The clicking stopped. She set the phone down and folded her arms over her chest.

"I shouldn't have spoken to you that way," he said. "I hadn't slept—still haven't, not much. But that's not an excuse. I was lashing out at you just because you were there, when you're the one person in my life right now who doesn't deserve it."

She unfolded her arms, her face softening a bit.

"I was disrespectful and inappropriate," he continued. "Can you forgive me?"

Paige reached behind her chair and produced a paper cup with a plastic lid. "I got you some chai tea," she said.

"Thanks." Parker smiled. If only everyone on earth were as forgiving and kind as Paige Carmichael.

"I brought you two different suits," she continued, pointing to a garment rack against the wall. "I think the pinstripe will look better against the set. Have you seen the set?"

"I'm just going to wear this."

"You're right. It's probably not worth changing. This is kind of small profile. Next time, tell Bishop Jackson's people to call me, and I'll let him down softly."

Parker plopped down on a velvety sofa opposite his assistant. He did not want to be here. The thought of having his name dropped on religious TV, of parading up onstage so that he and Bishop Wayne Jackson could slap each other on the back a few times and plug his book, turned Parker's stomach. He didn't think he could handle the carnival atmosphere—not in his present state.

"How did your call with Holton go?" Paige asked.

Parker wheezed. The last thing he wanted was to break their peace within ten words of restoring it.

"Things aren't great, Paige."

"I can tell you're stressed out. Do you want to talk about it?"

Before he could even have a say in the matter, Parker was crying. Sobbing like a child. Paige slid onto the couch next to him, rubbing his back and comforting him in a soft tone.

"What's the matter, Parker? You can tell me."

"I don't know how much longer I can do this."

"I understand. It's not fair. I'll have Mark Walsh call the prosecutor's office tomorrow. It's blackmail. They're holding your whole life hostage."

"I'm not talking about the police work. I'm talking about the TV ministry, the self-promotion, the dodgy interview answers. I don't recognize what I do for a living anymore. It's not what my father did, and it's *sure* not what my grandfather did."

Paige pulled a few tissues from her purse and offered them to Parker, who dried his face, blew his nose, and quickly regained his composure.

"Is this about tonight?" she asked. "Because we can cancel this. It's small potatoes."

"It's that. Exactly that. Treating ministry like some sort of show business."

"You're the one who calls it a show, Parker."

"I know. And I hate myself for it. When did that become my MO?"

"Your what?"

"Modus operandi." He chuckled. "I guess I've been hanging around those detectives too much."

"Do they really talk like that?"

"Oh yeah, all the time."

"Well, let's bang out a new modus operandi for you. When this legal mess is behind us, we'll block off some time and update your mission statement for the website. It's overdue anyway."

"Some tweaks to the website aren't going to fix this. It feels like everything is moving in the wrong direction."

Paige narrowed her eyes. "Have you been reading those blogs again?"

He shook his head. "I met a woman a couple days ago who watches *Speak It into Reality* every week. Never misses a program. Her son was one of the kids who got murdered. She said I let her down. She needed to hear some words of hope from the Scriptures, and I was talking about embracing 'moments of majesty.' And she's right. I dropped the ball."

"Parker, that sermon helped a lot of people. I've got folders full of e-mail, almost all of it positive."

"You know, my grandfather only gave me one piece of advice about preaching: when you've finished your second draft, read it over and ask the question: Could this sermon make sense without a crucified and risen Savior? If the answer is yes, throw it out, because it's not a Christian sermon. It's advice, life coaching, pep talks, whatever you call it, but it's not a Christian sermon. I honestly don't think one of my sermons in the past two years could meet that criterion."

Paige touched him softly on the arm. "Do you remember what you told me you were going to do when you hired me? You said you were going to save Jesus from his followers, from all those grumpy, miserable, Puritan types. God bless your grandfather, but you reach people he could never have reached, Parker. That's something to be proud of."

"But what am I reaching them with? I'm going to need some time, Paige. When the investigation is over and the Brynn thing is laid to rest, I want to take a month or two to study and pray and figure this all out."

"What about the book?"

"Letting it sit for a couple months won't kill anyone. I'll promote it when I get my head together. Besides, you said yourself—without Holton's endorsement, it's dead in the water."

Paige stood. "Will you do me a favor and put off this decision until you've caught up on your sleep?"

"That's probably a good idea." He looked at his watch. "They're going to want to wire me up pretty soon. There's no reason you have to stay for this circus. Why don't you head home?"

"Okay. Thanks." She bent down and hugged him around the neck. "I'm worried about you. Don't do anything rash without me."

"I promise," he said.

She looked back and gave him a little wave over her shoulder. He missed her the moment he heard the door click shut.

"My next guest needs no introduction, but I'll give him one anyway, because I like talking about him." Bishop Jackson loved riffing more than anyone Parker had ever met. The man was sweating profusely, but his composure was cool. "You've seen him on Joshua Holton's program. You've seen him on his own show, *Speak It into Reality*, casting vision, sharing the Word, growing his own congregation at Abundance Now Ministries. Now he's got a new book coming out in just a few months, which we're all looking forward to. You know what to say as Parker Saint takes the stage, folks. *God is awesome . . .*"

"And so am I!" roared six thousand people. A wall of applause met Parker as he strode out onto the stage, his practiced white grin catching the spotlights.

He shook Wayne's hand enthusiastically, as if they were old friends who hadn't seen each other in years.

"It's so good to be here, Wayne," he said. "I always say your church is the place to be if you want to feel the waves of the Spirit pulling us out into the divine, into a life of victory and blessedness." Parker found himself trying, unsuccessfully, to decipher what he had just said.

"We'd all like to hear a little more about this book of yours," Wayne said to another wave of applause, "but first, would you do me a favor and pray for a few of the blessed souls here tonight?"

"I'd love to." *I can't.*

An usher led a pudgy, middle-aged woman onto the stage.

"This is Leigh Ann," Bishop Jackson said, slyly referencing an index card. "She's been struggling with her work life. She knows that God has plans to prosper her—Amen—but she's having a hard time embracing them and calling them her own. Would you pray for her, Pastor Saint?"

"Absolutely," Parker said. He clamped his eyes shut, placed his hand on the woman's shoulder, and began a prayer full of buzzwords and clichés. As he prayed more or less automatically, his mind drifted. He thought of Meredith Ludema and her emotionless eyes as she told Parker, *I really needed something from God this morning. You let me down.* He thought of Evert Carlson and Geoff Graham, two very different men risking their relationships with Parker to try and warn him that something was very wrong in his life and ministry.

Parker suddenly realized that his prayer had gone rogue. "And we thank you, Lord, that you've paid for our sins through the blood of your Son Jesus," he was saying. It was the kind of prayer his grandfather would have prayed—not exactly the vague spirituality that had expanded his influence and success. But he decided to go with it.

"We thank you that you've not only taken our sin from us by the death of your Son Jesus on the cross, but that you've given us his righteousness in exchange." The words felt right, as if he were doing penance for his countless public prayers full of doublespeak and nonsense. "Lord, we pray for poverty of spirit."

He could hear Wayne issuing whispered orders, initiating some sort of emergency backup plan. An usher was bringing out the next volunteer for prayer, and the band was beginning to play, softly at first, but slowly swelling.

"Amen and amen!" Bishop Jackson shouted when Parker took a breath. "Powerful stuff, Pastor

Saint. Powerful! Our next guest on the stage this evening would like prayer for his destiny to become reality. He says he's being unfairly targeted by some of his adversaries. We know that's the enemy at work, don't we, folks? Parker, could you do us a favor and pray *specifically* for this man's destiny this evening?" He stepped back, revealing the man for whom Parker was to pray.

Damien Bane knelt on the stage, his long black hair partially obscuring his eyes. At the sight of Parker, his lips curled up wickedly.

Parker froze, his mouth clamped shut. He feared he might vomit on regional religious television in front of a potential audience of two hundred thousand. After two seconds of silence, Bishop Jackson began to panic, thumping Parker metrically on the back in an increasingly less friendly gesture. Damien was baring his teeth, his eyes wild, a quiet laugh pulsing in his throat.

Leaning up to Wayne's ear, Parker muttered something about not feeling well and quickly exited stage left.

It was only nine thirty when Parker slumped through his front door. He may have been humiliated and well on his way to alienating himself from his peers and colleagues, but at least he would get a good night's sleep. And that was as important as anything.

He was lugging in Ketcham's file box full of photos and statements relating to the church vandalism cases. Nothing sounded better than heading directly to bed, but Parker was not willing to walk into the police station empty-handed the next morning. He would have some notes, some clues, some insights, *something*.

A little cold water applied to his face brought him back around. He put in some teeth-whitening strips and settled in at the couch. Much to his delight, the box was two-thirds empty. One look at the handwritten incident reports and dense witness statements, and Parker knew this evening would be graphics only. Pulling each photo from the box, he surveyed it with some care before setting it down on the coffee table. The graffiti images were all similar, apparently drawing from a common source of inspiration.

Without a bit of police training, Parker immediately agreed with Ketcham's assessment. The symbols on the churches were not much different from ones he'd seen hundreds of times before, spray-painted on overpasses and railroad cars. The few objects that could be interpreted as religious or occult symbols were vague and could also be interpreted a hundred other ways.

Before long the entire coffee table and a large portion of the floor around it were tiled with photos—multiple angles of seven different incidents, some inside the churches, some outside, some both. The artwork on each was complex and interconnected, composed of many symbols and pictures woven into one another, making the task of examining each individually a pedantic one.

An hour into his review, Parker had nothing. He squished the heels of his palms over his eyes and rubbed vigorously. He was fading fast and on the verge of giving up when he saw it. As his vision came back into focus, all at once a pattern became plain. The importance of the photos was not in each individual element of the defiling artwork, he realized. It was under the surface in the white space.

When viewed at a distance with eyes relaxed, each and every picture bore an unmistakable image of the dingir. In order to spot it in some of the photos, Parker had to hold them at arm's length and let his eyes go blurry; as the image came back into focus, the dingir leapt out at him. It reminded him of the computerized posters one could buy in mall kiosks in the nineties—the kind that required you to blur your vision and let the hidden picture rise to the surface.

Whom to tell first? The priests would be at his house in two minutes if he called them, but what did that gain him except more lost sleep? He toyed with phoning Ketcham right then, just to show how seriously he was taking this assign- ment. But how would he explain the significance of the dingir? He wasn't supposed to have seen the photo of Isabella Escalanté's neck.

He could reference the image on Melanie Candor's foot, but that was a bit thin. After all, he had kept his distance, to say the least. Maybe it was better to try and gain legitimate access to the crime scene photos first, and pretend to make the discovery tomorrow. He pulled his phone from his pocket and stared at it, waiting for the decision to make itself. It didn't. He sank back into the cushions for a moment of rest.

At one thirty Parker awoke on the couch. His phone was vibrating in his hand. He cleared his throat forcefully.

"Parker Saint."

"Parker, it's Detective Ketcham. Are you at home?"

"Yeah. I'm still going through these photos. I actually may have something."

"Get dressed. There's a squad car on its way to your house to pick you up. We've got another victim."

"A car? What, right now?"

"Yes, now." The detective's voice was cold and distant.

Parker tried to counter it with a friendly tone. "I'll be of more use to you after a good night's sleep, you know."

"Parker, we'd be coming for you tonight even

if you and I had never met. The only difference is me calling to warn you, and that's just a professional courtesy. You're now a person of interest to this investigation."

One Week Ago

Danny had a spot of blood on his sleeve from the night's activities. This was unacceptable. He made a point of wearing latex gloves under a pair of black leather gloves whenever he went out killing for Them—a double precaution against leaving any of himself on his victims or bringing any of his victims home on himself. The last few times he had taken to washing the leather gloves with alcohol wipes and dropping them into one of many clothing bank donation bins around town. Hiding evidence in plain sight was better than bringing it back to where he ate and slept.

Melanie Candor had put up an unexpectedly hard fight, though, and Danny had not been able to control the environment as much as he liked. He was not sure if the blood on his sleeve was his own—he'd been cut shallowly along the forearm—or the girl's. Either way, it was best to burn the shirt rather than wear it again, even though he never crossed wardrobes. The clothes he used when feeding Them were never worn in everyday activities.

Well done, Danny, he felt Them say, as he fed

the shirt into the second-story fireplace of his old house. *You are our greatest creation.* They were the only ones who called him Danny anymore. He had left that name behind several years earlier when he'd adopted a public persona more conducive to his lifestyle—a persona that gave him growing power, resources, and a small band of loyal followers.

Adopting this persona had had its intended effect, namely freeing him up from his weekly trips to churches for exorcisms. That habit had become too much of a liability. Not only was the pool of candidates growing incredibly small, but Their leaving and returning was becoming too much to bear. Especially the leaving.

The last time he'd submitted himself to an exorcism, he'd fallen unconscious for three minutes. Fearing a lawsuit, the church's pastor had freaked and called an ambulance. By the time Danny woke and pulled himself together, he could hear the sirens in the distance. He'd pushed away their concerned hands, slipped out to his car, and made his escape. That had marked the end of The Project. And it had served its purpose. Danny had all the power he was going to have. Now it was time to use it.

He emptied his pockets into a large, plastic zipper bag. The various tools of the trade, many of which he'd been carrying for a dozen years, nearly filled it. The newest item was a black fine-tip permanent marker. He had marked the girl tonight, on the bottom of her foot. What the small star-shape meant was a mystery to Danny; They had written it, not him. He did not need to know its significance. What he did know was that Melanie Candor was only the first in a series of killings. Like the last spree, but bigger.

After marking the girl, he had prepared the scene with the public and media in mind. Classic misdirection. There was a plan, a design to this seemingly random string of murders. The girl tonight was no one Danny had ever met, the reason she had died known only to Them. Danny's contribution to the design would be the climax, the big finale.

He could not wait to execute the finale.

Eighteen

Parker knew what had happened as soon as the squad car slowed in front of Paige's building. He could not let himself think it directly, but the inevitability slowly sank in like poison as the policeman escorted him silently in the front door, up the elevator, and to Paige's door, where a large X of crime-scene tape did nothing to keep Parker from rushing in as if he could get there quickly enough to prevent what had already happened.

Paige was dead.

She lay facedown in the hallway between the bedroom and the bath. Parker could not see her face, but the bright red hair was unmistakable.

"Why would he do this?" Parker asked in a whisper, sinking to his knees at her side.

She wore a white nightgown that scooped low in back, revealing the canvas of her pale skin, upon which were painted an ornate dragon and a crown in dull brownish red. The detail was impressive; someone had taken his time on this.

"The dragon and the crown," Parker said. "Both showed up on a number of the vandalized churches." It was a feeble attempt at professional detachment.

Detective Ketcham took a knee beside Parker and placed a hand on his shoulder.

"We didn't bring you here to consult," he said, his voice full of empathy. "I have some questions to ask you."

Parker couldn't take his eyes off Paige's lifeless body.

"I take it you know this woman?" Ketcham asked.

"Yes, she's my personal assistant."

"Is that all?"

"No. She's my—*was* my friend." He choked on some tears. "I should call her mother, she's—"

"We'll do that, Parker. Right now, I need you to follow me into the next room."

"Sure." As Parker stood, his eyes were drawn to the dragon's bulbous eye, painted carefully on Paige's left shoulder blade. At its center, disguised as a twinkling gleam of light, was the same intersection of four wedge-shaped lines that Parker had spotted earlier in dozens of police photos. It was unmistakable. And yet Parker felt no thrill of discovery, no chill up his spine. He had no desire to point it out to the detectives—to solve the mystery or crack the case. What he did want, for the first time in his life, was revenge.

Ketcham led him into Paige's dinette and invited him to take a chair in front of an ultrathin laptop computer.

"Mark, come here and make this thing play," Ketcham called toward the door. "Mark!"

"I've got it," Parker said, using the touchpad mouse to press the Play icon.

It was a video of Parker's house, filmed from the street with a camcorder. The picture was crisp despite the waning light.

After a few seconds of inactivity, Paige marched into the frame, up the front walk, and pressed the doorbell. She waited briefly before whacking the large knocker against the door several times with obvious annoyance. Another pause and she retrieved a key from her purse and let herself in.

There was a cut in the footage. Now night, the front of the house was illuminated by porch light and street lamps. Parker arrived, crawling out the backseat of the Jesuits' Cadillac, and made his way up the steps, appearing almost drunk for all his staggering.

Another cut. The door flew open and Paige came charging out, slamming it behind her. The videographer was zooming in on her face, focusing in just as the anger melted away and she began to sob. She pushed her hands against her face and wiped her cheeks with a hard sweep. Another wave of tears hit her and she repeated the process, then walked quickly down the street, disappearing from the frame.

Another cut brought up the side entrance of the Rivers of Life Worship Center. Paige was seen entering. Then Parker. The footage was much lower quality, but the angle caught them from the side, and both were clearly identifiable. With the final cut, the vantage point changed. The person with the camera was clearly exiting the building alongside Paige. She was again fighting tears and resting her head against the splayed fingers of her right hand as she made her way out into the parking lot.

The picture went black and the words *She knew too much* filled the screen, almost immediately replaced with *So he killed her*. Then it faded to black. Ketcham gently closed the laptop.

"This video disc was taped to the door when we got here," he said. "You have no idea how much

I hate asking you this, Parker, but . . ." He swallowed hard. "Where were you tonight from the hours of nine to eleven?"

Parker put his head down on the table. "I was at the revival from seven thirty until I went home at about eight forty-five. Thousands of people saw me."

"No one thinks you had anything to do with this."

"I know."

Ketcham was silent for nearly a minute. "I'm sorry this happened," he finally said, his voice cracking slightly. "I can't help but think that she would be alive if I hadn't involved you in all this."

"It's not your fault. I don't hold anything against you, Detective Ketcham. I just want to see that psycho thrown into prison. I hope it's awful for him."

"We've got to pin it to him first. There are no prints on this disc; we're sure of that. But I've got people who can find the digital watermark in the video, which will give us the device's serial number. If it was filmed with a cell phone, which it looks like the second half was, we can probably pinpoint the account without breaking a sweat. And we're going to visit Damien first thing in the morning—visit him hard. We'll see if he's got an alibi."

"I'm his alibi," Parker said. "He came to the

revival, came up onstage so that I could pray for him. It was broadcast in four states."

Ketcham swore. "He's pushing our face in it again. Only this time, his face is the one that will get dirty. Idiot placed himself near the victim hours before her death. If we can tie the video to a phone or a camera that he owns, we've got him at the scene of the crime at the time of the murder."

"How long will all this take?" Parker was feeling a growing panic about his own safety.

"Techno-voodoo will take a day or so. But we're not waiting for that. Like I said, we're visiting Damien this morning. I've made a few calls tonight, cashed in most of my chips." He hesitated. "There are a hundred reasons why I shouldn't tell you this, but I owe you at least this much: if you really want to see Damien humbled, be at the corner of Sibley and Clemmens at five thirty tomorrow morning."

Parker checked his watch, although they were surrounded by clocks, both digital and analog. "As in three hours from now?"

"Right. No one's getting any sleep tonight anyway." He locked eyes with Parker. "Are you going to be okay?"

"I don't know. I'm just numb."

"If you don't want to be there, I understand."

"No. I wouldn't miss this for anything."

●●●

Parker hit a convenience store for some NoDoz and nicotine gum, then whiled away a couple hours at an all-night diner sipping coffee, his principles on the subject now right out the window. He focused entirely on what lay ahead—Detective Ketcham would be serving a search warrant on Damien Bane and had all but promised that the guy would be locked up in a cell before the sun came up.

This thought pleased Parker, but more than that, he was keeping his mind on the future to avoid any thoughts of Paige. Still, they squeezed in somehow, generally in the form of pining over missed opportunities. He wanted to go back in time, tell Joshua Holton to choke on his advice, marry Paige, and settle down to pastor a small church while she built up the PR firm she had dreamed of owning one day. He wanted to live the kind of life that would never intersect with Brynn Carter, Paul Ketcham, or Damien Bane.

When the time drew near to meet the police, Parker let his GPS guide him to the intersection around the corner from Damien's house, where five unmarked SUVs were parked end to end and about twenty men were gathered around Ketcham, getting their orders. Troy was there and Corrinne too, both wearing large Kevlar vests over their clothing. Almost everyone else was decked head to foot in body armor, pads, and goggles, a variety of long guns and submachine guns in their hands. The sight almost brought a laugh from Parker, who couldn't imagine that all this would be necessary to deal with the scrawny, maladjusted man who lived inside.

Parker pulled up behind the convoy and approached the group.

"Our team comprises three units this morning," Ketcham was saying. "Major Case, Vice, and Special Response Team. My thanks to Detective Donnelly and Sergeant Coleman for helping us out. For the uninitiated, the house we're executing on belongs to one Damien Bane, alias Daniel Banner, our prime suspect in the Blackjack Murders, now numbering five.

"We've managed to secure two warrants for this carnival fun house—one for narcotics and narcotics paraphernalia and one for weapons and physical evidence related to the murders themselves. These will give us access to every nook and crack. Let's be methodical and let's do this by the book. Our goal here is to get this man off the street this morning, however we can. I've got a whole buffet of evidence testing coming back today, but I can't risk another body in the meantime.

"So anything—and I mean *anything*—that could justify an arrest, you bring it to me. Rolling papers, knives, photographs, anything. If he's got a newspaper story about the murders in his recycle bin, you bring it to me. I also want any kind of cell phone, video camera, or other electronic device. And because narcotics are involved, let's secure the premises as quickly as possible. We don't want to give anyone time to flush evidence.

"One more thing: there are at least seven people we know of living in that house, probably more in there right now, crashing for the night. Half of them are minors. I've classified this a high-risk warrant to bring in the Special Response Team, but let's show some extra restraint. Keep it tight in there. Detective Kirkpatrick and I have reviewed the files on each of the known residents and we know who's who, so follow our lead."

Corrinne approached Parker, a bulky ballistic vest in her hand.

"Do you want to come in?" she whispered.

"You're not serious."

"Unfortunately, I am. Ketcham insisted you have the option. I think he's nuts, but if you want to . . ."

"Of course I'm coming."

She secured the vest to his torso with heavy Velcro straps and ordered, "You stay behind us, you hear me?" a command she repeated at least three more times as she adjusted the vest. When she was satisfied, she put a hand on his shoulder. "I heard about your friend," she said, tilting the word *friend* up slightly, fishing for confirmation. When Parker said nothing, she added,

"I'm sorry for your loss. We'll take care of this."

Ketcham had finished his pep talk. He pulled out his sidearm and racked the slide. The *ratchet* echoed across the still street.

"Let's go," the detective said.

With silent efficiency they rounded the corner and surrounded the house in formation, so quickly that Parker had trouble keeping up.

Ketcham thumped his fist against the front door. "Police! Search warrant!" he bellowed. No sooner were the words out of his mouth than a thick-necked cop, heavy-laden with tactical gear, slammed the door off its hinges with a battering ram. They poured in.

Inside, the house was thick with odor—a potpourri of dry rot, marijuana, and head-shop incense. Several young people were roused from their slumber on couches and tattered, old recliners, groggy and disoriented. Before they knew what was happening, they were being pinned to the floor, their wrists secured behind their backs with plastic flex-cuffs.

With a single motion Ketcham ordered two of the SRT members to remain in the front room and cover the door. Parker followed Ketcham and Corrinne through an arched doorway into a large sitting room, half a dozen cops at his heels.

"You Brownshirts!"

The redhead from Parker's backyard exploded into the room and lunged at Corrinne, swinging a wooden baseball bat. She absorbed the blow into her vest, trapped his wrist, and flipped him to the ground with such ease and grace that Parker wanted to initiate a slow clap. She rolled her assailant onto his stomach and held his arms in place while another officer secured his wrists.

"Look at the tactics of the Christian Elite," he grunted through the pain, "breaking into a man's house with machine guns, beating up teenagers."

Corrinne leaned in close. "Your mistake was turning eighteen last month, Dylan, my man. You're going to do some time for me now." She thudded his head against the floor and stood at the ready. At Ketcham's command they mounted a flight of stairs to a spacious landing, where they broke formation and quickly searched the four bedrooms, netting a sparsely dressed young couple in their early twenties and a very stoned teenager who laughed uproariously at the sight of the Special Response Team in their tactical gear.

Ketcham quickly exchanged status reports with the men downstairs via radio.

"No Damien," he said. "He must be in the attic." He pulled a rope dangling from the ceiling, and a retractable ladder came down. The smell of incense increased, and an orangish glow spilled down onto the landing.

"I don't like this, Ketcham," the sergeant whispered intensely. "Poking our heads into an attic with a suspected serial killer waiting up there, undoubtedly aware of our approach. I strongly suggest a flashbang."

"Negative," he answered. "Damien'll come with us quietly. Won't he, Parker?"

"I think so. He's definitely not up there with a gun, waiting to go down in a blaze of glory. Not his MO."

"You've got to stop with the MO stuff, okay?" He turned to Sergeant Coleman. "He's right though. I'll lead. You men hang back. We wouldn't want to frighten the delicate, little man, would we?" Ketcham scaled the ladder quickly, Parker right behind him.

Parker recognized the attic immediately as the setting for Damien's many video podcasts. The walls were plastered with occult symbols and psychedelic art. Damien sat cross-legged between the low table—upon which a thick book lay open —and the *Satan Self Will* banner, a hand palming each knee. He was smiling broadly.

"Hands where I can see them, Damien," Ketcham ordered, gun trained on his chest.

"Church and state, reunited," Damien proclaimed. "How touching." He flipped a page in his book.

"Hands where I can see them!"

"They are where you can see them."

"Put them on your head!" Ketcham took two threatening steps closer to Damien. "Interlace your fingers. The last thing you want to do right now is give me cause."

Damien complied. "Be careful. This is a hundred-and-fifty-year-old book of curses. It's worth more than Parker's shoe collection."

Three SRT members ascended the ladder into the attic, swept the open room, and trained their weapons on Damien.

"Shut your mouth and don't move a muscle," Ketcham said. "Not a sneeze. Not a twitch. In just a few minutes you'll be coming with us."

"For what? Is my religion illegal now?" His smile sickened Parker.

"No, but drugs and murder are. We're executing two search warrants as we speak."

"Show them to me."

"No."

"You have to show them to me. The Supreme Court said so."

"No they didn't, and no I don't. If you think our search is illegal, you can bring that up with your attorney. For now, shut your mouth and stay where you are. I won't tell you again."

All was quiet for fifteen or twenty minutes as the search continued below and all around him. To occupy his mind, Parker studied his surroundings, looking for anything that resembled a dingir, a crown, a serpent, or anything else that might bear out the theories of the Jesuits Militant. Nothing jumped out at him.

"You won't find anything," Damien announced, breaking the silence. "I don't use drugs. And I don't need to murder people. I have more sophisticated methods of dealing with my enemies. By the way, how's that curse going, Parker? Anything bad happen yet?"

Parker said nothing.

"Very effective, curses, but impossible to prove in a court of law. And I've got a never-ending supply. Plenty to go around for the detective and his Christian Imperialist thugs."

Ketcham spoke into his radio. "Give me a status update."

Three responses came, all reporting an as-of-yet fruitless search of the main floor.

Damien laughed. "You won't find anything," he repeated. "I operate on a higher level, a metaphysical level. I create reality with my words. Just ask Ben Ludema."

With a burst of rage Ketcham wound up and kicked the table in front of Damien. Parker jumped as the antique book flew across the room, followed by the dislodged tabletop.

Ketcham instantly regained his composure. "Please be quiet, Mr. Bane."

"What is *that?*" Damien asked, his eyes wide and round, glued to what remained of the table. Built in to its skirt was a shallow shelf, upon which were lined bag after bag of white powder and a neat row of five throwing knives.

"You have the right to remain silent," Ketcham recited.

"Those aren't mine."

"You have the right to an attorney." He was twisting Damien's wrists behind his back and securing them in handcuffs.

"Those aren't mine! You corrupt, lying, hypocrite pigs! You put those there!"

The detective yanked him to his feet.

"If you cannot afford an attorney, one will be provided for you."

For just a second, Parker caught Damien's eye. And forced a smile.

Nineteen

"You have two minutes, Parker. No more," Ketcham said, his tone sharp. "I can justify this because you conducted yourself well when we first questioned the suspect. But if you go nuts on him in there, you could endanger the whole case. He could walk."

"I understand."

Ketcham touched his ID card against a plastic sensor. The door to the interrogation room unlocked with a click. He held the door for Parker, and the two men sat in the same chairs they had occupied three days earlier. Across the table from them, Damien slumped, a combination of rage and defeat.

"Are you comfortable?" Ketcham asked. "Is there anything we can get you?"

"I'm not saying one word until I have a lawyer."

"You need a lawyer to tell you if you're comfortable?"

Damien glared.

"That's okay. I'll talk. You just listen. What you'll be charged with is capital murder. I just wish Michigan still had capital punishment to go with it. You're going to spend the rest of your life in a maximum-security prison, where you'll relive the nightmare of high school for the rest of your life, only the bullies will be gang members and hardened killers. You have no idea what's waiting for you inside. I don't tell you this because I want to make a deal or get a confession —I just want you to think about it. Honestly, I want you to cry all night tonight. That's my speech. My colleague has something to tell you as well." He fixed Parker with a firm warning look before exiting the interrogation room.

Damien stared at the table, his expression empty.

"I just wanted to tell you," Parker said slowly, "that I'm not praying for you anymore. I'm praying against you." He stood, sending the chair skidding along the floor. "And for the record, I do believe in hell. And I hope you burn there." He strode to the door and smacked it once with his palm. The lock buzzed open.

Ketcham was waiting in the hall. "Let's go debrief," he said.

"I'm so sorry about your friend," Troy said, rising from the conference table in the Command Center. He shook Parker's hand, firmly but gently. "We're going to make that little ghoul pay, believe me. DNA comes back today. Tomorrow at the latest. You can rest easy tonight."

Parker flopped down into a desk chair. "But can't he just pay some bail and get out until the trial?"

"No," Ketcham answered. "This is a capital crime. Bail has to be set by a judge at the arraignment, which won't even happen until next week. And with the nature of these charges, it'll be through the roof. There's very little chance Danny will be seeing the light of day anytime soon."

Troy smiled. "Sounds like good news, don't you think, Parker?"

"Good news. That's not my area anymore."

Ketcham exchanged a look with Troy then changed the subject. "Turns out you were right about the graffiti," he said brightly. "We found almost a hundred empties down in his basement. All the right colors in the right proportions. If you want, I'll even do some chemical tests against the samples from the churches."

Parker shook his head. "It doesn't add up for me. How could Damien be smart enough to mastermind this whole thing, but dumb enough to incriminate himself like he did? I don't get it."

Ketcham stirred some clumped powder creamer into his gray coffee. "I think it goes back to what you said before, Parker: it's pure arrogance. Everyone else was an idiot but him. In the end, that took him down."

Troy adopted a fatherly tone. "It's normal to feel like this, Parker. There's always something about every case that doesn't quite fit, and it can get inside your head if you let it. You have to just accept that it's not like on TV, where everything from the bullets to the pollen traces on the victim's lapels points to one person and then a last-minute surprise witness clinches it just before the credits roll. In real life we have to settle for good enough, and we've got that here. We've got more than good enough. Even if, by some strange twist of bad luck, these murders don't stick, the drugs will put him away for ten years."

"But did he actually seem like someone who was on drugs to you?"

"No, of course not," Ketcham said. "And his urinalysis came back clean. He wasn't taking the drugs himself, he was using them to control those kids. That's even better for us—trafficking, contributing to the delinquency of a whole soccer team's worth of minors. And we can add harassment if you feel like filing a complaint."

"No. I honestly don't feel like . . . anything."

Ketcham studied him for a moment. "Detective Ellis, could you excuse us for a moment?"

"Sure thing," Troy said, patting Parker's back on the way out.

When they were alone, Ketcham said, "You can't do this, Parker."

"Do what?"

"You can't let Damien take your faith from you. This is exactly what he wants."

"He hasn't done a thing to my faith."

"I can see it happening. We all can. We all liked you the way you were, Parker. That's all I'm saying—don't get hollowed out like us."

"I'll be fine. I'm stronger than you think."

"That's just it. *I'd* say that. You're supposed to be a man of God."

"With all due respect, Detective Ketcham, you don't know me."

"Maybe not," he said, turning his attention back to the gray coffee. "But I know what it's like to lose someone close to you and to rage against God. You know I'm not exactly a churchgoer anymore, but there's a hymn that I often remember when I think I'm nearing bottom: 'A Mighty Fortress Is Our God.' You know that one?"

"Yes."

"It reminds me that I may not be stronger than everyone thinks, but the Big Guy is looking out for me. There's this one line: *Deep guile and great might are his dread arms in fight; on earth is not his equal.* It's always been a comfort to me."

"That's about the devil," Parker said.

"What? No, it's not."

"Yes, it is. *The old and evil foe now means us deadly woe. Deep guile and great might are his dread arms in fight; on earth is not his equal.* That verse is about Satan."

"Oh."

"I appreciate your concern. I really do. But I've got to go through this on my own."

"I understand. But let me tell you something. And this might help raise your spirits—"

Troy burst in the door, out of breath. "I'm sorry to interrupt, but we need you, Ketch. We need you both."

"We're busy right now, Troy."

"Trust me. You're going to want to see this."

"His name is Chad Humbert," Corrinne said, handing Ketcham a printout of the boy's particulars. Parker and the three detectives were standing at the one-way glass in the observation bay peering in to Interview Room D, where a slight teenaged boy with blond hair sat, bouncing his legs nervously at the table.

"Okay. Who is he?" Ketcham asked.

"He's our mystery man from Melanie Candor's candlelight vigil."

Ketcham squinted through the glass. "Right. Was he at the house this morning? I didn't see him."

"No, he walked in the front door ten minutes ago," Corrinne said. "Said he wanted to talk to Parker."

"Could be a sleeper cell," Troy suggested.

"What do you mean?"

"As in, Damien tells this kid to stay below the radar unless we start to close in, then he's supposed to come in here and . . ."

"And?"

"I don't know, pour rat poison in the coffee, stab one of us with a shard of glass—you tell me."

"That's just stupid," Corrinne spat.

"It's stupid," Ketcham said, "but that doesn't mean it's not true. We're not sending Parker in there alone. We're all going in."

They paraded out through the hall, into the interrogation room next door, silent and solemn. Parker and Corrinne took the chairs. Ketcham and Troy stood on either side of the table, arms folded. Chad looked up and gulped.

"This is Parker Saint," Corrinne said. "What do you want to tell him?"

"No. No cops. I said I wanted to talk to him alone. Unofficial and stuff."

Ketcham planted a palm on the table and leaned down to eye level. "No cops? Son, you just walked into a police station of your own free will."

"Never mind," Chad said. "This was a bad idea." He made a move to stand.

"Sit," Ketcham ordered. "We've been looking for you, and you're not leaving until you tell us something we want to know."

Chad backed up against the wall. "Why would you be looking for me?"

Ketcham ignored the question. "And you're going to tell us everything you know about Damien Bane or you're going to share a cell with him tonight."

Chad's face twisted as if to tighten the valve on the tears that were building up.

"I wonder," Parker said, "if you three would excuse us for just a few minutes. I'd like to talk with my new friend here alone."

Troy and Corrinne looked to Ketcham. He nodded and buzzed them out, the three filing quickly back through the hall and into the observation bay.

"Have a seat," Parker invited warmly. "I'm here to help."

Chad sank back into the chair, noticing the large mirror for what it was for the first time. "Why would they be looking for me?" he asked again.

"You were with Damien at a memorial service for a young lady earlier this week. We think he killed that girl and several others."

"How do you know I was there?"

"I think we should talk about what *you* know," Parker said, almost able to feel Ketcham's approval through the wall. "What are you doing here?"

"I heard they arrested Damien for those murders."

"Yes, we did."

"I didn't know what to do. There was always a little fear in the back of my head, like a chance that Damien had done it. But if the police think so too, that's . . ." His voice failed.

"Scary."

"Yeah. I'm scared, man! Where else could I go? What if he comes after me too? What if he sends Dylan and TJ to my mom's house?"

"How do you know Damien?"

"Ben was my best friend."

"Ben Ludema? Did you go to school together?"

"No, I go to Catholic Central. At least I did until this year. I kind of dropped out. I met Ben through War of Ages."

"What's that?"

"It's an online multiplayer video game. You play with people over the Internet. I haven't really had many friends for the past couple years, and Ben and I started hanging out. Then like three months ago, he flakes on me and starts practically living at Damien's house all the time. He thought he was in love with this girl who went to all the parties out there. Anyway, all of a sudden, if I wanted to hang with Ben, I had to hang with Damien. I hated it there."

"Was Ben into drugs?"

"Drugs? No, that was totally not Ben's thing."

"Did you ever know Damien to give drugs to his followers?"

"Followers?" His face twisted up again. "I never thought of us as followers."

"Well, what would you call all those folks? Are they all Damien's friends? Does he treat them like equals?"

"No."

"Does he give them drugs?"

"Unlikely, man. I mean, yeah, he encouraged all of us to experiment with drugs or with anything that might 'break the chains of the Christian Emperor Elite' or whatever he called it, but I never saw him give anyone anything. Especially not something expensive like drugs. He freaked out on Dylan one time because he ate his favorite cereal."

"But you never actually lived with him, correct?"

"That's right."

"And you weren't exactly part of his inner circle."

"I'm pickin' up what you're throwin' down," Chad said. "Maybe he was giving everyone drugs all the time. I don't know."

"Did you cut yourself off from Damien as soon as Ben was killed?"

"No, I went back there a couple times after Ben died, but things were getting strange."

"Strange how?"

"It's like Damien started to believe his own lies. He told everyone that Ben died because he had put a curse on him. If people were a little freaked out by him before, well, after Ben died— let's just say Damien liked having everyone scared of him like that. He started talking about spells and curses a lot more. Like, all the time."

"And you just got tired of it?"

"Pretty much. One day I realized that Ben was the only one down there who knew where I lived or my phone number or anything—and he was dead—so I just stopped going."

"Did Damien talk about knives a lot, or did you ever see him practice throwing knives at a target?"

"No. But he's really private. Who knows what he does in the attic? No one's allowed up there but him. Still, though, he hates guns and knives and weapons. He thinks they're below him. That's why he hates cops and soldiers and stuff. He says weapons are for weak people who can't speak their own reality into existence."

" 'Speak reality?' He says that?"

"Yeah." Chad laughed through his nose. "I think that's one reason he hates you so much. You guys use a lot of the same phrases. When we started playing your drinking game—no offense—he'd hear you say things that were so close to what he said, and he'd go on these long rants. It was actually kind of funny."

"Five dead bodies are funny, are they?"

Chad stopped short. "No. I'm just . . . Do you really think he did it?"

"You tell me, Chad. In your gut, do you believe Damien Bane is capable of murder?"

"Absolutely."

The door clicked open, causing Parker and Chad to flinch. Corrinne walked in.

"Parker, Paul needs to talk to you," she said. "I'll take over here."

He saw the discomfort in the boy's face. "Chad, this is Corrinne. You can trust her, okay?"

Chad nodded. "Okay."

"What I was trying to tell you," Ketcham said, leaning back against the conference table and flipping through a legal pad, "is that I called the prosecutor's office this morning and informed them that you've fulfilled your obligation to this investigation. The charges against you no longer exist." He looked up at Parker. "You don't have to remain involved any longer."

"So I don't have to. But I need to. I need to see this through to the end."

Ketcham nodded. "If you want to come back on Monday, you're more than welcome. I'm not blowing smoke when I say you've been a tremendous asset to our work here. But I want you to take some time for yourself. Starting now. Take the weekend, go to church. Get your head straight. Cry a little bit. That's an order."

"Sure." Parker glanced at the door, fearing the world outside this place where he would have to deal with his grief and uncertainty—and do it all alone.

"Corrinne wanted to talk to you before you leave. Alone. I thought that might be weird considering what just . . . happened with your friend."

Parker buried his face in his hands and managed to say, "Yeah. I'll call her tomorrow or something."

"There's one more thing," Ketcham said, leaning in toward Parker and beckoning him to do the same. He spoke quietly. "What you said earlier about the drugs. You realize those were just to get him off the street, right? We don't need those to convict."

"I'm not sure what you're saying."

"Nothing. Just that those drugs could have been there or not, right? He's still our killer either way, and I'll prove it with solid evidence."

Parker felt a wave of dizziness. "Are you telling me that you"—he dropped to a whisper—"*planted* the drugs?"

"I'm not telling you anything. But if they *were* planted, would it matter? Everybody gets what they have coming, Reverend. That's what makes my world make sense." He straightened and turned his attention back to the pad in his hand. "Now get out of here. This is the last place you should be right now, considering. I'll tell Corrinne I bounced you."

"Right. See you Monday, Detective."

Parker's hand trembled, rattling the doorknob just a bit.

Twenty

They were back in the same booth at the Ming Tree. Evert reclined in his seat, arms folded, occasionally sipping his tea. Parker had left the police station that afternoon with no idea where to go. If he thought it would do any good, he might have argued with Ketcham a little, begged to stay. The last thing he wanted right now was to be alone.

His first thought was to call Paige, an impulse that only served to magnify his sense of loneliness. He considered going back to the church, but the only two offices belonged to himself and Paige. Everything else—from video production to custodial work—was contracted out. That was another of Joshua Holton's rules: the fewer possibilities for things to get personal, the better. There was always Corrinne, but that was a whole thing with baggage and expectations. Besides, she didn't really know Parker, did she? And, in light of the conversation he'd just had with Ketcham, Parker wondered if he really knew any of them.

Never in the ten years since his father died had Parker missed him more. He knew his dad would have the solution to all this, or at least the ability to listen, offer counsel, and make Parker feel as though everything could actually turn out all right. Evert Carlson seemed the closest connection to his father, and so Parker had called him.

"You're really not going to order anything?" Parker asked.

"No, I ate lunch two hours ago."

"Then why are we here?"

"You said you wanted to break bread."

"No, I said I wanted to talk."

"Same thing. Why don't you try the sesame chicken? It's spectacular."

"I'm really not hungry." Parker closed the menu and set it down on the table.

"Well, if we're not going to eat, then let's talk."

Parker had been hoping he'd find himself naturally opening up to Evert, talking about Paige's death, his involvement with the murder investigation, his growing unease with his current ministry. But it wasn't happening.

Evert tapped the table. "I can tell you've got something on your mind, son. Just spill it."

"I just wanted to ask you something about the old church," he said.

"All right," Evert replied, nodding his approval of the subject.

"Do you remember my grandpa ever talking about a treasure? Anything about a relic, specifically a crown—something that had been placed in his care."

Evert's face paled. "Son, that's not what you really brought me here to discuss."

"Or at either of the churches you pastored in town, did you hear anything about a crown or an artifact being protected by a group of churches?"

"Parker, you've been chasing the wrong crown for years now. The dragon's crown."

The image of Paige's back filled Parker's mind, the meticulously painted image of a dragon and a crown.

"What do you mean, Evert?"

"Look at this." He propped up the menu so they both could see. "The mythical Chinese dragon was meant to be a combination of the feet of a chicken, the head of a horse, the body of a serpent, and the mouth of a lion. But that's just one culture. The Vikings also had dragon myths, as did the Native Americans, the Slavs, the Hindus, and of course the Hebrews."

Parker sighed. "What's the point?"

"You know what the dragon looks like to me? Even this Chinese dragon here? It looks like a lion crossed with a serpent. Remember what we talked about last time we got together? How

Satan operates both as a roaring lion, openly attacking and devouring his prey, and as a seductive serpent, slithering his way into your life, into the Church? Well, in the book of Revelation, Saint John calls the devil 'the dragon.' I think what he saw was the combination of Satan openly persecuting the saints and cunningly convincing us to eat the forbidden fruit. You see, he's one and the same adversary."

"That's an interesting theory."

"This isn't theory, son. This is as practical as it gets. I told you how you remind me of Saint Peter. Remember, it was Peter who called Satan a 'roaring lion.' It was Peter who came face-to-face with the mob in the Garden, and he didn't back down. How did Peter respond?"

"He drew his sword."

"Exactly. Bring on the lion, and Peter turns into a dragon slayer. But how did Satan take him down? By using his tactic from the other garden. He used a slave girl asking a simple question: 'Weren't you with Jesus too?' A cunning invitation to join the mob, to renounce the Lord. Parker, I'm afraid you're on guard against the lion, but all too eager to wear the dragon's crown."

"Look, Evert. Not today, okay?"

"All we've got is today, son."

"You know what? I've had it with you and your lectures. I don't know if I've denied the Lord like Peter did. I never intended to. All I wanted to do was save Jesus from you miserable, funeral-dirge singing, negative-minded Puritans. That's all."

"You don't save Jesus, son. Jesus saves you. I don't know what's going on in your life right now, but I can sense that you're very near to hitting your moment when the rooster crows."

Parker was feeling a growing need to get away from this man. Had he really thought that talking to Evert Carlson might bring him some comfort?

"I've got to get going, Dr. Carlson. I'll give you a call. We can break bread again sometime soon."

Evert nodded weakly. "God willing."

Darkness was falling and Father Michael was waiting. Only a small square of light remained, projected through the attic window onto the south wall, offering a dim glow as it inched its way along the pine. Michael didn't mind the darkness, though. It could be a very useful tool.

He had been over every square inch of the attic, through each drawer and behind every beam. Damien did not seem to be hiding anything that the police had overlooked. But Damien was hiding something within himself: the truth. And Michael knew how to unlock it. He would wait as long as he had to.

The Jesuit sat utterly still in the shadows, where he had been crouching for nearly two hours. Part of his training had consisted of remaining motionless in a cramped space for a full day without food, drink, or any comforts. He had learned how to slow his breathing and even his heart rate, and how to keep the blood flowing to his extremities.

When one does not move, Michael had learned, all of one's surroundings and every sensation become amplified. He felt the familiar pressure of the clerical collar against his neck and the welcome heft of the .45 hanging from his shoulder—the two constants in his life.

It was uncommon for the Jesuits Militant to wear clericals when doing this kind of work—not exactly covert. But Father Ignatius had convinced Michael otherwise. Pairing the two—the gun and the collar—tended to throw people off-balance, made them quicker to break.

The dampened sound of voices and footsteps below alerted Michael. He breathed in slowly and let it out. With a crash, the ladder disappeared into the floor below.

Someone was coming up.

"Sleep deprivation" was the first subject Parker looked up after settling into bed with his laptop. A lifelong hypochondriac, he was immediately sure he exhibited each of the dreadful effects as he made his way down the list. Doing the math, he determined that he'd slept about ten of the past ninety hours, which seemed surprisingly high. He was afraid his mind would keep him awake yet another night with thoughts of murdered friends, dragons, crowns, and crowing roosters. To be safe, he popped an Ambien and returned to bed.

As he waited for the effects to kick in, he finally had a chance to run the words "Crown of Marbella" through an Internet search engine. Only four pages of results came back, most of them reviews of hotels or ads for real estate said to be a "hidden jewel in the crown of Marbella." Near the bottom of the second page, he found a reference to the Crown in a digitized version of a two-hundred-year-old book called *Treasures Lost*. The short entry on the relic confirmed what Parker had learned about its history, although it told him nothing more.

After a few more travelogues and hotel reviews, a cluster of three results linked to a website called "The Conspiracy Forums," where the Crown was occasionally included in extensive lists of missing artifacts, but never discussed directly.

Parker gave up and decided to spend some time boning up on the proper architectural terms used in describing churches. He would know his apses from his transepts when next he met Father Ignatius, he vowed. Yes, the content was dull, but Parker had a gift for absorbing the boring. Soon, though, the effects of the Ambien were clouding his ability to focus.

On an impulse he clicked his *Favorites* tab and

brought up Damien's Internet video channel. The last thing Parker thought as he drifted off to sleep was that the medication must really be messing with his head, because he could have sworn Damien had just said, "I made bail this afternoon."

Twenty-One

Parker slept until ten forty-five Saturday morning. He awoke to hear his phone making a brilliantly irritating, juddering noise next to the bed. He could sort of recall hearing it buzz while he slept the morning away, the sound becoming incorporated into his dreams along with the pain in his abdomen, where the corner of his laptop was digging in.

With twelve hours of sleep under his belt, he found himself able to survey his present situation with an acuity he'd been lacking of late. It wasn't the kind of fresh, bright perspective he might have hoped for, but at least he had clarity, and that was enough to get him out of bed.

Paige had been present—her old smiling, sarcastic self—in most of his dreams, and the renewed realization that she was gone took its toll on Parker's mood. Still, he was in a frame of mind for looking forward. Unfortunately, he had no idea where to start.

His television program was covered for this week, but what about next? The thought of taking the pulpit anytime soon did not sit well with him, and he was sure that a few weeks off was a pretty standard response to what he'd endured. But whom did he need to call? And when? Paige had handled everything, leaving Parker painfully unprepared to deal with his own life.

His phone buzzed along the nightstand again, complaining about the three voice mails it bore. Parker snatched it up and punched the button to retrieve them.

"Parker, this is Joshua Holton."

Parker had heard that tone before: guarded, one part hostile, one part pity. It was the voice of someone calling to break up.

"I just wanted to let you know that I've instructed my staff to cancel all of your scheduled appearances on *Live Your Dreams Now.* I'm not sure why you've stopped taking my calls or what is going on with you, but I can't be bothered with this brand of negativity."

Parker sat down.

"I don't know if I should even tell you this, but I had very big plans for us, Parker. You were going to be my Midwest campus, my first franchise. I even flew up to Grand Rapids on Wednesday to check out your operation in person. But you weren't there. You're never there anymore. I see now that you're not committed to the lifestyle we promote.

"I can't be the only one to give, Parker. Like it or not, this is show business, and if you don't scratch my back a little bit, I can't scratch yours. If you want to talk about this, give me a call back Wednesday morning between nine and nine fifteen. Good-bye."

Parker pushed the nine key to save the message.

"Mr. Saint, I don't know if you'll remember me. My name is Tammy Carmichael. I'm Paige Carmichael's mother." Her voice was low and quivering, the combination of crying and years of smoking. "I know you're probably as torn up as I am about what happened, but I was wondering if you would officiate her funeral. The police haven't released her body yet, so it may be a few days before we can finalize anything, but please give me a call when you get this. Thank you so much." She left a number for her cell phone.

Parker pushed nine again.

"Reverend Saint, this is Bruce Hansen of Van Kampen Funeral Home. I'm calling in regards to Dr. Evert Carlson, who I believe is a member of your congregation. As I'm sure you are aware, Dr. Carlson died last night, and he left instructions that you were to preach his funeral service. Please give me a call back as soon as you can to let me know about your availability, as well as where the service will be held. I'd also like information you might have on any family that Dr. Carlson may have left, because I can't find anything. My number is 616-555-8148. Thank you, and I hope to hear from you soon."

Parker slumped back onto his bed, stunned. The room tipped in every direction. Now he had no choice but to deal with his own life, starting this moment. He reached out and grabbed a pen and some paper from his nightstand. He needed to write down phone numbers, make calls, plan services, relaunch his television ministry, grieve the loss of two friends, catch a serial killer, and find a sacred relic lost for hundreds of years. Best to start by making a list.

The voice-mail lady was saying, "We're sorry you are having trouble. Good-bye." Parker was about to push the button to redial when he saw the words *RIP Dad* on his daily reminders. He tossed the phone to the ground. There were more late additions to the itinerary.

1. Buy flowers
2. Visit cemetery

The day was bleak and cloudy—sad, but not the fitting kind of sad you see in outdoor funerals on television. Parker would have preferred a steady rain beating down on his dull black umbrella, or perhaps a perfectly sunny afternoon, golden beams glinting off the orange and yellow autumn leaves. Instead, he found himself standing at his father's grave in an emotionless gray, a perfect reflection of the emptiness he felt inside.

He'd eaten a tasteless lunch of poached eggs on an English muffin and stopped by the church to pick up his mail, both the stack organized by Paige before her death and the bulging bundle of unsorted letters from the two days since.

The hour's drive to Fairplains Cemetery in Greenville had given him plenty of time to try and sort things out, but the "things" were immovable in their refusal to be sorted. He wasn't sure why, but he had chosen a route to the freeway that brought him past the old Presbyterian church and new nightclub. It hadn't helped his disposition.

The flowers were ugly, meant to be an afterthought impulse item—bleached, dyed, and wrapped carelessly in what looked like a botanical Elizabethan collar—picked up from an overpriced wine shop near Parker's house. In years past Paige had purchased the bouquet: a dozen white tulips, his father's favorite flower, the kind he had bought for Parker's mother every year on their anniversary.

Paige had always reminded Parker a few days in advance of the anniversary of his father's death. She always accompanied him to the cemetery, where she would stand respectfully behind him and place her hand on his back when he wept.

Joshua Holton had made it clear that men like himself and Parker had to exude an air of success and happiness at all times. Paige was the only one allowed to see Parker at his lowest. He had often wondered if that made her his only friend.

He thought again about the expectations that he would preach Paige's and Dr. Carlson's funerals. He couldn't imagine what he might say to do them justice or bring hope to the people mourning the young woman or the old man. He thought about Meredith Ludema's rebuke and how it—apart from all the other criticisms he'd received—stuck with him so stubbornly. He thought about his television slot. He could not imagine getting back up in front of crowds of people next week. Or the week after. Or ever.

His phone rang. The number belonged to Detective Ketcham.

"Parker Saint."

"Parker, where are you?" The detective's voice was edgy, almost panicked.

"I'm in Greenville. At a cemetery."

"Is there somewhere to sit down?"

"There are grave markers, but I'd rather not. What's going on?"

"I've got some good news and some very disturbing news."

"Give me the disturbing news first, I guess."

"No. The good news is that I just got DNA

analyses back from three different crime scenes. Damien Bane is a match for all three."

Parker leaned against, then sat, on his father's headstone. "What's the very disturbing news?"

"Our boy got himself a lawyer yesterday afternoon, who leaned on the prosecutor until she decided not to pursue the murder charge at this time."

"I'm sorry. What?"

"I was afraid this might happen. I can't blame her. The knives were circumstantial at best."

"But now we have the DNA, right? So it's back on."

"Yes, but you have to understand—the drugs were just barely under the legal limit for trafficking. He's only being charged with possession."

"Please don't tell me what I think you're going to tell me."

"He made bail yesterday. We don't know where he is."

In that moment it dawned on Parker that he was sitting in the middle of a deserted cemetery while the sky grew darker by the minute.

"Can't you arrest him again? Can't you put out an ABP thing?"

"We have an APB out on him now, but he's not at home, and he hasn't shown up on the grid yet. The good news is that his little army of delinquents has been bounced from the place. It was a condition of Damien's bail that he have no contact with non-family members under the age of twenty. We're camping out there. He shows up, we'll grab him."

Parker's hands were shaking. "I know you told me to enjoy myself this weekend, but I'd really like to come back in to police headquarters."

"That's not a good idea. There's another variable here, Parker. I can't discuss it on the phone. What are you, about an hour from home?"

"About that, yeah."

"I'll meet you at your house. In the meantime, be careful. Lock your car doors, keep an eye on the rearview mirror, and for God's sake, get out of the stupid cemetery."

Parker hated ending the conversation. He knew having a policeman on the other end of a phone call did nothing to make him safer, but a false sense of security was better than none.

It was a bit of a hike back to his car, during which Parker got the rain he had been wishing for. The wind picked up, and every shadow, every groaning tree made Parker reel in horror, certain he'd see Damien and his henchmen descending.

He castigated himself. Why had he tagged along on the raid? He had only ensured that Damien would want revenge. He could have faded into the background. He could have taken the hint and backed off when the cat went up in flames. Now it was too late.

He finally reached his car, anxious to get inside and lock the doors, but also apprehensive, as the heavy rain and fogged-up windows made it impossible to see inside. He couldn't stop thinking about the urban legend where the ax murderer lies down in the backseat of the car, waiting for his chance to behead the unsuspecting driver. Parker hung back and tried to squint through the rain and condensation.

Finally the fear of remaining in the open overwhelmed him, and he sprinted to the car, unlocked it, and threw himself into the front seat. He arched his back. No one lying down on the floorboards. No one crouched behind the passenger seat. So far, so good.

He brought the car to life and punched the gas. He longed to hear the tires squeal as he pulled away, but that would have required pavement. Instead they simply spun, slinging mud up in the air. In the distance he saw two headlights approaching. His pulse quickened.

He put the car in reverse and eased on the accelerator. A little movement. He quickly shifted back into drive and slowly pushed down the gas pedal. A bit more. The headlights were drawing closer. Back into reverse. Then drive. Reverse. Then drive.

The oncoming headlights were illuminating the inside of Parker's car. He wished he had heeded Ketcham's advice and gotten a gun, although he was sure he'd never have the nerve to fire it if he had.

The other car zipped by just as Parker cleared the mud and found traction on the gravel road. He would speed all the way home, he decided. And if he got pulled over, he would demand a police escort.

It was then he realized he hadn't checked the trunk.

Parker had thought of the phrase "white knuckling" as a figure of speech until tonight. His palms were sweating, his ears finely tuned to any movement at all from behind.

The rear console of his car could flip down in the backseat, revealing a small door between the trunk and the car proper—a useful feature when transporting lumber, but terrifying at the moment. He wasn't sure if the opening would accommodate a man, but he thought it more likely than not.

Ten minutes into the trip, he knew it wasn't his imagination—something was moving back there. He couldn't be sure, but it sounded like someone was slamming a fist into the little door separating the trunk from the car proper. He remembered that it opened with the car door key, but it was a flimsy mechanism, and he guessed a well-placed kick would dislodge it. He considered bailing, fleeing the car on foot, but opted instead to accelerate more.

Just forty-two minutes after leaving the cemetery, Parker turned onto his street. The rain had quit and the sun was beginning to set. On any other night it would be breathtakingly beautiful, but Parker had bigger things on his mind. What if Ketcham wasn't waiting for him, he wondered. After all, the detective wasn't expecting him for almost another twenty minutes. If his options came down to staying in the car or going into his house alone, he wasn't sure which he'd rather avoid.

As he neared home Parker saw that Ketcham's car was not in the driveway. But the Jesuits' Cadillac was. He could see a man sitting behind the wheel, probably Michael. Parker's car screeched to a stop at the curb and Parker sprang out onto the wet pavement, slipping and sliding his way to Father Michael's driver-side door.

He pounded on the window. "I think there's someone in my trunk!" he practically yelled. "I can hear him."

Michael emerged from the car, his hand bringing forth the bulky handgun from under his arm. "Do you have a remote for the trunk?"

"Yeah."

"Why didn't you just get going, like, ninety and pop it open?"

"I didn't think of that."

The priest positioned himself behind Parker's car, securing a small flashlight under the muzzle of the gun. "Well, pop it open now."

Parker pressed the release, and the trunk lid slowly opened about a foot. Michael yanked it the rest of the way and shined the light in. "Oh my," he said. "I think I found your 'perp.' " He reached into the trunk and pulled out a family-sized can of Massachusetts Bay clam chowder. "This must have been rolling around in there."

"I'm sure I'll feel stupid later. For now, you want to come inside and make sure there's no one skulking around?"

"Right. Might be some oyster crackers waiting to jump out of the cupboard."

Michael gave the house a quick sweep while Parker filled him in on the events of the previous day.

"She was more than your assistant, wasn't she?" he asked as they entered the living room.

"Yes."

"I'm so sorry for your loss."

The floor and coffee table were still covered with photographs of the church graffiti, and with very little prompting Michael was able to see the dingir in each.

"I was about to call you about that when I got word about Paige," Parker said. "It's looking like Damien really is the man we're after."

"That's just it, Parker. I came here tonight to tell you he's not."

"Sorry?"

"I spoke with him last night. Guy's an arrogant

jerk, but he's never killed anyone. Believe me. He's never been possessed either. He likes to talk about it, but he knows he's just talking."

"Well, someone killed five people."

"Yeah, someone did. But we don't believe it was anyone in that house. Ignatius and I followed up with a couple of Damien's flunkies this morning. They don't know anything about the occult that they didn't learn from bad TV and Jack Chick comics. The only main player we didn't get to talk to was Raggedy Andy from the other night. He's still in custody—apparently he took a swing at a cop."

"Dylan Eiler," Parker said. "He doesn't strike me as a criminal mastermind either."

"Agreed."

"Did you hurt Damien?" Parker asked, hopeful.

"I didn't lay a finger on him. I've never seen anyone flip so quickly. What a pansy."

"Did you scare him?"

"You have to remember, Parker, no one expects the Spanish Inquisition. Let's just say I'm afraid I may have reinforced some of his negative ideas about Christian clergy."

Parker was having trouble swallowing this new development. "What about the DNA?"

"I don't know. I suppose there are ways around that."

"But what about the video footage? Why would he have gone to Melanie Candor's candlelight service if he had nothing to do with it?"

"Oh, I forgot to tell you. We found that connection yesterday. They both spent time in the same foster home, overlapped by about a year. He was seventeen, she was fifteen. Seems they were still keeping in touch. In fact, she called Damien on his cell phone ten days before she died. It was his birthday."

"But the police went through her cell records. How could they miss something like that?"

"Could all be in the timing. If they went through her phone bill with a fine-toothed comb before Damien was even a suspect, they might not bother to look at it again. Believe me, Parker, the guy's not happening."

"So where does that leave us?"

"I don't know about you, but it leaves *us* leaving. We can't justify hanging around indefinitely. Father Ignatius has already flown back to Madrid to start the paperwork."

"Ignatius is gone?"

"Yeah, he left this morning."

"But you haven't solved anything. You didn't find the Crown. You didn't catch the killer. What have you accomplished here?"

"I told you, Parker, this kind of thing usually goes unsolved. We don't get many wins in this game."

Parker thought of Isabella Escalanté, Melanie Candor, and Father Ignatius's diamond-shaped throwing knife. Then he thought of Paige. Yet another lapsed Catholic was dead, and the militant priest with the medieval agenda was conveniently out of the country. Parker could only guess how much Ignatius hated the thought of a group of Protestant clergy keeping a sacred relic out of Holy Mother Church's hands.

"We'd love to stay until we've got it all figured out," Michael was saying, "but this whole thing has been one big web of dead-ends. We were all a little tentative about this investigation from the start, and there are cases on backlog with a lot more solid footing."

"Are you leaving right away?"

"No, we have a few loose ends to tie up. There are a few churches I'd like to revisit, and I've got a list for Father Xavier to check out too."

"Let me know when . . . you know . . ."

"Don't worry. I won't leave without saying good-bye."

The living room was briefly illuminated by a swash of headlights as a car pulled in to the driveway.

"I better go," Michael said. "Watch your back."

"Yes, that's comforting. Thank you." He walked Father Michael to the door and followed him out, throwing the dead bolt behind him. Ketcham was lighting a cigar behind the wheel. Parker knocked on his window, which the detective had to manually crank down.

"Who's that?" the detective asked, poking a thumb at Michael's Cadillac disappearing down the street.

"Just a colleague offering his condolences about Paige. So where are we going? A safe house or something? Should I pack a bag?"

"No, you won't need a bag. Get in."

"Can you tell me what's going on first?"

"Brynn Carter has been murdered," he said solemnly. "You need to come with me."

Five Days Ago

Danny was staring intently into the mirror, trying to get out of character before he went out hunting. He had stopped thinking of it as getting *into* character when he adopted a daytime persona not his own. Although he had just finished applying a good deal of black makeup around his eyes, there was no doubt that the true mask was the one he wore day after day, the only one most people knew.

He surveyed his reflection, letting Them boil behind his eyes. You never get a second chance to make a good first impression, they say, and Danny wanted to inspire terror, panic, and a sense of pure hopelessness tonight. He was working on his masterpiece, he had come to realize, but he had gotten off to a rocky start.

Tonight he would kill Isabella Escalanté. He

would also, as it turned out, kill her boyfriend. He was prepared for this possibility, having studied them both, mapped out their building, and run through every conceivable contingency. The boyfriend had a gun, but so did Danny—a 9 mm Beretta, which he felt tugging slightly at his waistband on the small of his back. The gun was plan D, and in the end Danny would not need it. He never did.

He retrieved the black wig from a hatbox on his dresser and placed it carefully over his scalp, securing it in five different places. He let the long, wavy locks fall down in front of his eyes, completing the effect. Keeping his hair long had been essential to The Project, helping him tap into the fundamentalist assumption that the unkempt and uncouth were more likely to be in league with the Prince of Darkness. But regulations were regulations, and the police academy required a close-cropped, respectable look.

Back when he was hitting a church every weekend, Danny loved the way it felt walking into a sanctuary, his ratty bangs obscuring his eyes, waiting for someone to glance through the tangles and see Them inside. The gasps of good, churchgoing folks were delicious. He had taken this show on the road with him everywhere, frightening checkout clerks, meter maids, and children. He would tell them with his eyes that he owned them, and in that moment they would know that he was capable of doing horrific things.

But that was all before the academy, before the act, before Danny was called Officer, and then Detective, Daniel Paul Ketcham.

Twenty-Two

The sign read Walter Hill Junior High.

Crawling with vines, the imposing Gothic revival would have been more at home on an Ivy League university campus than it was here in the inner city. The exterior was poorly lit with a smattering of mercury vapor lamps.

"What are we doing at a school?" Parker asked. He had said nothing during the fifteen-minute drive from his house, unable to process the news of Brynn's murder for all the questions crowding his thoughts. What did this mean to the now-closed case against him? What had caused Damien to single him out in the first place? What was Parker to make of Father Michael's latest visit? And why did he feel so incredibly unsafe right now, even with Detective Ketcham at his side?

"I need to show you something. Come on." Ketcham parked at the main entrance, and Parker followed him uneasily up the crumbling concrete walk to the door.

"Is this place even used anymore?" he asked.

"No, it's one of a growing number of abandoned schools. Sad really. They close the campuses in the worst neighborhoods first. Sure, they've got ways of justifying it, but we know it isn't right, don't we?" His voice changed just a bit, bringing a prickle of adrenaline up Parker's spine. "Then again, maybe these folks just need to grab on to their destinies and start *speaking reality.*"

"Why do you have a key?"

"It's city property. We use the gymnasium for storage." He unlocked the door and motioned for Parker to enter.

Ketcham pulled a small LED flashlight from his pocket and led the way down a long, oppressively dark hallway lined with lockers. Parker stepped twice on the heel of the detective's shoe, as he was trying to stay less than a step behind, feeling like he might be snatched at any moment and dragged off into some forgotten corner of the building. He suddenly remembered his cell phone and powered it on, holding the backlit screen up like a torch, to almost no effect.

"I'm still not sure why we're here," Parker said. "Is it a secret or something?"

"I told you. I have some evidence to show you. Now shut up and follow me. I shouldn't even be doing this."

"Can't we turn on a light?"

"There's no electricity, Parker. Can't afford it. That's the whole point."

They descended a flight of stairs into the basement, and Parker tried to get even closer to Ketcham. The small arc from the flashlight was no comfort at all, as a combination of claustrophobia, nyctophobia, and a not-unfounded fear of demonized serial killers had Parker nearer than he'd ever been to a panic attack.

"It's right in here," Ketcham said. "Hold on, I've got a better light."

A dappled orange radiance filled the corridor as Ketcham switched on a small battery-powered lantern. Parker's eyes raced to adjust.

"This is the big breakthrough we've been looking for, Saint," he said. Something was definitely different about the detective's voice, giving Parker pause. "What do you think?"

Parker's eyes—now in tune with the light—followed Ketcham's thin finger as it slowly uncurled toward the far wall. There, badly beaten and duct-taped to a plastic classroom chair, was Damien Bane, his mouth taped shut and his eyes frozen wide in terror.

Parker looked back toward the stairs twice, wanting to indulge his initial impulse to flee, but the unrelenting darkness behind him made that impossible.

"What is he doing here?" he asked.

"He's here to kill you. Don't you get it?"

"No. No, he shouldn't be here. We shouldn't be here." Parker glanced at Damien, reading the unmistakable fear on his face. It was clear that he'd been worked over quite a bit, between his swollen right eye and the crisscrossing lines of dried blood emanating from his scalp.

"I thought you'd be grateful," Ketcham said. "He killed your girlfriend. He stalked you, killed your accuser, and then he lured you here and finished you off."

"Thank God you got to him in time."

Ketcham shook his head slowly. "But we didn't, Saint. Sadly, we got here just a moment too late to save the good pastor's life." He crossed himself, mockingly. "Fortunately, though, we were able to end the killing spree and neutralize the murderer. We're going to be honest. This couldn't be better for our career."

"You're messing with me, right? This isn't very funny." He shouted into the darkness, "Corrinne! Troy! Are you guys back there? Come on out." The web of phobias was fusing into one paralyzing cord, wrapping ever tighter around Parker. Behind his back he was trying to dial 911.

"No one else is down here, Parker. It's just you and Damien. And us. And we think you'll find that there's no cell phone signal either."

The detective's body language had changed as well. His upright posture and uptight presence had melted away, leaving Parker with the impression that he was standing in the presence of someone else entirely—a complete stranger.

"Give us the phone, Saint."

As Parker handed it over, a horrible, inescapable truth dawned on him. "You killed them, didn't you?" he said. "You killed them all."

"That's not what the paper will say tomorrow. The official story will identify the late Damien Bane as the killer. And who would question the official story? Killer acquired, evidence piling up. And just look at this guy." He laughed, a deep, growling gurgle of a laugh. "It's almost like he was auditioning for the role of Serial Killer #3. The city will breathe a sigh of relief and try to put the whole unpleasant matter out of mind."

Everything was clicking at once for Parker. The DNA evidence, Damien's knowing about the pentagram, the hidden drugs and knives. It all made sense.

"You picked Damien as your scapegoat from the beginning, didn't you? And Officer Dykstra was your backup in case you couldn't make the murders stick."

Ketcham took a step closer. "You've got it all wrong. *You* were our backup. Dykstra was just a coincidence." He smiled coldly. "We always cover our tracks. Your god is a god of order. Well, we like order too."

"Why do you keep saying *we?*" Parker asked, knowing the answer and fearing it more than he'd ever feared anything before.

The smile broadened. "Why do you think?"

Parker whimpered involuntarily.

"Perhaps a better question," he continued, "would be why would a celebrated police investigator employ a clueless televangelist as an expert consultant in a series of murders?"

"Because I was part of your plan from the beginning too," Parker said. He was feeling drowsy, resigned, the fight-or-flight effects of adrenaline having more or less worn off.

"That's right. In fact, you should be proud. You were the inspiration for all of this. You're going to love this, Saint. We were standing in line behind you at the airport that day. We saw you throw your little fit when you didn't get your way. And we got to thinking . . . what could be better than a faithless hypocrite of a preacher right in the middle of our masterpiece? We knew there was no danger of you recognizing us, since you looked no one in the eye that day—so wrapped up in your own glory and fame. You have more in common with us than you'll ever know."

"You've been playing me from the beginning."

Ketcham snickered. "Do you really think *I'm* the one who's been playing Saint all this time?"

Parker swallowed hard. "Is Brynn really dead?"

"Look behind you," Ketcham growled.

Despite issuing himself silent orders to the contrary, Parker found his head craning back, following the dim beam of the flashlight. There, in an open closet, he saw Brynn Carter, her throat cut and her face decorated with occult symbols painted in blood.

"Someone had to shut her up. Right, Saint? I just saved you the trouble. Although, to be fair, she never really wanted to press charges. At least not when we first suggested it. But everyone has their breaking point. Brynn's was her sister. And her sister's meth habit. In the end she decided she'd rather send you to jail than see her sister get a third strike and spend twenty-five years in prison."

A dead sort of rage began to build up in Parker. "You killed Paige," he said, more accusation than observation.

"No, no. Haven't you been listening? Damien killed Paige. Then he killed you. Then we killed Damien. It really is tragic—losing a local treasure like Parker Saint. We're just thankful that justice was done at the end of the day. And in the meantime, of course, we got to slay some lambs, burn some churches, have some fun."

Parker did not remember beginning to cry, although his cheeks were streaked with tears. His mind was filling up with things he wanted to say, but "Why?" was all he could get out.

"*Why?* Because I'm a wolf, Parker. I'm a wolf and you're a little lamb, waiting to be slaughtered."

"But you're a policeman. A sheepdog, remember?"

"We play the part well, don't we? You asked how we deal with all the blood and the carnage, the chaos and the evil? The answer is that we *savor* it. We cherish every last morsel. Like the other morning. You should not have left the morgue in such a hurry. You missed the best part. We took that girl apart. Piece by piece. In that sterile medical environment, the good doctor and I finished the job begun in her apartment. And this Monday morning at nine—at my strong recommendation—we'll be having a look inside your precious Paige."

Rage flashed to the surface, and no one was more surprised than Parker when he squeezed his right hand into a tight fist and smashed it into Ketcham's ear. The blow seemed to catch the detective off guard, so Parker tried to follow it up with a haymaker, putting everything he had—all his fear, all his rage, all his confusion—into the punch.

He was stopped midswing and felt Ketcham's grip tighten around his wrist, locking his joint and sending a flare of pain from his elbow to his shoulder. His own inertia brought him down—or rather, seemed to bring the concrete slamming up to meet him. A wave of nausea came over him. The more he struggled, the more it hurt. Finally he went limp.

"One more outburst like that and we'll have to cuff you." Ketcham tapped his coat pocket. "We brought a second pair for you, just in case. But we'd rather not deviate from the script this late in the game. It just wouldn't look right."

Parker was disoriented, his fingers unable to grip the gritty cement floor. With great effort he pulled himself to his knees and gazed up at Ketcham, now pulling a black knife with a diamond-shaped blade from the folds of his coat.

"Recognize this, Saint? You've already held the weapon that killed Brynn. And Melanie and Ben. And Isabella and her boyfriend. And Paige. How easily we could have taken your good name from you. But we'll settle for taking your life."

He held the knife up, studying the blade in the dim light. "We've learned that if you put evidence in plain sight, slap a numbered tag on it, no one gives it a second thought.

"It's the same knife we used on two of the prostitutes a few years ago. But that's ancient history. The real question on everyone's mind right now is, what should we paint on your body? Any requests? Don't be afraid to think big. I can take my time with you." He tipped his head toward the man taped to the chair. "What do you think, Legion?"

Damien jerked in his seat and tried to swear.

"How about an ankh?" Ketcham asked. "Do you know what an ankh is, Parker? Hmm? Maybe you want to sneak out a minute and look it up on your smartphone." He wound up and hurled Parker's phone at the wall, smashing it into a dozen pieces. "Whoops. It looks like Damien did away with your phone so you couldn't call for help while he was carving you up. Good thinking, Damien.

"The ankh is out, then. Maybe something simpler, like that barbed wire circle—the one that death metal band stamps on all their merchandise. That would really resonate with the public, wouldn't it? I can hear the preachers now: 'Burn all your records!'" He threw his head back and indulged an enthusiastic laugh. "And Lee here and his kind will take the brunt of the backlash," he said, pointing back at Damien. "The sheep only see one side of evil, Parker. The obvious side. They'll rail all day against the diversion while they stand knee-deep in murky water, oblivious to the serpents slithering around their legs."

"Detective Ketcham, please. I know you don't really want to do this."

"Ketcham doesn't want anything. You know why? Because he doesn't exist. You can call me Danny."

Another fearful realization lighted on Parker, even as he tried to bat it away. "It was you. You're the one Dr. Graham told me about. The one from Broken Bondage Ministries."

"Ah, yes. Geoffrey. We were afraid he recognized us at the church that day. But we noticed him too late to back out. These things are delicate. Once you light the fuse, it can't be unlit. And, of course, it's for the best." He pointed to his head with two fingers. "Got to keep it swept clean."

Somehow, in the midst of all the fear, an idea was forming in Parker's mind. It was a long shot, but he knew he had to run with it now before he lost his nerve. Drawing himself up on one knee, he pointed his hand at Danny like a superhero shooting a laser beam.

"In the name of Jesus, I cast you out!" he shouted with all the authority he could fake.

The knife clattered to the ground and Danny doubled over, hugging himself violently around the abdomen. He wheezed and whined in an unnerving high squeal, his eyes rolling back in their sockets. Parker rushed to his side and shoved a hand up into his coat, searching for the 9 mm pistol that he'd seen there so often, hanging under the detective's left arm. After a few incredibly long seconds of grasping, he felt the cold metal of the handle on his fingers—and the hot flesh of Danny's hand around his forearm, squeezing, crushing, twisting, bursting blood vessels.

Danny's pitiful wheeze morphed into a dark, rhythmic laugh as he pulled Parker in close—an inch from his face. Parker could smell the stale cigar smoke and mint Binaca on his breath.

"Nice try, Parker. Here's the problem. Jesus, I know. And I know Geoffrey. But who are you supposed to be?" He smashed his knuckles into the bridge of Parker's nose, spattering blood.

Parker crumpled to the ground and went fetal, using his forearms to protect his head from the rain of blows. Danny kicked and stomped, a stream of curses and gutturals coming from the back of his throat.

Parker was on the verge of blacking out when the beating suddenly stopped.

"Is this what you were after?" Danny asked, drawing the handgun and pressing the barrel against Parker's temple. He cocked the gun.

Parker squeezed his eyes shut and thought for the first time in recent memory about what would happen when he died. Would he see his father and mother and Evert and Paige? Would he hear the words he'd recited at so many funerals, "Well done, my good and faithful servant. Enter into your rest"? Had he been faithful at all?

Danny eased the hammer back into place. "No such luck, Saint," he said, standing. "You see, the Blackjack Killer cuts people's throats. That's what he does." He slammed his foot into Parker's abdomen again.

Parker had never really been hit before tonight. Tears overflowed his eyes, and the pain was more than he could handle. He pushed his forehead to the ground and rolled onto his knees. "Oh, God . . ."

"*God?* That tired old song again?" Danny's laugh scooped up to a high giggle. "All right, we'll give you another shot, Saint. You go ahead and have your little meeting with God. See if he'll come on down here and save you."

Parker buried his face in his hands and prayed silently. For the first time in years, it was not for the benefit of an audience. *Lord, I know I can't resist the devil without submitting to you. I confess that I've been preaching a gospel with no scandal—a gospel with no blood, no substitution, a gold cross with no one dying on it.*

"Yesssss," Danny hissed. "Pray."

I know I've been trying to save you, when you are the one who seeks and saves the lost. I confess that I am wretched, pitiful, poor, blind, and naked. He was pouring his heart out for the first time in almost a decade, having replaced his nightly time of prayer with the rather neutral habit of Internet research.

"Tell him, Parker. Tell him how he let you down. What a pathetic shepherd. Just when the widdle wamb needed some help, he was nowhere to be found. Tell him he lost."

I submit to you. Not a little at a time when it's convenient, but everything. Now.

"Time's up," Danny said. "Time to take you apart." He scooped the knife up from the concrete.

Parker stood quickly, feeling taller than he'd been before, the pain of the beating leaving his body all at once. Everything in the room looked different somehow: Damien taped to the chair, Brynn's body in the closet, Danny standing there holding a knife in one hand and a gun in the other, the smile quickly fading from his face. Everything was smaller.

"Be quiet," Parker commanded, "and come out of him."

Danny convulsed, stumbling backward and falling hard onto the concrete steps. The gun clattered up the stairs behind him. He arched his back, his mouth gaping and foaming. A hideous sucking sound filled the room.

Parker quickly decided that his best chance of escape lay in shifting the odds. Gauging and analyzing, he rushed over to Damien, trying to determine the quickest way to free him from his bonds. What he saw was not encouraging.

Damien's ankles were taped to the two front metal legs of the chair; his torso was wrapped in duct tape many times over, holding him to the backrest; and his wrists poked out the back of the chair through a square hole in the green plastic, shackled together by a pair of metal police handcuffs.

Parker forced his eyes back toward the steps. Danny's violent jerking had subsided; he lay on the stairs, quivering softly, his eyes closed tight. Parker knew that he needed both the keys to the handcuffs and the knife to cut Damien's bonds. But how long would this condition last? When he came to, would Ketcham remember where he was, what was happening?

Walking tentatively toward the stairwell, the first thing Parker saw was the small flashlight rolling along. He grabbed it and clicked on the beam, shining it about the floor, searching for the knife.

Danny's eyes remained closed, his breath shallow, his right hand weakly grasping the railing and his left pinned beneath his body. Parker reached gingerly into the pocket of the trench coat, immediately feeling a cold metal ring with several keys attached. He pulled, but something was caught on them. He yanked harder and found himself holding a collection of keys and a pair of handcuffs.

Recalling every cop show he'd ever seen, Parker slapped one of the cuffs against Danny's wrist with a flick of his own. It surprised him by swinging closed and *ratcheting* shut. Parker secured the other cuff to the handrail, then tightened both.

That's when he saw Danny's eyes, now wide open, boring into him. He was trying to move, trying to wrench his left hand from underneath him. He hadn't dropped the knife, Parker thought. Parker leapt back from the steps just as the blade came swinging from underneath him. Danny was clearly disoriented, rattling the handcuffs and swinging wildly with the knife, back and forth across the stairway.

Parker grabbed the back of the plastic chair and

dragged Damien away—away from Danny, away from the stairs, and through a doorway, deeper into the dragon's lair. He needed somewhere to untape Damien and remove the handcuffs. He needed a phone, another set of stairs, an escape plan. Most of all, he needed to put as much distance between them and Danny as possible.

He moved along quickly, considering the hundred-and-sixty-pound load he was dragging behind him. Before long they'd covered a great deal of ground, having taken two turns, and Parker was feeling a little safer. As he dragged his one-time enemy, he was looking for exit signs—the glowing red kind that point the way out. Not surprisingly, there were none lighting up the basement of the abandoned school, but he kept looking, shining his weak stream of light into every corner, sweeping it above every doorway.

A noise from behind them caused Parker to freeze. He forgot to breathe for a moment, listening for the sound of footsteps. Instead, he heard the loud *clung* again. And again. It was distant, but hard to say how distant. Was it coming from the stairway, or had Danny managed to free himself? Parker felt a paralyzing fear grip him.

Damien was trying to say something through the tape on his mouth. He grimaced as Parker removed it, taking a good portion of his black goatee with it.

"That's far enough," he said. "Now help me get loose."

"You're right. There has to be another stairway somewhere, but I can't drag you up like this. Let's do it in here."

Parker opened a heavy door bearing a sign that read East Wing Boilers. He dragged Damien awkwardly through the doorway, somehow certain that Danny was indeed loose and lucid and would soon be bringing a legion of evil spirits through that very door.

Twenty-Three

It took Parker longer than anticipated to remove the duct tape. Danny had secured Damien from his chest down to his lap, crisscrossing the heavy tape back over itself many times. Removing it required a finesse Parker lacked at the moment. Strips of tape kept getting tangled and stuck.

The room—about fifteen by twenty-five feet— was feebly lit by the flashlight, now secured by a scrap of discarded tape to the pull chain over- head. Parker was cursing himself all the while for having removed the gag from Damien, who seemed to have been born without the ability to whisper.

"What happened back there?" Damien asked,

having already posed the question in different forms half a dozen times.

"I told you. Now be quiet."

"You really expect me to believe that?"

"At the moment I don't care what you believe. We can discuss it over goat's blood and burnt cat tomorrow if you like. Right now I just want to make sure we live to actually *see* tomorrow, okay? Let me concentrate."

The boiler room was cold; they could see their breath. Damien was bouncing his knees to keep warm, which did not help the process of freeing him.

"But why didn't it work the first time?" he asked again. "What happened there?"

"Do you know what a scapegoat is?"

Damien said nothing.

"I don't suppose you have a phone with you," Parker said, pulling off another three loops of tape. He could see more of Damien's black T-shirt than was obscured by tape, and soon he'd be able to access his pants pockets.

"He took it from me. Of course."

"Dang it."

"Dang it?" Damien craned his head back to glare at Parker. "Forgive me, but I don't think we've got a *dang it* or *gosh phooey* type situation here. Who would you call anyway? The police?"

"Yes, the police."

"Do you really think we can trust the police

right now? Don't you think your crazy detective friend has already called this in? *Officer down,* and all that? We'd go down in a hail of bullets."

"I know a detective who wouldn't betray us. She's a good person."

"You probably thought you knew this Ketcham character too, didn't you?"

Parker didn't answer. He was kneeling behind the chair, nearly done removing the last few layers of tape. "Then I'd call my friend Father Michael. That's who I'd call."

Damien wrenched backward and glared at Parker again. "You mean that psychopath priest who attacked my guys and broke in to my house yesterday? That Christian Imperialist thug with the gun?"

"That's the guy. I think he'd make short work of Ketcham. But his number's in my phone. And my phone is in a million pieces in the other room."

The last loop of tape came free, and Damien tipped forward onto the ground, breaking the fall with his right cheek. He groaned loudly.

"Are you okay?"

"I'm spectacular, Parker. Enjoying my *destiny*." He slumped sideways and stared at the ceiling. "I'm wanted for murder, stuck in a dark, dank, cramped room with my least favorite person on earth while a murderer roams the halls outside. I haven't been able to feel my fingers in three hours. Oh, and I can't even defend myself because my hands are cuffed behind my back."

"I can help you with the last thing," Parker said, reaching into his pocket. "I got the keys."

"If that's a joke . . ."

Parker held them up with a grin. "Have I become one of your favorite people yet?"

Damien's face fell. "You think *those* are the handcuff keys?"

"They were in Ketcham's pocket with his extra cuffs. It's got to be one of these. Hang on." He flipped through a car, ignition, house key, plus several smaller, less easily identified keys. "Turn around a minute."

Damien complied, but shook his head. "You really think cops keep their handcuff keys on a Redwings keychain in their coat pockets?"

It was immediately clear that none of the keys came close to fitting. "I didn't have a whole lot of time to think it through. I found some keys and I grabbed them. Guess you're stuck."

"Help me sit down."

Parker grasped him by both shoulders and directed him toward the chair.

"No, not there—on the ground." Once seated, Damien rolled onto his back. "Now help me get my feet under here."

"Let's take your shoes off first," Parker suggested.

Once the large black boots were set aside, the

two men were able—with much grunting and discomfort on Damien's part—to bring his cuffed hands under his stocking feet and up in front of his body.

"Much better," Damien said, pulling a boot back on. "Now what's our plan?"

"I still think we need a phone, first and foremost. There has to be one down here somewhere."

"There's no electricity in this building. Why would they have phone service?"

"We need to get out of here then. We find another flight of stairs, go out the back door of the school, head to the nearest house and call . . ." He trailed off. "Wait a minute."

"What?"

"If I don't have the handcuff keys, then . . ."

Their eyes met.

"We have to make our stand here," Damien said. "If we go out in the dark, he has every advantage. Weapons, the element of surprise, even the law on his side. But if we make him come to us, we take some of that from him."

"So, what, we dog-pile on him? Bum-rush him?"

"Can't you just do that thing again? *I cast you out?* That took him out of commission."

"You're assuming the spirits have already returned—not that you believe in such things. I have no idea how long that takes. Could be days before they come back. What if we're just dealing with Ketcham?"

"You mean just a highly-trained, mass-murdering policeman with a gun?"

"Right."

"We need weapons then." Damien yanked the flashlight from the pull chain and swung it around the room, illuminating two large boilers, a few rolling mop buckets, and three metal storage shelves laden with bottles and cleaning supplies. "Help me snap one of those broomsticks in half," he said. "We can stab him as soon as he walks through the door."

"No, that's stupid," Parker whispered. "You stab him, he's just going to start shooting. We need something heavy, something solid to knock the gun out of his hands."

"Maybe there's a fire ax in the hallway."

"You think there's an ax just sitting in a junior high school for anyone to grab?" Parker snatched the light from Damien and began rifling through the shelves of janitorial supplies. "It's a boiler room. Shouldn't there be a pipe wrench or some-thing?"

"There," Damien said.

"Shh!"

"Sorry. But look." Damien pointed at a stack of paint cans. He hefted several of them experi-mentally before finding a full one.

"That's good," Parker said, finding a can of his

own. "How about this? You wait on the right side of the door, back in that corner, and knock the gun out of his hands the moment you see it. I'll be on the other side, and I'll hit him in the head. You grab the gun, point it at him, and we make him hand over your phone and the handcuff keys. Then we lock him in here and make our exodus."

"Lock him in here how?"

"One of these keys opened the front door of the school," Parker said, examining them again, one at a time. "Could be a master key."

"You're not thinking. Closet door locks aren't designed to keep people *in*."

"Then we use these," Parker said, grabbing a handful of wooden doorstops from a cardboard box on the shelf. They looked like they had been zipped off from scrap wood, each one bearing the words, Doorstop, Do Not Throw Away in blue felt marker. Parker forgot himself for a moment and cringed at the poor use of punctuation, before continuing, "At gunpoint, we make Ketcham cuff himself to this shelf, then we use the paint cans to hammer these things in under the door. That should slow him down enough."

"Or we could just shoot him."

"Do you really want to add shooting a cop to the list of charges against you?" Parker asked, stuffing six of the wooden doorstops under his belt like shotgun shells. His eyes fell on a small plastic bucket.

"I have one more idea," he said. "Help me find some really noxious chemicals here."

Damien grinned. "I like it. We slosh a bucket full of corrosives in his face. Here, this has bleach in it."

"I'm not going to slosh it at him. I'm going to prop it up over the door. It'll fall on his head, distract him, maybe blind him. Then you make your move." He removed the cap and began emptying the bottle into the bucket. "In fact, why don't you get back in position now—who knows where Ketcham is."

Damien squeezed himself back into the shadows to the right of the door. "You're not seriously going to prop it up there."

"It's a good plan. It'll disorient him. Have you ever gotten bleach in your eyes? Or toilet cleaner? This gives us a chance to make our move."

"This is not a time for some Dennis-the-Menace-inspired hijinks. This man wants to kill us."

Parker was skimming the shelf for another ingredient. "The fact that you're familiar with Dennis the Menace sort of kills this whole cat-burning, brooding Gothic mystique you're going for." He began pouring another bottle—this one straight bleach—into the bucket. There wasn't much left, but the fumes were getting to Parker's eyes, which told him he was on the right track.

"That's not chlorine, is it?" Damien asked.

"No, why?"

"Make sure you don't mix chlorine with the bleach. There's a violent reaction, basically makes a chemical bomb. Trust me, I've done it before."

"Are you thinking of ammonia?"

"Oh, maybe. I'm not sure. I'd avoid both."

"Noted."

"The cat was a roadkill, by the way. I love cats. I'd never hurt one."

"Still messed up," Parker said, grabbing a bottle of bright blue glass cleaner and shining the light on the label.

"It was a statement about colonial Christianity's misuse of power. We were burning the cat at the stake."

"I guess the nuances were lost on me—just saw an animal burning in my backyard and some thug giving me the finger. I must not be very cultured." He began mixing in the blue liquid.

"Stop!" Damien shouted, then clamped a hand over his mouth. The word echoed through the room.

"It's vinegar based," Parker whispered harshly, holding up the bottle. He tossed it aside, clicked off the flashlight, and scurried to the door, bucket in tow, sloshing a trail of chemicals behind him. "We have to assume he heard that. Help me prop this thing up there."

Opening the door a crack, Parker held his

breath and stood perfectly still, sensitive to any indication of company. No light spilled in from out in the hall, but he was certain he heard soft, scuffing footsteps coming slowly in their direction. There was no more time to waste.

With Damien's help, he boosted the bucket to the top of the door and balanced it carefully.

"Do you want the light?" he asked as softly as he could.

"No, you keep it," Damien answered, finally achieving a true whisper. "You can always shine him in the eyes when your bucket prank doesn't work. I'll go for the gun when he's blinded."

The two men went to their separate corners, backs to the wall, each squeezing the handle of his paint can and trying to listen over the pounding of his heart. They could hear the sound of doors opening slowly in the hall and the scuffing footsteps drawing closer and closer until they were just outside the boiler room.

Lord, guide me, Parker prayed. *Help me to escape this man. And Damien too. He's had enough.*

He heard the rattle of the knob, the door scraping along the bottom of the bucket. Then he heard it give. Parker clicked on the flashlight, shining it toward the door just in time to see the bucket connect with the top of Danny's head, spewing the chemical concoction down his back, soaking his hair but coming nowhere near his eyes.

Though largely a failure, the trap had stolen Danny's attention for a moment. He flailed angrily, using his gun to bat away the bucket, which bounced noisily into the hall with a series of crashes. In the corner beyond, Parker could barely make out Damien, still gripping the paint can above his head, frozen in fear. His eyes were wide, but he seemed to be seeing nothing, withdrawn into the safety of his own head.

If someone was going to keep the Blackjack Killer from claiming two more victims, it would have to be Parker.

Twenty-Four

Chastising himself for betraying his location, Parker tossed the flashlight. It rolled along the ground, spinning its white light around the room like a disco ball. Then he swung with everything in him, bringing the metal edge of the can down onto Danny's wrist with a satisfying *whump* and sending the gun clattering to the ground. Parker lunged for it, the spinning light giving him the impression that he was falling slowly into a pit.

A kick sent him back eight feet, bouncing along the ground, both elbows smacking against the concrete. The paint can connected with his face and then with the floor, opening up and ejecting its contents everywhere while Parker crashed into the block wall and rolled onto his side, soaked in bleach and institutional green paint—the wind thoroughly knocked from his lungs.

He could see the detective reaching for the gun but could do nothing to stop him, jarred and shocked as he was. They had failed, he thought. He would die on the tenth anniversary of his father's death, a much lesser man with nothing to show but his own inconsequential little media empire.

Then he heard Damien's scream, the overflow of his rage and fear.

Damien swung his paint can—fuller than Parker's—connecting with the back of Danny's skull, sending him down to one knee. He swung again, pushing his advantage, and again connected. But Danny was slowly standing, unhindered by the beating. He slipped aside as the bucket came down a third time, then grasped Damien around the neck, flinging him across the room as if he weighed nothing.

Parker thought of the Gadarenes demoniac breaking chains and shattering irons. He thought of the demonized man in the book of Acts, beating the seven sons of the high priest within an inch of their lives. Danny was not alone here. *Then it returns,* he remembered, *and takes with it seven other spirits more wicked than itself.* Parker knew what he had to do. He had to cast them out again—he had to buy a window of escape.

Damien had bounced back up, jumping onto Danny's back, where he was ferociously digging the chain of his handcuffs into the flesh of Danny's throat. They went down together and grappled, each pulling the other away from the gun, Damien grunting and gasping.

Parker pulled himself to his knees, then to his feet, struggling to recover his breath. A few words and they could be out the door. He could leave Danny trapped and convulsing once again, while they made good their escape. If only he could speak. But first he'd have to draw in a breath.

A sharp *pop* filled the room, followed by an unnerving howl. Damien's left arm was bent the wrong way at the elbow, a starburst of broken blood vessels encircling the wound. He screamed and gawked at the broken joint, nostrils flaring, involuntary tears beginning to flow. He went limp and made no move to further defend himself as Danny sent him spinning along the ground with a kick to the ribs.

Parker shook his head hard, trying to focus on the gun lying three feet behind the demoniac. Danny was turning, his own eyes searching for the weapon in the faint light. If he recovered the pistol, Parker knew that would be it. As long as they had him off-balance and outnumbered, they stood a chance, however slim.

He hurled himself in the gun's direction,

colliding with Danny, but managed to swat it away, sending it skidding into the darkness toward one of the boilers, where—with any luck—it was now underneath, inaccessible.

Before he could even think of dragging himself off the cold floor, he felt it suddenly drop out from beneath him. A half second later his body slammed against the ceiling, a light bulb exploding against the back of his head. The ground came back quickly, bouncing against him twice, then disappeared a second time. Parker's vision went white with pain as the broken glass in the light socket dug into his scalp, drawing blood. He landed hard.

He couldn't speak. Not only was the pain overwhelming, but his throat was closing in under Danny's long, viselike fingers. Overcome and unable to breathe, he went limp, allowing himself to be dragged to his feet and shoved against the wall.

"Apparently, the Blackjack Killer has broadened his MO," Danny smiled. "Now he suffocates his victims before he cuts their throats. Always evolving, always branching out."

Parker could see his own green footprints spanning the width of the room amid shimmering puddles of paint and chemicals. The flashlight was lying back there somewhere, bouncing its light off the far wall, keeping them just this side of complete darkness. From just beyond its reach, he could hear Damien's labored breathing and intermittent groans.

"Remember, Saint," Danny growled. "God is awesome. And so are you."

Parker's vision was beginning to swim, his airway constricting tighter by the second. He had to struggle to make out the image of Danny's hand disappearing into his coat, reaching for the knife on his belt.

Jesus, help me.

With a sudden flash of clarity, Parker reached into his own coat and pulled one of the door-stops from his belt. With a final desperate rush of adrenaline, he connected the sharpest corner of the wooden wedge with Danny's temple. The knife fell to the ground and Danny took a step back, stunned.

Parker struck a second time, aiming for the soft flesh under his eye, but again connecting with his temple. The blow spun Danny a hundred and eighty degrees. Parker sloughed off his Melton peacoat and pulled it over Danny's head, tying the sleeves tightly around his neck and yanking the man off-balance.

"Damien," he rasped with all the volume he could muster, "we're leaving!" To Parker's surprise, he saw Damien roll to his feet and stagger out into the hall.

Danny was circling and cursing, yanking at the coat with one hand and swinging wildly with the other. Stepping into a mixture of paint and bleach solution, he slipped and fell to the ground.

Parker moved quickly around him, snatched the flashlight from the floor, and made his exit, slamming the door behind him. Damien was leaning against the wall across the corridor. His heavily tattooed chest was bare, and his injured arm was wrapped tightly in a ripped black T-shirt, tied off at the metal cuff on his wrist.

"So that's what you were doing," Parker said. He stuck the flashlight to the doorknob with the tacky strip of duct tape and began wedging the doorstops into place, spacing them evenly along the bottom of the door. He was feeling surprisingly good about their chances and felt his spirits rising all the more at the ongoing sound of Danny flopping around behind the door.

"Are you going to be able to run?" he asked.

"I'm fine," Damien said hollowly. "I can run." His eyes were heavy and his shoulders slumped. Parker thought of the picture in the file folder—Daniel Banner, age 6, with a black eye and fractured collarbone.

"I think you're in shock," Parker said, pushing the last doorstop into place.

"No I'm not."

"You are. But shock is good right now." Somehow, analyzing their situation made it seem less hopeless. "You can deal with everything when we're safely out of here." He used his heel to kick the doorstops, one by one, hammering them into the narrow space beneath the door. There was no more sound coming from within.

"Did you get the gun or the phone?" Damien asked.

"No, neither," Parker answered, ramming the last wedge into place. "Now let's get out of here."

The door buckled with an ear-splitting *wham*, moving the whole line of wooden doorstops an inch and launching the flashlight down the hall. Parker—still sprawled on the floor—kicked the door shut and began stomping the doorstops back into place. Light returned, Damien having detached himself from the wall long enough to rescue the now-dimming flashlight.

Whump! Again the door popped open, farther this time. Parker jammed it shut with both feet and scrambled to relodge the doorstops. One was missing. He could hear breathing and laughing from behind the door.

The third impact opened the door two inches, and Danny's hand emerged through the crack, reaching, grasping. Parker kicked the door again, trying to uncoil like a jackhammer with every possible ounce of pressure. The hand retreated, and Parker was able to close the gap again. This was unsustainable, he realized, and glanced back to where Damien had been. But the light was gone now, along with his companion, and Parker's outlook sank further.

"Damien?" His voice echoed down the hall. "Are you there?" No response. The laughter grew louder from in the boiler room.

"Damien, where are you?" he shouted.

Another explosion of weight against the door fired another of the doorstops across the hall into the darkness, leaving only three in place. The hand appeared again, groping for the doorknob. Parker thought of running for it, wondering if he could retrace his steps in the dark—when he heard the squeaking of wheels and a rumble of sheet metal coming in his direction. Then he saw the light.

Using the shoulder of his good arm, Damien was wheeling an enormous, old lever-style voting machine toward the door.

"Help me tip this over," he commanded.

Parker jumped up and wrapped his arms around the top of the machine, pulling with all his weight. It teetered, then came crashing down, lurching forward into the door.

"There are more," Damien said, and disappeared, leaving Parker in darkness again. He returned moments later with an identical machine, which the two of them tipped against the first.

"Now follow me," he said authoritatively as he took off down the hall with great speed and surprising lightness, leaving Parker struggling to keep up. Damien hurdled chairs and dodged tables, unhampered by his gruesome injury. They took a left, heading back the way they had come.

"Stop a second," Parker demanded, doubling over and fighting to catch his breath. All that time on the treadmill had been far more leisurely than this. "I think we're—"

Damien shushed him. "What's that? Do you hear that?" There was a rumble behind them and a scraping sound—quiet, but growing louder.

"I hear it."

The two voting machines thundered past them, skidding down the hall on their sides as if they weighed nothing.

"Go!" Parker shouted. They took another left and then a right, pushing themselves, both sure they could feel Danny closing in. They raced past Brynn's body, up the stairs, and down the hall.

"This way," Damien huffed, veering left.

"No, the entrance is over here," Parker said. He was indulging the idea of stealing the detective's car. After all, he had the keys in his pocket.

"Trust me. I used to go here. We can lose him this way."

They dashed through a large cafeteria, staying low, through a narrow kitchen, and out a back exit near a loading dock. The sharp, cold air brought no sense of freedom, serving only to heighten the terror that gripped Parker.

They were behind the school, an area illuminated only by the full moon and light pollution, yet surprisingly bright.

"Kill the light," Parker whispered. "Let's regroup at those trees."

The trees in question were bare, diseased, and leaning precariously on a chain-link fence. Parker arrived first, pushing himself as far back into the scant darkness as he could.

"This isn't exactly cover," Damien observed, his voice a shrill whisper. "And I can't climb this fence with handcuffs and a broken elbow."

Parker noticed the makeshift T-shirt cast coming loose at the bottom.

"I don't think he got his gun," he said, looking for an upside, "and if he had a backup piece, I think he would have used it."

"Did you see what he did back there?" Damien asked. "Those voting-booth things must weigh fifteen hundred pounds each. He doesn't need a gun and he knows it."

"So what do you suggest we do?"

"Go on without me."

"No, Damien. I won't."

"We have no choice. I'm done. Look at me."

Parker put his hand on Damien's bare shoulder and looked him squarely in the eyes. "I'm not going to abandon you like everyone else."

"I'm not being noble, you idiot! If we separate, he'll follow you."

"Oh." Parker wanted nothing less than to split up. He knew Damien was useless as an ally and would only slow him down, but there was something unbearably frightening about being hunted alone. "Why do you think he'd go after me? You're wounded."

"He can afford to let me get away. I'm *the killer*, remember? No one would believe my version of what happened here tonight. You on the other hand—he can't have you talking to the police, the papers, the prosecutor. You're a giant liability."

"You're right." Parker surveyed his possible routes of escape. "Try and find a phone. Call the police and ask for Detective Kirkpatrick. Tell her I need her to rescue me."

"Take the light," Damien said, holding it out to Parker.

"You think that'll help lead him away from you?"

"Can't hurt."

Parker snatched the light, leapt up on the fence, and began climbing—something he hadn't done in twenty-five years. To his surprise, he was able to swing over the top on his first try. The neat landing he envisioned did not pan out, however, and his feet slipped out from under him. His elbows made contact with the ground again, sending a shock of pain in both directions. He clawed his way off the ground, up the chain-link fence, until he found himself face-to-face with his new ally. Their eyes locked for a moment, wrapped up in adrenaline, fear, and the strangeness of it all.

"Be careful," Damien said.

"You too."

Twenty-Five

Parker made his way up the alley, emerging from between two shuttered storefronts. Despite the demon-possessed serial killer on his tail, he took a moment to fret about the safety of the neighborhood. The street was deserted, save for a homeless man pacing and mumbling at the litter as it scooted by in the strong breeze.

Ten years ago Parker would have expected to find a pay phone or two in the vicinity, but there were none. Across the street, two nearly identical red-tagged homes sat side by side. They were either abandoned or full of squatters, Parker decided. Either way, he was sure that introducing a dark, deserted old house to the present equation was a move in the wrong direction. Instead, he moved north up the street.

Parker weighed his options, reminding himself that Danny would not hesitate to kill anyone who got in the way. He needed to avoid families, homes with children or old people. He needed a phone. He'd try to contact Corrinne. Or Troy.

He'd even take Officer Dykstra right now. Failing a telephone, a business—someplace crowded or at least public—would do.

Cresting the hill, Parker saw nothing of the sort below. There was an old church—and Parker had certainly had more than his fill of those recently. Beyond that, another row of houses all dark and foreboding, a brownfield, and a factory or plant of some strain, likely idle.

I should never have stopped asking which way to go, he prayed. *I'm asking now. I need wisdom or a sign. Anything.*

At the top of the steeple, light from an unseen source glinted off the cross. It seemed to be beckoning. Parker didn't hesitate; he threw himself down the hill, at times stumbling on the old brick street until he found himself smacking up against the door of the church, his lungs collapsing in on themselves.

The front doors were solid, each bearing a tall, narrow window, reinforced with wire mesh. Clearly, he would not be able to break in here, although he imagined Father Michael could gain access in no time at all. Even if he managed to break through the glass somehow, the windows were high up, far removed from the handle and ostensibly the latch. Desperately, he yanked on one of the doors—locked—and then the other.

It swung open easily, sending Parker tumbling back onto his butt. As the door closed slowly on its hydraulic arm, he saw the hand-lettered sign: Saturday Night Mass: 8:00, Open for Meditation Until 11:00. He could almost hear his grandfather approving. Security be damned, the church should be open for the people.

Pulling himself to his feet, Parker entered the church and was presented with an immediate choice: head up a few stairs into the rear of the nave, or down a few stairs into a drab hallway. He put off the decision and turned his attention to covering his back. What he needed was a way to lock the door behind him, to barricade himself in. The two wooden doorstops on the floor wouldn't do the trick—he knew that from experience. Besides, this door swung out, not in. But maybe that was a good thing, Parker thought. Perhaps Danny's strength would be less useful pulling than it had been slamming forward. After all, at some point, wouldn't the door handles just break off?

The doors themselves were substantial. Antiques by the look of them. Their outer hardware was apparently original to the building. But inside, they had been retrofitted with the same sort of crash-bars as Parker's own facility—the kind that locked and unlocked with a hex key. On a hunch, he went up on his toes and slid his fingers along the ledge above the door. A shower of dust came swirling down and an L-shaped Allen wrench clattered to the floor. Parker recovered it, his fingers sweaty and hands shaking, and on the fourth try was able to insert it into the lock mechanism and spin it counterclockwise until the bolt was in place.

Feeling significantly safer, he pocketed the key, took another few seconds to catch his breath, and descended the stairs, intent on finding a phone. Somewhere between the alley and the church, he'd remembered the Kent County Sheriff's Department. They had authority throughout the city, Parker knew from one of his recreational fact-finding missions, but were officially unaffiliated with the Grand Rapids Police. He'd start with a call to them, then he'd access his voice mail and get Corrinne's number from the message he'd saved. He thought of her walking him to his car and the way she'd pinned Dylan Eiler to the ground with such ease. He'd happily be rescued by her tonight.

The hallway downstairs smelled strongly of new carpet. It took a few tense seconds to find the light switch, and a few more for the fluorescent bulbs to stop flickering. The hall was a straight shot, undecorated save for a large print of Jesus—hair feathered, teeth white, cheeks rosy and high-boned. There were six or seven windowless white doors on either side of the hall, each with a carefully stenciled label.

Pastor's Office, Church Office, Christian Education, Children's Minister, Social Services. They'd all have phones, Parker realized. Jackpot.

He gave the first door a yank. It was locked. As was the second. And the third. He rushed from door to door, down the hall then back up, praying for a forgetful staff member, an absent-minded janitor, a poorly constructed mechanism. He kicked the door to the church office with as much force as he could muster. It didn't give. A minute later, Parker was back where he started, having spent the hallway's potential. He left the light on and remounted the stairs to the vestibule.

Plan B.

The church proper was gorgeous, lit up like Christmas, particularly at the front where the sanctuary and transepts were filled with burning candles. Parker chided himself at the sight. What was he doing skulking around the bowels of the church? The building was open, the lights on, candles burning—there would be a priest here, an ally, a sympathetic man with keys to the offices below. Parker tore up the aisle, feeling irresistibly drawn to the large crucifix suspended in the apse, the outstretched arms of the likeness of Christ offering comfort and safety.

"Hello?" Parker called, the word disappearing into the high ceiling. No one answered, and he saw no one. "Is anyone here?" he shouted. Still nothing.

Parker's newly acquired knowledge of church architecture brought him to the chancel and up the choir aisle, where he expected to find a door to the vestry, likely continuing into the sacristy and eventually out the other side of the church.

The door was indeed where Parker expected to find it, and it was wide-open. And standing in the doorway, blood caked along the side of his smiling face, was Daniel Paul Ketcham. He charged into Parker, sending him tumbling along the chancel, crashing into the altar.

"Too predictable, Saint," Danny said, approaching with long, quick strides. "You thought we couldn't enter a church. Admit it."

"Sort of," Parker muttered. With the aid of the altar, he pulled himself to his feet, surprised at his lack of surprise.

"Where's your little friend?" Danny asked, scanning the church. "Rigging up a bucket of holy water? With a pinch of garlic and a little silver, maybe?" He stepped closer. "Or how about a cross? Maybe that will keep us away." He snatched the brass cross from the altar and hurled it at Parker's chest, knocking him again to the marble floor and clattering down next to him.

"A cross." He scoffed. "Is there anything more pathetic than a bunch of Jesus freaks celebrating under the emblem of your own god's death?" He pulled his knife from the scabbard on his belt. "Tell me, Saint, where is my little freethinker?"

"He's far away by now. He's safe, which means you're through."

"Nice try. But he's safe nowhere. The man's an

escaped prisoner. His face is on every TV channel in the city. And who are they going to believe: a self-professed Satanist or a highly decorated detective? His blood is all over you, Parker. When Damien turns up, he'll be placed back in our custody. And when he tries to escape, we'll be forced to kill him. But first we're going to kill you, before you squirm out of our grip again."

The *ka-chung* of a door closing echoed up the church, followed by footsteps ascending the stairs. A man came walking up the aisle evenly. Despite his blurred vision, Parker could see the clerical collar and black garb.

"Get out of here!" Parker warned. "Run! Call the pol—" Danny silenced him with a foot to the chest.

The priest pulled a handgun from within his coat and leveled it at Danny. "Drop your weapon," Father Xavier commanded, "and put your hands on your head."

Danny wheezed a laugh. "Sign of the times, I guess," he said, raising his hands but not dropping the knife.

"I haven't called the police yet, my son," Xavier said. "Why don't you just leave this house of God and let me tend to your victim?"

"I *am* the police, Padre. I'm a detective with the GRPD, and this man is a murder suspect. Now, please lower *your* weapon and allow me to do my job."

"Since when do policemen use knives?"

Danny shrugged. "Since when do priests carry guns?"

"Father Xavier!" Parker yelled. "He's the one!"

Xavier squinted. "Parker?"

With a snap of his arm, Danny put the knife squarely into its target. Xavier fell to his knees, his gun clacking to the ground. He pulled the knife from his throat in a wide arc, sending blood spurting everywhere. His other hand went tightly around his throat—a vain attempt to hold it all in—then he went facedown to the floor, a deep red puddle growing around him.

Danny's eyes, wide and ecstatic, were locked on the gruesome scene. Parker tore his own eyes away from the dying priest and again found them drawn to a cross—the one lying on the floor, inches from his face. He knew he wouldn't get a better opening. He needed to act now, while Danny was distracted.

He grabbed the cross by the very top and swung it toward Danny with all his might. It made a full rotation, an inch from the ground, and its heavy base connected solidly with Danny's ankle. He stumbled back a step, his feet getting locked up against the brass crossbar, then caught the curved communion rail midthigh and flipped backward. He fell several feet into a small city of burning votive candles.

Instantly, Danny's paint-and-chemical-soaked

coat and hair went up in flames. He rolled to his feet and ran down the side aisle, shedding his coat as he went, the only sounds the puffing of his breath, the clapping of his dress shoes against the floor, and a loud, unsettling click from his ankle with every step.

Parker rolled under the rail, down the steps, and scrambled over to Father Xavier's still form. The pool of blood around him was now several feet wide and still growing slowly. Parker squeezed the vomit back down his throat and pushed two fingers to the side of Xavier's neck. There was no hint of a pulse.

Danny had reached the font in the back of the church and was baptizing himself by immersion, headfirst, extinguishing the flames. Parker knew he had just seconds. Where was Xavier's gun? He frantically looked around the body, under pews, lifting kneelers, coming up empty.

Another glance to the back of the church revealed that the baptismal font was once again without occupant, and Danny was nowhere to be seen. Parker felt a surge of terror. Between facing Danny empty-handed and rolling Father Xavier onto his back, the latter was preferable, but not by much. He took a deep breath and yanked up on the priest's arm. The body slid several inches on the wet tile but refused to turn. He tried again, surprised by the thin man's dead weight.

In three large waves, the overhead lights in the

church went out, leaving Parker and Xavier in the dark save for the glowing of some candles and the streetlights filtering in through the stained glass. Parker shoved his hand under the priest's body, soaking his sleeve in blood. He grappled for a moment before locating the gun and struggled to extract it. He quickly wiped the weapon on his shirt and stood.

He remembered passing the three rows of light switches on the way into the nave, which placed Danny there just a moment ago. There was a slim chance that the killer had doubled back past Parker in the meantime, but Parker would take those odds. He took off for the altar again, then stopped himself and returned for the knife, which he had to pry from Xavier's lifeless hand.

By any account, the detective was now completely unarmed and badly injured. Probably on his way to the hospital. Parker, on the other hand, had a gun and a knife and had only taken a beating, albeit a severe one. *This changes everything,* he told himself. Now able to put up a fight, he could make his way out the rear of the church. If he passed a phone, he'd make a call. If not, he'd draw the attention of someone with a badge. That much he was sure of.

This is the knife that killed Paige, Parker suddenly realized. An alms box a few yards away in the north transept had a slot large enough to accommodate the weapon and was secured with a small padlock. Parker shoved it in blade-first and forced the handle through with a blow from the butt of the pistol. He returned to the chancel.

This time no one stopped him from passing through the door into the vestry, which was dark except for the red glow of the exit sign at the rear. Parker pulled the small flashlight from his pants pocket and held it up under the barrel of the gun as he'd seen Father Michael do. He swept the room, imagining that Danny might jump out from any corner or crevice.

One wall of the narrow room was dominated by three tall wardrobes, presumably housing a large assortment of robes and liturgical garments. Opposite these were a number of file cabinets and a large full-length mirror, which sent Parker several inches into the air at the sight of his own reflection. Thank God he hadn't shot at the man in the mirror.

He headed out the exit into the ambulatory, through a narrow corridor, and down a curved flight of stairs lit by a small, tasteful chandelier, where he came to a halt. The stairway ended at a pair of double doors, and in front of them on the stone tile floor, lay another body. It was a priest in full vestments, stabbed several times. Before Parker could resolve himself to step over the corpse and walk out into the dark night, he realized it was a moot point: the handles of the two doors were secured to each other with a pair of handcuffs.

There were no windows in or near the doors. He briefly considered trying to do something clever like removing the pins from the hinges, but he hadn't a clue how to go about it. He glanced back up at the door to the dark ambulatory and the vestry beyond. The gun in his hand was offering less comfort by the second. He'd gladly trade it for a phone.

A phone! *There's not a clergyman alive without a cell phone,* he thought. Of course, this particular clergyman was not alive, but Parker forced himself to descend the last few stairs all the same and approach the priest's body. He reminded himself that he'd been in the presence of more than half a dozen dead bodies in the past week— all murder victims—and that he was beginning to think of himself as something of a professional. *It's just an investigation of a crime scene,* he told himself as he began riffling through the priest's pockets. He turned up a handkerchief, a case of business cards, a wallet, and a pocket missal, but no phone.

Of course a priest wouldn't have his cell on him while saying Mass. Parker rolled his eyes at his stupidity. *It's probably locked in his office downstairs.*

And that was it. He would get into the office, whatever it took. He'd call the police on the landline and the sheriff on the cell phone. And maybe he'd fax the National Guard too. He needed heroes right now, and he was surer than ever that he wasn't one. He climbed the stairs and made his way back into the vestry. His resolve was mounting with every step, although the dread of reentering the sanctuary was growing in equal proportions.

He'd just walk right through, he told himself. He wouldn't even look at Father Xavier's body, just head right out the back and down the stairs. He'd get into the church office even if he had to shoot the door open.

Idiot! He stopped in his tracks. *How can the chain on a pair of handcuffs keep you locked inside when you have a gun?* Maybe he should go back, he thought. A single bullet might not separate the cuffs, but Parker was sure he had quite a few—somewhere between six and fifteen was his guess. He wanted to save one or two in case he ran into Danny again, but that still left plenty for opening the door. He stood in paralyzed indecision for what seemed like minutes, putting off commitment in any direction as long as he could.

A revived prickle of fear climbed up Parker's skull, as the eerie sound of a cappella singing drifted into the vestry.

"The old and evil foe now means us deadly woe." It was slow and mellow and just slightly out of tune—coming from the sanctuary, by the sound of it. Parker doubled back toward the rear entrance. "Deep guile and great might are his dread arms in fight." Now it seemed to be coming from both directions. "On earth is not his equal."

Knowing it was a stupid move, Parker pocketed the flashlight and climbed into the middle wardrobe, sliding in behind a dozen robes and then pulling the door shut as quietly as possible. He was holding the gun out straight from his hip like an old West gunfighter, listening intently but only able to hear his own heavy breathing and his pulse pounding in his head.

Twenty-Six

Damien waited twenty minutes, wedged shirtless and shivering between the trees and the fence, before he dared to move. His body was getting steadily colder, particularly his T-shirt-wrapped broken arm—a source of growing concern. If he had been in shock, it was wearing off.

He silently made his way up to the school and crept around to the front, hugging the outer brick wall. Ketcham's car was still parked by the entrance, stopping Damien midstep and stealing his breath. The space beyond the school was dark, and he could only assume that a street lay beyond the darkness. He cursed himself for sending the flashlight with Parker and for not getting the keys from him. He'd love to drive out of here right now and never look back, but he had no idea how to hot-wire a car.

Gathering his wits, he breached the darkness in the direction of the street—or at least where he expected to find one. The blacktop of the parking lot was cracked and cragged. He stumbled twice before going down, instinctively trying to break his fall with his cuffed hands. The pain in his injured arm was incredible, and he couldn't stop a shriek from escaping. He rolled onto his back on the jagged ground and began to sob.

He allowed himself only a moment of self-pity. *Enough,* he told himself. *Get over it! They can't hurt you. They can't hurt you.* He'd been repeating this mantra to himself for decades. It was a trick he'd learned as a child: use your fear to fuel your defiance. Never show weakness, especially not when attacked by someone stronger than you.

A seedling of hope was trying to break through the surface of a week's worth of compounding despair. The charges against him, the injustice of the system, the prospect of prison—if he could just get some aid to Parker while the hypocrite was still alive, the two of them might have a chance of setting the record straight. Unlikely, but worth a shot. Damien began planning the complex project of rising to his feet without bending or burdening his broken arm.

He carefully rolled to his knees, then rose and

pushed on. Another twenty yards and he came upon a chain-link fence, probably connected to the one Parker had jumped, he thought. He could see a little better now, by the light of a few streetlights, and were those headlights drawing nearer? Yes, he was sure they were.

Hope sprang up in Damien at the sight of the car, and then fell just as quickly. Again, a fence stood between him and freedom. Receiving a second wind, he raced along the chain-link fence toward the oncoming car. He could make it out now, an old red coupe full of rust. It would pass him in seconds and disappear into the darkness behind him. Damien pushed himself physically— something he hadn't done in years before tonight —knowing this was a gamble. If he tripped and fell now, it would take him out of commission for hours.

A gap appeared in the fence, wide enough to drive through, and Damien veered out into the road and thrust himself in the path of the red car, knowing immediately that he'd miscalculated, as there was no room for the driver to stop. Instead, he veered and locked up the brakes, missing Damien by only a few inches. The car skidded, then recovered, and squealed to a stop.

The driver emerged, a ruddy, muscle-bound man with a bald head and a nineteen-inch neck. His button-up black shirt read Eagle Security.

"I know who you are," he said.

Oh no. Damien looked down at himself, the tattered, shirtless, tattooed escaped prisoner in handcuffs, running through the night; the serial killer whose picture had been everywhere for the last two days. Yes, he had miscalculated indeed.

The big man closed the space between them quickly and slammed a fist in Damien's stomach, crumpling him to the ground.

"You're a psycho," the man said. "I don't like psychos. So you get a free ride in my trunk down to the cop shop." He pushed a button on his keyless entry, and the trunk lid popped open. "I wonder if there's a reward," the man mused.

Sweat was beading up on Parker's nose, forehead, and upper lip. He scrunched up his face, afraid that Danny might actually hear a drop fall to the floor. The wardrobe was getting hotter by the moment and seemingly smaller, but he dared not move. He could hear Danny whistling now, still "A Mighty Fortress," and it sounded like he was drawing closer to the vestry.

By the next stanza, there was no doubt—the demoniac was in the room, just a few feet away, clomping past the wardrobe, the click of his ankle still punctuating each step. Then the footsteps stopped altogether.

The overhead light came on. Parker could see the diffused glow spilling in around the edges of the wardrobe's door. He slid his finger onto the trigger guard and waited, willing the steps to resume and fade away into the sanctuary.

A rush of air rippled the vestments as the wardrobe door was yanked open.

Before he could react, Parker felt his cover of robes and albs disappear along with the bar they'd been hanging on. Sudden, harsh light paralyzed Parker, who brought his left hand up to shield his eyes and felt an explosion of pain in his right. He screamed.

The gun was gone, knocked to the floor by something heavy and pointed—something that had come roaring out of nowhere and broken bones in Parker's hand. His eyes were adjusting to the light, and the image of Danny's face coming into focus was the most horrifying thing Parker had seen yet. Most of his hair was burned away and the skin around his eyes was charred and curled up slightly. One eye was swollen and sagging, almost completely closed. But he was smiling wickedly and holding a bronze censer, suspended by a chain.

"Look what we found, Saint," Danny said. He swung it back and forth, mockingly. "Hocus pocus, dominus ominous." With a jerk of his arm, he smashed the bronze globe into the side of Parker's face, knocking him down into the soft piles of vestments. Parker rolled to his knees and scrambled through the folds of fabric, looking for the missing gun.

Danny was hovering over him, swinging the censer in hard, tight circles, occasionally letting out some chain and bringing the bronze globe down on Parker's exposed back or neck. After the third impact, Parker rolled defensively onto his back and tried to deflect the blows. Each time the globe made contact, it coughed a little cloud of black dust. The smell of coal and incense was floating all around him, and for a moment Parker could only think of Saint Maurus, the patron saint of coppersmiths and charcoal burners.

The next blow glanced off Parker's knuckles and connected with his head, leaving him dazed —his vision blurred and his limbs slow to respond to mental orders. Another swing connected with his jaw, knocking three teeth to the back of his throat, where they were momentarily batted about by his gag reflex.

Danny chuckled and paused the beating. "I'm feeling inspired, Saint," he said. "Let's burn this place down. We don't know where your friend Damien is or who he's been talking to. But we do know it's impossible to establish time of death from charred remains. Maybe Damien escaped and burned down the church. We always cover our bases."

Parker felt himself beginning to fade again. He knew that if he had one more move to make, it would have to be now. An experimental opening of his mouth brought a wave of terrific pain, causing him to choke on his own spit. Another verbal command to the spirits was out. He grunted in frustration.

"We know what you're thinking," Danny said. "Don't bother. We're more than we were last time. Sevenfold more. And 'this kind only comes out by prayer and fasting.' We're afraid you just don't have the time."

Parker glanced at the far wall. A desperate idea was budding somewhere in his mind that, if he could just get to the switch and kill the intense light emanating from that bare hundred-watt bulb in the ceiling, he might be able to escape the room under cover of darkness and find a new place to hide.

He clambered for the switch on the wall, realizing too late that the catlike speed he had envisioned was impossible at the moment. He took a wobbly step and then another toward the door, then felt the censer's chain wrap tightly around his ankle and yank him back to the ground. Parker landed gracelessly on his hands and knees, having gained all of three feet toward his goal.

"Come on, Saint," Danny growled. "You've got to *speak it into reality*. Be positive. Hit me with your best shot."

Parker grabbed a white cassock from the pile on the floor and tossed it up toward Danny's face, hoping to wrap him in it, to re-create his success from the boiler room. The garment was easily batted away, bringing another derisive laugh from Danny.

"Look at you," he spat. "You thought you could stay off the dragon's list if you didn't ruffle any feathers. You thought we'd let you slide."

"I don't know where it is," Parker wheezed.

"It's okay, Saint. You're not cut out for this, anyway. You could never shoot another human being."

"No," he huffed. "The Crown. We never found it. It's probably gone forever."

Danny paused for a moment. "Crown? What are you talking about?" He nudged at Parker with his foot. "Don't get delirious on me yet. We want to enjoy this."

Parker slumped. Danny didn't even know the Crown existed. The Jesuits had been on the wrong track all along. Just like Parker, chasing the wrong crown all these years. The dragon's crown. And now the rooster was crowing, and he had nothing left. The fight had left him.

He was waiting for the final blow to come when he saw it, right there on the carpet in front of his face, where the cassock had lain a moment earlier: Xavier's gun. Behind him, Danny was still offering mocking encouragement intermixed with blasphemous epithets. Parker snatched up the pistol and struggled to insert his finger into the trigger guard. His enlarged knuckle was a tight fit, and his fractured bones complained at being wrapped around the cold, hard handle, but he managed.

Shuffling around awkwardly on his knees, Parker looked up at his enemy's face. Standing was probably out of the question, he realized. Without much conviction, he raised the pistol with both hands and managed to grunt, "Back off."

Danny perked up, swung the censer faster. "You don't know what you're doing, Saint. You were right: lambs and guns don't mix."

Parker tried to pull the trigger. He squeezed with every muscle he could access, but his hands were in knots and his fingers too swollen. Danny struck with his makeshift weapon, knocking the pistol away. It discharged a shot into the wall and bounced across the floor, once again obscured amongst robes, stoles, and chasubles.

Parker had never fired a gun before, and the sheer volume of the gunshot disoriented him all the more. He wilted and watched Danny circle around behind him, breathing heavy. He felt the cold chain wrap twice around his neck and then tighten, slowly lifting him up off the ground. He could smell the burned flesh and hair, not unlike the smell of the cat in his backyard.

"It's a shame," Danny whispered into his ear. "We had hoped to take our time with you, but we have some other loose ends to tie up. My colleagues will likely be on their way after that gunshot, and there's still the matter of disposing of the evidence." Parker's vision was dimming, but the words were still getting in. "Poor Pastor Saint, burned up in the church fire. Of course, as the papers will report, one heroic detective rushed in to the inferno to try and rescue you—with utter indifference to his own safety. Even sustained some horrific injuries. I'd say we're looking at another mayor's commendation. Probably be captain in a few years."

Parker's arms were moving up and down frantically, although he wasn't sure why. He had no idea how long it took a man to choke to death, but he had to believe he was nearing the halfway point. He flailed all the more. With his right thumb, he felt the soft, slick flesh of Danny's burned eye and instinctively drove it in, feeling strangely as though he were stronger now, without oxygen holding him back. He felt his thumbnail digging deep into the rubbery tissue of the eye socket.

This time, Danny shouted and loosened his grip long enough for Parker to steal another panicked breath.

"Bad move, Preacher," he said. "I was going to let you drift off peacefully."

Danny yanked the end of the chain back hard, spinning Parker three hundred sixty degrees and dumping him down on the ground. He looked down at his mark, lying there limp and semi-conscious, and resumed spinning the censer in wide, easy circles.

"If you do see Jesus on the other side, do us a favor and tell him he can—"

"Shut your mouth, devil."

Father Michael stood in the doorway, gun drawn.

"Oh, good," Danny sang. "More friends. I suppose you heard this poor man's prayers."

"I heard the gunshot."

"Listen, this is not what it looks like. I'm actually—"

"No," Michael said. "You listen. That dead man in the aisle was one of my best friends. I know you killed him, Detective, and I'll admit that I want nothing more than to put a bullet between your eyes. But some of us don't give in to our every carnal desire. So you get this one chance: drop the thurible, step away from Parker, and put your hands on your head."

Danny scoffed. He was still spinning the censer lazily. "You think you have—"

"Last chance. Drop it."

"Fine," Danny said. He released the chain on an upswing, sending the globe rocketing forward. It passed through the light bulb, shattering it, then collided with the ceiling and crashed open, ejecting a curtain of thick black dust onto the priest. Danny exploded from out of the swirling ash, blasting into Father Michael. The gun disappeared into the choir seats, and the two men careened out onto the chancel.

Twenty-Seven

Parker could hear the two men fighting from his spot on the floor of the dark room, but his interest was waning. What he wanted to do was pull some of the vestments up over him like a blanket and drift off to sleep. Instead he began the process of once again drawing himself to his knees. This proved more difficult than ever, as Parker's left arm now ached like fury and refused to bear any weight. But Xavier's gun was in here somewhere. And if he could, he would find it.

Thank you, Lord, for sending Michael. I needed an archangel. Now I pray you give me the strength to help him.

He waded through the fabric on hands and knees, squinting through what dim candlelight managed to find its way in from the sanctuary, not remembering that he still had a flashlight in his pocket. He felt his way blindly through fold after fold, realizing with the gradual return of oxygen to his brain that this was a hopeless search. As he drew near the door on hands and knees, he decided to check in on his would-be rescuer. Perhaps there was a more pressing need than the gun at this moment.

Head spinning, he slowly rose to his feet in the doorway and took in the scene. What he saw would have seemed beyond surreal on any other day. The two men were locked in intense combat, more or less evenly matched—Danny possessing more strength, but Michael more speed and skill, having been trained by the best.

They traded blows, grappled, evaded. The priest moved smoothly, in combinations, getting inside his opponent's reach and landing flurries of blows with the heels of his palms, his fists, his knees—but these barely seemed to faze Danny, who occasionally struck Father Michael with such force as to knock him back several yards. Parker watched the action unfold, standing slack-jawed in the doorway, as if he were watching it on a screen.

It slowly dawned on him that Michael's hand-gun was also unaccounted for, having been lost in the melee, and must be somewhere nearby. Through the fog and the ash, he thought he had seen it fly off into the distance when the two men collided. Lighting was sparse out here, but sparse was better than the blackness of the vestry. He moved along the wall as stealthily as he could, trying to mentally re-create the trajectory and bounce of the gun. It would probably be in the choir stalls, he decided.

Feeling far from sure-footed, Parker propelled himself from the wall and staggered the four steps into the stalls, bracing himself against the ornately carved partition. He willed his eyes to adjust to the blackness around his feet, without success.

The flashlight came to his mind and out of his pocket. It was low on juice, but still made a world of difference, its dull glow revealing folders full of music, water bottles, boxes of Kleenex. But no gun, at least not in the slight circle of light directly beneath him.

He glanced up toward the sanctuary and saw Father Michael upside down, his feet swinging through the air in an arc. Danny threw him hard onto the altar, smacking his back against the stone surface, upsetting the chalice and candles. The priest grunted in pain, spun on his back, and frantically pushed his adversary away with both feet.

Parker turned his attention back to the floor, hunching his way down the choir stalls, searching with his fast-dying beam of light. Still nothing. A hollow thud and a cry of pain from Michael resounded through the perfect acoustics of the church.

"Get out of here, Parker!" Michael barked, pulling himself again to his feet. His eye was seeping heavily, and his breathing was labored. Parker could see that he was slowing, tiring. And that Danny was not. The priest rushed full bore back up to the chancel, teeth clenched, intent on knocking the demons right out of his opponent.

With a single blow to his center of mass, Danny sent Father Michael sprawling down the steps, onto his back. The priest slid ten feet along the stone floor of the aisle like a hockey puck, only coming to a stop when he collided with Xavier's body. The tide of the fight was turning—slowly but inevitably—in Danny's favor.

Then Parker spotted the pistol amid a pile of spilled cough drops. He rushed over to it, leaning heavily on the rail. His hands were in worse shape than the last time he'd tried to fire a gun, and he knew his nonexistent marksmanship would be handicapped further by the semi-darkness and his own mental fog. He needed to get the gun to Michael, who could actually use it.

Praying he wouldn't fall flat, Parker wobbled as swiftly as he could back to the wall and down the stairs on the epistle side of the church. Father Michael hadn't moved from the aisle, where he lay more or less on top of his deceased friend. Was he even conscious? Parker ducked low and pushed ahead between two pews, drawing nearer to his friend. Before he knew it he was ten feet away, close enough to slide the gun to Michael.

Danny suddenly filled his field of vision, blocking his path.

"We'll take that," he sneered, wrenching the pistol from Parker's throbbing hands and shoving him down onto the pew. He took aim. "Good-bye, Saint."

The sound of three shots filled the church.

Danny lurched forward, landing on Parker with

some force. He wheezed long and loud, then began to convulse. Parker slithered out from beneath him, letting the detective's body fall to the floor. Grouped closely in the center of Danny's back were three bullet wounds.

A shrill whistling sound, like a thousand shrieks all wrapped together, threatened to burst Parker's eardrums. The holes in the detective's shirt were bubbling and billowing as his body quivered.

Parker could feel the dark spirits coming out of his enemy, looking for a place to go, and he thanked God for providential timing. Earlier that day he'd been swept clean and in order, a perfect home for Ketcham's demons. But not now.

A moment later, Ketcham's body was still and the church perfectly quiet.

Parker shuffled over to Michael, still sitting on the floor next to Father Xavier, whose pant leg was bunched up to the knee, revealing a small, empty ankle holster.

"So that's the unauthorized exorcism," Parker managed to say, his jaw tight and sore.

"I told you it was messy," Michael said. "Are you all right?"

"I'll live, I guess. I think I need an ambulance, though."

"On its way. I called 911 before I burst in on you two." He tipped his head back against a pew and closed his eyes. "We shouldn't have split up. I came by to pick up Father Xavier. Waited in the car fifteen minutes before I came in to check on him. He could still be alive if it weren't for me."

"How could you know? Besides, if you two had stayed together, I'd probably be the one lying dead on the church floor. He gave his life to save mine."

"Right," Michael replied. He opened his eyes and straightened his clerical collar. "I suppose I should call Ignatius and tell him to hold off on that report."

Parker nodded. "I guess you finally got a win."

Michael shook his head slowly. "We didn't win here, Parker. Look at this." He gestured at the bodies on the floor. "It's a draw at best. But this is only one battle. The war against darkness goes on, and I think even Father Ignatius would agree, you're more than ready to wage it."

Parker looked at Xavier's still form. "I'm not so sure we didn't win," he said. "We stopped a madman from killing again. And yes, we both lost friends, but we gained something too, didn't we?"

Michael was unconvinced. "What did you gain, Parker?"

"You said yourself that I might rediscover the most precious lost treasure of the Christian church. And I think I did."

As it turned out, Parker's ambulance ride would have to wait. The medics stabilized him, bandaged him, and applied a splint to his arm and two fingers, but the police would not delay their questioning. They needed an explanation as to how one of their own had come to be burned up and shot in the back, in a church of all places—along with two other bodies, both priests.

Damien—also splinted and temporarily taped up by paramedics—had already told them where to find Brynn Carter, bringing the night's body count to four. The one-time suspect had been hand-delivered to police headquarters an hour earlier, but found himself unable to convince the arresting officers of the night's events. At Parker's insistence, Corrinne had brought him to the church as well after some initial questioning, so all three survivors could give a statement together, which she emphasized she was only doing out of "professional courtesy."

They gathered in the library of the church to be debriefed, first by Troy and Corrinne—both trying to hide their shock at learning Ketcham's secret—and then by Homeland Security when Father Michael's diplomatic status came to light.

A man in a black suit, exuding authority, breezed in shortly after midnight and took the seat next to Damien at the head of the conference table. He identified himself merely as Agent Jones and rehashed the same line of questioning to which they had already been subjected, challenging every statement that each of them made.

After several hours of interrogation, it had become more than clear, even to Agent Jones, that the evidence squared with their individual statements and their collective story. A series of phone calls went up the chain—how high Parker never knew—until a decision was made. The federal agent tersely explained that charges would not be leveled against any of them, provided they agree to the official version of the evening's events.

In order to avoid an international incident, the involvement of the Jesuits Militant would be redacted from the official story and a field officer from an unnamed state agency would be credited with taking down the Blackjack Killer. Damien and Parker were free to go, he explained—presumably to the hospital, and then home—but Michael would have to leave the country, never to return.

A smirk bit at the priest's lips. "I understand," he said, "and I can assure you that Michael John Faber will never set foot in the United States again."

Before the questioning wrapped, Parker brought up the issue of Damien's drug charges, which were clearly fabricated in light of recent developments. A call from the feds to the prosecutor's home at 3:40 a.m. confirmed that all pending charges would be dropped.

That settled, the meeting was adjourned. As

papers were gathered and briefcases clasped shut, Parker felt as if a business deal had just been closed. Except that nine people were dead, some of whom had been strangers, some his friends, and others his enemies. With those who had survived, Parker wasn't quite sure where he stood.

"Your name's not really Michael Faber, is it?" Parker asked the young priest, as the agents arranged his trip to the airport and, from there, back to Vatican City.

Michael just winked. "Can't tell you, buddy," he said. "I took an oath."

Parker's mouth fell involuntarily open.

"Different oath," he chuckled. "I'm glad I met you, Parker. You've got my number if you ever need anything." He gingerly embraced his new friend, both men grimacing at the pain, and then disappeared out the door amid a sea of gray suits.

Damien was on his way out as well. Having declined the feds' offer of a ride, he'd called some friends to drive him to Butterworth Hospital. He paused just inside the door and gave Parker a sheepish grin.

"Sorry about the cat," he said.

"I forgive you."

"And thanks for not leaving me taped to the chair back there. That was decent of you."

"You're welcome. How's the arm?"

"The bad news is I'm not in shock anymore. The good news is they gave me some really funky pain-killers. Paramedic said it will probably need surgery." His eyes betrayed a good deal of apprehension at the prospect.

"What would you say if I offered to pray for you?"

"I wouldn't say anything."

"Well, I guess that's progress."

They shook hands simply and parted ways.

Epilogue

Parker was admitted to the hospital with a fractured skull, a concussion, two broken bones in his hand, and a stress fracture in his right ulna. All this in addition to his three missing teeth, which rendered his perfect white smile—for which he had given up so much—a goofy, hillbilly grin. After two days he was sent home with a cast, a stack of prescriptions, and orders for a week of bed rest.

He disobeyed the doctor's instructions, emerging from his bed on the third day to get a temporary dental bridge before performing Paige's and Dr. Carlson's funerals—both at Hope Presbyterian's sanctuary in the Holy Ghost Tabernacle.

For the next three weeks Parker rested, healed, and reassessed the direction of his life and ministry. To fill the slot on his weekly TV program, he featured some of his father's old sermons from the early days of the television ministry. The response was positive enough that he decided to continue that for the rest of the season.

As for Abundance Now Ministries, Parker simply dissolved it, donating its considerable assets to H.I.S. Youth Center on Division Avenue. He sent letters to everyone on the donors' list, explaining his reasons for pulling back from the spotlight.

To that end, despite a major national buzz surrounding the televangelist who helped track down a serial killer, Parker's own media involvement was limited to Damien Bane's newly rebranded *Skeptic Humanist* video podcast, record viewership to date: 242. They recounted their harrowing experience in the school and discussed philosophy and theology, even sharing a laugh or two. Within a week Damien had broken his record by more than half a million views.

As soon as he felt able, Parker met with his editors at Charter House, intent on returning the advance for *God Is Awesome (And So Are You)*. To his initial shock and annoyance, they were unwilling to let him out of his contract. They did, however, offer to roll the advance over to a new book instead—one about rediscovering the faith of his father through a series of grisly murders.

One month to the day after he began his consultant work with the Grand Rapids Police,

Parker hand-delivered his résumé to the elders of Hope Presbyterian Church. The next day he had an interview with the Pastoral Nominating Committee. A week later, all seventy-one active members showed up to unanimously vote him in as their new pastor.

It was a Thursday—Parker's fourth day on the job—when he finally called Joshua Holton. Parker had been meeting with Reverend T. Charles Watkins every morning for coffee and prayer in his office at Holy Ghost Tabernacle.

That morning, after saying "amen," Charles had looked Parker in the eye and said, "Listen to me, son, you won't have peace until you forgive this man. And you need to forgive him man-to-man. Understand?"

"Did you premeditate that rhyme scheme, or did it just happen?"

Charles laughed and waved him away. "I've got work to do."

Parker walked out of the office and a short distance down the hall to a door that read Reverend Brian Parker III. The office was small and full of dreadfully outdated furniture, but functional enough. Parker slid into the shabby desk chair and reviewed his to-do list for the day. First and foremost, he needed to finish preparing his Sunday message—his first at Hope in eight years.

He knew word was out that he had landed another church, and he had no idea how many of his former fans to expect on Sunday morning. The only person who had promised to be there was Corrinne, even though it was neither Christmas nor Easter. She had checked on Parker by phone every day his first week out of the hospital, and at his invitation stopped by his house with dinner.

The elders moved their service back an hour so they could use the new, larger auditorium if needed. No matter how many attended, though, anyone expecting to hear about Moments of Majesty and seizing his destiny would be surprised by the message of repentance and forgiveness of sins in Jesus' name—a message of the cross, grace, and self-denial.

At the top of Parker's to-do list, he added *Call J. Holton,* then immediately crossed it out and picked up the phone, dialing the familiar number from memory. He was deposited directly into voice mail.

"Josh, it's me, Brian Park—er, Parker Saint. I just wanted to call to thank you for all the opportunities you've given me and the trust you placed in me. The time we spent together really made a significant impact on who I am. I mean that. If you ever want to talk, I'd be more than happy to. Or if you're ever in town, I'd love to get together. Blessings on you and your ministry."

The door opened and Ruth, the volunteer

secretary, walked in. Of the seventy-one members of Hope Presbyterian, six were named Ruth. "At least we're not a Ruthless church," went the joke that Parker had heard about thirty-five times now.

"There are two messages for you, Pastor Brian," Ruth said, handing him a couple illegible notes on small slips of paper. He smiled and accepted them.

"What does this say here?" he asked, pointing to a particularly cryptic word.

"Halligan Moving Company," she answered. "They called about an appointment tomorrow, but I didn't understand what it was for."

"It's my office furniture," he said. "I miss my office furniture. This stuff has seen better days."

Ruth wrinkled her forehead. "I don't think there's anything wrong with it. Some of these things arrived with Reverend Brian, Senior."

He tipped back in his seat, intrigued. "You actually remember when Grandpa started pastoring this church?"

"I sure do. He did my wedding in 1949. And I knew your father when he was only this tall."

"So which of these priceless treasures belonged to my grandfather?"

She squinted her way around the room. "That rocker in the corner was his. That love seat. This desk blotter, I believe. And this lamp. Your grandmother thought it was the ugliest lamp on earth, but Reverend Parker would never dream of parting with it."

Parker picked up a plastic Bic. "What about this pen? Was this my grandfather's pen?"

Ruth frowned and left the office.

He chuckled. This was going to take some getting used to. He thought of his sleek, spacious office at Abundance Now and let his eyes drift from the threadbare love seat to the rocker to the lamp . . . Honestly, the lamp wasn't half bad. The shade was cheap and cracked, but the base was interesting, made of yellowed glass—almost an amber color—and filled with what appeared to be very realistic artificial flowers. And thorns.

Lots of thorns.

Pastor Brian picked up the phone and reached for Father Michael's card.

Author's Note

Like most readers, I am often interested in the genesis of the novels I enjoy, as well as which aspects are rooted in reality and which sprang full-form from the author's mind. Along those lines, I have been asked who some of the characters in this book are modeled after—generally by people who are reasonably sure they know the answer. The truth, however, is that the tension Parker feels between following Joshua Holton and following in the footsteps of his grandfather and Evert Carlson is a tension felt by almost every pastor I know, myself included, and on a certain level by every disciple of Jesus. The twelve certainly felt it (Mark 9:33–34; 10:37) and Christians—especially Christian leaders—have been tempted to chase the dragon's crown ever since.

As far as the historical and ecclesiological devices are concerned, while the Sudarium of Oviedo is very much a real (and, I believe, true) relic, the Crown of Marbella and its provenance are products of my imagination. Likewise, the Jesuits Militant do not exist as such, although there is no shortage of claims that the Society of Jesus has functioned or does function as something of an ecclesiastical spy agency. Among such claims one finds frequent appeals to the so-called "Jesuit Extreme Oath of Induction," which one can indeed find in the Library of Congress and the Congressional Record (including the text Parker highlights). Parker's brief research and debunking of the oath's veracity is a succinct recounting of my own conclusions on the topic, reached after a much more in-depth study of the matter.

If you take away anything from this book, I pray it will be that positivity in and of itself is powerless to save you and without the cross it will lead you in the opposite direction. Only Jesus's substitutionary death and triumphant resurrection have the power to raise a broken sinner from death to life (Luke 11:24–26, Matt. 23:27).

Soli Deo Gloria,
Reverend Zachary Bartels

Reader's Group Guide

1. Do you accept Evert Carlson's assessment of Satan, the dragon, as a combination of a lion (I Peter 5:8) and a serpent (Gen. 3:1)? Why would the enemy need both strategies?

2. Where in Scripture do you see Satan using his *serpent* strategy (i.e. slipping past a person's guard undetected)? Where in your life have you seen this? Where in our broader culture?

3. Where in Scripture do you see Satan using his *lion* strategy (openly attacking, trying to shatter a person's faith)? Where in your life have you seen this? Where in our broader culture?

4. Does worldly success necessarily open us up to temptation as it did with Parker? How can we guard against falling into a spirit of self-sufficiency (Rev. 3:17) when God blesses us with success?

5. What did you think of Parker's evasive answers to the reporter and Father Michael's philosophy that we should avoid glossing over differences and difficult truths? Is it ever wise to gloss over the truth?

6. Parker's journey, while filled with trials, pain, and missteps, ultimately leads him back to the cross and to a place of being stronger than ever in his faith and more effective in his ministry. Have you ever gone through a similar valley, only to see in retrospect how God was refining and re-making you in His image?

7. Danny scoffs at Christians who are quick to see Satan in the obvious places (e.g. Damien) and to rebuke him there, while missing the "snakes slithering around their feet." Do you think this is happening in the church today? Where and how?

8. Damien is outwardly hostile to Christianity because of the pain he has experienced at the hands of self-professed Christians. Only when Parker is forced to ally himself to Damien does the protective shell of hostility begin to crack. Can you think of opportunities in your own life to remember that people who are openly hostile to the Church are also broken people who need Jesus? What helps you maintain this Christlike mindset?

9. Did Jesus and the Apostles react more harshly to the Damiens of the world who rail loudly against the church or to those who slip in

undetected and teach falsehoods? (See Luke 23:34, Matt. 23:15, Acts 16:25–28, Gal. 5:12)

10. Do you believe that there is any veracity to curses or spells? When the Bible speaks of "cosmic powers over this present darkness" and "spiritual forces of evil in the heavenly places," (Eph. 6:12, ESV) what do you think that looks like in our world today?

11. What do you think of Dr. Graham's assessment that effective spiritual warfare is comprised of two steps, which are simple but not easy? (See James 4:7)

12. Danny's descent into full-blown demoniac status began with dabbling in darkness and the enemy slowly taking hold. Do you believe this can happen to a believer as well? Why or why not?

13. At the end of the story, it seems as though Parker will not be able to recover Hope Presbyterian's former building. How important are physical church buildings to your faith? Is a church building simply a convenient place to meet or is there more to it?

14. What do you think Parker means when he says he has recovered the "greatest treasure of the Christian church"?

Acknowledgments

The writing of this book took literally years and many people were of great help. First and foremost, unending thanks goes to my wife, Erin, who is the greatest teacher, encourager, guide, and friend an aspiring novelist could ever want. Her skill as a writer is matched only by her patience in helping me along the way. My congregation at Judson Baptist Church has offered encouragement as well and has gladly put up with their pastor's writing habit. (By the by, we'd love to have you worship with us any time —www.ChurchLansing.com.)

Of course, my deepest thanks to my agent Ann Byle of Credo Communications, my editor Amanda Bostic and the whole incredible fiction team at HarperCollins Christian Publishing (for a large company, "y'all" feel suspiciously like a family), as well as Allen Arnold and LB Norton.

My boy Ted Kluck (as well as Chaz Marriot and the whole Gut Check Empire) was also instrumental in this book becoming a reality, as were Bill and Jen Colin and WAC Productions. And I appreciate everyone who was willing to slog through a pretty rough draft early on and offer advice and encouragement: Terry and Shelly Bartels, Noel Harshman, Mike Wittmer, Helen

Patscot, and Noah Filipiak. And, oh, let's say Turk.

I am also grateful to Lt. Col. Dave Grossman for his book *On Combat*, from whence comes the metaphor of sheep, wolves, and sheepdogs, and to the men of the *White Horse Inn* for getting me thinking about a lot of this stuff.

About the Author

An award-winning preacher and Bible teacher, Zachary Bartels serves as senior pastor of Judson Memorial Baptist Church in Lansing, Michigan. He earned a BA in world religions from Cornerstone University and his Masters of Divinity from Grand Rapids Theological Seminary. Zachary enjoys film, fine cigars, stimulating conversation, gourmet coffee, reading, writing, and cycling. He lives in Lansing, Michigan, with his wife Erin and their son.

Visit Zach on his website zacharybartels.com
Facebook: AuthorZacharyBartels
Twitter: AuthorZBartels

Center Point Large Print
600 Brooks Road / PO Box 1
Thorndike, ME 04986-0001 USA

(207) 568-3717

US & Canada:
1 800 929-9108
www.centerpointlargeprint.com